Praise for the Alexandra Cooper series

'Engaging characters, an intelligent story full of twists'
The Times

'Chilling stuff' *Hello!*

'Fascinating reading in a mystery which stretches far
beyond New York' *Sunday Telegraph*

'Romantic tension, the fast-paced plotting, and the New
York setting will keep fans of Fairstein's series engrossed'
Booklist

'There are so many legal functionaries showing up in
fiction . . . that it's a mark of Linda Fairstein's class that
she stands out' *The Weekend Australian*

'Impeccably plotted and thoroughly engrossing novels'
Daily Mail

'Her novels pulsate with catchy police jargon and a
bustling, warm, down-to-earth reality' *TV Week*

Death Dance

LINDA FAIRSTEIN

sphere

SPHERE

First published in the United States in 2006 by Scribner
First published in Great Britain in January 2006 by Little, Brown
This paperback edition published in 2006 by Sphere
Reprinted in 2006

A CIP catalogue record for this book
is available from the British Library.

ISBN-13: 978-0-7515-3571-6
ISBN-10: 0-7515-3571-0

Typeset in Adobe Garamond by Palimpsest Book Production Limited,
Polmont, Stirlingshire

Printed and bound in Great Britain by
Clays Ltd, St Ives plc

Sphere
An imprint of
Little, Brown Book Group
Brettenham House
Lancaster Place
London WC2E 7EN

A Member of the Hachette Livre Group of Companies

www.littlebrown.co.uk

For
Matthew and Alexander Zavislan

About, about, in reel and rout
The death fires danced at night.
       – Samuel Taylor Coleridge

Chapter 1

'You think we've got a case?' Mercer Wallace asked me.

'The answer's inside that cardboard box you're holding,' I said, opening the glass-paneled door of his lieutenant's office in the Special Victims Squad.

I placed my hand on the shoulder of the young woman who was slumped over a desk, napping while she waited for my arrival. She lifted her head from her crossed arms and flicked her long auburn hair out of her eyes.

'I'm Alex Cooper. Manhattan DA's office.' I tried not to convey the urgency of what we had to get done within the next few hours. 'Are you Jean?'

'Yes. Jean Eaken.'

'Has Detective Wallace explained what we need?'

'You're the prosecutor running the investigation, he told me. I've got to go through the details with you again, and then make a phone call that you're going to script for me. Is Cara still here?' Jean asked.

'She's in another office down the hall,' Mercer said. 'It's better we keep you separated until this is done. Then we'll take you over to the hotel and let you get some rest.'

I had been the assistant district attorney in charge of the Sex Crimes Prosecution Unit for more than a decade, and Mercer had called me into the case to try to add something from my legal arsenal to speed the arrest process and increase the likelihood that Jean Eaken would be a successful witness in the courtroom.

Mercer told me that the twenty-four-year-old Canadian graduate student had met the suspect at a conference on adolescent psychology at the University of Toronto, which she had attended with her friend, Cara, four months earlier.

I sat opposite Jean, who stifled a yawn as I asked the first question. It was almost midnight. 'When you met Selim back in January, how much time did you spend with him then?'

'I sat next to him at a couple of lectures. We made small talk during the breaks. He bought Cara and me a glass of wine on the last afternoon, at happy hour. Told us he lived in Manhattan, that he was a doctor. Nothing more than that.'

'He invited you to New York?'

'Not exactly. I told him that we'd never been here, but that we had a trip planned for the spring. He was very friendly, very kind. Cara asked him if he knew any inexpensive hotels, since we're on student budgets, and he told us we could stay at his apartment.'

'Did you talk about the sleeping arrangements?'

'Yes, of course. Selim told us he had a girlfriend, and that he'd either stay over at her place or sleep on a futon in the living room. He offered us the twin beds,' Jean said. 'He gave me his card, Ms Cooper, with his office phone and everything. He's a medical doctor – a psychiatric resident. It seemed perfectly safe to both of us.'

'It should have been perfectly safe,' I said, trying to

2

reassure her that it was not her own judgment that precipitated her victimization. 'Did you correspond with him after that first meeting?'

Jean shrugged. 'A couple of e-mails, maybe. Nothing personal. I thanked him for his offer and asked him whether he really meant it. Then I sent him another one a month ago, after Cara and I set our travel dates, to see if those were still good for him.'

Mercer nodded at me over Jean's head. He was keeping a list of things to do, and getting subpoenas for the e-mail records of both parties would be added to his tasks. We had worked together often enough to know each other's professional style, especially for documenting every corroborating fact we could in this often bizarre world of sex crimes.

'Were there any phone calls between you two?'

'Just one, a week ago. I left him a voice mail explaining when our bus arrived at the Port Authority and making sure it was a convenient time to show up at his apartment. He called me back late that night and we talked for a while.'

'Can you reconstruct that conversation for us? The details of it, I mean.'

There would be skeptics on any jury that was eventually impaneled, people who would assume that there must have been verbal foreplay between the time of the first meeting of this attractive young woman and the stranger at whose home she later arranged a sleepover. I needed to know that before Mercer and I took the next steps.

'Selim asked me if we had made plans for the days that we'd be in the city and what we wanted to see. Things like that.'

3

'Did he say anything at all, Jean – anything – that made you think he was interested in you, maybe socially or even sexually?'

She answered quickly and firmly. 'No.' Her green eyes opened wide as she looked at me to measure my response.

'Nothing inappropriate?'

She thought for several seconds. 'He asked me why my boyfriend wasn't coming with me. I told him I didn't have one,' Jean said. 'Oh, yeah. He wanted to know if I liked to smoke marijuana, 'cause he could get some while I was here.'

Mercer moved his head back and forth. This was a fact he was hearing for the first time. It didn't necessarily change the case at all, but it reminded us that we had to constantly press for things that often seemed irrelevant to witnesses – and for the truth.

'What did you tell him?'

'That I don't like weed, that it makes me sick.'

'Did you expect to spend any time with him, Jean?'

'No way. Dr Sengor – Selim – told us he'd be at work all day and with his girlfriend most evenings. I just thought he was being a nice guy, letting us crash at his place.'

Most of my prosecutorial career had involved women meeting nice guys who had other things in mind. Cops and prosecutors – and often Manhattan jurors – found young people from west of the Hudson River and north of the Bronx a bit too trusting much of the time.

'So he didn't come on to you at all?'

Jean forced a smile. 'Not until I was ready to go to bed the first night.'

'What happened then?'

4

'It was after nine when we got to his place. We sort of settled in and talked for an hour. Just stuff. Psychology and how hard grad school is and what were our first impressions of the city. When Cara went into the bath-room to take a shower, Selim came over to the couch I was sitting on and like, well, he tried to hook up with me.'

'Tell Alex exactly what he did,' Mercer said, coaxing the facts we needed out of her as he had done earlier in the day.

Jean was a well-built young woman, almost as tall as I am at five-foot-ten, but much stockier. 'I was tired from the long bus ride, and kind of leaning back with my head against a pillow. Selim reached over and tried to kiss me – right on the mouth – while he was fumbling to get his hand on my chest.'

'What did you do?'

'I just pushed him away and stood up. I asked him to give me the telephone book so I could find a hotel to stay in.'

'How did he react to that?'

'He was very apologetic, Ms Cooper. He told me how sorry he was, that he had misinterpreted my body language. He pleaded with me not to tell Cara. He told me that in his country—'

'His country?' I asked.

'Selim's from Turkey. He said that back home, if anybody did that to his sister, he'd be pilloried in the town square.'

He'd be short one hand and castrated, too, no doubt. 'So you stayed?'

'He was a perfect gentleman from that point on. He

5

was just testing me, I guess. It's happened to me before. Maybe that's why I thought I could handle the situation.'

'And Cara?'

'You'll have to ask her about that,' Jean said, blushing perceptibly.

Mercer had already told me that Selim Sengor hit on Cara, too, after Jean fell asleep the first night. They stayed in the living room talking, and she engaged in some kissing and fondling with him, but had stopped short of further sexual intimacy. That was another reason to keep the witnesses separated. They were likely to be more straightforward with us out of each other's presence. Cara might blame herself for what happened thereafter – an unfortunate but typical reaction when some of the sexual contact was consensual. She might even be less candid in front of Jean.

'Did you socialize with him during the week?'

'No. In fact, he actually did spend the night before last with his girlfriend. We hardly ever saw him.' She bit at the cuticle of one of her nails, until she noticed me watching her. Then she straightened up again and began to wind a strand of her long hair behind her left ear.

'And yesterday?'

'In the morning, after Cara and I made our plans, I beeped him at the hospital. When he called back, I told him that we were going sightseeing and planned to pick up some half-price tickets to a Broadway show, in Times Square. We invited him to join us, to thank him for letting us stay with him.'

'Did he spend the evening with you?'

'No, he didn't seem the least bit interested in doing that.'

'Did you and Cara go to the theater?'

'Yeah, we saw that new Andrew Lloyd Webber thing. Cara loves him. We got back to the apartment after eleven o'clock and Selim was waiting up for us. We bought him a gift, an expensive bottle of Kentucky bourbon,' Jean said, smiling again, now braiding the length of hair as she talked. 'It sounded very American.'

'What did you do then?'

'He offered us a drink and we both said sure. We sat in the living room while Selim went into the kitchen and mixed the cocktails.'

'Mixed them? What did he make for you?'

Again she shrugged and shook her head. 'I don't know. I never drank bourbon before. I heard that loud kind of noise that a food blender makes, and he came out with something – I don't know – it looked very frothy when he brought it to us.'

I couldn't imagine anyone adding something to a good Scotch, and I doubted there was much to improve on in a fine bourbon either.

'Had you changed your clothes, Jean, to get ready to go to sleep?'

'No. Cara turned on the CD player and we started listening to the soundtrack from the show. Selim came back into the room and handed us each a drink. He offered a toast to our friendship and we clinked our glasses together.'

The young woman rested her elbows on the desk and cushioned her head in her hands while I asked her how much of the cocktail she drank.

'Three sips of it, Ms Cooper. Maybe four. I swear I didn't have any more than that.'

7

'Any marijuana?'

'No. I mean he had some in the apartment – he offered me a joint that he took out of a drawer in one of the tables, but I didn't smoke any.'

I needed her candor. The blood and urine that had been collected by the nurse-examiner would confirm her answer.

'Did he smoke?'

'Not in front of us. Not that I saw.'

'What's the next thing you remember?'

'There was no next thing. That's the last memory I have, really. I felt dizzy and weak – so weak that I tried to stand up but I couldn't. The room started spinning and then it was dark. Completely black. That's all I know.' Jean pushed herself upright again, looked at her nail – the bed red with irritation from her biting – and then back at me.

'Until . . . ?'

'Until I woke up this morning.'

'In the living room?'

'No, no. No. I was in one of the beds in the other room. That's what's so strange about this, Ms Cooper. I was dressed in my nightgown, my clothes were folded neatly on top of my suitcase,' Jean said, dropping her head back in her hands and lowering her voice. 'And I ached. I ached terribly.'

'I need to know where it hurt. Exactly where you felt it.'

Jean Eaken didn't lift her head. She rubbed her lower abdomen with one hand.

Mercer and I both knew what she meant, but that wouldn't be specific enough for the purposes of the law. 'On the outside of your body?' I asked, speaking softly.

8

'No. Inside me. Like someone had sex with me. Too much.'

'Do you remember having intercourse with Selim? Do you think you might have consented to it after you started drinking with—'

Jean flashed another look at me as I gently challenged her and cut me off abruptly with a single sharp word. 'No.'

'Tell me what you did this morning, Jean.'

'I was frozen. I didn't know what to do. At first I couldn't even remember where I was. I looked at my watch and saw that it was eleven thirty in the morning. We'd had the alarm set all week for seven, but I didn't even hear that go off. I got out of bed – I was still a little dizzy – to lock the bedroom door. Selim had been working rotating shifts – different hours all week. He told us he had to work sixteen hours today – eight a.m. to midnight – but I was scared he might still be there. Then I woke Cara up.'

'Where was she?' I asked.

'In the other bed. Same as me – dressed in her night-gown and her jeans and sweater all folded up neatly. She was sleeping so deep, I had to keep shaking her to get her up. She didn't remember anything, either. She started crying, so first I had to calm her down. It was my idea to get dressed and go over there to the hospital.'

'That was the best thing you could have done, Jean. Very smart.'

'But the doctors haven't told me anything.'

'We won't let you go home until they've explained their findings to you,' Mercer said, watching Jean nervously twist and untwist the same plait of hair.

9

'Did you leave your things at Selim's?'

'Are you crazy? I never wanted to see that guy again. We brought our suitcases with us.'

'The glasses you drank from,' I said, 'did you see them in the apartment this morning?'

'I didn't look around. I just wanted to get out of there as fast as possible.'

'Did you have any reason to go into the kitchen, to put things away or clean anything up?'

'No. That's his problem.'

Even better. It meant there was a shot that we might get lucky and still find some inculpatory evidence if Mercer and I could get going on this.

'I know it's been a long day for you, Jean. Just give us a few minutes to put things together and we'll be back,' I said, stepping out of the room behind Mercer, who had picked up the cardboard evidence collection kit that had been prepared by the nurse-examiner at the hospital. We were in the hallway of the quiet corridor that Special Victims shared with the Manhattan North Homicide Squad.

'How long will it take to get the tox screening back on these?' he asked, referring to the slides and plastic bottles inside the compact box.

In addition to the traditional testing of fluids and stains recovered from a patient's body during the emergency room treatment of a rape victim, the latest kits required samples be taken of blood and urine for the most refined testing, as assailants used more sophisticated methods to overcome their prey.

'Seventy-two hours, if they jump us to the front of the line.'

10

'I'm sending this whole thing to the ME's office, to Serology?'

'It starts there,' I said. Mercer knew that our medical examiner's serology lab did most of the analyses we needed. 'Unfortunately, if there are any exotic drugs involved, it'll go out to a private lab and take even longer.'

'Damn. I hate to give this bastard a three-day pass. We'll even have the DNA results by this time tomorrow.'

'DNA tells us next to nothing in a case like this. We know they spent the night in his apartment. We know the docs recovered semen specimens from both women. None of that's a crime unless he used force—'

'No sign of that,' Mercer said.

Even the aches that Jean described could be consistent with consensual sexual activity if it was vigorous or prolonged – or infrequent, since she had told Selim she did not have a current boyfriend.

'Or he spiked their drinks to render them unconscious. We're nowhere without the toxicology,' I said.

'How do you want to take it from here?'

My deputy, Sarah Brenner, had stayed behind at the DA's office to draft the search warrant with the facts Mercer provided to her, and she would take it before the judge who was sitting in night court to sign while we set the rest of the operation in motion.

'I'll work up the conversation for Jean to have with Selim,' I said, 'but I don't want her to make that call until your team is stationed outside the door of his apartment. His shift ends right around now and he should be home within the half hour. The minute Jean hangs up, I'll be on the phone to you and you'll go in with the warrant.

11

If her questions raise his antennae, I don't want him to have a chance to clean house before you get there.'

The glass-paneled door with the gold-and-black lettering – HOMICIDE – opened from within and Mike Chapman called out to Mercer Wallace. 'Your witness is getting antsy in here. She wants to know when you and Coop are gonna move on the perp.'

I walked farther down the hallway to greet Mike, whom I hadn't seen in several weeks. I smiled at the sight of him back in his natural habitat in the Homicide Squad – his thick shock of straight black hair, the long, lean body, his personal uniform of navy blazer and jeans. All that was missing was the infectious grin that had been good to bring me out of every dark situation and mood I'd faced in more than a decade that we had worked together.

'Hey, stranger. When did you come on?'

'Doing steady midnights. I'm not sleeping much, so I might as well have a place to hang out.'

'When Mercer and I finish up in another couple of hours – around two a.m. – why don't we take you downstairs for something to eat?' I asked.

Mike walked to his desk, seated himself with his back to me, and put his feet up while he examined his notebook. I paused at an empty cubicle next to his and started writing the lines I wanted Jean Eaken to deliver to Dr Sengor.

'I'm sticking here,' Mike said. 'Just got a scratch I got to sit on.'

A scratch wasn't a formal report of a crime, but rather a notification to the NYPD of an unusual circumstance.

'What's so serious you'd pass up the greasiest bacon and eggs in Harlem with me?' I tried to tease a familiar smile out of my favorite homicide detective and still-grieving friend.

'Right up your alley, twinkletoes. There may be a swan on the loose. Lieutenant Peterson has me on standby.'

'What are you talking about?'

'Ever hear of' – Mike looked down at his notes to get the name – 'Talya. Talya Galinova?'

'Natalya Galinova.' The world-renowned dancer who commanded more curtain calls in a month than most performers would ever know in a lifetime was as famous for her artistry as for her ethereal looks and regal bearing. 'She's starring with the Royal Ballet at Lincoln Center this week.'

'Well, sometime between the second act and the curtain calls tonight, she pulled a Houdini. Me and the loo got other plans for the weekend than breakfast with you. Personally, I'm hoping your missing swan doesn't morph into a dead duck.'

Chapter 2

'Hello, Selim? I didn't wake you up, did I? It's Jean.'

'Jean? Where are you?'

We were sitting in a room with two phones, one of which was attached to a digital recorder, so that I could listen on an extension as my witness confronted her assailant and give her direction in case she needed it. It was now twelve forty-five in the morning.

'I'm at the Port Authority, waiting for—'

'You were supposed to be on a three o'clock bus this afternoon, weren't you?' Selim's English was heavily accented as he cut Jean off before she could answer.

'Yeah, except Cara and I were a bit sick today. Nauseous and dizzy. We just couldn't face a ten-hour bus ride.'

'But you're still going tonight, aren't you?'

'Nothing leaves for Toronto until the morning.'

'You want to come back here? I'm still up. I haven't been home very long. Wait at my apartment until then.'

'Oh, no. I think I'm going to take Cara to the hospital. She's really feeling bad and I think she should be examined before she travels. I was wondering if—'

'You don't want to start with that, Jean,' Selim said, sounding almost angry as he raised his voice to get her attention. 'I'm a doctor. Tell me what her symptoms are and I can figure out if anything's wrong. Probably something she ate. You'll waste too much time waiting in an emergency room. You don't have any insurance coverage in this country, do you? So it's going to be very expensive for her.'

He seemed to be scrambling for any ideas that would keep the women away from a medical exam.

'We didn't eat anything unusual, Selim. Each of us had a salad. And we didn't drink anything except bottled water until we got to your place.'

'Yeah, well, maybe there was something wrong with the salad. Like it wasn't clean or the dressing had turned already.'

'That's a good enough reason for us to go to the hospital. Could be food poisoning. At least they can do blood tests there, can't they?'

Jean was quick. I had told her not to be confrontational with Selim, knowing that might anger him and cause him to hang up the phone. Roll with him. Bring him back to talking about the cocktail he mixed for you.

'That drink you gave us tasted kind of weird. Lucky I didn't have more of it.'

'Hmm.'

'Hmm' didn't tell me anything I needed to know. Selim was probably trying to think of an excuse for her observation. I scribbled a note to Jean and slid it across the table. I wanted on record that she had not been drinking more alcohol than she told Mercer and me. I wanted to hear it from Selim. The defense at a trial like this would just try to convince the jury that she and Cara were blottoed.

15

'I mean, you saw me, Selim. I don't think I even had more than a few sips, did I? I didn't finish a fraction of the drink you poured.' Jean was wide awake now, the receiver in one hand and her other one gripping the papers I had prepared.

'No, no, you didn't. You hardly touched it. Maybe you were already feeling sick before you came here.'

'I felt fine when we got to the apartment. Both of us did. I'm worried about Cara. She's been throwing up and everything. C'mon, what was in the drink you gave us?'

'Bourbon. Just the bourbon that you brought me.'

'You gotta be kidding, Selim. It wasn't even the same color as what was in the bottle. It was all fuzzy and white.' Jean didn't like being challenged any more by him than she had by my questions. Her green eyes were focused with determination now.

He was silent.

'You still there, Selim? I mean, I don't have to tell Cara, but it would help me to know that we can get on that bus and she's not going to need to have her stomach pumped or be throwing up on me all the way home. I can't think of much worse than that on a long ride, can you?'

Still, silence.

'My problem has all cleared up – you don't have to worry about that. It's just between you and me, but you gotta give me a hand with Cara.'

Good pitch, girl. Let him think it's no big deal.

'Bourbon and what?' Jean said. 'I heard you working the blender in there.'

A nervous laugh. 'Oh, that. I usually put a little cordial in with my drink. Do you know Bailey's?'

16

'I know what it is, but I've never had it.'

'I think you two just weren't used to the taste of the bourbon.'

'But that combination of liquors wouldn't make me feel all drugged up, would it? So quickly?'

'Oh, sure. It could do that. Everybody has a different reaction, depending on their metabolism.'

'Really?' Jean paused for several seconds before her next question. She put down the crib sheet, gnawed once at her cuticle, and stared down at the tabletop. 'Selim, did you have sex with me last night?'

Again he seemed to snap at her. 'Why are you asking me that? You wanted to do that?'

I held my hand up at Jean to try to get her to back off, but it was clear to me that she was frustrated by the doctor's answers and understandably anxious to know whether she had been violated after he sedated her.

'No. You know I didn't have any interest in having sex with you. I made that clear the first night we got there. But I had this sort of dream that you were—'

'Maybe you drank the bourbon too fast. Maybe you're just imagining things. I never touched you. Look, it's really late and I have to go to—'

'How about Cara? She swears you made love to her.'

I had written out that choice of language for Jean to use. If she'd confronted Selim with a highly charged word like 'rape', he would have known immediately that she was talking about a crime. I was hoping that an expression like 'making love' would cause him to lower his guard and explain away the conduct to his accuser as consensual.

'I think you better go home, Jean. I think you're acting

17

really crazy. Nobody's going to believe the stuff you're saying. They'll just think you were drunk.'

The call ended abruptly. Jean tried to keep him talking, but Selim wasn't having any more of it.

I dialed Mercer's cell phone number and walked out of the room so Jean wouldn't hear my conversation with him.

'Where are you?' I said when he answered.

'Right down the hall from the doc's apartment. Top of the stairwell,' he whispered. 'I got two guys with me for backup, and Kerry Schreiner, in case the girlfriend's inside. Four of us ready to roll.'

'The judge authorized nighttime entry, didn't she?'

'Yeah, Sarah argued exigent circumstances so we could go in any time. By morning, the kitchen sink might be clean as a whistle. Before I put my finger on the door- bell, did Jean get any admissions from him?'

'Not enough to collar him yet. Denies drugging them. Denies sex. She did a really good job but he got spooked when she pressed too much. It's all up to what you find inside. Keep me posted.' I wished him luck and clicked off the phone.

I took Jean back to the Special Victims office to reunite her with Cara McDevitt. When Cara saw us enter the squad room, she stood up and rushed forward to embrace her friend.

'What took so long?' Cara asked. 'Are you okay?'

She was tearful and anxious. Jean nodded without emotion and stepped away to sit in one of the chairs. 'I'm fine. Exhausted is all. I just talked to the pervert—'

'You did?' Cara asked, wide-eyed and still sniffling.

'Can I let her know about it now, Ms Cooper? I'm

only sorry I couldn't tell him what I really wanted to say.'

'I promise to give you that chance down the road. It's better for the case that you stuck to my script. You nailed down some very important points, and I know how hard that was to do.' I smiled at Jean, admiring her courage and her fortitude. 'Sure you can tell Cara about it.'

One of the detectives from the squad was waiting to take them to the hotel room we had arranged so they could get some rest. I wanted them to stay in town to testify before the grand jury the next week if we came up with evidence of the commission of a crime.

My file was still in the Homicide Squad office, so I went back to retrieve it and wait for Mercer.

'What's got you up past your bedtime?' Mike asked. 'You're looking a little short in the beauty sleep department.'

'Think we've got a DFSA.'

Drug-facilitated sexual assault had been around for a very long time. There were mickeys slipped to femmes fatales in half of the noir films and pulp fiction of the forties and fifties. And the occasional Mata Haris who used similar techniques to betray their seducers. But the nineties had ushered in a roster of designer drugs that made it sport for college kids, street thugs, and professionals to lace drinks of unsuspecting dates with ecstasy and Seconal, roofies and GHB – known more formally as Rohypnol and gamma hydroxybutyrate. Not only did the druggings often lead to sex crimes, but also to lethal combinations of chemical substances in these muscle relaxants that triggered a range of reactions, from seizures to comas, and even death.

'Why don't you go home?' Mike asked.

'The call didn't go as well as I had hoped. The guy didn't give us much, so I want to see what Mercer comes back with. Anything new on Natalya?'

'The artistic director of the company wants to lowball it. She's got a bad rep as a prima donna—'

'She *is* a prima donna. She's one of the best dancers in the world. Julie Kent, Alessandra Ferri, Natalya Galinova – they're breathtakingly brilliant artists. What does that have to do with the fact that she disappeared?'

'Your pal Talya sports a fierce temper and a foul mouth. She had a battle backstage in her dressing room after the second act, stormed out of there, and wasn't around to take her bow at the end of the evening.'

'She's too much of a pro not to finish the performance.'

'No, no, Coop. She was dancing only one piece. It was – what do you call it? A gala or something. They weren't doing a full-length ballet, just excerpts, and hers was done.'

'That makes more sense. Who was she fighting with?'

'Maybe her lover. Maybe—'

'Her lover? I'm sure her husband back in London will be thrilled with the news.'

'Could be why the director wants to keep a lid on this one for a few hours, till we see where she shows up,' Mike said, looking over his notes. 'Thirty-eight. That's pushing it for a dancer, isn't it? It's even an advanced age for a prosecutor.'

'I'm not there yet. Don't rush me. And yes, ballet is ruthless in that regard,' I said. 'Who called in the scratch?' I asked.

'Talya's agent. He phoned the precinct to ask how to file a missing persons report. The desk sergeant told him it was too early but kicked it up here to cover his ass.'

The long-standing NYPD policy didn't allow adults to be declared missing unless they hadn't been heard from in more than twenty-four hours. More than eighteen thousand reports of missing persons came in to city cops over the course of an average year, and all but a handful turned out to be runaways or people who had chosen to leave whatever scene they had disappeared from.

'Who's the lover?'

'Depends who you ask. The artistic director claims the guy's a major producer. Theatrical, like Broadway shows. He says they've been working the couch in her dressing room pretty hard. The agent admits Talya knows the man, but claims it's just a professional relationship.'

'What's his name?'

'Joe Berk. Ever hear of him?'

'I've seen it in the papers but I don't know anything about him.'

'Seems there's no accounting for the lady's taste. He's twice her age, thick like a stuffed boar, filthy rich, and vicious as a rattlesnake, according to Talya's agent. But he's sleeping at home like a baby tonight. Rinaldo Vicci – that's her agent – tried calling Berk to find her. Says if the guy did anything evil, it's not keeping him awake. Besides, Talya also argued with the stage manager about the lighting, and earlier in the evening with the guy who partnered her about nearly dropping her on a lift at today's rehearsal. Might have just pirouetted off in a huff.

21

Something you've done to me more times than I can count on all my fingers and toes, blondie.'

The door opened and Sergeant Maron from Special Victims signaled to me. 'Need you inside, Alex. DCPI wants a briefing in case anything goes down.'

The deputy commissioner of Public Information had to be ready for reporters when any police matter threatened to be high profile. I picked up my folder and started out.

'Hey, Mike,' Maron said. 'Where you been holed up?'

'Took some time off.' He wouldn't turn his head in Steve's direction.

'Sorry to steal Alex away from you.'

Mike waved the back of his hand at us. 'You're doing me a favor. Coop was threatening for a month to plaster my picture on the side of milk cartons, send a task force out searching for me. It's a relief to be back on the job.'

Mike's girlfriend had been killed in a freak accident on a ski trip a few months back. The grief had overwhelmed him and he had distanced himself from even his closest friends as he tried to find a way to deal with the loss.

Steve Maron and I were still in his office half an hour later when Mercer and his team of detectives walked into the squad room. He was holding the arm of a man whose hands were cuffed behind his back.

Mercer led his prisoner into the barred holding cell, unlocked the cuffs, and told him to take a seat on the wooden bench against the wall. The sullen suspect was about five-foot-eleven, looked to be in his early thirties, had short brown hair parted neatly on one side, and large

22

dark eyes that swept the room as though he was trying to figure out who each of us was and why he had been brought here.

'Dr Sengor, I presume?' I asked Mercer, as he crossed the room to talk to me in Maron's office, our backs to the larger room.

Mercer nodded.

'And probable cause to go with him?' I asked.

'Check out the boxes,' he said, closing the door and pointing at the cartons that the other two detectives placed on Maron's desk. I opened the lid of the large one and saw a blender and three dirty drinking glasses. Two of them were coated with residue that streaked their sides and bottom.

'Where were these?'

'On the kitchen counter. The sink was full of dirty dishes.'

I lifted the top off the shoe box next to the carton. Pills. Dozens of pills. All of them in vials with prescription labels or sample cards from pharmaceutical companies.

Mercer removed a glassine envelope from his pants pocket. In it was an empty pill bottle. 'This was sitting beside the bourbon the girls brought him last night. See what those red letters say next to the warning symbol?'

I twisted the bag and looked at the highlighted print. 'Avoid alcohol while taking Xanax. Alcohol increases drowsiness and dizziness.'

Mercer picked out one of the samples from the shoe box. 'You don't have to read the fine print on this to find out what we already know – an overdose of the drug causes unconsciousness. It's up to you to make the charges stick, Alex. I just couldn't walk out of that apartment without cuffing the bastard.'

Chapter 3

'I'm asking you to remand the defendant, your honor. I don't think there's any amount of bail that's sufficient to ensure his return to face the charges in this case.'

I hadn't counted on standing in front of Harlan Moffett in the arraignment part on a Saturday morning at eleven o'clock. He was too senior to have drawn that duty, but the court officer told me he was covering for a young judge who had taken ill during the night. The case I had tried in front of him last year still haunted me, and it was a sure sign of bad luck for me to be stuck under his thumb again with a new matter.

'Alexandra,' he said, chuckling at me, 'don't give me a hard time today, okay? Bad enough I had to give up my first golf date of the season, now you're gonna go overboard on some cockamamie rape allegation? Remand is for murderers. He's a doctor, this guy. Am I right?'

Moffett smoothed the thinning gray hair that framed his lined face. He was short, and liked to place his elbows on the bench before him to pull himself up straighter and taller. He lifted the yellow-backed felony complaint while Sengor's court-appointed lawyer, Eric Ingels, answered, 'Yes.'

'Sengor Selim?'

'Selim Sengor,' I said.

'Whatever. Thirty years old. Nice-looking boy. I got a granddaughter who can't get herself a steady guy to save her life. What kind of name is Sengor? If he was Jewish, I might parole him to her custody and take him home with me.'

'You know what, judge? I'm going to step back to counsel table. I'd like this entire application to go on the record.'

'Whoa, whoa, whoa, Alexandra. Mr Ingels, don't get on this lady's bad side, I'm telling you right now,' Moffett said, tapping his fingers on the railing in front of him. He pushed up the sleeves of his robe and started to play with his pinky ring. 'Stay right here for a minute, sweetheart, while we talk this out.'

I didn't want this conversation to happen at a bench conference any more than I wanted to be held in contempt by a judge who had never made the effort to understand the nature of sexual assault nor to address 'lady lawyers' appropriately.

Eric Ingels had been catching cases for Legal Aid this morning and had been tossed Sengor's matter when the papers were docketed by the court clerk.

'Whaddaya got? I mean for real,' Moffett said. 'You got a witness?'

'Two of them.'

'What do they say?'

I repeated the stories that Jean and Cara had told.

'The doctor, he make any admissions to you?'

'He refused to talk to me when they brought him into the squad this morning,' I said.

'Aha! Maybe I should try the same tactic sometime. I'm the judge – I can't even control my own courtroom when Alexandra here gets a hard-on for some miscreant,' the judge said, talking to Ingels. He turned his attention back to me, drawing his handkerchief from his pocket to wipe the remains of cream cheese off his chin. 'So how are you going to prove your case?'

'The toxicology will confirm that Sengor drugged the women.'

'How long is that going to take?'

Nobody would even open the evidence collection kit until Monday morning. 'I should have preliminary results by Wednesday.'

'Judge,' Ingels said. 'You can't possibly hold my client that long on Ms Cooper's speculation. He's a physician who—'

'Who has been in this country for three years, whose entire family lives abroad – in Turkey – and who has the means and opportunity to flee this city the minute you let him loose.'

'You honestly think this guy is going to run home to the land of black veils and burkas when he's got college kids knocking on his door for a slumber party – coming all the way from over the border – just asking to be shtupped?' Moffett asked.

My adversary laughed, so Moffett carried on. 'Miss Cooper has no sense of humor about these things. Imagine her on a date? First time a guy makes a pass she probably whacks him across the face. No wonder she's still single.'

I turned and walked back to my position in the well of the courtroom. The stenographer put down his magazine and poised his fingers over the keyboard.

'For the record, your honor, I'm repeating my request for the remand of this defendant.'

'So how do you get a first-degree rape charge with no force, missy?'

'Missy' me and 'Sweetheart' me again, you moron, so it's recorded in black and white and I'll whip these minutes right over to the judiciary committee. Moffett had barely squeaked by them the last time he was up for reappointment.

'Incapacity to consent, judge. The defendant rendered them physically helpless by administering a drug without their knowledge.'

'Your honor,' Eric Ingels said, 'there's no evidence that my client gave these witnesses any drugs. Half the young women in America are on some sort of antianxiety medications.'

'Yeah, Alexandra. How do I know your girls didn't pop the pills themselves? Just because they don't remember taking them doesn't mean anything. Maybe they were too drunk to recall it.'

'Neither of these young women was on any sort of medication, prescription or recreational. They did not voluntarily ingest the Xanax. That's what makes this a crime. They weren't drinking heavily and they weren't drunk. Even the defendant admitted—'

'To you?'

'No, judge. We did a consent recording with one of the victims.'

'I thought he didn't admit anything.' The cheap garnet-colored stone in Moffett's ring looked like a giant wart on his gnarled finger as he waved it in my direction.

'Not to me. But he acknowledged to one of my

witnesses that he knew she had not been drinking much alcohol.'

'This drug, what does it do to them? It's an aphrodisiac?' The judge was smiling now, twisting the ring round and around his finger. 'They should have tried to stay awake.'

I had gotten up early to do my homework. 'It's a central nervous system depressant.'

'So is alcohol, your honor,' Ingels said.

'That's the point, if I may continue. My victims were sipping bourbon, which is in itself a central nervous system depressant. Sengor slipped—'

'*Doctor* Sengor, Ms Cooper.'

'I don't care if he's a doctor or an Indian chief, he's charged with several counts of the most serious felony on the books short of murder,' I said.

'Prematurely.'

'May I be heard, your honor?'

'Sure,' Moffett said, flapping the wing of his black robe at Eric Ingels. 'Let her do her thing. I know Alexandra. Once she puts her hand on her hip like that and loses that Colgate smile she marched in here with, she's not happy till I hear her out.'

'The instructions for the pills that we believe were used last night caution that because they're for extended release, they are explicitly *not* to be crushed or chewed. That's why the defendant took a vial full of Xanax—'

'How many pills are you claiming he used?'

'I don't know, your honor. The container was empty, and it holds twelve capsules when completely full. The lab will be able to give me an estimate of the quantity after they've examined the blood and urine samples of both women.'

'Go on.'

'The combination of the two powerful depressants causes immediate sedation, possible unconsciousness, often leads to respiratory cessation, which—'

'What's that?' Moffett asked.

'Death, judge. An overdose like this mixed with a combination of alcoholic beverages could actually have killed these women.'

'Your honor, you can't expect me to stand here and let Ms Cooper go overboard with her imagination, can you? Nobody's dead.'

Moffett was digging back forty years, trying to remember how to cross-examine a witness. He seemed more interested in the consummation of the sexual acts than in the involuntary drugging. 'These girls, they don't remember the sex?'

'There's an amnesiac effect from this type of sedative. Even if they had been conscious for any portion of the encounter, they wouldn't be able to remember it. I'm going to submit the literature packaged with the drug as part of the court record.'

'Yeah, Alexandra. How's a guy supposed to know they'd pass out?' Moffett held the handkerchief over his nose and honked into it before stuffing it back in his pocket and picking up his red pen.

'Judge, Sengor is a resident in psychiatry. His area of specialty is pharmacology. He knows the property of sedatives and that's exactly why Xanax was his drug of choice.'

Moffett looked over at the defense table and shook his head. 'I wouldn't expect a medical doctor to have to—'

'Cardinal rule of drug-facilitated rape, your honor. Expect the unexpected. It's for guys who might never

30

resort to force to act out their twisted fantasies. They let the drugs subdue the victims for them.'

I went on, hoping that Moffett would stop doodling on his legal pad and listen to me. 'There are four parts of this puzzle, and Sengor had every one of them in place to accomplish his goal.'

The judge looked at the defendant and held up a finger for each piece of the modus operandi as I ticked them off for him.

'He's a physician, with the knowledge of the properties of a CNS depressant and its effect when combined with alcohol. Couple that with the ability to write prescriptions for sedatives, and that gives him the means to commit the crimes – his weapon of choice. Next he needs the setting in which he controls the environment. What better than his own home? Third, he had to have the opportunity, which usually requires gaining the trust of his victims, and he'd had the first three nights of their visit to do that. Finally, Sengor had to have a plan to avoid arrest. The victims generally sleep off the effects of the drugs, and here, they would have gotten on a bus to go home to Canada, no wiser for the occurrence of the crime.'

Eric Ingels was on his feet. 'C'mon, judge. There was no "plan" to do this. These women wound up in a hospital, right down the street from Dr Sengor's home. What kind of lamebrain scheme to escape detection is that? Only a complete idiot or a man who'd never had intercourse could think that a woman might wake up and not realize she'd been . . . been . . . well, been—'

Moffett laughed out loud in agreement with Ingels. Even Sengor was smiling, perhaps sensing an ally in judicial

31

robes. 'Yeah. Been had. That's what you mean, isn't it? What do you say to that, Alex?'

'I'd say this is all completely inappropriate for a bail application, your honor. Do I need expert testimony here, to explain to both of you that one of the advantages of sedating someone with a muscle relaxant is that it makes it possible to consummate a sexual act without the victim's awareness? And many of these cases occur without transmission of seminal fluid?'

Moffett looked down at the papers and then glanced at Eric Ingels, probably hoping my adversary would interrupt me.

I went on. 'The crime of rape is accomplished, as I'm sure your honor recalls, by penetration of the victim, however slight. There's no legal requirement that he ejaculate in each of these women.'

Moffett knew he was out of his element. The colloquy was too graphic for his old-fashioned courtroom style. 'Save that talk, Alexandra. Eric says the hospital these girls went to is near his home. You heard him. What kind of scheme is that?'

'A pretty foolproof one, if my victims had used the bus tickets they told Sengor they had for yesterday afternoon. Do you know how many victims of drug-facilitated rape ever get to a hospital in time to be tested?' I asked. 'Less than ten percent. It's almost impossible to prove these crimes because some of the drugs work their way out of the system so quickly that by the time the victims sleep off the effects of the sedatives and feel well enough to get themselves medical attention, nobody even knows what toxicological tests to perform.'

'What you're telling me, missy, is that this healthy male

specimen,' Moffett said, an elbow resting on the ridge of the bench in front of him, his forefinger wagging at Selim Sengor, 'would rather make love to somebody who doesn't even know what the heck is going on. Now why would anyone want to do that?'

'It's deviant behavior, your honor. Obviously.' Don't try to compare it to your own sexual experience, I was tempted to tell him. Don't try for a minute to think outside the box. He looked even more puzzled as he licked the tip of his finger and used it to smooth down the wisps of hair that were flipping up behind his ears. 'We'll have experts to explain the psychology of it at trial. I'm just dealing with the strength of my case for the purpose of this arraignment.'

Moffett's ruling about whether or not to detain Sengor would be grounded on two major points: the likelihood that he would return to stand trial rather than be a risk to flee the jurisdiction, and the probability of my obtaining a conviction when the case went to a jury many months down the road.

'So, let me understand this, hon. You got two women who were shacking up at Dr Selim's place, drinking liquor with him, who wake up with a hangover and miss their bus ride home. You maybe have some seminal fluid—'

'And both women tell me they hadn't had intercourse in more than a month.'

'The only thing you haven't got is any evidence that the drugs were even in their cocktails, no less slipped there by the doctor,' Moffett said.

Eric Ingels had very little left to do, with Moffett so obviously in his corner. A physician didn't fit the stereo-typical profile of a rapist, and a man whose arousal came

33

from sedating women for the purpose of subjecting them to sexual assault was an even bigger stretch for this jurist's small mind.

'It seems to me, judge,' Ingels said, 'that until Ms Cooper gets her lab results, you have absolutely no reason at all to detain my client. He's got strong roots in this community. It's where he lives, it's where he works. He's got no history of criminal conduct – a perfectly clean record.'

'What kind of bail can he make?' Moffett asked Ingels.

'Your honor, most respectfully,' I said, 'I don't think you should approach the matter that way and accommodate the pocketbook of the very person we're charging with these crimes. We're talking about two counts of first-degree rape. I'd like to suggest bail in the amount of two hundred and fifty thousand dollars.'

'*What?*' Ingels said, pounding the table in front of him with a closed fist. 'You know how much a medical resident earns?'

'Calm down, both of you. Here's what I'm gonna do. She's gonna holler at me anyway, Mr Ingels. I'm going to release Dr Sengor on his own recognizance – no bail. You, Alexandra. Stop with the grimace and the smoke coming out your ears. I'll put the case over for a very short date. Next Friday, in my part. You'll have lab results by then. I'll hear you from scratch on this issue. If the case looks stronger then, I'll give you the opportunity to make your application all over again.'

Screwed twice. Not only would Sengor walk out the courthouse door before I made it up to my office, but Moffett had kept the matter in his own court part.

'I'd like him to surrender his passport to you, judge. How about that?'

Ingels whispered to his client, who told him something in response. 'Of course, Dr Sengor doesn't have it with him. The detectives rousted him out of his home in the middle of the night, with no warning.'

'So get it to me at the beginning of the week. You're not planning any vacations, are you, son?'

Selim Sengor smiled at the judge and shook his head. 'Thank you, sir. No, sir. I – I didn't – it's not what—'

Ingels put his hand on his client's arm and told him not to speak.

I gathered up my papers and medical research and walked the length of the courtroom with Mercer beside me.

'You didn't want me to collar him when I was in the apartment, did you?'

'I can't fault you for that,' I said. 'I never dreamed the pills would be there in plain view. I figured you'd execute the warrant, we'd test the findings, and the arrest would go down later during the week. You couldn't do anything but lock him up once you saw what you did in there. I'm fine with it.'

'And now you've got to argue this case before that Neanderthal?'

'Not if I can help it.' The district attorney, Paul Battaglia, occasionally pulled strings to move high-profile cases after too many embarrassing episodes of trials in front of the handful of judges who couldn't manage the more notorious crimes.

Mercer's cell phone was vibrating in his jacket pocket and he removed it to speak while we continued through the rotunda within the 100 Centre Street lobby.

'No, we're done with that,' I heard him say to his caller. 'On our way to her office. You want to ask her?'

He handed me the phone, telling me that it was Mike.

'What's up?'

'Nothing good,' Mike said. 'I'm on my way to Lincoln Center. The Metropolitan Opera House.'

'Natalya? Has anyone heard from Natalya yet?'

'Nope.'

'No one's even seen her?' I asked.

'They found some stuff. She'd been dancing a scene from *Giselle* – that's the one with the Wilis, right?'

'Yes.' Mike knew I had studied ballet all my life.

'Like a headpiece, and some tulle from the costume that must have caught on a nail and ripped off.'

'A garland of white flowers, with a veil?' There was a standard costume for Giselle's graveyard scene.

'That sounds right. Would dancers like her go out on the street after a performance, Coop, in a full-length tutu and toe slippers?'

'Very unlikely. Even if she had a coat over her costume, she'd put shoes on so she wouldn't rip the satin pointe slippers on cement sidewalks or asphalt. Why, Mike? Where did they find the clothing?'

'In a hallway, going up to the third floor, a few flights above the stage and the dressing rooms. Along with a glove – a man's white kid glove. A dressy one, if you know what I mean. I had a pair like it once that I had to wear when I was an usher at a wedding at St Patrick's. And blood, there's a few droplets that look like blood on the wall.'

'That could mean any number of—' I said.

'Did I mention a contact? One contact lens. The agent confirmed she wears them.'

I thought of what kind of blow to the socket could cause the lens to be forced off the surface and expelled from the eye. 'You're ruling out everything but some kind of struggle, aren't you?'

'They're checking all the corridors, top to bottom – every room and cubbyhole. That place is just massive. I can't sit on my ass anymore and wait for the twenty-four hours to pass.'

I could picture Talya – a magnificent creature whose fragile appearance masked the incredible strength and stamina possessed by the great ballerinas. I had seen her at Lincoln Center just months earlier, commanding the enormous stage as though it was her natural home.

'It's unthinkable,' I said.

'What is, Coop?' Mike's personal tragedy had made him more cynical than ever. 'That Talya Galinova might have been unfortunate enough to put herself in the running for this year's homicide stats?'

More than a decade in this business had made me mindful that no one was guaranteed immunity from that often random list. But to disappear inside the most famous theater in the world, with more than four thousand people under the same roof at the very moment she vanished?

'It's not possible she was murdered at the Met.'

Chapter 4

Mercer parked in the driveway that arced away from Broadway and ran the entire length in front of the plaza at the Lincoln Center for the Performing Arts, from 65th down to 62nd Street. The travertine complex of theater and music facilities was built in the 1960s at a cost equivalent to more than a billion dollars today.

Bright April sunshine bounced off the waters in the enormous fountain in the center of the buildings as streams gushed in the air at timed intervals, delighting the tourists who gathered around it with their guidebooks. We ignored the structures to the north and south – the Philharmonic's Avery Fisher Hall and the City Ballet and Opera's home, the New York State Theater. The block-long giant that dominated the plaza set back on its western end was the Metropolitan Opera House, and I tried to keep pace with Mercer's great strides as we both hurried to hook up with Mike Chapman.

'I hope you didn't read him wrong.'

'He wants you here, Alex. That's why he called.'

'I'm familiar with this world. That's really why he called. I'm not sure Mike's ready to let me back into his life.'

People with cameras were everywhere, snapping photos of one another against the backdrop of the imposing buildings on this great urban acropolis. Large silk banners with the Royal Ballet's logo billowed from the flagpoles, heralding the visiting company in the calm afternoon breeze.

The three of us had worked as a team on more murder cases than most prosecutors would ever handle in their entire careers. Mercer had transferred from the Homicide Squad to Special Victims. Like me, he got satisfaction in helping women find justice in a system that had denied them access for so long, with archaic laws and even more stubborn human attitudes. The legislative reforms and stunning advances in scientific techniques brought us successes not dreamed possible even twenty years ago.

Mike preferred the elite world of homicide cops – no living victims to hand-hold, few eyewitnesses to have fall apart in court – coaxing from lifeless bodies the secrets of how they met their deaths and then ferreting out the killers. All too often our professional worlds intersected and we shouldered the cases together, trying to restore moral order to a world in which lives ended so violently and abruptly.

'You think he's ready to settle down and work, Mercer, if this turns out to be what Mike thinks it is?'

'He's got to be ready. He lost his focus after Val's death, and nobody knows that better than he does. The man needs to get back in the mix now. Lieutenant Peterson gave him time – lots of time. I'm working with him, whatever he wants on this. You stick, too, Alex. He'd like that.'

39

I was practically running to keep up with Mercer. 'You may think so, but Mike might not say that to—'

'I'm saying it. He doesn't have a better friend than you. We got to think for him now, we got to be there when and if the center doesn't hold.'

Inside the Met's lobby, straight ahead, I could see the brilliant yellow-and-red panels of the two Chagall murals – each of them three stories high – celebrating the triumph of music with figures of musicians and dancers, instruments and whimsical animals.

Mercer guided me into the revolving door and pushed from behind. Several uniformed cops stood casual guard within the lobby, keeping up an air of business-as-usual for theatergoers who queued on the lines to buy tickets for next week's performances.

One of the only African-American first-grade detectives in the city, Mercer's six-foot-six figure commanded attention wherever he went. Here he flashed his badge at a young officer, who responded by removing the red velvet rope from the brass stanchion and sending us down the carpeted staircase to the lower lobby without even questioning why I accompanied Mercer.

The long flat counter of the bar would later be filled with cocktails served up for the crush of dance aficionados during intermissions of this evening's program. Now it was covered with paper from end to end. Mike Chapman stood with his back to us, his left hand in his pants pocket and the right one combing through his thick hair.

Mercer tapped his shoulder, interrupting Mike's conversation with the two men who stood across from him behind the bar. They were all studying architectural

40

drawings of the vast corridors, below- and aboveground, which made up this imposing theatrical venue.

Mike turned to introduce us. 'Mr Dobbis here, Chet Dobbis, is the artistic director of the Metropolitan Opera. He's overseeing the ballet company's visit because it's part of a series of fundraisers for the house.

'Mr Dobbis, I'd like you to meet Mercer Wallace – NYPD Special Victims. This is Ms Cooper, Alex Cooper. Alex heads the Sex Crimes Prosecution Unit in the Manhattan DA's office. And she's a mean dancer.'

I reached over to shake Dobbis's hand. He was taller and leaner than the photos of him I'd seen in the *Times* when he was hired two years ago by the great Beverly Sills – just before her retirement – and her board of directors. Forty-five, maybe older, he was dressed in a black shirt and slacks with a sweater over his shoulders, tied loosely around the neck.

'And this is Rinaldo Vicci. He's Ms Galinova's agent.' I towered over the diminutive Vicci, who bowed in my direction. I guessed him to be fifty, too portly for his height, with pasty skin that looked blotchy and irritated. The glen plaid suit he sported was in need of serious alterations, the buttons pulling across his belly as he stretched out a hand to each of us.

'Any developments since we spoke?' Mercer asked Mike.

'The commissioner gave us a green light to start searching the joint.'

'That's a big concession.'

'The missing person status would go real-time – twenty-four hours since Talya disappeared – in the middle of tonight's show, which would certainly disrupt the crowd. Everybody here thought we needed to ratchet it up as soon as possible.'

'Where is Talya staying?' I asked.

'The Mark. But she hasn't been back to the hotel room since yesterday,' Mike said. 'Never called her husband, and they usually speak three or four times a day.'

'Her street clothes?' I asked.

'They're still in her dressing room,' Vicci said with a trace of an Italian accent. 'Sweater and pants, her boots. Even the purse she carries. It's all still there. I – I can't tell you how worried I am about her. I'm absolutely frantic at the thought of anyone harming her.'

'Bet you are,' Mike said. 'What does an agent get these days? Fifteen percent of nothing is nothing. That's why we need your help, Mr Vicci. You got a better reason than anybody to keep her alive and well.'

'Joe Berk?' I asked. 'Have any of you spoken with him today?'

'Nobody can find him,' Chet Dobbis said. 'The office is closed for the weekend and he's not answering calls. I'm told that's not unusual, Ms Cooper. In the middle of a Saturday afternoon, he might well be attending a performance of one of his shows.'

'Mind if I take a few minutes with Detective Wallace?' Mike asked.

'I'll step inside and watch the dress rehearsal, if you don't mind. Rinaldo, why don't you wait with me?' Dobbis said, leading Vicci to the theater doors at the far end of the bar. There was a quiet elegance about him, a gracefulness in the way he moved that fit so precisely with his role in the theater.

Mike waited until they were out of range. He leaned

both elbows on the bar and rested his head in his hands. 'Sorry. It's been an uphill battle all night to get these guys to let us in. They'll go nuts when ESU shows up with all their gear.'

'You called for Emergency Services?' I asked. They were the unit of last resort, teams of fearless cops who got into and around places that no others could manage. They rescued jumpers from bridges and building cornices, recovered bodies from tunnels and train tracks, and broke down doorways and barriers to get into wherever their colleagues needed to go. 'Battering rams and the jaws of death? Isn't that giving up the ghost a little bit early?'

'Jaws of life. They're what get you out of the jaws of death. I guess you've never been backstage here, have you, kid? You're in for an eye-opener.' Mike swiveled around to look at me. 'Remember how old you were the first time you came to Lincoln Center?'

'Maybe eight or nine.'

'What for?'

'To see the *Nutcracker*, next door at the State Theater. My mother brought me there every Christmas.' It was almost a ritual for little girls who loved ballet and who had grown up in the city or, as I had, in the suburbs less than an hour away.

'And the Met?' Mike asked.

'A year or two later.'

'How many times since?'

He knew the answer to that question. I subscribed to the annual repertory season of American Ballet Theater and frequented the opera whenever I had the chance. 'Dozens of times, Mike. Maybe hundreds.'

He was going somewhere with this and I waited patiently for him to make his point.

'I know you don't like the parking garage much, but did it ever scare you to sit inside the Met?'

'Scare me? To be in the audience? It's where I come to get away from the tawdry things we see and hear every day at work. It transports me to be here, to put it mildly.'

I truly loved to sink into a velvet-cushioned seat at the end of a day at the prosecutor's office, wait for the 1,500 yards of Scalamandre silk curtain to lift and drape in Wagnerian style, and the thirty-two crystal chandeliers to rise up against the twenty-four-karat gold-leaf ceiling as they dimmed to darkness. For two or three hours I was able to lose myself in whatever world of make-believe the artists drew around me.

'Let me tell you about the first time I came here,' Mike said. 'Same age as you – maybe ten at the time.'

Mike had turned thirty-seven a few months earlier, and I would celebrate the same birthday at the end of this month. Mercer was five years older than us, now married to another detective named Vickee and father to a baby born a bit more than a year ago.

'My old man and I were out together for the afternoon, a weekday in late July. It didn't happen often that I got to spend a whole day with him,' Mike said. We knew all about his father, who'd been on the force for twenty-six years. Brian Chapman was a legend in the department, and the heart attack that killed him forty-eight hours after he turned in his gun and shield made Mike even more determined to follow in his footsteps.

'Somebody gave him tickets for the Yankees game and, man, was I psyched. He got off duty at eight a.m., slept a couple of hours, took my buddies and me out on the street to pitch to us so we could play stickball, see how far we could whack the ball. Three manhole covers or more.'

Mercer nodded his head, familiar with the New York City street game.

'Something you never did in the burbs, right, Coop? It was before cell phones. My mother shouted him in from the stoop to take an emergency call from his boss. When he got back out, my dad pulled me aside and asked me if I wanted to take a ride. Told me he wouldn't be able to go to the game after all, 'cause something had come up with work. He knew how unhappy that made me, except he told me I could come along with him this time. Me, I'd give up every Yankee from the Babe to Mantle to Guidry to Piniella – and throw in Jeter and A-Rod now, too – just to hang out on the job with my pop.'

'I know what you mean,' I said.

'He let me choose what I wanted to do, so I gave the other kids the ball-game tickets and we got in his jalopy, drove over and parked on Amsterdam Avenue, right behind Lincoln Center. I remember coming in the back door that day, through the garage, everybody stepping aside as soon as he palmed the gold shield. "On the job" – I still hear his voice saying that to people. He told me a girl was missing, a musician who played in the orchestra, and that lots of guys were already here looking for her. The big boss was interviewing her husband back at the squad. They needed every cop they could get because of the size of this place.'

'She went missing like Natalya, in the middle of a show?' Mercer asked.

But I had my own question. 'Why'd your dad take you into a breaking case?'

Mike answered me first. ''Cause he had the same logical thought that you did, Coop. It's the Metropolitan Opera, for chrissakes. The Big House is what they called it. Four thousand people – *four thousand* – were sitting in that very room on one side of the curtain,' he said, pointing to the auditorium door, 'four hundred more working their asses off to make the show go on, and somebody disappears from the orchestra pit without one person in the whole joint hearing a peep? Not possible.'

I nodded at him. I understood what his dad had been thinking.

'She must have been upset about something and walked out between acts. That's what he and every other cop thought. Same as her friends in the orchestra. The woman behind her just moved up and shoved the girl's violin under her seat, and the conductor kept right on going with the show. Hey, you know the stats as well as anybody. Women are far more likely to be hurt or killed by someone they know and love than by a stranger in a crowded theater.'

'That's why they were grilling the husband at the same time the cops were searching the place,' Mercer said.

'You bet. Garden-variety domestic violence is what he figured it was. You're missing the point. This wasn't about the case – not about the police work,' Mike said, looking at me.

'What then?'

'My old man had never been inside the Met. Didn't know the first thing about stuff as grand as opera or ballet. My house, you heard Sinatra and Dean Martin, Judy Garland and Dinah Shore. No Pavarotti or Caruso or

46

Callas. Entertainment was the living room television set, big deal was going out to an occasional movie or a night at the fights.

'This was a chance for my father to show me some culture, Ms Cooper, something as foreign to me as stick-ball and warm beer are to you.'

Mike liked to underscore the differences in our upbringings. My mother was trained as a nurse, but stopped working after she married my father and gave birth to my two older brothers and me. Their middle-class lifestyle changed dramatically when my father, Benjamin, and his partner invented an innovative medical device that thereafter was used in most cardiac surgery for more than thirty years. The tiny Cooper-Hoffman valve was responsible for providing me with a superb education at Wellesley College and the University of Virginia School of Law, an old farmhouse on Martha's Vineyard that was my refuge from the turmoil of my job, and lots of small luxuries that wouldn't have been afford-able on the salary of a young public servant.

I knew Mike loved and respected his father as deeply as I did my own. That thought took me back to his story. 'He must have delighted in having you by his side,' I said.

'I remember how he brought me through the corri-dors – endless gray cinder block walls with doorways going off in every direction. It's the size of a football field and a half from the front door to the back. Somehow, we wound up in the wrong place – on the main stage, looking out into the empty house, tier after tier of seats. I had to crane my neck to see to the top row.'

'You remember that?' Mercer asked.

'Like I was inside St Peter's for the first time. That it

was the most magnificent place I'd ever seen in my life. There was so much gold on every surface, and the biggest crystals in the chandeliers – well, I thought they were diamonds the size of baseballs. I'd never been near anything like this. People were walking around backstage in costumes – the girls hardly had anything on and the men were dressed in tights with bare chests.'

'What did your father do with you?'

'I guess he thought he'd sit me down and let me watch a rehearsal while he worked,' Mike said to Mercer, 'but most of the artists were too distracted to perform with the searches going on in every corner of the building. So I went along with him. He wasn't expecting any trouble, right? And all the guys knew me – you remember Giorgio and Struk, don't you? It was their case.'

Two of the smartest detectives I'd worked with as a young prosecutor, they had handled major cases long before I came on the job.

'Sure. Didn't Giorgio train you?' I asked.

Mike nodded at me. 'Jerry G. was just breaking in at the time. Asked Dad to go up to the fourth floor. Along the way, every time we passed somebody in a costume, my old man'd stop them and introduce them to me. I don't know what the hell he was thinking, but he wanted me to shake hands with people he thought might be famous, like maybe the class would rub off on me,' he said, laughing at the memory of it.

'Sweet,' Mercer said, smiling back at him. 'Sweet idea.'

'Those girls were something else. They all looked so soft and so beautiful. Each one he put a hand out to greet had creamier shoulders than the next, with jewelry sparkling on their ears and in their hair.'

48

Mike smiled at Mercer as he talked on. I hadn't seen him this animated and happy since before Val's death. 'I don't think I'd ever seen women in makeup before, elegant women – not all that much older than I was – who tousled my hair and stroked my cheek as they went past me; each of them seemed like a fairy queen to me. You ever dress up like that?'

'Only for our recitals,' I said. 'My favorite day at the end of the year.'

'We got up to the fourth floor and it was like a city unto itself. There was the scenic design room, with a few guys building a palace for some opera and others making a fantastic tree out of Styrofoam. There were Roman columns and castle parapets, papier-mâché mountains, Egyptian pyramids and Hindu temples, like a giant play-room. Cops were everywhere, looking behind plywood frames twenty feet high, stacked against every surface.

'Then came a clothing studio where thousands of costumes were made, with tailors and seamstresses hunched over drafting tables. Life-size figures were standing in the hallways, and a pole – a spaghetti rack, they called it – hung from one end of the corridor to the other. There were soldiers' uniforms and kings' robes, and still cops sticking their noses in every nook and cranny 'cause you could have hidden ten bodies just about anywhere up there and not found 'em for years. And me? I was mesmerized by the costumes – touching the gold braid and holding the different fabrics against my skin, wondering if I'd ever feel anything that silken again.'

'How about Brian?' Mercer asked.

'Pop did what he had to do, asking the workers if they'd seen or heard anything, writing down all their names. He was happy just watching me, 'cause I really was entranced by the whole thing. Exactly what he wanted to bring me for. Till one of the rookies came running to get him, whispered something to him.'

Mike paused and when the storytelling stopped, the smile was gone with it. When he went on, there was no trace of a pleasant memory.

'I can remember the look on my dad's face. He didn't seem to know what to do at that very moment, and I wasn't used to seeing him like that. I think he wanted to leave me right where I was, but he knew he couldn't do that. The guys were all working too hard to ask any of them to look after me. He gave me one of those very stern, hand-on-my-shoulder commands in his best brogue: "Mikey, my son, just follow me and stay out of everyone's way."'

'Where to?' Mercer asked.

'Back through the maze of shops and studios, till someone put us on an elevator that took us up to the roof. We stepped off and I saw Giorgio and Struk. One of them called out to Brian and pointed at me, telling him to leave me back, right where I was.'

Mike stopped again. 'My old man was wrong. That's the first thing I remembered thinking that day. I didn't believe the guy ever had a bad instinct in his life and maybe this time he'd screwed up for once. I was so shaken and disappointed, I thought I was gonna be sick. I knew he'd catch hell from my mother for bringing me along, for his thinking the missing musician was alive and well someplace else, and for his idea that the Met would be a good afternoon outing for his kid.'

'You mean they told you what happened to the girl?' Mercer asked.

'Tell me? Nobody was paying any attention to me from that point on, with good reason. So I got down on the floor and held on to a pipe along the edge of the building, leaning out just enough to see what they were all staring at below us.

'There was her body, crumpled on the top of a setback, six floors down from the roof, four stories above the street. Long blond hair down most of her back, spattered with blood, her legs twisted and bent like a wishbone torn apart at a Thanksgiving dinner.'

I thought immediately of the missing Natalya Galinova.

'I still can't shake that memory,' Mike said. 'You never forget the first time you see a corpse.'

Chapter 5

Murder at the Met. If it could happen a quarter of a century ago, it could happen again today. No matter how elegant the setting, no matter how benign the business going on inside, no matter how familiar the great urban institution, there was nothing that made any place in the city safe from violence. No wonder Mike was urging the police brass to get inside and moving on this case.

'Who killed the musician?' I asked.

'A twenty-one-year-old stage carpenter. Must have intercepted her when she got lost in a hallway, trying to get backstage to meet one of the dancers. He was a baby-faced kid with a bad alcohol problem. Pretended to show her the way, tried to rape her, and she fought him off. Got him the old-fashioned way, before DNA. Fingerprints on the pipe near where she went off the roof, and then a confession. That judge you're always flirting with?'

I laughed. 'Roger Hayes?'

'He tried the case for your office. Brilliant job. My dad kept a scrapbook with all the clippings. I've got it at home – and the killer, he's still rotting away upstate.'

Mike opened the auditorium door and asked Dobbis and Vicci to come out.

'Where would you like to start, Mr Chapman?' Chet Dobbis asked.

'Crime scene is processing the site where the objects were found,' Mike said to Mercer and me. 'There's another area near that where a nail's sticking out of the wall. Looks like Talya's hair got caught on it. Pulled out a clump from her scalp.'

He turned back to Dobbis. 'Where's a good place to talk?'

'There's a rehearsal in the auditorium. I don't think that's a good idea. Perhaps Natalya's dressing room, Rinaldo?'

'Sure. That'll be fine.'

Dobbis pointed to a doorway. 'Behind stage right.'

It was to the left of the great auditorium, and Mike reversed his course as he must have realized that stage directions were sited from the perspective of the artist facing the audience.

'Why don't you tell us what the security is like here?' Mike asked.

I was walking alongside Dobbis, with Mike and Mercer behind us and Rinaldo Vicci waddling in the rear.

'Until today I would have answered that it's been quite good.'

'Talk about during the performances.'

'Front of the house, of course, you can't get in without tickets. Thirty-eight hundred seats – center orchestra starts at ninety dollars, on up through six tiers, balcony at the top.'

'The nose-bleed section,' Mike said, poking me in the back. 'Bet you've never been up there, Coop. You'd get vertigo just thinking about it.'

'Two hundred seventy-five people pay for standing room at the back of the orchestra. That's your four thousand tally.'

'Employees?'

'Several hundred. Stagehands, electricians, makeup artists, costume and set designers. Every piece of scenery, every item of clothing or headdress, every prop for more than twenty-five operas that are mounted here throughout the season is made in-house. And then we have guests who rent the space, if you will, ballet companies like the Royal, who bring their own people in.'

'So every day . . . ?' I asked.

'You've got hundreds of employees, and hundreds more transients passing through. Tours are conducted daily – schoolchildren, tourists of all ages and nationalities, visiting performers and dignitaries, materials are delivered from morning until night. Artists have visitors – family, friends, other producers they're auditioning for. We've got coaches and prompters and conductors. A cast of thousands, you might say.'

'Screened by security?'

'They come in through the stage-door entrance. They've got to show identification, of course. Do they sign in or have we lists of their names? For the employees, certainly. For everyone else, I think not.'

The gray cement corridor was cheerless and cold. Its walls were lined on one side with enormous trunks stamped with the Royal Ballet name in white stencils. A few were open, revealing peasant dresses and pirate shirts, all part of the repertoire that would be danced during the week.

Mike rapped his knuckles on a trunk and called to a

uniformed cop at the far end of the long hall. 'Get more guys in here. Open every one of these. I don't care if you have to break the locks to get inside, just check each of them.'

We were single file going through now, Dobbis leading us as he talked. 'That's the doctor's office,' he said. 'Nurses are on duty all throughout the day, and there's a physician in the house for every performance. Talya knew that as well.'

Past another door. He turned the knob, but it didn't give. 'Animal handlers. SPCA requirements. Whenever we've got an opera with a horse or a donkey or a camel, we've got to have someone who meets humane society regulations. In *Giselle,* there are a couple of borzois – Russian wolfhounds – so even this room was occupied last night.'

Mike yelled again to the cop. 'Yo. You doing anything? Get a custodian with keys or a sledgehammer to get through these doors.'

Chet Dobbis showed his annoyance for the first time. 'We're going as fast as we can manage, detective. I've given orders to have everything unlocked for you.'

'After the show, Mr Dobbis,' I said, 'suppose Talya had gone somewhere on another floor in the building, for a legitimate reason. How soon would the backstage area be emptied out of all the workers?'

'It never is. The Met stage is alive for the better part of twenty-four hours. The show will go on tonight, and when it's over, the stage crew will strike the sets that were used. The night gang will take over and they'll start working to put up the scenery for whatever the next day's dress rehearsal will be. When the rehearsal is finished,

55

they strike that set and get things in place for the following night. The work is endless and the place is always bustling.'

'Even Sundays?'

'Often. There are usually practice sessions, even if the house is dark. And then you've got charity benefits and special events that we put on quite frequently.'

Another left turn and we were at a door marked DRESSING ROOMS. Dobbis entered and the string of us followed him in. A small wall unit held a series of locked boxes. 'This is where the principals keep their valuables while they're dancing. Talya's wallet and hotel key are still there,' Vicci said. 'I've got her spare.'

Mike took the key from the agent, unlocked the box, and removed the items. 'Hold on to these,' he said to me. 'I'll voucher them if she doesn't show up for dinner tonight.'

Straight ahead was a T-shaped intersection. 'The corps has lockers in another part of the building. This area is just for the stars,' Dobbis said. 'There's even a pecking order in here. In opera season, the soprano and the tenor have the center rooms. The baritone, the mezzo, and the bass are off to the side. So Natalya had this room, of course.'

He ushered us into a private suite, bare of any personal items except an index card tacked to the door with Natalya's name in black marker, and her clothes hanging on a rack inside. I checked the bathroom and stall shower, but saw nothing. Dobbis offered me the chair in front of the mirrored dressing table.

There was a piano against the opposite wall, where Vicci seated himself. Dobbis perched on the edge of a sofa, while Mike and Mercer remained standing.

'There aren't many windows in this joint,' Mike said. 'What are we looking out at?'

Except for the five glass arches that faced the plaza, the Met seemed completely encased in its marble skin.

'That's Amsterdam Avenue behind me,' Dobbis said. 'It's actually the only window that opens in the entire building. Rudolf Bing was the general manager when the company moved to Lincoln Center back in 1966. His favorite diva was Renata Tebaldi, and she wanted fresh air whenever she sang. So, voilà, a window.'

Dobbis thought Mike was interested in the history of the house, but I knew he was only studying means of entering or exiting the building.

'You mind getting up off that sofa?' Mike said, motioning to the director and then speaking to Mercer. 'Let's get this sill dusted and see if there are any footprints on the couch.'

Mike picked up the phone on the wall next to the piano.

'That's just an intercom, detective. You can't ring out,' Dobbis said. 'The stage manager calls in to give the artist her cue. It's a three-minute walk to the wings from this room, almost six to get to stage left for an entrance.'

Mercer turned to the door and called back to Mike. 'You want the guys from the Crime Scene Unit to come down and process this next?'

'Yeah.'

'Easier for me to see what they're up to.'

'So what's the story with this guy Joe Berk?' Mike asked as Mercer walked out. 'How'd you know he was in here with her last night?'

'The Wizard? He'd be hard to miss.'

'Wizard of what?'

'That's what he likes to call himself. The Wizard of the Great White Way.'

'More like a lizard,' Rinaldo Vicci said. 'The venomous kind.'

'What does Berk do?' Mike asked. 'He's a producer?'

Chet Dobbis laughed. 'Joe Berk owns Broadway. That's what he really does. Everything else flows from that.'

'You gotta explain that to me. How does somebody *own* Broadway?'

'The theaters themselves, detective. There are four families in New York that control every single one of the legitimate theaters.'

'You mean, like the Shuberts?' I asked.

'Exactly. The Shuberts, the Nederlanders, the Jujamcyns, and the Berks. There are thirty-five Broadway theaters. You want to bring a show to town? You got the next *Cats* or *Phantom* in your back pocket? Nothing happens unless you get through to the head honcho of one of these families. There are nice guys and smart guys and decent guys in this business, and then there's Joe Berk.'

'What's his relationship with Ms Galinova?' Mike asked.

Vicci wanted to do the spin on this. 'Joe has been courting my client, but strictly in the professional sense,' he said, rolling his *r*'s for what he must have thought was dramatic effect. 'He's got an idea for a project that she might be able to star in.'

Dobbis interrupted him. 'Rinaldo, you're talking to the police. Try telling the truth, for a change.'

'Why don't you give him a hand?'

'The fact is that it's Talya who's been chasing after Joe Berk, Mr Chapman. She's gotten to the age when most dancers have to give some thought to the next phase of their careers. By the time these ladies reach forty, it becomes harder and harder to convince an audience they're a fourteen-year-old Juliet or an adolescent sleeping beauty. And the injuries – the injuries really take their toll on their feet and knees and hips.'

'Broadway?'

'That's what she's been exploring,' Dobbis said. 'Talya is as stunning an actress as she is a ballerina. The Russian accent's a bit thick for a lot of roles, but that hasn't stopped her from trying to develop ideas. She's ready for a star turn that would introduce her to millions more people who don't have the first clue about ballet. Popular culture for the masses, rather than an elite crowd.'

'And Berk?' Mike asked.

'The way I see it,' Dobbis said, 'she thought seduction was the best way to audition.'

Vicci was unhappy. 'You've got no business saying that, Chet. I know everything that goes on in Talya's life and there's nothing at all to that gossip.'

'How old is Berk?' Mike asked.

'Seventy-four.'

'Vigorous?'

'Overweight, but as strong as he is tough. He's got a stranglehold on Broadway real estate,' said Dobbis. 'No reason he couldn't have one on a human being.'

'And you say he was here last night?'

'Not in the house. Not in the audience, I mean.'

'Wasn't he coming to see Talya?'

'He was late for the second act,' Rinaldo Vicci said.

59

'The Met's policy – maybe you know it – is you can't be seated once the performance has started. They've got – how you call it? – a little auditorium offstage right where you can watch it on a big screen. Berk had a fit.'

'Why?' I asked.

'He doesn't like crowds. It's not in his nature to sit there with the tardy bridge-and-tunnel folk, looking at the action on a monitor,' Dobbis said. 'That's how I found out he was in the dressing room. Bullied his way in past the ushers – made a scene doing it – and waited for Talya to get offstage.'

'The fight?'

'She was peeved that he hadn't bothered to get there in time to watch her dance.'

'He likes ballet?' Mike asked.

'Berk doesn't like anything until it makes the cash jingle in his pocket. I think he's used to something with catchy lyrics to keep him awake during the show.'

'His antics with the ushers,' I said to Dobbis, 'and then the argument with a diva, didn't they get everyone's attention?'

'The staff expects a few nasty latecomers most evenings, Ms Cooper. Once they realized he wasn't an autograph hound, Berk's tiff with them blew over. And any arguments between Talya and Berk – or anyone else who crossed her – well, the acoustics in this building are extraordinary, maybe the best in the world. There's not a corner, not a ninety-degree angle inside the Opera House. The ceiling and wall panels are rounded so that sound bounces off and back into the theater.'

'But I'm talking about outside the auditorium.'

'The rest of the building is made up of scores of soundproofed compartments. It has to be, if you think about it. Stagehands are moving around enormous pieces of scenery and equipment – even in the middle of a performance – while singers and musicians are rehearsing in studios throughout the building, and other artists are practicing,' he said, tapping the top of the piano, 'often until the moment they walk to the stage. You aren't supposed to be able to hear anything else from anywhere else behind the scenes.'

'So Talya could have been—'

'Having a tantrum? No way for me to know.'

'Then how come you told me that?' Mike asked. 'That was part of the first information from the scratch that came in last night.'

'The masseur called it to my attention. I was already aware of the brouhaha about Berk storming back to the dressing area to wait for the end of the act. Talya got there and threw the poor man out of the room, then began her tirade at Berk.'

'A masseur in her dressing room in the middle of a ballet?' Mike asked. 'Coop, you're in the wrong line of work. What's his name and when can we talk to him?'

'You'll have it. You'll have whatever you need.'

'Did anyone see Berk leave the theater?'

Vicci and Dobbis looked at each other. 'No one's mentioned it to me,' the agent said. 'But we haven't exactly been concerned about him, to tell you the truth.'

Mercer opened the door and signaled to Mike and me to come out into the hallway. I had seen him at crime scenes and hospital bedsides, in courtrooms and prison holding pens. There was no facial expression of Mercer's that I couldn't read. This one broadcast bad news.

'It's Natalya,' I said.

'Let's get up there before the whole area is compromised,' he said, shaking his head.

'If you hadn't ramped up this search like you did, Mike? They wouldn't have found her till summer.'

'Where?'

'You'd have to know this place as well as the guys who built it.'

Mike started walking to the bank of elevators behind stage right. 'What floor?'

'They're up on six. Like a roof—'

'The roof's on ten,' Mike said, a fact seared in the memory of a ten-year-old boy.

'It's an enclosure then, with a walkway that leads outside, over a great square pit. It's where the air-conditioning units are – with fans bigger than I am.'

What better to mute the sounds of a final struggle.

We were there in less than four minutes, precinct detectives and uniformed rookies stepping aside and pressing their backs against the dirty gray walls as they saw Mike Chapman approach, everything about him signifying the arrival of a homicide cop who had come to take over control of the grim corridor.

The closer we got to the rampart that led outside, the bellow from the giant rotors made it more impossible to hear conversation. The pipes seemed to be vibrating as the monstrous blades circulated air and blew it up at us.

'What's the drop?' Mike asked a janitor who had apparently made the discovery and was standing closest to the opening.

'Thirty feet, easy.'

Mike stepped down onto the rim of the fan pit – a

platform a couple of feet wide – and was followed by Mercer, who held out a hand for me. I wanted to clutch one of the black pipes to steady myself, but knew they might hold trace evidence of value.

I glanced over the edge and at first saw only the blackness below. It took seconds for my eyes to adjust to the dark as my body braced against the roaring blasts from the giant fan blades.

Even as the soot whirled around me, I could see the flash of a white tulle costume lifting with the current, revealing the motionless, broken body of Natalya Galinova, wedged into the remote corner of the filthy air shaft.

Chapter 6

The janitor led us down to the third floor, through the electrical shop and the multistory paint bridges where crews of workers were constructing scenery, back to the interior point within the building where the air shaft bottomed out.

Only Mike, Mercer, and I entered the narrow passageway. The air circulation system had been turned off at Mike's direction and he led us in to check for any signs of life while we waited for someone from the medical examiner's office to make the decision about how to move Talya.

Mike kneeled at the wire-mesh cage, shining a torch-size flashlight into the hole, trying to get as close to her body as he could.

I flinched when the beam found Talya's head. Not much of it was intact. It didn't matter how many corpses I'd seen. The moment never got easier.

Mike was talking to Mercer, framing a description like the ones he'd heard week after week as he stood witness at the autopsy table in the Office of the Chief Medical Examiner. 'Probably a circular fracture of the cranial vault. Can you see that split through the hairline?'

The long, fine strands of Talya's hair were plastered against her scalp. She had gone into the shaft headfirst, it appeared, her neck twisted under the weight of her slim body.

The skull was actually split in pieces, looking like the bloodstained map of an intersection of five major highways.

Mercer differentiated the injury from a depressed skull fracture, the kind that occurs when an object crushes a small area of the head. 'Must have been alive when she was thrown over.'

The circular fractures radiated out from the point of impact, aggravated by the velocity of the dancer's descent and the height of the drop.

Blood was everywhere, pooled beneath Talya's ear and splattered all over the satin torso of her costume.

'You see her arms?' Mercer asked.

'Looks like they're behind her. Probably tied.'

The legs that had been so distinctly Galinova's – long and lean, well muscled and with extension that had been remarked upon by every reviewer since her debut in Moscow more than twenty years earlier – were visible from beneath the ripped tulle skirt. The left one was twisted inward, the knee apparently knocked out of its joint as it bounced off the wall of the shaft. The right one, closer to us, seemed broken in half at the calf, the bone protruding through the Lycra tights that covered Talya's leg. There was no toe shoe on that foot, as there appeared to be on the other.

Mike moved the light like a wand, up and down the lines of the body, looking for any other marks or signs of injuries unrelated to the fall.

Behind me I could hear the voices of new arrivals. 'Chapman? We're comin' in.'

'Move it, Coop. That's Emergency Services.'

I backed out of the space and greeted the crew from ESU. They were lugging just about every kind of device that could be imagined to cut through the metal grating.

While I listened to them work their way into the small cell – the caged area above the giant fan – that held Talya Galinova, one of the death-scene investigators appeared to do a cursory study of the body, declare the matter a homicide, and supervise the delicate removal of the remains to the basement of the morgue.

Mike and Mercer joined me to make way for Hal Sherman, who had to photograph the body from every aspect before anyone could move the dancer from her painful pose.

When that was done, Dr Kestenbaum, the medical examiner on duty, put on his lab suit, gloves, and booties, looking more like a space traveler than a forensic pathologist as he approached the air shaft. Within minutes, Kestenbaum returned and signaled the ambulance crew to bag the body.

We circled around him to see what he had to say. 'I think you could have done this without me.'

'Yeah, doc,' Mike said. 'But what killed her?'

'Skull fracture. Broken neck with cervical spinal injuries. Hands bound behind her back so nothing to cushion the blow before the head struck. Massive contre-coup contusions – a classic result of a fall. You and I had one like that before, Mike.'

I had seen the photos of the brain in Mike's case in which a man was pushed off the roof of one of the city's great museums. The brain rebounds backward from the skull after striking with such great force, leaving the devastating marks at the location directly opposite the point of impact.

The young doctor turned to me. 'Doesn't look like your bailiwick, Ms Cooper. The leotard and tights are in place. No signs of an attempt at sexual assault.'

Mercer wasn't giving up the connection that would keep a Special Victims Squad detective in the case. 'The murder may have been the result of a relationship she was involved in. Too early to tell. Alex and I are in this for the long haul.'

I couldn't tell whether Mercer said this because he was professionally interested in who killed Talya or because he wanted to remain in the case for the purpose of shoring Mike up as we got him back in the saddle for what would now be a high-profile investigation.

'You'll want these things,' Kestenbaum said to Mike, handing him several brown paper bags.

Mike opened the first one and passed it to me. Inside was one of Talya's pointe shoes – soft white satin with the hard surface at the front that allowed her to dance on her toes. The two ribbons that crisscrossed and laced around the ankles seemed to be missing.

'Did this tear off during the fall?' I asked.

'No,' Kestenbaum said. 'Check one of the other bags. The perp must have made her take one slipper off before he killed her.'

Each piece of evidence was bagged separately, to prevent the transfer of any substance – even microscopic amounts – from one item to another. It was collected in ordinary brown paper, so that surfaces damp from blood or water would dry out, rather than mildew in the plastic. In a second bag, then, were two strands of ribbon.

'The shoe landed underneath her body. We'll have to study the pattern of the blood to see exactly how it spattered or dripped. Those ribbons were used to tie her hands behind her back. Much easier to toss her into the pit without her able to struggle or resist. I'm actually surprised there's no gag.'

'That's 'cause this monster's turned off now. Sounded like a fleet of 747s on takeoff when we got here,' Mike said. 'Would have drowned out anything.'

Mercer's gloved hand reached for the smaller bag. He removed the two pieces of ribbon, an ivory white satin that matched the color of the pointe shoes exactly, and examined them. The ends that had been sewn onto the shoe had been ripped off. He sniffed at the ribbons.

'Smells like mint, don't they?' he said, extending his hand to me.

'Yeah. Could be flavored dental floss. The girls are each responsible for their own shoes – breaking them in, coating the toes with resin, sewing on the ribbons,' I said. The class that I took on Saturdays had several of American Ballet Theater's soloists in it. They often relaxed between sessions, stretched against the wall below the barres and covered in their leg warmers, preparing some of the dozens of shoes they danced through every season for the week's performances.

'Floss?' Kestenbaum asked. 'We'll have the lab test to make sure.'

'That's the latest thing in the studio – it's replaced old-fashioned thread 'cause it's stronger and thicker.'

A small manila envelope was the third package

Kestenbaum handed Mike. 'Looks like your victim pulled a tuft of these out of somebody's head.'

There were eight or ten strands of hair, white and silky. 'Were they in her hand?' I asked.

'Not when she landed. Hard to say, after being bounced against the walls on her way down. A few were clinging to the tulle skirt in the back, so they may have been in her fist before she got banged around.'

'Will you be able to do mitochondrial DNA?' It was a much slower process used for human hair – and a different one – than that used with body fluids, and still more controversial in regard to acceptance in the court-room.

'If she didn't get these out by the root, then, yes, we'll have to do mito. We'll send them down to the FBI overnight.' This form of testing could be done when the entire root of the hair was not available for tradi-tional nuclear DNA work, using just the shaft that often rubbed or sloughed off against clothing or other surfaces.

'Where'd this come from?' Mike asked, removing a small black object from the last envelope.

'Not to worry. Hal got a picture before I moved it. It was likely to fall out when they picked up the body,' the pathologist said. 'It was caught in the netting of the skirt. Most likely an artifact of some sort that she picked up during the drop to her death. I didn't want to leave it behind because some defense attorney will end up seeing it in the photos and accuse me of throwing it away. I don't know what it is.'

'You've been spending too much time under the micro-scope. You need to give your brain a rest and work with your hands every now and then,' Mike said. 'Never saw a bent twenty in your life?'

I leaned over for a look. It was a nail, bent at a ninety-degree angle in the middle.

'They're everywhere here. Go back to the design shop, they're probably what hinges every piece of scenery you see. When workers put the different panels of plywood together, after they've moved them onto the stage, they hammer 'em in place using these little suckers to hold them. I bet there's more bent twenties in the Met than there are peanut shells at Yankee Stadium.'

'You getting ideas?' Mercer asked.

'Tell the commissioner this one will take a task force the size of an army. By the time we interview everyone on staff, run raps on all of them, check alibis, and begin to think about strangers who might have worked their way inside, I'll be old enough to put in my papers for retirement.'

We started back toward the elevators. 'Don't you think we ought to get this theater shut down for the night?'

'That's the first subject that reared its ugly head before you and Mercer got here this afternoon. I was turned down flat. Not even the PC can get it done, but he's got the mayor working on it. Why should a frigging murder get in the way of a few hundred thousand bucks at the box office?'

When the elevator doors opened on one, Chet Dobbis was waiting for us. 'Word's spread around here pretty quickly. Rinaldo Vicci has gone to call Talya's husband, and I'll have to deal with the media. May I – may I see her before . . . ?'

'Nope. You can pay your respects at the funeral home.

This stuff isn't for amateurs,' Mike said. 'Better make some space for us. We'll be living under your roof for a while.'

'I thought you'd do this from the station house, detective,' Dobbis said, pulling tighter on the knot of the sweater wrapped around his neck. His narrow, elongated face looked pinched, as though he'd tasted something sour. 'It's going to be rather disruptive to the other artists, to the people who work here. To our patrons, of course.'

'Funny thing about murder, Mr Dobbis. It often is. Put some of your divas on tranquilizers, but I expect this to be our headquarters till we find the phantom.'

'And what do I tell Joe Berk, Mr Chapman?'

'What do you mean?'

'He called here half an hour ago, looking for Talya. Do you want to break this to him or should I?'

Chapter 7

The green velvet smoking robe with its coordinated paisley cravat over bare hairy legs was a striking choice of outfits for Joe Berk, who received the three of us at five thirty on a Saturday afternoon, but I was mostly fixated on his mane of fine white hair.

'You'll forgive me for not getting up, won't you? Which one of you is Chapman?'

Berk was reclining in a Barcalounger, unable to see me behind Mercer and Mike.

'I'm Chapman. This is Detective Wallace, and that's Alexandra Cooper, from the Manhattan DA's office.'

'I didn't notice the young lady there. Sorry,' Berk said, kicking down the footrest and getting to his feet. He approached us, exchanging greetings with the men, then bowed at the waist and reached for my hand, gesturing as though to kiss it.

He looked younger than I had expected, and more fit. Mike had used the word *thick* to describe Berk, but it was burliness rather than weight, and it gave him a powerful air that was consistent with the arrogance he exuded.

'My secretary said you wanted to see me about a

missing person. Who's that?' he said, picking up a cigarette holder, sticking a Gauloise in the tip and searching for his lighter. Berk moved behind his desk and offered us three chairs that were arrayed in front of it. 'Who'd you lose?'

It was easier to get people to cooperate with investigators – especially if they could be linked to the crime in any way – by asking for help with someone who's gone missing rather than invoke the word *murder*.

'Natalya Galinova,' Mike said.

'You're a little behind the breaking news, aren't you, boys?' Berk looked back and forth between Mercer and Mike. 'Who're you kidding here? Joe Berk? Talya is dead. You think I'm an idiot?'

'Seems to me that half an hour ago you didn't have a clue where she—' Mike said before being interrupted by the buzz of an intercom.

Four of the buttons on Berk's large phone console showed flickering red lights and he pushed the one closest to him, holding a finger up in Mike's direction. 'Yeah, babe? Tell that rat bastard when his check clears, *then* I'll take his call. And release all my house tickets for tonight. Anyone on your list. It looks like I'm going to be with these comedians for a while.' He disconnected the call. 'Gentlemen?'

'Who told you about Ms Galinova?' Mike asked.

'Told me what?'

'That she's dead.'

'It's some kind of secret?'

'It was until—'

'Yeah, I heard you. Half an hour ago. You know how many people call Joe Berk every thirty minutes?' he

73

said, sweeping his hand over the blinking dials on the console.

'Nathan Lane comes down with a sore throat, my phone rings. Bernadette Peters gets indigestion, somebody rings me. The Lion King has diarrhea, I'm the first to know.'

'Miss Galinova didn't work for you, did she?' Mike asked.

Berk dragged on the cigarette. 'Footlights and fantasy, Mr Chapman. That's what I'm about. Anybody who ever walked the boards wants to work for me.'

The intercom buzzed again. Berk gave Mike a full palm now. 'Yeah, babe?'

He listened while the secretary told him who was on the line. 'Gotta take this call, guys.'

Berk rested the cigarette holder in an ashtray and pressed his fingers against his temple. 'Bottom line, that's all I wanna know. Yesterday you told me thirty-five. We going over that yet?' He waited for an answer. 'You kidding me? It's grossed over three billion worldwide. Soup it up, Joey. Hands down, it's the most popular entertainment property ever. Don't screw with me – I got a lady here, Joey, or I'd tell you how I really feel.'

'Can you hold these calls till we're done?' Mike asked.

'Hey, for thirty-five million, I'd suggest you hold your questions till *I'm* done, buddy,' Berk said, turning his attention to me. 'We're taking *Phantom of the Opera* to Vegas. Custom-made theater at the Venetian, a flying chandelier bigger than a boat, and very few people with Joe Berk-size pockets who can make it happen. Broadway goes Vegas. Get a hundred bucks a seat without even blinking.'

'We were talking about Ms Galinova,' Mike said.

'Look, Mr Berk, we understand you were at the Met last night.'

'Absolutely.'

'But missed the show.'

'Not my thing, ballet. The music puts me to sleep, the broads are too skinny for my taste, the boys run around with pairs of socks wadded in their crotches to make themselves look like they're well hung. Give me Shakespeare or give me schmaltz and I can pack you a full house. Not the ballet.'

'But you were going there specifically to see Ms Galinova, weren't you?' Mike asked.

'Talya invited me to the gala. Look, I tried very hard to make it. She's a classy dame, but I got a schedule of my own. We had an understudy going on in one of our shows last night and I had to see the first act for myself to figure out whether she's got the stuff to take over the lead. I was late for Talya's scene. So sue me.'

'What happened when you arrived at the Met?'

'Nothing happened. Meaning what?'

'Meaning what did you do when you found out they wouldn't seat you?'

'I thanked my lucky stars for my brilliant timing and went back to the dressing room to wait for her.'

'The ushers just let you inside? No problem?'

'Why? Some jerk didn't know me, I had to spend a few minutes educating him? Next time he will.'

'You knew where the dressing room was?'

'Yeah, sure I did. I've been there before.'

'Recently?'

'Yeah, yeah, yeah. Talya wanted to talk to me, I went. She had time off during the rehearsals, I went.'

'To talk about ballet?'

'Don't be funny, detective. I told you that doesn't interest me. Talya needed Joe Berk, Mr Chapman, not the other way around,' he said, poking his forefinger into his broad chest. 'She wants to be – wanted to be – in a production of mine. She wanted me to make her a Broadway baby.'

'Any show in particular?'

'That would make a difference to you? You want to put up ten percent, be a backer?'

Mike was as annoyed as if Berk were scratching a finger-nail along a blackboard. 'The only difference it would make is whether I believe you.'

'Like I have to worry if you do or you don't.' Berk laughed. 'You know the story of the girl on the red velvet swing? Evelyn Nesbit.'

I recognized the Nesbit name and knew she'd been involved in some kind of scandal, but couldn't bring it to mind. Mike answered. 'Harry Thaw. Stanford White. The old Madison Square Garden. Sex, infidelity, money, murder – the story's got it all.'

'Bravo, detective. Opening-night seats for you, sir, on the aisle. Murder, Miss Cooper. A good old-fashioned Manhattan murder. Your detective friend clearly knows his true-crime stories. He'll tell you later. Otherwise you'll have to buy tickets. You,' Berk said, winking at me, 'I might invite you myself. Leave the coppers home.'

Mike had majored in history at Fordham College. There was nothing he didn't know about military history – foreign and American – and his congenital fascination with the world of policing made him an expert on New York's darkest deeds.

'It's a Broadway show?' Mike asked. 'A homicide case that's a hundred years old?'

'Eighteen, twenty months down the road I expect it will be. A blockbuster musical. You're too young to remember *Sweeney Todd*. Hey, look at *Chicago*. The Weisslers, now they're fucking geniuses. Came to me with the idea to do a show for Broadway about a dame who shoots her lover and I turned them down flat. How many years running and nine touring companies abroad? Forget about what the movie did to keep the show alive and kicking. The Shuberts had more goddamn sense than I did, for once. What the hell was I thinking? Murder set to music sells great.'

Berk flicked his ashes. 'I've got Elton John doing the score, Santo Loquasto on the costumes – gowns, furs, that famous bearskin rug – and the swing will be gaudier than the bullshit chandelier they're building for *Phantom* in Vegas. How does that song go? All I need now is the girl.'

'Talya Galinova?' I asked.

'Ask Mr Chapman to fill you in on the story, Miss Cooper. Evelyn Nesbit was one of the most gorgeous dames of her day. But she was only sixteen years old when all of this happened. Great role for an ingénue. Talya? She would have been a bit too long in the tooth by the time we launch this production. Give me nubile.'

'Did she know that?' Or could it have been what they fought about in the dressing room?

'It doesn't matter if she knew it. I certainly did.'

'And Ms Galinova, she was glad to see you last night?' Mike asked.

'They really sweat, you aware of that? You think it's

all floating around on your toes and flapping your wings out there onstage, but those girls do some kind of workout. She came in all sweaty and hot, dripping with perspiration. And very pissed off that I'd missed the show. What a temper,' Berk said, walking away from us and untying the belt on his robe as he opened a door and turned on a light.

He had entered a bathroom, leaving the door ajar behind him and continuing to talk to us as he urinated. 'You can hear me, right?'

'A little too well. The city doesn't pay me enough for this,' I whispered to Mike. 'Remind me to tell Battaglia he owes me.' I was scoping the top of Berk's desk and the area of floor around my chair, hoping to see a stray piece of his hair.

'Talya let me have it, unloaded on me like a shrew. Jeez, she should have saved some of her strength for the guy who attacked her.'

He was washing his hands now and I stood up to walk behind his lounge chair to look at some photographs on the wall, thinking there might be a few white hairs on the headrest that I could pocket for a comparison to the ones Kestenbaum found with Talya's body.

When Berk emerged from the bathroom, he was still knotting the robe around his thick waist. 'You like that picture? It's me. You'd never guess from that one, would you?'

The faded black-and-white image was of a toddler in knee pants, holding his mother's hand, her dreary house-dress blending into the backdrop of their small, dreary house.

'Little Yussel Berkowitz. Taken more than seventy years

ago, back in Russia,' he said, patting his hands against his bloated abdomen. 'It's been quite a ride, folks.'

I could never have imagined that the child whose family escaped some impoverished upbringing in what looked like a foreign village would be sitting in his duplex apartment above one of the theaters he owned, wearing a smoking jacket and matching green velvet slippers with gold crests on the throat that looked like something the Duke of Windsor might have worn at The Fort.

'We were talking about the argument you had with Ms Galinova,' Mike said.

'Argument? Who told you anything like that?'

'Well, you said she was mad at you, that her temper flared. I'm wondering whether it had to do with any of these professional matters you've been discussing with her or if it was something more personal.'

'Personal what?' Berk plunged the tip of his cigarette into the ashtray and ground it down until what remained fell out of the holder.

Mike was getting short with him. 'Were you and Miss Galinova having a sexual relationship? Did this start as some kind of tiff that got out of hand?'

'You got no business coming in here and insinuating I had anything to do with whatever happened to Talya. You got no business asking anything about my personal life,' Berk said, looping one finger over the belt of his robe and jabbing the other through the air in Mike's direction. 'Do you know who you're talking to? Do you know who I am?'

Mike stared back at the red-faced impresario.

'Do you know who I am?' Berk's voice rose louder and

79

louder, each time he asked a question. 'Do you know who I am? Do you?'

None of us spoke.

'Do you know . . . who I *am*?' Each word spit out at us, spaced to reverberate in the room, underscoring Berk's power and control.

'Yo, Mercer,' Mike said, turning to look at us. 'Do you know who he is?'

Mercer shrugged and stared at Berk with the same implacable expression Mike had.

Berk seemed ready to explode at my partners. I thought it was time to intervene.

'Look, Mr Berk,' I said. 'All we know is that you may have been the last person to see Talya Galinova alive. Why don't you tell us when you left her? The time, the place, who else was around.'

Berk started walking back to the bathroom. 'Argument? You people are nuts. Like I have to take any kind of crap from an over-the-hill ballerina? Like Joe Berk had the least bit of interest in letting that bitch tell me how to run my operation? I walked out on her screaming just like I'll walk out on you if you don't watch your place.'

He was mumbling now as he again made no effort to close the door that separated us. 'Talk to my driver. He knows what time I got into the car. Damn, I knew that rotten *corva* was trouble.'

Mike looked at me, puzzled by the word. 'Italian?'

'Yiddish. It means "whore".' It had been my grandmother's ultimate insult for any woman whose conduct she disdained.

Berk called out to us. 'You want to know why Talya couldn't keep her tights on, detective? Talk to Chet

80

Dobbis. He spent way too much time poking around where he shouldn't have been, all in the name of art. Ha! Ask Mr Dobbis where he was when it came time for last night's curtain call.'

Chapter 8

We were standing on West 44th Street, under the marquee of the Belasco Theatre, where Joe Berk's duplex apartment sat atop the 1907 neo-Georgian landmark. Diners looking for preshow bargains were jamming the sidewalks as they studied menus in restaurant windows, and scalpers trying to make a score were hawking tickets for tonight's return engagement of Ralph Fiennes's *Hamlet* at three times the going price.

'You want to try and hit Dobbis with this right now?' Mercer asked.

I looked at my watch. 'If we can get to him before the performance starts.'

Mike was less than enthusiastic. 'Odds are we got a repeat of the first murder at the Met. Somebody who works backstage, maybe even with a rap sheet. Probably intercepted Galinova in a corridor or elevator. She was steaming mad from whatever Joe Berk did to blow her off. Blue-collar guy comes on to her, she freaks out, and so on. The lieutenant will flood the Met with guys from every squad in Manhattan North and he'll have a suspect by the middle of the week.'

'You're willing to wait that out, it's okay with me,' Mercer said.

'Yeah, we may have latents. Maybe some DNA by then.'

'Hey, I understand. You're tired and not ready for the whole routine yet. You go on home. Alex and I'll put in a few more hours.'

Mike combed his fingers through his dark hair. He knew Mercer was goading him to get back in the game. 'You two'll feed me when we're done?'

'Wine and dine.'

Mike had left the car in a 'no standing' zone half a block down from the theater. We circled around the one-way streets, passing through the swelling crowds in Times Square, and drove up Tenth Avenue to park behind the Met at 65th Street.

This time we entered the building through the stage door in the rear of the parking garage. Carloads of patrons were beginning to stream in, some to keep their dinner reservations at the Grand Tier restaurant, below one of the colorful Chagalls, others to enjoy the mild spring evening on the plaza with a glass of wine.

The security guard now had the company of two uniformed cops, one of whom recognized Mercer and waved us in.

At a second checkpoint, Mike asked the man inspecting identifications to call Chet Dobbis for us. We were told he wasn't in his office.

'Page him, will you? It's urgent we see him before the show starts.'

When the call had not been returned in ten minutes, we became impatient and decided to try to find him in the area around the stage.

Now the hallways were teeming with people. Musicians

dressed completely in black so nothing in the orchestra pit distracted from the stage action, carrying instruments of every shape and size, squeezed between the costume trunks and workmen pressing ahead in the opposite direction.

Dancers in the obligatory leg warmers and turned-out foot positions, most carrying bottles of water, practiced their variations or sat along the wall stretching their legs and backs. Carpenters and electricians carried pieces of scenery and props, dangling drills and hammers as they maneuvered the turns of the endless gray walkways.

Mike approached a man who seemed to be a supervisor, calling out instructions to other workmen. 'Dobbis. I'm looking for Chet Dobbis.'

'Last I saw him he was at the rear wagon.' The man pointed in the direction we were headed. 'Keep going that way.'

'Did you see any wagons this afternoon?' I asked. 'Where do you think he means?'

'Must be some part of tonight's show. Let's just get over to the stage and someone will show us.'

We rounded the last corner and found ourselves in the cavernous opening of the Metropolitan's stage. The curtain separating us from the six tiers of seats was closed, and at least a dozen men were readying sets for the performance that was due to start in about an hour. One woman was dabbing paint on the scratched surface of a fake boulder, making details perfect for the evening event. If anyone had concerns about the murder of one of last night's artists in an air shaft several hundred feet away, nobody showed it.

'Hold it up right there,' a voice shouted at us, although I couldn't see the speaker.

'We're looking for—' Mike said.

'I don't care what you're doing. It'll have to wait until after the show.' A lanky man with wire-rimmed glasses stepped out from behind a control panel on stage right. 'You mind stepping back? We've got a big move to make.'

'Look, I'm a detective. Mike—'

'Nice to know. And I'm Biff Owens. Stage manager. I got an audience to please tonight, you three want to step out of the way?'

'Sure. I'm looking for Chet Dobbis. Where's the wagon?'

We stepped around the wires on the floor and he motioned us into what seemed to be his workspace, an area with four television monitors and more switches than the controls of a space shuttle.

'I got four wagons, and if you stay perfectly still, you won't wind up underneath one of them while we check this out. Harry?' Owens called out to someone farther upstage. 'Let's roll out the main and bring in the turn-table.'

With the sound of a low rumble, the entire main stage of the Met began to sink out of sight, dropping almost ten feet. From the rear of the building, another enormous platform, sixty by sixty feet, rolled forward into place.

Biff Owens clapped his hands in approval and then studied the second hand of his watch to time the move-ment as the entire surface rotated in a giant sweep of a circle, making a full rotation in two minutes.

'Okay, Harry. Swing it back,' Owens said, turning to Mike. 'Those are my wagons. Why'd you ask?'

'I'm looking for Chet Dobbis. Somebody told us he was near the wagon.'

'This is one of the things that makes the Met unique, detective. We have four separate stages here, each one full size. That area off stage right is one, off stage left is the second, the rear stage with the turntable is the third, and this here's the main,' Owens said, as the solid floor crept back up into place. 'Stagehands call them wagons.'

'Hydraulic?'

'Nope. They're on an electrical system. When the main one lowers, the others are attached by cables that supply the electricity and pulleys that move them into place. They move 'em like wagons.'

'Must be noisy, no?'

'During performances, you mean? There's sound-proofed doors between each of the stages. Nobody can hear a peep.'

Owens confirmed the acoustical needs that made the musical experience so pleasurable for the audience and treacherous for a woman in peril behind the scene.

'None of you ever saw *Bohème* here?' he asked, walking back to his monitors. 'You got the Bohemian house on stage left, dragged right in on top of the main stage for the opening. Takes a minute to slip it off – bingo – you got the Parisian street scene. Over on stage right the café is all set up, and on the back wagon you got the whole thing gradually elevated so when Mimi's dying, back in her garret, you'd think you were up on the heights of Montmartre.'

'During last night's performance, what kept you busy?'

'Me? Think of it like I'm the air traffic controller,

detective. If I leave my post for even a minute during the performance, there's likely to be a disaster. I'm responsible for giving all the cues to the principals, making sure the scenery gets moved when it has to, and knowing when every scrim and curtain needs to be lowered or raised. That's several hundred commands per hour. The show don't go on without me.'

'These monitors,' Mike said, sweeping a finger across the small television screens, 'what do they tell you?'

'This one lets me see the conductor, down below stage center. The second one – that's dark during the ballet. Don't use it when nobody needs lyrics. Usually it's my window on the prompter, who is giving all the lines to the opera singers. Third is the lighting controls, and the fourth one shows me the full stage, so I can follow how the production is going.'

'And Mr Dobbis, where was he during last night's performance?'

'In the director's booth.'

'Where's that?'

'Very back of the orchestra. He'll be there again when the show starts tonight.'

'Hey, Biff,' a man called from high above the stage. 'You ready for me to drop the trees?'

'Who's that?' Mercer asked.

'One of the flymen,' Owens said, before clearing the stage with a loud bark. 'Everybody out of the way. Let 'er rip, Jimmy.'

I craned my neck and looked up to the blackened interior, almost ten floors above. With lightning speed and incredible precision, an enormous painted forest fell from the heights and stopped a quarter of an inch above the floorboards. If someone had been beneath it, he would have been sliced in half.

'What's up there?'

'The fly system. Ninety-seven pipes, each one the width of the stage, and each one capable of holding half a ton of scenery. We can fit an entire show up there, dropping the pieces in a flash.'

The network above me was ringed with catwalks and galleries, painted black pipes against a painted black background. Three or four figures in dark clothing moved on opposite sides of the grating.

'Looks like an accident waiting to happen,' said Mike.

'Dangerous stuff. That's why we're so meticulous about rehearsing the timing of it.'

'Who calls the shots?'

'I do,' said Owens. 'I need a scrim down, the hands have the number that corresponds to what pipe it's hanging from in their script. I yell out "Go" to the head flyman, and he calls out to the others to move. Takes eight, ten guys to man the bigger shows.'

'So, if a man took a hike before the act ended—'

'Couldn't happen with my crew. They work in pairs, both sides coordinating with each other. Anybody slipped off, there wouldn't have been a close to the second act or a scene change to start the third. One guy can't manage it alone.'

'And Dobbis,' Mike said, 'you could see him in that booth last night?'

'You got that backwards, mister. His equipment can see me, and he can talk to me by phone. But I can't see him. He gave me the signal to raise the curtain at eight fifteen, and when we were striking the sets at the end, he came by to say good night. Everything in between, that's his business.'

'Can we get out into the theater from here?' I asked.

Owens led us away from his post and pointed to another series of doors. The three of us continued on our way, practically pinning ourselves against the wall from time to time as we went against the flow of ticket holders trying to claim their seats.

I asked the usher for the director's booth, and he led us to a narrow doorway, midway between the elongated bar and the rear entrance to the orchestra. I turned the handle but it was locked, so I knocked.

Chet Dobbis opened the door, seeming rather startled to see us. 'Let me call you back later. I've got company,' he said into the phone receiver before hanging up.

'May we come in?'

Dobbis had changed into a business suit and his mien had become as formal as his dress. 'This isn't a particularly good time. We're ready to get the program started here,' he said, stepping back as he reluctantly let us into his small room.

The glass-fronted booth was about ten feet wide, furnished with two stools and several monitors. 'The ballet mistress will be along any minute. We watch the performances together.'

On one monitor I could see the conductor's baton waving from the orchestra pit as he seemed to be rehearsing the tempo of a piece. Another had a frozen shot of the great curtain while the third displayed the lighting devices high above the back of the auditorium.

'Would you prefer to step out for a few minutes? There

are some questions we need to ask you before the story of Natalya's death hits the morning papers.'

He parked himself on one of the stools, fidgeting with something in his left hand that made me think of Captain Queeg and his marbles. 'If you don't mind holding off until the end of the performance, we can certainly talk again.'

Three hours was longer than I was willing to wait. If Dobbis and Galinova had been involved in a relationship, both my boss and Chapman's needed to know. 'I'd rather get the answers—'

I was interrupted by the opening of the door. 'Sandra, come in, of course,' Dobbis said, rising to make room for the woman he introduced to us as the ballet mistress.

'Sorry,' she said, kissing Dobbis on both cheeks before stepping in front of me to perch on the second stool. 'I just couldn't shake whatever was bothering me yesterday. Some kind of twenty-four-hour thing. I didn't mean to leave you alone last night, and then – oh, then with this dreadful thing about Talya.'

'In or out, Ms Cooper. I can't let you open that door once the performance begins. The light draws the dancers' attention from the stage.'

There really wasn't room for the three of us to stand in the booth behind both of them, and I nodded to Mercer to open the door. The three thousand lightbulbs in the theater started to dim and the crystal chandeliers circling the parterre boxes began to lift up out of sight.

Dobbis thanked us and said he'd see us later. He stopped playing with the small object in his fingers and placed it on the ledge in front of him.

The booth was almost dark but the light that glowed from the monitors settled on the thing that Chet Dobbis had carried in his hand. It was a two-inch-long black nail – the kind the stagehands called a bent twenty.

Chapter 9

'Dewar's on the rocks for the blonde. No fruit. You have Grey Goose?'

The bartender set up the glasses and took Mike's drink orders. We three were alone in the lobby of the Met, at the foot of the grand staircase, while all the balletomanes were in their seats for the performance.

The added police presence at entrances and doorways leading behind the stage hadn't seemed off-putting to most spectators, who would not know about Natalya Galinova's death until they heard the late news or read the morning paper.

We sipped our drinks and talked through the forty-minute first act of *Coppélia,* Mercer and I both trying unsuccessfully to draw out Mike. It was clear to me that he wasn't ready to expose the emotional upheaval he had suffered after Val's death, and he didn't even bother to feign interest in Mercer's stories about Vickee and their baby boy.

When the doors from the auditorium swung open and the crowd emptied the rows for the intermission, Mike stepped around the corner and fought his way to the director's booth. As I followed behind him, I could see that his instinct had been right. Chet Dobbis was walking briskly toward the front of the house, against the flow of the people, as though he was trying to distance himself from us.

Mike called out to him, but Dobbis didn't turn his head. I was zigzagging through the lines of annoyed patrons, as I slowed their efforts to get their plastic glasses of champagne or stand on the endless lines for the restrooms.

Mercer was more direct. He scooted across a row of seats that was empty but for one elderly couple, and then he vaulted over the chairs in front, beating Dobbis to the exit that was closest to the backstage door.

'You know how this one ends or you just trying to catch an early train?' Mike asked.

The angled nail was again twisting between the director's thumb and forefinger. 'I've got to talk to the stage manager, detective. Our lead dancer has missed half of his cues and his performance is entirely off.'

'Why don't you let the ballet mistress take care of that?' Mike said, backing out the door with his hand on Dobbis's elbow. 'This will only cost you a few minutes.'

The usher saw Dobbis coming toward him and opened the door to the backstage area that said NO ENTRANCE. Once inside, the three of us stopped, surrounding the director before he could go any farther.

'Am I making you nervous, buddy?' Mike asked.

'Not at all. I'm sure you don't like being interrupted when you're doing something important at a crime scene, and I'm asking the same respect for the business at hand tonight. I'm in the middle of a major production.'

'What a coincidence. This *is* the middle of my crime

scene, Mr Dobbis. You wanna watch out for that nail you got? I'd hate to lose you to a bad case of tetanus before we even get to talk.'

Dobbis opened his palm and looked down, as though he'd surprised even himself by the discovery that he was holding something. 'This? Not nerves at all, detective. Just for good luck,' he said, pocketing the black nail.

'How so?'

'Something I picked up in the days Pavarotti sang here. Luciano Pavarotti?'

'Yeah. The fat man.'

'Hardly a distinction among tenors, detective. Pavarotti was wildly superstitious, did you know that, Ms Cooper?'

'Why does everybody ask *her* the culture questions? She didn't know it – trust me on that – and neither did Mercer. What about it?'

'It got so Luciano wouldn't go onstage until he picked up a bent twenty. He found one, just by chance, the very first time he did *Tosca* here. A tremendous ovation and sixty *Tosca*s later it remained his personal good luck charm. They actually had to have a pocket sewn into every one of his costumes to conceal a nail. He'd spend the last few seconds before his entrance scouring the floor for these,' Dobbis said, showing it off to us again. 'I got in the habit of carrying one around just so that I could hand it to him if he couldn't find any.'

'Some habits die hard,' Mike said. 'Didn't he retire a few years back?'

'His superstition must have rubbed off on me. I still think it's a charm.'

'Not so lucky last night, was it? Or maybe you dropped it?'

'They're all over the place, Mr Chapman, as I'm sure you've seen. Are you here to talk hardware or something more serious? There's a second act to stage.'

Mercer had walked a few feet away and turned his back to us, making it seem as though Dobbis could reveal any secrets he had only to Mike and me.

'Ms Cooper and I are easily confused, Mr Dobbis, so maybe you could straighten this out for us. You were quick to point the finger at Joe Berk and his relationship with Talya, and in the meantime, Berk says that you've been scoring with her, too.'

'Such a way with words, detective. But Joe Berk is wrong.'

'I'm gonna let you be the guy to tell him that. Do you know who he is, Mr Dobbis?'

Dobbis didn't appreciate Mike's effort at humor. 'Who he is, or who he thinks he is?'

He adjusted his tie and the collar of his shirt before speaking again. 'Talya and I had an affair ten years ago, maybe more. Long before either one of us was married. Neither she nor I had any reason to hide it. It drained me of a fortune in yellow roses every time she curtsied to the crowd and caused an ulcer I'm still nursing today. When Talya decided to end the whole thing, it was actually a blessing.'

'Never got the urge to revisit the territory?'

'Not even to look at the map, detective.'

'Artistic differences? Anything to squabble about?'

'Of course we had those. She wanted things to be all Talya all the time. She liked a good fight, and the older she got, the more unwelcoming she was to the young dancers who were getting the starred reviews. I spend an

95

inordinate amount of time juggling personalities instead of directing talent.'

Dobbis tried to walk around me, but Mike didn't give up. 'Last night, did you see Talya after Joe Berk left the dressing room?'

'I had a third act to worry about, Mr Chapman. The scene with the golden idol from *Bayadère*. Major set changes with the destruction of the temple, two primas and two male leads onstage as well. It wouldn't have mattered to me if Talya had decided to dance naked in the fountain on the plaza. I had to be in my booth making every second of that performance look seamless. May I?'

I stepped back to let Dobbis pass through and walk away.

'I'm beginning to agree with Mike,' I said to Mercer. 'Let's knock it off for the night. Maybe we'll have some preliminary findings from the autopsy tomorrow that will jumpstart the conversation.'

'You up to going?' Mercer asked Mike. It was part of his duty as the homicide detective who caught the case to attend the autopsy. This would be the first time he'd have to view one since Val's accident.

'You two are spending way too much time psychoanalyzing me. I didn't know this Talya broad. Sorry she's dead but I'm not about to throw myself on top of her grave. The way you look at me, you act like I should be in a transfer to the Auto Theft Squad. C'mon. I haven't had a decent meal in weeks.'

'Now that's what I like to hear. Any cravings?'

'Nothing that you could satisfy, Coop. I'm thinking pasta.'

'I can't tell you how lonely it's been without your

insults. Here you go, putting me down, and I'm smiling about it like you just asked me to the prom,' I said, looping my arm in Mike's. 'I'll call Primola.'

We had to make our way to the front of the opera house and walk around the entire complex to get to where we'd left the car. We drove through the transverse in Central Park and across 65th Street to one of our favorite watering holes on Second Avenue.

Giuliano hadn't seen Mike in two months. He embraced him enthusiastically and led us to the first table in the corner, ignoring all the couples with nine o'clock reservations who were piled deep at the bar.

Adolfo took the drink order and uncorked a bottle of Tignanello that Giuliano sent over with his compliments. Each of us was familiar with the sophisticated menu that was the restaurant's famous fare but opted for the delicious comfort food that was Primola's Saturday-night special – an appetizer portion of fried zucchini along with three orders of spaghetti and meatballs.

No matter how tired I was from the work of the last twenty-four hours, I could feel myself come alive again in the reuniting of our trio. Family and close friends have provided my emotional sanctuary during years of prosecuting intimate violence for which no formal education could have prepared me. The women I had lived with at Wellesley, my study group from law school at the University of Virginia, and the colleagues with whom I stood shoulder to shoulder in the trenches of the criminal courthouse at 100 Centre Street all played a role in maintaining my faith in the goodness of humankind.

But no professional relationship had been forged that

97

compared to my friendship with Mike and Mercer. They had seen the darkest side of man's nature, regularly witnessing the taking of lives by killers motivated by greed, lust, and every other deadly sin. They had helped nourish victims back to stability after the trauma of the most personally invasive violence imaginable. And they understood the meaning of loyalty in ways I had trouble expressing to people who couldn't fathom why each one of us derived such satisfaction in restoring dignity to those who'd been attacked or to their survivors.

Mercer's beeper went off while we were gnawing on thin strips of zucchini and enjoying our wine. He stepped out on the sidewalk to return the call.

'If you're gonna try to ruin my dinner with new business,' Mike said when he sat down again, 'get yourselves another table for two.'

Mercer smiled at me and lifted his glass. 'We're one step closer to nailing the Riverside rapist.'

'Another attack?'

Joggers who ran the pathway in the slice of parkland along Riverside Drive had been battling an assailant who hid himself in the thick bushes that had started to bloom in March, lying in wait for women who exercised alone. Police expected that the man had some kind of sexual dysfunction, since he had not ejaculated in any of the cases. Lacking a DNA profile of the attacker, we had been unable to search databanks for convicted offenders or links to other unsolved crimes.

'Not quite,' Mercer said. 'This one was running with her dog, a small mixed-breed special she rescued from the pound. The perp tackled her to the ground and started to tear off her shorts but the mutt wrapped his mouth around the guy's wrist till he pulled free. I've got to go over to the hospital to interview her.'

'You want me to come with you?'

'Stay here with Mike. This one will be easy.'

'Your man get away again?'

Mercer smiled. 'For the moment. But they've got the dog down at the ME's office. Docs are swabbing his teeth. There's still enough of the perp's blood on his canines for a DNA profile this time.'

Chapter 10

Mike and I both lived on the Upper East Side in circumstances as different as our backgrounds. He referred to his tiny, dark fifth-floor walkup on York Avenue as 'the coffin', while I lived on the twentieth floor of a high-rise, in a large sunlit apartment with twenty-four-hour doormen who enabled me to separate myself from the day's demons when I settled in at home.

There was a comfortable chill in the early-spring night when we left Primola, and Mike offered to walk me the few short blocks north to my building.

When I tried to bring the conversation back to the subject of Valerie, he countered by asking questions about my personal life.

'So what are you going home to, Coop? Grind your teeth over the Saturday *Times* crossword puzzle and sink into a steaming-hot bath to avoid your empty bed? Anything new in your life?'

'Ouch! You're beginning to sound like my mother. I think you and Mercer are going to be stuck with me for a while.'

'How much longer you gonna do this?' he said, steering me across to the west side of the avenue, dodging couples arm in arm on their way home from local eateries and bars. 'Running around to crime scenes, getting mouthed off at by scumbags, giving up your nights and weekends—

'Like you do.'

'Shit. I get paid for overtime.'

'You know anybody who has a better job than I do? Every day I wake up and want to go to work. I like how my gut feels, I like knowing we make things a little bit easier for people who don't expect the system to get it right.'

'But you've got to vent somewhere, other than to Mercer and me.'

Mike had come to depend on Valerie's love and support after years of trusting no one outside the job. She had fought to get him to open up to her, and now he was struggling to regain the tight grip he'd always held on his emotions.

'That's why my friendships have been so important to me. You know that.'

'I'm talking about something else, Coop. Not pals, not girlfriends, not drinking buddies. Don't you ever worry it's all gonna pass you by because you're in over your head with this blood-and-guts stuff? You've taken yourself out of circulation.'

More than a decade ago, before I started the work that had so absorbed my interest, the man I had been hours away from marrying had been killed in a car accident. I had experienced a loss as great as Mike's and could give him no assurances that a love as important as this last one – like my love for Adam – would ever sustain him again.

'Don't be ridiculous. I thought the reason I had no takers was because you've been spreading the word about me for so long.'

'Nobody listens to me,' Mike said, veering away from me as our elbows inadvertently rubbed together, looping his thumb over the top of his belt. 'You're your own worst enemy. You might as well be wearing a sign that warns guys to keep their distance.'

There was no moving Mike from his morose mood. 'What are you doing next weekend?' I asked. I took a few steps ahead of him and walked backward, forcing him to look me in the eye.

'I'm catching.'

'You could switch with someone, couldn't you?' I was trying to get him to lighten up, but when he ignored me and kept walking, I planted both hands on his chest to stop him.

'I think I've used up all my favors lately, don't you?' Mike brushed me aside and pretended to laugh.

'I'm supposed to fly up to the Vineyard after work on Friday. Open the house for the spring. Jim's away,' I said, referring to the fiancé of my friend Joan Stafford, 'so Joan will probably come with me. Sit me in front of the fireplace and both of you can pile in on me with pointers about turning around my love life.'

We had reached my building's driveway, which cut through between two streets. Opposite the entrance was a pocket park for the residents, planted with daffodils and crocuses, the quarter moon reflecting in the shallow flagstone pool surrounded by granite benches.

The doorman held the door open for me. I gave it another try. 'Want to come up for a while?' I cocked my head and smiled at Mike, who was staring down at the pavement – oblivious to the moonlight and flowers – but he wouldn't even meet me halfway.

Mike shook his head and told me he'd call me after the Galinova autopsy. I walked to the elevator and pressed the button. As I waited for it, I looked out the lobby windows and saw Mike leaning back on one of the benches, staring at the heavens as though the brilliant constellations weren't obscured by the bright city lights. I wasn't used to being pushed so far away by him and wondered whether someone else was helping him deal with his grief.

I didn't have the strength for the Saturday *Times* crossword – the toughest puzzle of the week – but I drew a hot bath and counted on its soporific qualities to help me stop reviewing the last hours of Talya Galinova's life. I was too tired to fight sleep and too resigned to the current state of my social life to mind that there hadn't been a crease on the other half of my sheet for several months.

The dancer's death was headlined below the fold on the front page of the *Times* when I reached for it on my doorstep at eight thirty Sunday morning. A triumphant photograph of her as Odile, in arabesque, ran behind the news of the rising unemployment rate and the latest political skirmish in North Korea.

The *Post* never disappointed when it came to bad taste. The front-page banner, MURDER AT THE MET – AGAIN, was featured in bold caps over the shot of the body bag being loaded into the ambulance in the docking bay of the opera house. The subtitle beneath Talya's name identified her latest role: CORPSE DE BALLET.

A gentle April rain drizzled down the windowpanes and gave me license to spend a lazy day at home. I caught up on paying bills, answered dozens of accumulated e-mails, napped in the late afternoon, phoned family and friends, and put on my hooded rain slicker to cross the street for a late-afternoon pedicure and manicure. Dinner was a salad and turkey sandwich delivered from PJ Bernstein, and I hibernated in my den for the evening with a slightly foxed copy of a collection of Raymond Chandler stories that I had picked up for a dollar at the Chilmark flea market.

I had expected Mike's call after the autopsy, but with the morgue understaffed on weekends and a recent upsurge of violent deaths, there was no predicting when he would report in to me.

I had just turned on the ten o'clock nightly news when the phone rang.

'Not much to help us with,' Mike said. 'The fall killed her, pretty much like we expected.'

'Kestenbaum is certain Talya was alive when she was thrown over?'

'A lot of bleeding in the brain when he opened the skull, so her heart was still pumping when she hit. Terminal velocity, going headfirst down the shaft with hands tied behind her back, slamming into the fan casing at about a hundred twenty miles an hour. Fractured skull, ribs, pelvis and massive internal injuries. And the doc was right when he said you might not be along for this ride, kid. No sign of sexual assault. No semen in the vaginal vault, so that won't even solve who she was cozy with yesterday.'

'Has Talya's husband flown over to claim the body?'

'Nope. He told the morgue attendant that he and Talya had separated several months ago, that her lawyers had notified him she'd be filing for divorce. They talked frequently but that was all business. He wasn't having anything to do with this.'

'Well, how about her agent? What's his name again?'

'Rinaldo Vicci. He came down to do the ID, but we're still waiting for someone to confirm the arrangements. Vicci has no authority to make any decisions either. Galinova's husband claims she fired him more than a week ago.'

'Why? Did he say why?'

'Vicci denies it. Says she often threatened to do that whenever she had tantrums, but the husband says this time it was meant to stick. The husband's been in constant contact with Talya's lawyers because of the legal separation status and that's what they told him as recently as a week ago. It's one more thing to sort out.'

'You just can't let her lay there on ice indefinitely, Mike.'

I clamped my jaw shut as soon as I said the words.

'Why?' he asked. 'She deserves any better than Val?'

The accidental death of Mike's girlfriend in a glacial crevasse was still foremost on his mind. There was an edge to him now, a bitterness that had never hung between us before. I struggled to bring back the intimacy of our friendship but was beginning to realize it was going to be a very long road to regain it.

'How about the evidence you submitted to the lab? The physical items, and the blood and hair?'

'Calm down, Coop. Nobody worked today. They'll get going on it tomorrow.'

105

'And the Met employees? Has their screening started?'

'Those guys won't know what hit them. Forget the borough. Every squad in the city is giving us some men to do interviews, run rap sheets, check backgrounds. We'll saturate the place. How'd you like the morning papers?'

'I've often thought of putting my English Lit background to work and helping them out. You just hold your breath and hope nobody who cared about the victim ever sees those tabloid bombs.'

The courthouse pressroom was plastered from ceiling to floor with page-one stories that had won it the nickname of the wall of shame. High-profile cases like this one would result in several more offerings for the coveted space.

'Don't think tomorrow won't top this one, kid. I got a chance for you to come scoop up some of those long white hairs you were dying to get your mitts on yesterday when we were in Joe Berk's office. Ready for a late-night date on Broadway?'

'Where are you? What's—'

'A little too much juice on the street, Coop. Berk was electrocuted tonight.'

'*What?* Joe Berk? How'd that happen?'

'Stepped on a manhole cover outside the theater an hour ago. Faulty insulation in the junction box.'

'But he's our prime—'

'Accidents happen, kid. Con Ed has these freak hot spots all over town and Joe Berk happened to put his fat foot on this one. Sometimes justice is swift and certain, and I wouldn't want to miss an opportunity like that.'

'You're sure it's an accident?'

'The Lord works in strange and mysterious ways. Berk

stepped on the wrong manhole cover and spared the state some aggravation. I'm going upstairs to take a peek at his apartment. Wanna come?'

'You picking me up?'

'Be ready in ten. And save yourself fifty cents on tomorrow's news. It's curtains for Joe Berk. Another banner day for the tabs, photo of the old guy lying in the gutter – that's their money shot – his life captured in a single word: *ZAPPED!*'

Chapter 11

'Times Square, Crossroads of the World,' Mike said, stepping out of his department car just off the main intersection of Broadway and 44th Street, a few minutes before eleven o'clock on Sunday evening. He pointed up at the sky. 'You can fly into LaGuardia at night and read a book sitting by an airplane window without your overhead light on, just from the electricity generated in this neon canyon.'

One hundred years ago, when Adolph Ochs moved his daily newspaper to this midtown site known as Long Acre Square, it was renamed Times Square in honor of the great publication. This once elegant residential neighborhood had given way to what were then called silk-hat brothels, and when railway hubs and subway stations made the area the commercial center of Manhattan, the theater district followed here soon after.

This time there was no yellow crime-scene tape. Uniformed cops had cordoned off the hot zone with orange no-parking cones and three Con Ed trucks blocked off the entrance to the street as workmen scrambled to repair the damage.

'Works on the same principle as Old Sparky,' Mike

said, referring to the electric chair at Sing Sing that had not been used since 1963. 'One good jolt and you're off to meet the devil. Joe should have known those friggin' velvet slippers wouldn't have grounded him.'

One of the cops led us to the chief of the crew, who was explaining the problem to a couple of guys from the mayor's office. We introduced ourselves and joined the conversation.

'What does it look like?' Mike asked.

The Con Ed crewman pointed to the apparatus down on the street across from the marquee of the Belasco Theatre at 111 West 44th Street. 'It's that junction box. Another damn maintenance situation. Improper insulation.'

One of the mayor's men was already doing the math. 'This'll cost the city a few million. Shit. It's only the first quarter of the year and we've already had more than forty complaints about hot spots. That's way ahead of last year.'

'How does it happen?' I asked. 'I mean these accidents.'

'The wires in the boxes, ma'am, they're supposed to have two layers of insulation, one made with plastic tape and the other with rubber. When the rubber wears off, the exposed end of the wire comes into contact with the metal frame on the service box.'

'The manhole cover?' Mike asked.

'Looks like about fifty-five volts of electricity ran up the side of the box to the plate – the manhole cover – above it. More than enough to kill you.'

'You got more of these?'

'Two hundred fifty junction boxes in the city.'

'Any other deaths?' Mike asked. 'I haven't seen one of these before.'

The guy from the mayor's office, who was measuring civil lawsuits if not human lives, answered. 'A month ago they had one downtown. Manhattan South responded. Woman walking her dog in the East Village. This seems to be the season.'

'Why's that?'

'There was a lot of snow this winter,' the Con Ed man said. 'When the city salts the streets, the cable insulation corrodes and cracks.'

The mayor's representative shook his head, not willing to shoulder the liability for the anticipated lawsuit. 'Salt is not the reason Joe Berk died. That last service box was too small and crammed too full of cable. It pushed those wires to the top, snapped them, and electrified the whole thing. You should have had a limiter in there.'

'What's that?'

'It's like a fuse,' he said, answering Mike before continuing to excoriate the Con Ed chief. 'When's the last time this box was inspected? You haven't got enough workmen on the street and you haven't developed an adequate way to test the manholes.'

'Forty complaints?' Mike asked. 'You don't mean forty people have died.'

'No, no, no. Hot spots. Electrified metal utility covers like this or even on areas of sidewalk. Usually it's only twenty or thirty volts – enough to give you a good scare or bounce a dog in the air. People call them in every week. Wastes a hell of a lot of our time because these hard hats can't get it through their hard heads to fix the problem.'

110

Mike stepped away from the huddle and we walked around the orange cones, crossing the street to the front of the Belasco, its wide façade of warm red brick set off by the white stone pediments of its neo-Georgian architectural style.

Another rookie cop stood at the door that led upstairs to Joe Berk's apartment. Mike flashed his badge. 'Anybody inside?'

'There was a gentleman with Mr Berk when he went down in the street. Might even be his son. He went back upstairs when the ambulance took off with Berk. Said he had to make some calls, then headed over to the hospital. I asked him to leave the key with me. There's nobody up there right now.'

'Good thinking. Ms Cooper and I are going to take a look around.'

The kid passed over the key. We walked to the elevator in the rear of the building and took it up to the fourth floor, which was as high as it went, letting ourselves in to the dead man's quiet apartment.

The room we entered was the office in which we'd talked to Berk yesterday afternoon. The dark oak paneling on the walls and ceilings took on a somber cast now, and all Mike could find for lighting was the single bulb of the desk lamp.

'We're looking for . . . ?'

'Anything to link Joe to Galinova. Anything to point us in another direction, in case he didn't really deserve that last blast of energy as his final send-off.'

'So how do you feel about a search warrant, Detective Chapman?'

'The mope is dead. Why? He's still got standing in a

court of law? Clarence Thomas is gonna go out on a limb on this one?' Mike had put his rubber gloves on and was pushing and lifting pieces of paper on Berk's large desk. He tossed another pair to me. 'You can just stare at me and continue to be useless or you can poke around here.'

I pulled the latex over my fingers and reached for several small manila envelopes that Mike removed from his jacket pocket.

He pointed at the lounge chair. 'You want those long white hairs, don't you?'

'I won't be able to use anything I take out of here in Talya's case, if that's what you're suggesting.'

'Abandoned property, Coop. Guy passes on and leaves stuff behind. Think of the poor cleaning lady who has to pick up after him. You're doing her a favor. C'mon. Help yourself.'

I brushed some loose strands into the envelope and put it in the pocket of my jeans.

Mike handed me a memo pad with a 'to do' list for Monday, the following morning.

There was a list of names and phone numbers, meeting times, and a luncheon appointment. I grabbed an empty sheet of paper and copied all of the notations.

The correspondence was stacked in neat piles. One tall stack seemed to be all about the settlement of a grievance between Broadway producers and the union that represented stage actors and managers. Negotiators had reached a tentative accord to avert a major theatrical strike, and Berk seemed to be in the middle of the mix, refusing to give in to demands from Actors' Equity and drawing the ire of union leaders.

Another folder overflowed with papers on the

upcoming Tony awards, the equivalent of Hollywood's Oscars. The televised ceremony was a couple of months away.

'Just make a list of these files,' I said to Mike. 'We can't take this stuff with us, and I can't find anything at all relevant to Galinova. This one's all about the Tonys. Looks like some of Berk's shows are up for the big prizes.'

'They make a difference?' Mike asked, opening drawers and scanning their contents.

'No question about it. Winning an award usually keeps a show running or fills up the house by introducing a new audience, so it's got to help the producer. We can always get someone to give us more info about the business side of the theater world.'

Almost everything I could see on the top of the desk had something to do with show business. There was nothing with Galinova's name on it and very little that seemed to relate to Berk's personal life.

Mike stood in the threshold of the room and called over to me. 'Check this out.'

Past the door of the bathroom there was another enormous dark room, with a staircase leading up to the second floor of the duplex, where a balcony ringed the entire perimeter. The two-story height was capped with a stained-glass dome. Around the sides of the room were niches, all filled with Napoleonic memorabilia.

I joined Mike and we circled the floor, looking at the brass labels on the displays. In one corner was a statue of the Little Corporal himself, while other cases held his swords, his campaign maps, and even his underwear. A burgundy leather chaise longue with the emperor's initials was in the center of the room, and built into the walls

113

were bookcases that housed what looked to be a library of theatrical works.

Mike started up the winding oak staircase and halfway to the top, signaled me to join him. 'I think I've found the old boy's boudoir.'

At the top of the stairs was a foyer that led into a large bedroom. The king-size bed was made up with a plush set of linens, Berk's monogram sewn into some kind of crest on the spread and pillow shams.

On the far wall was a display with four television monitors, similar to the ones that cued the stage director at the Met, but bigger. Mike parked himself on the side of the bed and picked up the master remote control, clicking on the first screen. He changed the channels until he found the Yankees game.

'Look, this is a waste of time,' I said, switching on the small lamp on the bedside table, looking for any notes or photographs.

'Tied up at two all against the Sox in the bottom of the twelfth? One out, Jeter just stole second, and you're in some kind of a rush? You got something better to do than this?'

He left the set on and clicked the next monitor. The image came up but there was no movement on it, and Mike couldn't seem to change the channel from the fixed camera view that was focused on a white-tiled wall. He moved the remote to the third set and got a similar shot. It looked like the same room from a different angle. Neither of us was surprised that the fourth set displayed a background setting much like the two others.

'What do you think we've got here? Think these are his theater properties?'

I stepped closer to the screens and kneeled in front of them. 'If they are, we're not looking at the stage or the orchestra.'

Mike walked over and leaned in against my shoulder. 'What do you see?'

'This one looks like – well, like it's in some kind of dressing room, doesn't it?' I pointed at a mirrored wall opposite a sink, with a clothes rack that had a dress and a woman's blouse hanging from it. 'And this one's a bathroom. You can see right into the shower. There's some mosaic design in the background. Looks like flowers – maybe tulips. Same for the last one.'

'That old bastard was sitting up here watching the showgirls undress,' Mike said, breaking out into one of his classic grins. 'What a frigging racket this is. Perfect business for an old pervert.'

Suddenly, there was a loud creaking noise that seemed to come from behind a doorway in the wall next to the bed. It startled me and I grabbed for Mike's arm.

'What's that?' I asked, anxious to get out of Berk's apartment before anyone found us here without any legitimate business to do. 'Seems like it's coming from the closet.'

The grinding sound of elevator cables stopped and the door opened into the room. The young woman who stepped out of the narrow space hissed her words into my face.

'Who the hell are you and what are you doing here?'

Chapter 12

'I'm Mike Chapman. NYPD. This is Alexandra Cooper. Are you a – um – related to Joe Berk?'

'Was I? Yes. Mona Berk. Joe was my uncle.'

'I'm sorry about your loss, about his death—'

'I'll pass along your condolences to the rest of the family. You waiting for the cartoons to come on or what?'

She positioned herself next to Mike, in front of the bank of monitors.

'Maybe you can help tell us what we're looking at. Could it be he's got cameras concealed in bathrooms or a dressing room in one of the theaters your family owns?'

'That wouldn't surprise me. Joe Berk was a pig.'

She took the remote from Mike's hand and clicked off the sets. 'I have no idea where those cameras are installed, and I still don't understand why you two are here,' Mona said, turning away from the screen and batting her long black eyelashes at Mike.

'Routine. We were talking to your uncle yesterday about an investigation. He apparently had my business card in his pocket so the cops on the scene called me after they put him in the ambulance and the EMTs took him away. Ms Cooper and I came up here to see if we could find any next-of-kin information so we could make the proper notifications.'

'Consider me notified.'

'I was wondering, actually, how you got the news so quickly.'

'My cousin was with his father when it happened. He called some of us. Briggs and I are very close.'

'Briggs?'

'Briggs Berk. Joe's son.'

'Where is he now?'

'At the hospital, I guess, dealing with Joe's affairs – the funeral home and all that. I didn't really expect to hear from him after the first call. Anything else I can help you with tonight?' Mona asked, walking in the direction of the staircase as though hoping we would follow.

'I'm afraid we can't leave until we have some more information,' Mike said. 'I'll have to complete all the paperwork for the medical examiner's office.'

She smiled at him. 'Routine?'

'That's why they sent me here, Ms Berk. Would you give me your cousin's address and phone number, date of birth if you know it? I take it he was a witness to the accident.'

'Briggs is two years younger than I am. I guess that made him twenty-six last November,' she said, telling him the rest of the information he asked for.

Mike held up the apartment key that the rookie had handed him on our way in. 'How'd you get in, Ms Berk? We've got your cousin's key, and we used it to come in through the front elevator. What's your secret?'

Mike obviously didn't think the young woman had any more authority to be in her uncle's apartment than we did and was holding his ground rather than leave the place to some other family interloper.

Mona Berk leaned against the stair railing. 'What do you know about David Belasco?'

'Never heard of him,' Mike said.

She held up her arms and waved around the open space. 'This is his home, detective. Belasco lived in it till he died. My uncle and his oversized ego moved right in. Room to spare for his Napoleonic complex, as you can see.'

'Who's Belasco?'

'One of the great figures in the history of the American theater, but I guess you didn't know that. He acted a bit and wrote some plays, rode bareback in the circus, peddled patent medicine that his mother cooked up in her own kitchen. He was entirely self-made, and he went on to become one of the most prolific producers of his day. Flamboyant? Belasco was outrageous. He's been dead since 1931. Uncle Joe kind of saw himself as the second coming.'

'How do you mean?'

'Belasco built this theater in 1907 – the second-oldest one in midtown Manhattan. It's a jewel of an auditorium, meant to be very intimate. Only four hundred and fifty seats in the orchestra, another five fifty upstairs. Designed by the same architect who built the Apollo.'

The 125th Street theater that had a white-only admissions policy when it opened as a burlesque house in 1914 was renamed the Apollo twenty years later. A great showplace for black entertainers, it had headlined Bessie Smith and Billie Holiday, Duke Ellington and Thelonius Monk, Aretha Franklin, and Gladys Knight. The two houses could not have looked more dissimilar.

'And this apartment?'

'A few years after the theater opened, Belasco built this ten-room duplex on top for himself to live in. That dome?' Mona said, pointing above us to the rich tones of the stained glass. 'It's by Tiffany. That chair in Joe's office? It's a pew from the church where Shakespeare worshiped in Stratford. Belasco was over the top. He collected all this, but it was mostly broken up after he died. A lot of the antique furniture was bought by Sardi's, to make a private dining room.'

'Berk bought it back?' Mike asked.

'First Uncle Joe bought the theater itself from the Shubert Organization. You don't even want to know what he paid them for it. Then he hunted down all the trophies – the artwork, the furniture, the library.'

'But why this theater? There's bigger ones in town. Aren't they more profitable?'

'Joe fancied himself a great showman, just like Belasco. And a ladies' man, too,' Mona said, looking at me, maybe for the first time. 'The baby pink spotlight? Belasco invented it. Made all his girls look good onstage. The first dimmers on a theatrical stage? Again, David's idea to flatter the babes. Meanwhile, he paraded around town in a bishop's robe and white collar. That's all he ever wore.'

'Because he was religious?'

Mona dismissed me with a sneer. 'Please. His father was Jewish and his mother was a gypsy from Spain. You can't see Joe's inspiration? Here's Belasco – a guy who came from nothing, yet he was the man who discovered Mary Pickford, Jeanne Eagels and Lillian Gish, Lionel Barrymore and Katharine Cornell. He starred Humphrey

Bogart in a Broadway play in 1929. You wanted to know how I came in without using the front elevator that brought you upstairs?'

'Yeah.'

'Belasco had that small lift installed after he moved in. While the performances were going on in the theater, he'd send for his favorite showgirl of the moment – sneak her up by this private elevator – so he could ply her with oysters and champagne in his bedroom and make love to her during the evening. Uncle Joe? Loved that contraption. He's been doing the same thing right up until he croaked, only he was too damn cheap to pay to oil the cables. Everybody backstage knew exactly when he was getting serviced. The code on the keypad never changed. Hit *J-O-E* and you wind up right in Joe Berk's bed. Impresario and lecher. Lovely legacy for the family, don't you think, Mr Chapman?'

Mona Berk continued to descend the staircase. 'Why don't you throw on some lights?'

'If I knew where they were,' Mike answered, following her down the steps, 'I'd be happy to.'

'That makes two of us,' she said, turning to face Mike and putting her hands on her hips. 'Now you can probably think like Joe Berk. It's kind of a guy thing. Some sort of gadget, some flashy device that would do the trick more dramatically than an ordinary switch.'

'When was the last time you were here?' Mike asked, sensing that Mona's visit was as exploratory as our own.

'It's been years. Since my father died, more than five years ago,' she said, pushing aside the folders on the desktop that we had been looking through. 'Ah, the Empress Josephine.'

She held up a small statuette of Napoléon's consort that was in a cradle next to the telephone. 'I'm betting it's her breasts, detective, what do you think?'

Mona Berk pressed on Josephine's chest and the lights went on in wall sconces all around the room. She swiveled the nipples and they dimmed. 'At least Uncle Joe was consistent. He never let propriety stand in the way of a quick feel.'

'If you're so close to your relatives, why haven't you been here in that long?'

'Close to my cousin, Mr Chapman. As you can tell from my profound lack of sympathy for the dearly departed, I didn't have a lot to do with my uncle.'

'The business Joe Berk ran, isn't it a family enterprise?' I asked.

'I'm sorry. Did you say your name was Alice?'

'Alexandra Cooper. Alex.'

Mona Berk was saving all her charm for Mike. A few months ago it would have worked well for her, but now he wasn't in the mood to respond.

'Family? Don't make me laugh. We're not exactly cut out of the pages of a Louisa May Alcott story,' she said, parking herself in her uncle's desk chair. 'But that's probably more than you need to know. You want to leave one of your cards for me, Mike? I'll call you if there's any way you can be helpful. Maybe some security for the funeral. That's going to be a mob scene.'

'I don't do funerals, Ms Berk. I'm a homicide cop.'

He had Mona's attention now. 'Homicide? Briggs told me this was an accident. You said you were here for a routine notification. What are you?'

'The investigation your uncle was helping us with is

121

actually a murder case. Maybe you heard about it on the news today.'

'I don't listen to the news. It's too depressing. Who died?'

I looked at Mona Berk, slumped back in the oversize chair, a ribbed turtleneck clinging to the outline of her well-toned body. The bottom of the sweater didn't meet the top of her jeans, and she rubbed the exposed crescent of her flat abdomen with her left hand. The only thing that distracted me from the petulant expression on her face was the large sapphire she sported on her ring finger.

'A dancer. Galinova. She was killed at the Metropolitan Opera House.'

'And what does that have to do with Uncle Joe?'

Mike sat on the edge of the desk. 'First of all, Ms Berk, have you ever heard of Galinova?'

'You don't need to be all "Ms Berk". I'm Mona, you're Mike, she's Alice.'

'Okay, Mona. Did you ever—'

'Talya? Is that the one they call Talya?'

'Have you ever met her?'

'Nope.' Berk was pulling open desk drawers and flipping through piles of paper, fidgeting mostly, rather than examining them like Mike and I wanted to do.

'Did you know anything about her relationship with your uncle?'

'Professional? I didn't think he was into dance.'

'How about personal?'

She grimaced. 'Spare me the details. A classical ballerina falling for his shtick? So how did she die?'

'She was accosted by someone backstage who got her

122

to a remote hallway upstairs. Tied her hands behind her back and threw her headfirst down an air shaft.'

'Awful,' she said, covering her mouth with her hand. 'That's really awful. Joe had something to do with her?'

'I think she wanted to be in one of his shows,' Mike said.

'Which one?'

'See, Mona? We ask you a few simple questions about the family business and you're ready to show me to the door, but now you want answers from us.' Mike stood up and motioned me toward the elevator door.

'Okay. The Berk Organization. The most dysfunctional family to hit the boards since the Sopranos. What interests you about us?'

'I'm looking for links between your uncle and Galinova. He was with her at the Met just a short time before she died, and witnesses tell us they were arguing. It might have had something to do with a plan she had to work with Joe,' Mike said. 'Maybe it's my own ignorance about the theater. I always thought that producers were responsible for the creative oversight of a show, and that the rich backers were like silent partners. They didn't really have any influence on the creative side.'

'Angels, Mike. You're thinking about angels.'

'Well, what was your uncle's role?'

Mona played with the dimmers on Josephine's chest and laughed. 'The last thing I'd call Joe is an angel. Not even a dead angel. Anyway, Broadway has changed a lot. The angels *are* the producers. It's all economics, Mike. It's become so prohibitively expensive to stage a show – millions of dollars in most cases – that raising the money has become a huge burden.'

123

She stood up and started to walk toward the elevator. 'You know what you need now to become a great producer? A checkbook. Find material that's worked well before, package some popular talent with familiar names that people will pay big ticket prices to come see. Why do you think revivals dominate the Broadway theater? You don't need ideas to produce them. You just need a deep pocket.'

'And Joe Berk had that.'

'So now you're going to tell me what show he was talking with Talya about, aren't you?' Mona said to Mike.

'When I find out what it is, I'll let you know.'

'If it's anything to do with a story about Evelyn Nesbit and Stanford White, be sure and give me a call,' she said, testing Mike now but getting his best poker face. 'That project is my idea and nobody's going to steal it from me.'

Mona pressed the button and the doors opened. 'I take it we're all leaving? I've got to be ready to help my cousin in the morning. That nice young cop at the door won't let anybody in, if that's what you're worried about.'

I knew Mike wanted to stay but couldn't come up with a reason to offer Mona Berk. We stepped into the elevator with her.

'Exactly how are you related?' Mike asked.

'My dad was Joe's older brother. Isidore Berk. Izzy.'

'He worked with Joe?'

'Yeah, but my dad was the class of the business.'

'And you, you're part of the organization?'

'I've got my own office. Around the corner – 1501 Broadway. The Paramount Theatre building. Do you know it?'

'Yeah,' Mike said. 'That great-looking tower with the clocks and the globe? Sinatra's old hangout.'

We were on the ground floor, in the narrow corridor that led to the street. 'Have you seen the house?' Mona asked. 'I mean inside the Belasco Theatre?'

She turned the knob and a door marked EXIT opened. This time, the light switch panel was on the wall and she illuminated the front orchestra of the fan-shaped auditorium. We followed her in and she lowered herself into one of the plush gray seats in the first row.

'Pretty spectacular, isn't it?' Berk said, looking up at the brilliantly painted murals that lined the proscenium and arched over the boxes on stage right and left. 'Can you see?'

Mike and I leaned our heads back and studied the ceiling.

'Each portrait is a tribute to one of the great dramatists – Goethe, Molière, Shakespeare. Those figures over the stage? They're all allegorical. Everett Shinn, the Ash Can School – he was the painter,' she said, pointing at the nudes represented against the lush green-and-gold background. 'That's Mother Love, sheltering Innocence, and the other? It's Devotion dispelling Grief with a kiss.'

That was her only reference to grief since we'd encountered her.

'You know this place well,' I said.

'You can't imagine how many hours I spent in Broadway theaters, waiting for my father while he made deals with other producers or tried to sweet-talk actors into coming to work for him. Going to rehearsals and openings, going back again whenever there was a cast change to see if the understudy could handle the part.

Going a third or fourth time if a new song was added or a dance number cut. I could probably draw the interior of every one of them from memory.'

'Would you mind giving me your number, in case we need to talk with you again?'

'Sure. My cell's the best.' She smiled at Mike as she gave it to him.

'Can we see you out?' Mike asked.

'I'm just going to sit here for a while. I think it's my favorite place to be – an empty theater at night. All the artifice is gone, all the things that directors impose on our imaginations. Now it's just a stage that's full of possibilities. We'll hang out – just me and Belasco's ghost.'

Mike started for the door ahead of me.

'Hey, Mike,' Mona said, 'I'll give you something to tell those dancers over at the Met. They know about ghosts?'

Mike wasn't amused.

Mona got up from the seat and walked to the edge of the stage, boosting herself up to sit on it. 'Every theater has a ghost. Ask anyone who's ever worked on Broadway. There's a ghost in every house. And now that someone's been murdered there – at the Met – they'll never get rid of it.'

It's not the first time, I started to say, but she wasn't playing to me in any event.

'Maybe Joe threatened Galinova. Maybe it's another Belasco trait he tried to imitate.'

'What are you talking about, Mona?' Mike asked.

'The theater world thrives on superstition and legend. You won't get anywhere if you don't understand that. Belasco fell in love with one of his actresses. Carter – I

126

think her name was Leslie Carter. He was a total control freak, just like Uncle Joe. Starred her in a lot of plays but wanted complete control of her life, even though he continued to have other mistresses.'

Mona went on. 'She surprised Belasco by getting married to another man, and he went completely berserk. He forbid her to ever enter this theater again. There was a big row, and she ended it by placing a curse on him – a curse against his vindictiveness.'

'Yeah?'

'You ought to find out if Galinova had another lover, Mike. Jealousy – there's something to enrage my uncle, I can promise you that.'

'What about the ghost?'

'I'll let you know tomorrow, detective. Rumor has it that all throughout the night you can hear the blood-curdling screams of Belasco's ghost echoing in this theater,' she said, winking at Mike. 'I'm just praying I don't have to listen to Joe Berk screaming, too. I spent enough of my life doing that.'

Chapter 13

'*Aha!* What's the matter with you two? You look like you've seen a ghost,' Joe Berk said, propped up against the pillows in his private room at Roosevelt Hospital. '*Cats* was the longest-running show on Broadway. Fifty million people around the world saw it and what? You jerks didn't make it? Couldn't buy a ticket? Nine lives, baby – just like a cat – and Joe Berk still has five or six to go.'

Mike had called me at five in the morning to tell me that the paramedics had revived the self-proclaimed wizard in the ambulance on the way to the emergency room. The cops who had originally notified Mike of Berk's collapse on the street had gone off duty an hour later and never learned that the EMTs had saved the man's life minutes after picking him up. It was only after we'd been home a couple of hours that Mike – struggling with insomnia since Val's death – heard the news story about Joe Berk's rescue on the radio.

Dr Lin-So Wong, who admitted Berk to the hospital, was standing with us at his bedside at seven a.m. on Monday, explaining to us the effects of electrocution as his patient listened intently. Wong patted the older man's hand and checked the readings of his pulse and blood pressure.

'Mr Berk is quite fortunate not to have suffered very severe burns. It's the vital organs that are so susceptible to disruption by the flow of the electric current.'

'So how come he's alive?' Mike asked.

'Because the EMTs had just finished their pizza in one of those joints on Broadway,' Dr Wong said, pursing his lips into a smile. 'Because they were there within ninety seconds after he went down, and they had a defibrillator on board. A minute more without oxygen to the brain and we'd have a different result.'

'I'm walking across the street with my kid, going up to Baldoria for something to eat,' Berk said, giving his own version of the events. 'You know that scene in the Frankenstein movie where they juice up the monster? You see those lightning bolts flashing when they bring him to life? Lemme tell you, I saw stars when I landed on that manhole cover. I take a few steps, I think to myself, No way Joe Berk is gonna die by frying on top of a goddamn sewer. I deserve better than that.'

Mike asked the doctor, 'He really kept walking? I thought they'd declared him dead at the scene.'

'Very common reaction for an electrocution victim to keep moving for several seconds. Yes, his son said he actually walked a few feet farther and then collapsed. Apparently he'd sustained ventricular fibrillation and went into cardiac arrest. The paramedics were right to think he was dead. If it weren't for the defibrillator on the ambulance, well—'

'Finish the sentence, doc. The lights would be dimmed all up and down the Great White Way tonight, no? Banner headlines everywhere.'

Berk looked paler and weaker than he had on Saturday, but hadn't lost much of his moxie.

'He'll be staying with us awhile. He's not out of the woods yet.'

'Now they'll really try to kill me. Hospital food.'

'What's the danger?' I whispered to the doctor, taking him away from the bedside while Mike looked at Berk's medical chart, copying down his date of birth and some of the legible medical notations.

'Blood offers less resistance to the electrical current than other body tissues. Usually there's a large amount of current that flows through blood vessels, and that can cause damage to the lining. Increases the risk of thrombosis. Stroke is always possible.'

'What's your guess? How long will you keep him in?'

'If he doesn't fight it, I'd like him here for the rest of the week.'

Wong walked back to Berk's bedside. 'I don't want him agitated, detective. He needs plenty of rest.'

'Agitate me? What do they care, doc? They're looking to beat up on an old man, they came to the wrong place.'

'We're not here to do that,' I said, stepping closer to calm Berk, knowing Mike would want to ask a few questions and hoping he would ease his way into them. 'It's a good thing your son was with you last night.'

'Thank God for Briggs is damn right. You meet him? He still hanging around?'

'No. No, we haven't met him yet.'

'Handsome kid. Takes after his mother. But I'm the one who gave him the name. Briggsley.'

'That's his real name?' Mike asked.

'Briggsley Berk. Found it in a book, something about

130

the peerage. Imagine what a favor I did him. Yussel Berkowitz. Try growing up here with a name like that.'

'Does Briggs work for you?' I asked.

'So I go to court, here in Manhattan. Supreme Court. Must have been the late fifties,' Berk said, not interested in paying attention to me. 'I made an application to change my name. Who's the judge? You're a lawyer, listen to this. You ever know Judge Schmuck?'

I laughed. 'Before my time, but I've heard of him.'

'Why should I grant your motion? the guy asks me. What's wrong with being Yussel Berkowitz? he wants to know. What's wrong? I hated the damn name. I wanted to sound like I was an American, not some hustling immigrant. The judge, he says to me, "You know what my name is? I'm Peter J. Schmuck. My father was a Schmuck, my grandfather was a Schmuck, and I've lived all my life being a Schmuck." Bang! He slammed down the gavel and kicked me out of the courtroom.'

'So you waited a bit and went back to a different judge another day.'

'Waited, my ass. I asked around, found a friendly clerk who liked the color of my money, and next thing you know I'm Joe Berk. Whole thing took five minutes. Figure the one sure thing I could do for my kids was give them good old Anglo-Saxon names.'

'How many children do you have?'

'Five. You really interested in this personal stuff about me or you still nosing around where you don't belong? You catch whoever killed Natalya?'

'Not yet.'

'You do, I got a manhole cover you could sit him on.'

'Does Briggs work with you?'

131

'Nobody works with me. They work *for* me. They'd all be living in a trailer park somewhere if I didn't put this empire together for them.'

My elbows were resting on the metal railing on the side of the bed. Berk lifted his arm, which seemed to be trembling, and took one of my hands in his.

'All by yourself?'

'Me and my brother. Izzy, he was my older brother. Smartest man I ever knew.' His eyes were closed now and he seemed overwhelmed by the realization of how he had escaped death so narrowly.

I looked to Mike and he cupped his hands, waving his fingers toward himself. He wanted me to keep Joe Berk talking.

'Did Talya tell you that she was going to be leaving her husband?' I asked.

'What? You don't want to know about Izzy? You just asked me whether I built the business myself. You know what we got?' He was patting my hand now, anxious to show off. 'Real estate. We own more commercial real estate than there are square acres in the state of Rhode Island. It's true. Don't look at me like that, young lady. I'm telling you the truth. You like hotels? The Berkleigh chain. Makes the Hyatts look like they ran out of properties on a Monopoly board. Jet plane leasing? BerkAir's got the biggest private fleet in the world.'

I tried to disengage my hand from Berk's grasp. He opened his eyes and reached out for my wrist. 'We're going to have to go, Mr Berk. You need to rest.'

'I'll rest when I'm good and ready.'

'Mike and I have to get to work.'

'You mean if I don't answer your questions, you're

132

gonna leave me alone in this place? Don't go until my son gets back. It won't be very long. You want to talk about Talya?'

'That would help us.'

'First I gotta explain how Izzy and I got into the theater business, right? I wouldn't be having anything to do with fancy dancers and Tennessee Williams and all that jazz if we hadn't moved the organization into the stage world. Can't make sense of my relationship with Talya until you understand what my business is about.'

The man didn't want to be alone. He didn't have the least interest in cooperating with us, but he didn't want to be on his own in the alien and uncontrollable world of the sterile hospital room.

'I think I'm more interested in your personal relationship with Talya than your professional one.'

Again he ignored me. 'Real estate. Simple as that. We were buying up so much commercial land in midtown when the market went to hell in 'seventy six, we found ourselves competing with the Shuberts and Nederlanders for property. We wound up with four legitimate theaters. The stage – I told Izzy – that's where the magic is. Forget television and the movies, people still want to come out at night and touch the stars.'

I looked to Mike and now he was shaking his head.

'We've got to go, Mr Berk. Is there someone you'd like me to call to come sit with you? One of your children?'

'Briggs'll be back any minute now. He promised me. The others are scattered all over the country. We got offices in LA, in Chicago, in Miami. I only got the youngest kid here with me.'

'How about nephews or nieces? Izzy's kids.'

133

'Same story. Spread out all over the place. I'll give you my secretary's number. Let's get her over here, okay?'

'We can do that,' I said. 'How about Mona?'

'Who?'

'Mona, your niece. Izzy's daughter.'

'Oh, so now she's Mona? Desdemona Berk, Ms Cooper. The first Broadway show Izzy ever saw was in 1943. *Othello*. Paul Robeson as the Moor. Trust me, that's an actor who'd never have done bullshit ads for the telephone company like – like – what's his name? What a talent Robeson was. Uta Hagen, she was Desdemona. Izzy was a kid, but he was entranced. Another marriage and four sons later, he finally gets the baby girl.'

'Mona's office is here in town, though, isn't it? Would you like me to call her?'

Berk dropped his hold of my arm, turned his head to the other side of the bed, and pretended to spit on the floor. 'Bite your tongue. I'd rather eat nails.'

Mike walked to the foot of the bed. 'Briggs called your niece last night, while the ambulance was on the way to the hospital. She came over to the theater right away. Maybe he can tell you why he wanted her to be there.'

'Where? In my office? My home?' Berk was trying to pull himself up. 'I'll tell you why she was there. She wanted to be the first one to drive a nail in my coffin. Nobody let her in, did they? Did they?'

He was shouting now and a nurse opened the door and displaced me at the side of the bed. This was a giant step beyond the level of agitation that Dr Wong didn't want us to provoke.

'We're not the ones who let her in,' Mike said, omitting the fact that she hadn't needed anyone's help in

134

gaining access through the secret elevator in the apartment.

'Talk to my lawyers, detective. That little *vonce* – that cockroach – shouldn't be anywhere near my place. She's filed a lawsuit against me. She's trying to break up the business organization and my family. Desdemona Berk – my brother Izzy should rest in peace – she's a greedy little bitch.'

Chapter 14

'Want to grab some coffee before I go downtown to my office?' I said to Mike.

'Nah. I'll go up to the squad and put in a few hours.'

'So how come you didn't ask him about the monitors in his apartment?'

'He was holding your hand, not mine. I thought you'd get to it. That's not homicide work, that's some kind of Peeping Tom stuff, right up your alley.'

Mike was a detail guy. It was rare for him to let a single fact slip from his grasp. It was even more unusual for him to turn down my offer of a free breakfast.

'Are you going to talk to Mona?' I asked.

'About what? Right now all I'm interested in is who else saw Natalya Galinova before she disappeared and why her personal life seemed to be in such turmoil.'

'I'll be in my office if you want anything,' I said, hailing a Yellow Cab on the corner of Tenth Avenue and 59th Street.

It was only eight fifteen when I bought two cups of black coffee from the cart on the corner of the Hogan Place entrance to the courthouse. I scanned my ID card and pushed through the turnstile, greeting the cop whose fixed post was security in the cramped lobby of the District Attorney's Office.

The eighth-floor corridor was still empty when I pushed open the anteroom door, passing my secretary's desk and turning on the lights in my office. I had left hurriedly on Friday evening to get to work with Mercer on the Jean Eaken case up at the Special Victims Squad. The case memos and screening sheets from the forty senior assistants who worked in my unit were still scattered on my desktop for review and response, so I spent time making comments on them until the phones started ringing at nine.

Half of the morning was occupied with phone calls to press for special attention to the new cases. I needed the toxicologist to do the routine drug screening in the Eaken case, but also to be aware that Xanax had been recovered from the doctor's kitchen counter. I begged the chief serologist to rush the DNA profile from the blood on the teeth of the dog who saved his owner from a rape in Riverside Park. A match to a known felon would launch a search that might prevent other women from being victimized.

I had no official role in the death investigation of Natalya Galinova, but knew that Mike could navigate the most professional medical examiner's office in the country with a skill that would produce the best results possible in a timely fashion.

At eleven, after I had set my secretary, Laura, to work on some correspondence, I walked across the hall to the executive wing, to see whether Rose Malone, the district attorney's assistant, could fit me into his schedule. I waited through a series of phone calls from the governor and several lesser public officials before I was summoned into the large office from which Paul Battaglia supervised the work of the six hundred lawyers on his staff.

There wasn't an hour of the day or night that Battaglia was without a cigar stub in his mouth. He could talk straight for thirty minutes without bobbling the unlit Cohiba that was stuck to his lips, and when he was actually smoking, as he was now, he would remove it occasionally to waft a ribbon of smoke in my direction.

'Good morning, Paul. Thanks for giving me some time. There are a couple of new cases that are likely to get some ink, that I thought you'd want to know about.'

'Like what?' he asked, drawing back one side of his lip and speaking out of the corner of his mouth.

'Like a physician who drugged two women in order to rape them. Canadian tourists.'

The press always played up the foreign element in crime stories. Politicians hated any mentions that might scare people away from the city's most profitable industry. 'And the good news is that we finally have DNA from the Riverside rapist, so we're likely to have a profile to put in the databank by midweek.'

I expected his usual barrage of precise questions about the pedigree of the doctor who'd been arrested or the breed of the heroic dog. 'You think I think that's why you're in here to see me?'

I blushed and that drew a wide smile around the cigar clenched in his teeth.

'The commissioner called me about the Galinova woman. He seems to know that you were up at the crime scene.'

138

And didn't call to tell Battaglia about it, which was the unspoken part of the district attorney's 'gotcha'.

'We were working on my rape case up at the squad when Homicide got the news she'd gone missing. Chapman thought I might be useful because of my familiarity with the ballet world, and the possibility that Galinova had been assaulted before she was killed.'

'Chapman always finds a way to make you useful, doesn't he?'

I ignored the shot. There wasn't a rumor that circulated anywhere within the office that escaped Battaglia's radar. 'Paul, I'd really like to ask you to assign me to the investigation.'

Homicide cases were controlled in the Trial Division by Pat McKinney, a rat-faced prosecutor whose legal ability was obscured by the pettiness of his personality and the longtime affair he'd conducted with an incompetent young lawyer for whom he'd carved out a protected place in the bureau. I had challenged McKinney too many times to be favored with investigations that fell on the outer borders of my own unit. Battaglia's reliance on my sex crimes prosecutors for the resolution of so many high-profile cases – our ability to exonerate falsely accused suspects before charging them and to nail those guilty of such heinous crimes – had given me direct access to him whenever I wanted it.

'Nobody's got the case for us?'

'No suspects yet. The squad's just getting on all the employees today. Nobody's been tapped to work on it.'

'It's not a rape, according to the commissioner. Any reason to think the perp was trying?'

I had gone online to find the old news stories about

the first murder at the Met. I reminded Battaglia of the facts, since the case had occurred before he was in office.

'That wasn't a completed rape either, Paul, but it was certainly an attempt at one. The best those detectives could reconstruct, the violinist ran into the stagehand when she was lost. He got her in an elevator and tried to assault her. He probably killed her when she resisted, when she was struggling.'

'So you want to keep that option open?'

'Yes. We've got four hundred guys who were some-where backstage that afternoon and evening, so detectives have got to talk to every one of them, in case this was random – or to see whether one of them had been stalking Galinova since she'd arrived here. And we're developing a very complex personal life. A lover's quarrel – a domestic – isn't so far out of the question.'

'How so?'

'Galinova recently put her husband on notice that she wanted a legal separation. She had something going on with this guy called Joe Berk, and a former lover is the artistic—'

'Slow down, Alex. Don't just throw Joe Berk's name in here and slide by it.'

'Is he a friend?'

'He's everybody's friend. And he'd be your worst enemy.'

There were no powerful businessmen or -women who had somehow not been in Battaglia's orbit throughout his several terms in office as one of the most influential law-enforcement figures in the country. Every prominent New Yorker had been solicited for campaign contributions over the years, and most had benefited from the services of the great lawyers mentored in their careers by Paul Battaglia. Among his prosecutorial alumni were partners in every major firm, litigators sought to battle in the most controversial trials, judges on the state and federal bench, commissioners leading government agencies of every type, and one protégé who had been a contender for the position of attorney general of the United States – the country's premier legal post.

'Anything I need to know?'

'Don't turn your back to him, Alex. He's vicious.'

'I assume the commissioner told you he was with Galinova – arguing with her – just before she disappeared?'

'Take it wherever it goes. You don't need a pass from me.' Battaglia's mantra had been consistent, no matter where the tentacles of an investigation led. I'd been given a green light to do the right thing, which is all he asked of each one of us.

'So your answer is yes? I can stay on the case? And you tell McKinney, please. I don't even want to see him.'

'I want to know everything you develop before I read it in the *Post* with a Mickey Diamond byline. Got that?'

Diamond was the veteran courthouse reporter who snagged the best leaks from the NYPD brass, and when facts failed to fall in his lap, he fashioned the most creative sidebars in journalism.

'And when you know where you're going with Berk, I'll give you some background about his other run-ins with the law.'

Battaglia always delivered one of his throwaway lines while I was on the threshold of the door. I turned back. 'Crimes?'

141

'Nothing violent. Tax fraud. Some pretty sophisticated planning that's made him and everyone around him worth billions. Not millions. The *B* word. I've been trying to get the bastard for years. The feds took the investigation away from me when I couldn't put together a case that'd stick, but then in the end, neither could they,' he said, smiling broadly again. 'I may have some leverage for you when you come to need it.'

'You want to tell me now?'

'I don't want to muddy the waters.'

Maybe another tidbit would help. 'The commissioner fill you in on the fact that Berk got hotfooted on a manhole cover late last night? And survived it?'

'Yeah. I wanted to make sure the PC thought it was accidental. You agree?'

'Had all the right signs. His favorite son was taking him out for a lobster dinner, and his driver was parked next to the manhole. Con Ed said they'd had more than—'

'I know, I know. Forty reports this year. We're going to do a grand jury investigation on the one from downtown. Throw last night's matter into it, too. See if it rises to criminally negligent homicide on that poor dogwalker who got hit last month.'

I left out the fact of the television monitors in Berk's bedroom. There would be time for that story when we figured out where the cameras were concealed. Otherwise, it would be one more question for which I couldn't provide an answer – a very bad way to start a Monday morning with Paul Battaglia.

Rose interrupted on the intercom. The mayor wanted Battaglia immediately, which suggested there was friction between him and the governor on an issue in which the district attorney figured centrally. He wanted me out of the room before he talked and made it clear by dismissing me before he picked up the phone from its cradle.

I called the squad to tell Lieutenant Peterson that I was officially attached to the case. From this point on, any legal decisions – whether applications for warrants or sufficiency of probable cause for a suspect's arrest – would be made in consultation with me. Peterson mentioned that he had seen Mike earlier in the day but didn't know whether he had gone down to the Met to work or was sitting out this shift.

The rest of my day was filled with the routine of my prosecutorial duties in the sex crimes unit. Lawyers on trial took precedence with often urgent issues that had arisen during the current courtroom proceedings. Detectives dropped in regularly for guidance about how to handle new complaints for which our pioneering unit had developed protocols. Advocates and victims themselves called to ask questions about the process they faced if they chose to report their crimes to the police. And friends came by every day to hang out with one another, tell war stories, and vent about the array of characters who presented themselves to us with endless stories of bad and bizarre human behavior.

Mercer Wallace phoned in shortly after six. 'Heard your weekend took an interesting twist.'

'Mike called you?'

'Let's say I hunted him down.'

'Does he know Battaglia's put me on Talya's case?'

'Good going. No, he didn't say. He's at Lincoln Center. He's going to meet me for something to eat at Shun Lee West at seven o'clock. Want to join us?'

'Is it okay with him?'

'Hey, who's making the ask here? You're my date.'

'I'll be there.'

'You're not passing off Dr Sengor's case, are you?'

'Not a chance. I'm getting antsy about the tox results. You think Jean and Cara are willing to hang around this week?'

'Another day or two. What are you going to do about the grand jury?'

'I'm ready to go as soon as we get confirmation on the drug testing.'

'You talk to anyone in administration at Sengor's hospital?'

'Yes,' I said. 'Our perp has been suspended. Risk management didn't want to take the chance he'd be exposed to any other patients.'

Liability in medical centers had become such an expensive prospect that most legal offices had been renamed 'risk management units', responsible for the oversight of all problems that might lead to litigation.

'Double-edged sword. I hated to think he'd still be with patients, but this way we have no idea of his daily whereabouts.'

'They wanted him to keep his beeper so they can stay on top of him, too. They've required him to respond to them twice a day. Suspended with pay is the way they handled that one. He's already called in twice, so the doctor in charge of the psychiatric department says he's cooperating.'

'I'll see you at the restaurant?'

'Absolutely.' I called my friend Lesley Latham to break my dinner date, apologizing for the last-minute

144

cancellation. I took the cab to West 65th Street and found Mercer and Mike seated at the bar.

I walked past his stool and patted Mike's shoulder.

'Of all the gin joints in all the Chinese restaurants in the world, you had to walk into mine?' he asked. 'Who invited you?'

'Maybe I'm in the wrong place. I was supposed to meet a couple of my friends here. I guess that really is a gun in your pocket and you're not so happy to see me.'

'I'll take the weight,' Mercer said, embracing me. 'I needed some Peking duck and the service is so much better when we cut Alex in. Figured it was time to get back in the *Jeopardy!* habit, don't you think?'

For as long as I could remember, since we'd started working on cases as a team more than a decade ago, the three of us stopped whatever we were doing when we were together to bet one another on the Final Jeopardy question at the end of the show. Mike had kept witnesses waiting at the morgue, interrupted cocktail parties in full swing, and put the police commissioner on hold more than once to test his trivia knowledge against ours for twenty bucks a shot.

By the time the bartender served my drink, Mercer had coaxed him into turning the wall-mounted television set to the quiz show. We made small talk until Alex Trebek revealed the category of the final question: Sports.

Mike and Mercer were both jocks who followed college and professional sports with great enthusiasm. Mercer had turned down a football scholarship at the University of Michigan to join the NYPD. I put my twenty-dollar bill on the bar and brightened only slightly when Trebek's final answer involved a Yankee legend.

'Field named for Native American tribe where Babe Ruth hit his longest home run.'

I could think of rival teams in the long history of my pinstriped favorites, but nothing about the names of any of their fields that qualified in this category. Fenway and the Jake wouldn't do it. Mike wanted to double the stakes, but Mercer was as puzzled as I and we held our ground.

The music ticked away the time as all three of the contestants seemed to be stumped.

'I'm so sorry,' Trebek said, ready to reveal the question.

'What is Sing Sing prison?' Mike asked, sweeping the three bills off the bar. 'Home of the Sint Sinck Indians as well as the aforementioned Old Sparky. Yankees played an exhibition game against the inmates every year and the Bambino slammed the longest ball of his career there one time. Something like six hundred and twenty feet or more. You know why the state built the prison on the Sint Sinck land? 'Cause there was enough marble for the thugs to be put to work quarrying it – it was murderers and rapists who dug the stone that built Grace Church and New York University.'

Mercer led us to our table, a corner in the sunken pit beneath the giant mouth of the long black dragon that was suspended from the ceiling.

'You know that I'm officially catching Talya's case, don't you?' I asked Mike.

'The lieutenant just gave me the news.'

'I figure you could bring me up to speed over dinner and then I'll go back to the Met with you.'

The West Side branch of our favorite Chinese restaurant was just across Broadway from the Lincoln Center complex, a popular dining spot for theatergoers.

Mike was crunching on a handful of crispy noodles as we waited for our order of hot-and-sour soup. Not only did the task force have to deal with the several hundred employees who were in the opera house on the day and evening of the murder, but they learned that more than two thousand other workers had been on the payroll within the last year.

'Each time we start to question somebody, seems he adds three names nobody gave us before. It's a union shop, and most guys who work there have had a father or uncle or cousin who got their foot in the door earlier. If someone's covering for a relative, we'll never get to first base.'

It was rare to hear Mike sound so discouraged in the initial stage of an investigation.

'We've still got forensics to shed some light.'

'The droplets of blood near the place she went down?' Mike said. 'Preliminary run of the DNA looks like it's Natalya's. Autopsy findings included dried blood in her nasal cavity, probably from the same blow that knocked the contact lens out of her eye. Hair seems to be torn out of her scalp. That figures, too. Those don't connect to anyone else.'

He slugged his vodka and gritted his teeth. 'Serology lifted two different profiles from that white kid glove that was found near the bloodstains in the corridor. Remember, that man's glove I told you about? One profile from skin cells on the inside, another from the outer surface. For whatever it's worth, they don't match each other. He might have something more to work with by late tomorrow.'

'And the white hairs? Did you ask him to submit them

147

to the FBI for comparison to the samples we got from Berk's office?' The more difficult processing of mito-chondrial DNA still had to be outsourced to the FBI lab.

'Forget you ever saw Joe Berk's hair, Coop. The strands that were found with Galinova's body? They weren't human. The guys at the ME's office didn't need the feds to tell them these came from some kind of animal.'

Chapter 15

I was at my desk at eight the next morning, structuring a grand jury presentation on the drug-facilitated-rape case in hopes I'd have the toxicology results before my witnesses got restless and bolted home to Canada.

By eight thirty, Mike was standing in my doorway, looking more together than he had last evening, now dressed in a navy blazer, pink oxford-cloth shirt, and neatly creased chinos.

'Have I forgotten that we were supposed to meet?'

He walked to my desk, took my unopened second cup of coffee, and began to drink. 'Won't be the last time I take a bullet for you, kid.'

'What now?'

'I got a call from the PC in the middle of the night. Had to be in his office at seven. And no, it wasn't for a promotion,' he said, sitting opposite me and stretching his legs out in front of him.

'Something on the case?'

'Can you believe this dirtbag, Joe Berk? Gets his personal physician to check him out of the hospital around dinnertime and send him home with private-duty nurses. Calls the precinct and reports a theft from the

149

apartment. Says the thief is either the niece, or more likely, whichever member of the department was present.'

I thought of all the valuable artworks and antiques that filled the duplex. 'What'd he say was stolen?'

Mike smiled as he answered me. 'Three television sets from his bedroom.'

'The monitors he had hooked up so he could watch women undressing?'

'Not the way he tells it. Just his entertainment center. Any theatrical mogul would have multiple screens to watch different presentations simultaneously. He didn't happen to mention that they were wired into somebody's bathroom.'

'So how about Mona? Didn't you tell the commissioner we left before she did?'

'Mona denies ever being inside the apartment. IAB goes to interview her at midnight,' Mike said, referring to the Internal Affairs Bureau detectives who would have been assigned to a complaint of official misconduct. 'They pry her out of bed, away from her boyfriend. She says she was stopped at the door by me when she showed up at Uncle Joe's home to help her cousin through the night – and that I was inside with another woman, going through the place. Never let her inside.'

'Tell Joe to check the nipples of that little device that dimmed the lights if he wants a few of Mona's skin cells.' I kicked back my chair from the desk. 'Were the monitors really gone? Did someone take them out after we left and before Berk got out of the hospital?'

'IAB searched the apartment. No sign of them.'

'Well, I'll certainly tell the commissioner—'

'Your name never came into this. You were right about

Mona paying no attention to you at all. She assumed you were another detective.'

'I'll let Battaglia know as soon as he gets in.'

'Let it go. Don't you see what Berk's trying to do? He just wants to jam it down my throat that he knows we're on to the concealed cameras. It's a great big "fuck you" he's sending me, telling me to keep away from his private perversions. He could have said I took ten thousand bucks in cash from the apartment or some other valuable object. This is mainly to stick me under the PC's nose and remind me that Berk can play rough any time he wants to.'

'And the PC?'

'C'mon, Coop. The commish had to stroke the old bird but he knows I'm not rolling over for a few lousy television sets. He just wanted to know how I got into the apartment and make sure my ass was covered on that.'

The phone rang. 'Alexandra? Dr Kestenbaum here. I'm looking for a little legal guidance, if you don't mind. It's on Galinova.'

'Sure. What's come up?'

'There's a gentleman who called last evening. He says he's cleared it with her estranged husband and he's going to claim the body and take it home to London for burial. I'm going to have written confirmation from the husband later today, but I just wanted to make sure it's okay with you and the police that I release the remains.'

'Who is he? What's he to—'

'His name is Hubert Alden. I don't know much about the ballet, but this guy claims to be Galinova's patron. Does that mean anything to you?'

'Yeah. I'd like to talk to him before you sign off on it. Do you have a way for us to contact him?'

151

Kestenbaum gave me the number. 'He's flying in on the shuttle this morning. He's got some meeting to attend today. You'll be able to reach him at his office after five.'

I repeated the news to Mike. 'What do you mean, patron?' he asked.

'One of the more controversial subjects in the refined world of the dance. There's very little public funding of the arts these days, so some ballet companies are offering this kind of sponsorship as a way to raise money.'

'I don't get it.'

'American Ballet Theater, the Atlanta Ballet, the other companies that do this, they actually hold auctions. For the right price—'

'How much?'

'For a regional company, maybe ten or twenty thousand. For a prima ballerina at ABT, maybe one hundred thousand or more. We can get a copy of last week's program. It'll have a photo of Talya and say something like "the artistry of Natalya Galinova is supported by"' – I looked at the name I had scribbled on my Post-it – '"Hubert Alden".'

'So Mr Alden, he *owned* her?'

'I think the dancers would tell you no. But that's what makes the whole concept so awkward. Most of the companies claim they urge distance between the patron and the artist, but other directors want them to bond with each other. They want them to hang out so that the rich donor can introduce his or her friends to the dancers and hope they want to jump on the same bandwagon.'

'So Alden after five? Then you can take a ride with me right now.'

Mike was much more animated now than he had been

at dinner last evening. Berk's antics had goosed him and he was getting back into the chase.

'I'd like to polish up this presentation. Where are you going?'

'To drop in on Mona Berk. Leave a note for Laura. Tell her you're in the field.'

Laura would find assistants to cover the walk-ins who appeared on my doorstep when they were apprehensive about calling the police to report a crime. There was nothing on my desktop that couldn't wait until the afternoon.

We drove to midtown in Mike's department car, littered with empty soda cans, packs of red licorice twizzlers, and a stack of the weekend's tabloids announcing Talya's death.

Mike's NYPD laminated parking plaque allowed us to leave the car just off Times Square in a loading zone on the already double-parked length of West 45th Street. The first of the tour buses was beginning to disgorge passengers into the eclectic canyon that remained the crossroads of the city, if not the world. Above the tacky billboards rose the gleaming profiles of the Condé Nast and Reuters buildings, new entries in the booming and gentrified district.

The army recruiting station was already open and operating at Duffy Square, tourists were lining up for the evening's half-price seats at the TKTS booth, a palm reader was reaching for my arm and urging me to come upstairs for holistic healing and advice on all matters of mind and spirit, and a street missionary was handing out cards that told me exactly what I could do and how much it would cost to save my soul.

The electrified morning headlines were crawling

153

around the ledges on several of the skyscrapers that had revitalized a neighborhood which had boasted little more than XXX-rated movie houses when I first started working in the prosecutor's office. Galinova's death and the fact that it was being mourned by balletomanes all over the world ran fifth behind the dismantling of a terrorist cell and a political scandal in New Jersey.

'You know what that's called?'

I looked up at the moving signage. 'No idea.'

'It's a Motogram. First one in the world was here, running on the old New York Times Tower, starting with the presidential election returns in 1928. Used fifteen thousand lightbulbs to wiggle the news around four sides of the building.'

'Your dad?' Mike's father had filled the boy's head with stories of every corner of the city's history.

'Nope. This one's my mother. You know her postcard collection,' he said, referring to the vintage photographs she had saved since childhood. He pointed at the giant Barbie billboard display that now garishly controlled the airspace in Times Square. 'In the 1930s, there was a forty-two-foot-long angelfish advertising Wrigley's Spearmint gum. In the forties, there was a thirty-foot-high waterfall with a gargantuan woman – like an Amazon – draped in a Grecian toga. In the fifties it was a huge Pepsi bottle, which gave way to pouring Gordon's Gin a decade later. First one I remember is that giant Camel cigarette ad – don't you? – with the huge smoke ring blowing out of it. Those images are all classics – it's the most monumental advertising arena in the world.'

1501 Broadway was a throwback to another age. The business center of the theater world, its gilt-and-marble lobby had been refurbished to reflect its century-old splendor. The directory of offices listed on the wall reflected a warren of cubbyholes in which production deals and partnerships were made, and wannabes hitched their wagons to star vehicles.

Mona Berk's company was on the eighth floor. The old wrought-iron elevators still required a manual operator, who knew the stops of all his regulars and punched them into the keyboard.

We got off the elevator and found the entrance to 807, the corner suite. The secretary, who didn't appear to be more than eighteen, looked up from her fashion magazine as we entered the reception area.

'Mona Berk, please? We're here to see Ms Berk,' Mike said.

She scanned her appointment book. 'She expecting you?'

'More or less.'

'She'll be here any minute. She's already got a nine thirty, though.'

'We'll be quick.'

She picked up her pencil to make a notation in the book. 'Is it about a property? Would you mind giving me your names?'

'Yeah. I'm Jack Webb. It's about a musical version of *Dragnet*.'

'Cool. Have a seat, Mr Webb. And you are?'

'Alice. She just knows me as Alice.'

Ten minutes later, Mona Berk walked in the door, laughing and talking to the man who accompanied her. She pulled up short when she saw both of us.

'Well, good morning. It's detective – detective . . .'

'Chapman. Mike Chapman. This is Ms Cooper, from the District Attorney's Office. Mind if we come in for a few minutes?'

'Does this mean you haven't solved that murder case yet?' Mona said, turning to her companion to explain who we were. 'These are the officers who were figuring poor Uncle Joe had taken enough Viagra last week to attack that poor ballerina.'

She picked up her mail from the in-box and motioned us to follow her into her office.

The man held the door open for us.

'And how about that encore performance for your uncle? That must have made you and your cousin very happy,' Mike said, taking a seat in a black leather armchair and pulling one up beside it for me.

'Hallelujah! Joe Berk lives another day to screw some other sucker out of his hard-earned cash. What can I help you with now?'

'Would you mind if we spoke to you alone?'

'Frankly, I would. This is Ross Kehoe. I'd like him to be here. He's my business partner and my fiancé.'

Kehoe shook hands with Mike and me, and remained standing, perched on the windowsill over Mona's shoulder. He was about forty years old, six feet tall and solidly built, with sharp-featured good looks and teeth that had been recently whitened to show off his broadly artificial smile. His European-cut shirt and tight jeans were the perfect complement to Mona's black twinset, cigarette-leg slacks, and two-inch slides that clicked as she crossed the floor.

'Funny, I didn't notice your name on the door,' Mike said.

'I'm shy,' Kehoe said, the smile disappearing as quickly as it had been flashed.

'How long have you two been partners?'

'Almost a year,' Mona said.

'What's your role in the business?'

'Same as mine, detective. We're into production. Legitimate theater. Now what is it that we didn't finish discussing the other night?'

'It seems like after Ms Cooper and I left the Belasco, you went back upstairs and helped yourself to some of Uncle Joe's property. I got blamed for the snatch and I'm hoping to make good on those monitors.'

'I haven't the faintest idea what you're talking about. What monitors?'

Ross Kehoe folded his arms and waited for Mike to explain.

'So it's going to be like that? You know damn well there were four screens in the bedroom when you stepped off that elevator. Uncle Joe says he's short three.'

'Briggs called me on my cell about ten minutes after you left. He told me that by the time he got to the hospital, he found out that his father had been resuscitated and was going to pull through, so he didn't need my help after all. Ross was back at our apartment, so I went right home.'

'Which is where?' Mike said.

'SoHo. We have a loft.'

'Damn. SoHo, of course. They better send me back to the academy. Can't believe I asked a stupid question like that when you've got "trendy" written in block letters all across your forehead.'

'And what the hell do you think I'd be doing with television monitors?'

157

'Cleaning up Uncle Joe's clubhouse 'cause your cousin asked you to. Looking around the apartment for things you weren't entitled to see. If it's got something to do with the lawsuit against your uncle, then maybe his attorneys would be interested in knowing about your midnight house call.'

Mona Berk glared at Mike. 'That lawsuit is nobody else's business but ours. We're a very private family and we intend to stay that way. Stick to dead bodies, Mr Chapman. Maybe you know something about them that'll keep you occupied in your spare time and out of my hair.'

The intercom buzzed and Mona Berk stabbed the button with her forefinger. 'Yeah?'

'Your nine thirty's here, Mona.'

'You want more of my time, detective, make an appointment.'

She walked around the desk to usher us out. She picked up a bound manuscript from the table next to the door. It was entitled *Platinum*, and beneath that had the words 'The Girl on the Red Velvet Swing'.

The first person I saw in the reception area was a six-foot-tall blonde, half the age of Natalya Galinova with twice her measurements in all the significant places. Behind the young woman, seated in a chair and flipping through what appeared to be a copy of the same manuscript that Berk had picked up, was Rinaldo Vicci, the agent Talya had fired just before her tragic death.

Chapter 16

'Maybe we just ought to go downstairs to the Booth Theater and convene a grand jury, Coop? All the world's a stage and we've got most of the players right here. Mr Vicci, who's the talent?'

Vicci got to his feet and stammered an answer. 'Lucy, meet Detective Chapman. This is Lucy DeVore. Ms Cooper. That's Ms Berk, in the doorway, Mr Kehoe behind her. Your meeting's with them.'

'All of them?' The showgirl seemed surprised. 'I thought you said—'

'No, no, only Berk and Kehoe. You go on in the office with them and—'

'This could be kind of interesting for me,' Mike said. 'Just a minute, Ms DeVore. How long have you been working with Mr Vicci?'

She looked at Vicci and shook her head. 'Maybe a—'

'I don't represent the young lady, detective, if that's what you're thinking. I'm doing a favor for a friend. Lucy, *bella* – go on inside with Ms Berk.'

Lucy DeVore walked with the grace and attitude of a runway model. Ross Kehoe closed the door behind her so that she and Mona Berk were alone in the office, and he took hold of Vicci's elbow to steer him in the same direction.

'From what I hear, you no longer represented Ms Galinova either,' Mike said. 'So it's a bit odd that you were at the Met the night she died.'

'You don't know many prima donnas, then, do you?' Vicci said, wiping the sweat off his nose with a mono-grammed handkerchief.

'Only one. I take her with me everywhere I go. Keeps me humble.'

'Hire, fire – fire, hire – threaten to fire, rehire – rehire, prepare to be fired,' the chubby Italian trilled, as if it were a diction lesson. 'Talya was famous for it, detective. Of course she wanted me with her that night. She had nobody else to represent her interests.'

'How about her patron? How come nobody told us about Hubert Alden?'

'Alden? That whole thing is just a gimmick. The company uses it to raise money.'

'How much did Alden contribute to be Talya's patron?' I asked.

'You want to sponsor one of the children in the second row who spends half her life in – how you call it? – a mazurka costume, it's cheap. Primas go for the big bucks,' Vicci said. 'Five hundred thousand.'

'What the hell kind of privileges did that buy him?' Mike asked.

'Prestige – in the dance world, anyway.'

'I mean with Galinova. How far did that get him?'

'You're asking me if it was a romance?'

'The hell with romance. For half a million, it must have gotten him under the tutu, no?'

160

Vicci blotted his forehead and shook loose of Ross Kehoe's grip. 'Look, I managed her business, not her social life.'

'So if you were doing such a bang-up job as her agent, how come you weren't backing her for the Evelyn Nesbit role in *Platinum*?'

Vicci looked at Kehoe for help, but there was no response.

'Mr Kehoe, how well did you know Ms Galinova? Why does Mr Vicci think you've got the answer?' Mike asked.

'I never met the lady.' Kehoe threw up his hands in the air. His voice was raspy, as though if he were able to clear his throat the harsh edge might disappear.

'Ball's back in your court, Mr Vicci.'

'Look, detective. This wasn't any part for Talya. Maybe Mary Martin could play Peter Pan till she was a hundred and fifty years old, but this is a blockbuster part for new talent. It could put a kid like Lucy into the stratosphere.'

'Help me, Coop,' Mike said. 'Isn't this what they call a conflict of interest?'

Vicci's eyes moved back and forth between us like he was watching a tennis match.

'Could be exactly that. Depends on how Mr Vicci was dealing with his two clients.'

'I told you, Lucy isn't my—'

'Who's got the rights to the show? That's what I want to know,' I asked. 'If Mona and her uncle have two separate development companies, which one has the property?'

Vicci started to answer but Ross Kehoe cut him off. 'That's still being negotiated, Ms Cooper. Nobody has the rights yet. Have you met Mona's cousin?'

'Briggs? No, we haven't.'

'They'd like to join forces with each other on this project. Maybe repair some family rifts. Now if you'll let us get on with our meeting,' Kehoe said, nudging Rinaldo Vicci, 'maybe we'll all have the answers you want.'

We made our way back downstairs and around the corner to the car. The sidewalks were as crowded with pedestrians – working, walking, or gawking – as the roadways were with cars, trucks, and buses.

I called Laura while Mike took Broadway north to Lincoln Center. 'What's it like down there? Anybody looking for me?'

'Relatively quiet day so far.'

'Mike and I are headed for the Met to check on how the interviews are going. Beep if you need me.'

The NYPD had taken over the elegant boardrooms above the atrium in the main lobby of the opera house. Normally curtained off from the grand staircase, it was an odd sight to see through the glass walls to the staging area now occupied by the task force, shoulder holsters and cardboard coffee cups replacing evening bags and champagne glasses. Long conference tables had been put together end by end and were loaded with packing boxes that held everything from lists of employees to the growing files of completed interviews. Against the tables leaned blown-up floor plans of the immense complex.

At the far end of the room, six detectives were seated at makeshift desks. Each was talking one-on-one to men we assumed were part of the permanent Met crew. The auditorium doors were open and Prokofiev's music from the late-morning rehearsal drifted up as soothing background for the serious conversations about observations, alibis, and incriminating evidence.

Lieutenant Peterson greeted us and told us to claim some empty piece of tabletop as our own. 'Don't get too comfortable, either. Rule is we got to clear out of here by six o'clock. Everything gone from the room, ashtrays empty, soda cans and Krispy Kremes carted along with us. Doors open at six and curtain's up at eight. All cops and other forms of lowlife have to be out of sight.'

'What, loo, you surprised? The show must go on. Guess all that gilt and crystal and marble must distract people. Make them forget someone was murdered right under their noses.'

'You still got your contacts up at the Botanical Garden, Alex?' Peterson asked.

The last case we had worked together had taken us to the most exquisite land in the five boroughs, a piece of the city with a pristine native forest, acres of cultured gardens, and a river with a deceptively deadly waterfall. New York's Botanical Garden was renowned for its spectacular conservatory filled with rare plants from all over the world, seasonal displays of orchids and exotic flowers, and a scholarly staff dedicated to the understanding and conservation of the plant kingdom.

'I'm sure they haven't forgotten us.'

'The head of the police lab called me an hour ago. They're stumped. You know that odor of mint you both smelled on the two ribbons from Galinova's shoe? It's not from floss like you thought, Alex. Crime Scene picked up a couple of crushed leaves with the same scent from the hallway she was thrown from. She must have stepped on them during the struggle. They're thinking maybe

163

someone at the garden can identify the greens, give us a source for the kind of plant it is.'

'The research department there is first-rate. You tell the guys at the lab to transport a sample to the Bronx,' I said. 'I'll find you a botanist.'

'How's the talk going?' Mike said, gesturing at the interviewers.

Peterson picked up his clipboard. 'So far, we've gotten through eighty-six guys. Fourteen with criminal records – minor stuff – a few driving intox, a couple of petty thefts and harassments, some drug possession. Nothing to get excited about.'

'You find the masseur who was rubbing the swan's feathers when Joe Berk showed up in her dressing room? I imagine he's got some upper body strength,' Mike said.

'He's covered,' Peterson said, flipping to the page of notes for that interview. 'No shortage of dancers waiting for him when he left Galinova's room. I got one sugarplum fairy and two bluebirds who swear he was working on them, one after another, the rest of the evening.'

'Did he tell you what Berk fought with her about?' I asked.

'Says she starting cursing at him for being late – then went off on a tirade in Russian. The masseur didn't get a word of it – just the volume and tone of voice. Berk told him to get lost so he folded up his table and slipped away while the temperamental duo went on shouting at each other.'

I was impressed at the progress Peterson's men were making. 'Did anyone have a chance to speak with the ballet mistress? Sandra – I think it's Sandra Braun. She came in when we were talking with Chet Dobbis,' I reminded the lieutenant. 'She didn't show up Friday night. That leaves both of them without an alibi.'

Peterson thumbed back through the pages of notes. 'Bad for him, good for her. Twenty-four-hour pharmacy around the corner from her house confirms delivery of antibiotics that she signed for at eight thirty-seven. We got a Xerox of the slip she signed.'

'You're really moving on this, loo.'

'That's not counting the walk-ins, Alex.'

'Who?

'Like one of the girls from New York City Ballet,' he said, referring to the legendary company founded by George Balanchine and Lincoln Kirstein, housed in the adjacent State Theater, which shared the Lincoln Center plaza. 'She came in this morning to file a complaint about a stagehand who tried to molest her on her way home one night last year. Never reported it to the precinct.'

'She ID him?'

'Yeah. He was fired six months ago. Bad cocaine habit led to a sloppy attendance record. It's the no-shows that got him kicked out. We'll run him down.'

'If she'd reported the damn thing when it happened,' Mike said, 'we'd have had a lead on him by this time. You fingerprinting?'

'Every damn one. Fingers and palms, photographs, buccal swabs.' The last technique, putting each man's saliva on a Q-tip, would give us DNA for every employee.

'Anybody balk yet?'

'Most of 'em are really decent guys, very cooperative. There are a few who don't want to go the whole route. One guy's got a paternity case pending and doesn't want anybody to have his DNA. And then there's some of the crew that haven't even been back here since Friday night, 'cause of shift changes and all that. So we don't know if people are avoiding us or just out of the loop till they show up for work.'

'So this could take—'

'Don't even think days. You could be vested by the time we're through here. I could be in my retirement home in Key West, sucking margaritas through my IV tube before we even finish with the house crew.'

I stood at the glass partition, looking at the carpeted staircase that wound down to the lobby. There was a surreal air to this investigation, cops on one side of the glass talking murder and autopsy, palm prints, and genetic profiles, while below me, Sleeping Beauty's father – dressed in his crown, robe, and tights – was strolling out of the theater into the sunshine to grab a soda with the witch whose knitting needle felled the young princess.

'Has Chet Dobbis been any help?' Mike asked.

'The artistic director? All he cares about is keeping us out of the way of the people who give him money. I'm telling you, every damn one of these ballets and operas is about somebody getting killed. In every single one of them somebody dies,' Peterson said. 'But the minute life imitates art, nobody wants to know about it.'

'You need me here?'

'You and Alex do what you gotta do. When we narrow this down to some viable suspects, you'll get the first crack at them.'

Mike was a skilled interrogator. He had exacted admissions to murders in which there was no physical evidence, building solid cases with little more than his exquisite understanding of the criminal mind and his ability to elicit confessions that would have impressed the most accomplished priests.

We took the elevator up to the executive wing and found Chet Dobbis's office. There was no one with him and his assistant waited until he got off the phone before she showed us in.

'Anything wrong, Mr Chapman? Or should I expect to see you every day till you've put this matter to bed?'

'What do you call all those extras in the opera?'

'Supernumeraries, detective. Supers.'

'Well, think of me as a super-whatever. I'll be in and out all the time till we close a noose around the bastard who killed Galinova. Hope it doesn't rattle your nerves.'

Dobbis's suite held an assortment of Met treasures. A framed poster of the very first performance – Leontyne Price and Justino Diaz in *Antony and Cleopatra* – dominated one wall, surrounded by signed photographs from many of the divas who had sung here over the years. There were grateful inscriptions from Placido Domingo and Renée Fleming, and a triumphant photograph of the brilliant Beverly Sills in her Met debut as Pamira, in the 1975 production of *The Siege of Corinth*, which won her an eighteen-minute ovation.

'The lieutenant seems to have everything he needs downstairs.'

'So far. But I'm hoping you'll help us behind the scenes,' Mike said.

'What do you mean?' Dobbis asked, as I studied the costumes he had hung on wall displays and in shadow boxes.

'You're likely to hear things because of your position. I'm talking about things no one will tell us. Workers who

167

may be reluctant to give up their colleagues or supervisors who may try to protect one of their own might not spill the beans to the police. It happens in whatever setting we're looking at. Museum staff, hospital employees, teachers – you're far more likely to hear the rumors and gossip about the internal goings-on that we may never get wind of.'

'Surely, Mr Chapman, you're not going to operate from rumors and gossip to solve a murder?'

'I'm not going to ignore them, either. Sometimes they just lead us the right way, sometimes they're dead-on accurate. Not all gossip is unfounded.'

Chet Dobbis seemed to flinch at Mike's statement, as though he was taking it personally. He turned to me and changed the subject.

'You're interested in my collection?' he asked, smoothing the front of his suit jacket. 'That's the outfit Grace Bumbry wore when she did the dance of the seven veils. *Salome*. Do you know it?'

I nodded my head. 'And this one?'

'*Turandot*. The emperor's costume,' Dobbis said, stepping over to finger the elaborately woven silk kimono that hung from the wall. 'Zeffirelli may be the most brilliant director we've ever had at the Met, but he cost us a fortune in costumes and scenery for every production.'

'Why are these particular things here, rather than on display downstairs?'

'Naturally, everything in the collection is archived. It's one of my perks to choose some of the more colorful items, some of my personal favorites, to decorate my office. It's a good hook when I'm trying to raise money from people who come in for meetings.'

Mike pointed to a long pole across the near edge of Dobbis's desk, too shiny and modern to be part of a traditional costume. 'That looks lethal. Where did that come from?'

'It has nothing to do with the Met, I assure you. I'm a rock climber, Mr Chapman. And a spelunker – you know, caves and that sort of thing. That pole is for trekking. It's got a precision steel tip at the point, to help get a foothold in the ice or between rocks, and it probably is pretty deadly. I live across the river, near the Palisades, and I was setting out to climb on Saturday morning when I was called back here because of Talya. I never leave my equipment in the car – it's an easy target for thieves and quite expensive to replace, so I carried it in when I parked.'

I was staring at the assortment of wigs that were mounted on shelves next to the door.

'Tell me about these.'

'We make everything in-house, Ms Cooper. Every single piece of clothing, even the wigs. You've got wonderful examples there,' he said, pointing at the variety of styles, 'from Dr Faust's receding hairline to Madame Butterfly's thick upsweep.'

'This one? The one on the top shelf with the long white hair?'

'Falstaff. I'm quite sure that's Falstaff.'

Mike picked up my cue. 'Pretty natural looking. What are they made of?'

'Human hair, of course,' Dobbis said, lifting the closest wig from its stand. 'Very costly, but that's still the way we do it here. Manon Lescaut, this, with all the curls and pompadours of eighteenth-century France. You see?

169

There's a very fine mesh, which is actually glued to the singer's forehead during the performance. The hairs are knotted through that mesh. It takes three or four days to make each one of these.'

'Besides you, Mr Dobbis, who else has costumes and props available to them?' I asked.

He thought for a minute. 'I'm not really sure. I don't suppose they're easily accessed. Occasionally, when they're worn-out and need to be replaced, I guess the employees get to keep some of them. The ones in better shape are auctioned off at our annual gala, along with the used pointe shoes of the dancers, as you probably know.'

'These wigs,' I asked, 'where are they normally kept?'

Dobbis handed the one he was holding to Mike. 'In the wig shop, upstairs, under lock and key, I'm sure. They're all made from human hair except for these white ones,' he said, pointing at the one he had just given to Mike.

Mike rubbed the strands between his fingers. 'Could have fooled me. These don't feel artificial at all.'

'Nothing here is artificial, detective. It's just that human hair that's white,' Dobbis said, 'well, it tends to turn yellow under the stage lights. We like to keep everything natural, everything real – so all the white wigs that are used at the Met are made from animal hair. It keeps its color better. The hair in every one of the white wigs comes from albino yaks, actually. Tibetan yaks.'

Mike's raised eyebrows gave away his surprise. 'Have I startled you, Mr Chapman?' Dobbis asked, smugly strutting back to his desk as though he had scored a point in a sporting competition.

'You got that right. I'm thinking blondie here, with all

170

her peroxide, is no match for an albino yak. I got my niece's first holy communion coming up in two weeks and I just about freaked thinking Coop is such a stickler for detail that she's likely to send me on an extradition to the Himalayas for a live yak.'

Dobbis couldn't figure whether Mike was trying to be funny or not. 'This matter about the hair – the wigs – is it serious?'

'Nothing that the Dalai Lama and I can't figure out,' Mike said, walking to the door of Dobbis's room. 'Excuse me. I meant the Dalai Lama, Richard Gere, and I.'

Chapter 17

Mike stopped to tell Peterson the news about the animal hair. 'Let's see if we can get a fix on the wig shop upstairs. See what kind of inventory they keep. Maybe there's something missing from last week. That stuff must be expensive to make so they've got to keep careful track of it. Maybe we can get a photo or duplicate. If the killer who intercepted Galinova was wearing a white wig, it would change his entire appearance.'

Employees were being questioned not only about their own activities on Friday night, but about strangers they saw in the hallways and backstage area before and after the performance. These descriptions might have less use to us if the perp had altered his appearance during the course of the evening.

Peterson asked about Dobbis's collection. 'You think he had access?'

'I could kick myself for letting him see how thrown off I was by his answer. Anyway, the wigs he's got on display are period costumes. He'd draw a little attention to himself walking around like he's the French king, but who knows what he's got in his drawers? A wig with a contemporary cut – well, whoever was wearing it might just look like a distinguished gentleman. A diversion, a strong feature you'd be sure to remember if you passed him in a hallway or rode up with him in an elevator.'

'Or maybe,' I said, 'the killer wanted someone to think he was Joe Berk. See a shock of white hair – or even better, just plant a few on the floor to throw us off base – knowing Berk was having some kind of liaison with Talya. Create an illusion – that's what costumes are all about. Launch a red herring to send us in Berk's direction.'

'So who knew that about Berk and Galinova?' Peterson asked.

'Dobbis, of course. Rinaldo Vicci, her agent. I can't imagine it was a secret from some of the crew who worked backstage with her the past few days, and at rehearsals the week before. Talya was very visible, and Berk picked her up from the Met a few times.'

'And then there's Berk's family,' Mike said. 'I could put on some protective armor and get into that hornet's nest.'

Peterson turned back to his temporary squad headquarters. 'All nice to know once we get past the most obvious likelihood. I've studied the case file from the old Met murder case. The odds are pretty good that Talya was a random pick – bumped into the wrong guy in a deserted corridor or staircase, just like that doomed violinist. He makes a pass, she rejects it, and he goes wild. A scenario Alex has seen dozens of times before.'

'You're right about that.'

I frequently lectured to women's groups about sexual assault and domestic violence. The question I was most often asked was whether victims should offer resistance to an attacker, especially if he's armed. There are far too many variables to suggest answers that would work in every situation, decisions that would have to be made by women in the several seconds they had to assess the nature of the danger.

Sometimes, women with the confidence and strength to try to counter the threat of force with a kick or punch or scream before running would be able to prevent the completion of the assault. But all too often I had seen an effort to struggle thwarted by a rapist who was stronger than his prey and more prepared for the attempt, who became more enraged by the resistance, escalating his force to a deadly level to subdue his target. It was impossible to know yet whether that had been the motive that led to Talya's death.

'The ME called me about the release of Galinova's body to this guy – this – uh . . .'

'Her patron. Hubert Alden,' Mike said.

'I kicked it over to you.'

'We're dealing with it, loo,' Mike said. 'C'mon, kid. Let's hit the road.'

We left the building by the front door and walked to the car, warmed by the bright April sunlight. Mike dialed the number for Alden's office and asked the receptionist whether he was in town and might be available for a meeting earlier than five o'clock.

'Depends on what?' he responded to her comment.

She didn't ask his purpose but said something to Mike that made him smile as he flipped his phone closed.

'Ever been to a walk-through?'

'Walk through what?' I asked.

'Like a reading for a Broadway show proposal. Mr Alden's availability depends on what time the walk-through at the Imperial Theatre ends. The one Mona Berk wanted him to see. Chatty little thing, this receptionist. Some of the prospective backers will be there, she said. The angels. Call Information. Get an address for the theater.'

I dialed Information for the box office, and once connected, repeated the address aloud for Mike. 'Two forty-six West Forty-fifth Street. How do you think we'll get in?'

'Keep your sunglasses on. Haven't you always wanted to be an angel?'

'I'm willing to start sometime. So I don't remember anything about this deadly affair. What was it that happened?'

'You know who Stanford White is, don't you?'

'Sure.' The accomplished architect's firm – McKim, Mead and White – had created some of the most notable buildings in New York. Among them – Fifth Avenue's University Club and the classic Hall of Fame for Great Americans – were sites that had played a role in cases Mike and I had investigated together.

'Did you know that he designed Madison Square Garden?'

The huge sports and entertainment complex had opened in the 1960s on Seventh Avenue and 33rd Street, but I knew that White had lived more than a century ago. 'That's impossible.'

Mike was driving down Seventh Avenue. 'Not this one. The old one.'

'Where was that?'

'Who's buried in Grant's tomb, kid? White built the one on Madison Square – you know, Madison and

Twenty-sixth Street. It was a musical theater and concert hall. White was in his fifties when all this happened, but he had a thing for young girls. I mean teenagers like Evelyn Nesbit. You'd have been after his ass.'

We parked half a block from the theater and walked toward the entrance.

'How old was Nesbit?'

'Probably fourteen or fifteen when Stanford White met her. She was a great beauty, and had one of those domineering stage mothers who brought her to New York to model for artists.'

'Real artists?'

'At first. Then fashion photography, and by fifteen she was a showgirl.'

There was a young man at the door of the theater with a list of names in a notebook. He was leaning back in his chair, eyes closed as he listened to his iPod. He must have heard us and sat up. 'You are?'

'Mr Alden's expecting us. Hubert Alden.'

He saw Alden's name checked off at the top of the list of twenty or so others and pointed us to the entrance. On a small bronze plaque, I noted that the building was owned by the Shubert Organization.

'What's Mona doing in a Shubert theater?' I asked Mike.

'Probably avoiding Uncle Joe. If she held this audition in a Berk property, he'd be the first to know about it. Might spoil her party.'

We intentionally bypassed the orchestra and found the staircase that led to the top tier of this vast theater, which had none of the intimacy of the Belasco. The plaque described it as the home of such musicals as *Fiddler on the Roof* and *Dreamgirls*; its walls and ceiling were covered with elegant panels of floral and geometric motifs. One had only to return to the original Broadway theaters to see some of New York's most distinctive and elegant interiors – frescoed walls and ceilings, sculptured reliefs crafted by the great artists of the day, cartouches and decorated glass panels, chandeliers and Tiffany lamps – many restored today to their early splendor.

Mike kept going until we found side seats in the next-to-last row of the balcony. The entire upper half of the house was unlighted and although we could see down to the stage, it would be hard for anyone to notice us.

'The gang's all here,' Mike said, in a whisper, 'and I'm in my usual seat. Bet you've never been up this high.'

The large stage was empty of everything except a baby grand piano and a pianist, and Lucy DeVore, script in hand, dressed only in an ecru-colored lace-trimmed teddy and matching tap pants.

Scattered in the first couple of rows were some familiar heads. Mona Berk was sitting next to Rinaldo Vicci, and Ross Kehoe was rising to walk up the steps to the stage. I guessed that Alden was among the other spectators.

Kehoe called out to whomever was operating the lights. 'Give me something cooler. Bring it down a bit, can you?'

The adjustment was made.

Kehoe signaled his approval with a wave and added another direction. 'Be ready with an amber spot for Lucy, okay? Something that will really glow, goldenlike. You know how to do that or you need me to come up there?'

From somewhere above us a voice called out, 'Got it.'

Ross Kehoe nodded and walked into the wings. There

was some conversation between Mona Berk and Lucy DeVore, but we couldn't hear it.

'So Evelyn Nesbit?' I asked Mike.

'Everyone wanted a piece of the kid. John Barrymore tried to marry her, but she dumped him for Stanford White. She became White's mistress.'

'Did he ever marry her?'

'He already had a wife, and a bunch of children. But he also had a fantastic studio, an apartment at the top of Madison Square Garden – a duplex, just like Joe Berk. On the second floor, suspended from the frame of a skylight, White had a red velvet swing. Story was that he'd give the girls champagne, undress them, and watch them play on the swing – back and forth up to the ceiling of his loft – naked. That was his thing.'

A young man, also with script in hand, came out from stage right, and it appeared Lucy was ready to go on. His sleeves were rolled up and he wore khaki pants; Mona called to him to get in place, closer to Lucy. 'Harry, I want you right on top of her. It looks more threatening that way when you get mad, when you react to what she says.'

'Harry Thaw,' Mike said. 'Millionaire kid from Pittsburgh who married Evelyn. Total psycho.'

'Did he know about Stanford White?'

'Not enough. Not at first. He knew White liked young chorines – preferably blondes – but Evelyn claimed to Thaw that she was a virgin.'

'I take it that Thaw found out she wasn't?'

'One of the papers published a photograph of Evelyn. She looked like she was sleeping, stretched out on a bearskin rug in White's apartment. Her long platinum hair was the only thing covering her.'

Mona Berk was standing now, shouting directions to Lucy DeVore.

Lucy was speaking Evelyn's words, the teenager beginning to whimper as she disclosed the story of her deflowering by Stanford White. 'I didn't want to be there, Harry. Really, I didn't. I didn't want to drink the champagne, but St – but Mr White, he made me do it.'

Mike was in my ear. 'How many times have you heard that excuse in your office, Coop? How do you force someone to drink champagne? Hold her in a headlock and pour the stuff down her throat? I don't get it.'

Harry Thaw wasn't buying Lucy's version of events, either. He ranted at her, raising a hand as though to strike his young bride.

'He drugged me, Harry. He must have put something in my drink to make me pass out. You know I wouldn't have given myself to an old man like that willingly.'

'Drug-facilitated sexual assault,' Mike said. 'A hundred years ago.'

'False reporting, too. She wouldn't have made it past Mercer's first interview.'

Lucy DeVore dissolved into tears pretty effectively as she described how she awakened in White's bed, naked and helpless, and how he took advantage of her without her understanding or permission. Thaw reached to embrace her and the pianist broke into the music for his soliloquy about stolen innocence. Nobody would leave the theater humming that one on opening night.

Ross Kehoe came back onstage and put his arm around Lucy, and together they disappeared off stage left.

A few leggy chorus girls, older than Lucy DeVore and just as well built, sauntered onto the stage, dressed in

179

black leotards that highlighted their blond locks and high-heeled shoes laced at the throat. They limbered up and showed off their talents with stretches and splits, while the pianist vamped some ragtime to invoke the spirit of the Gilded Age setting in which these events had occurred.

Mona was talking to the assembled angels scattered in the theater seats. 'So this is the big scene on the roof of Madison Square Garden. Climax of the first act – we'll go to intermission with this one. It's a hot summer night in 1906. A very elegant gentleman is sitting alone at a table, closest to the dancers. That's Stanford White.'

A handsome man, prematurely grayed – I guessed – by a dash or two of talcum powder, came onto the stage pushing a small table on wheels and carrying a chair that he placed beside it on which to sit.

The piano player kicked up the rhythm and the girls did a stylized dance routine, which Stanford White watched with great enthusiasm, applauding wildly and calling out their names from time to time.

From within the folds of the burgundy curtain on stage right, Harry Thaw slipped onto the stage, pretending to make his way through the imaginary tables of crowded theatergoers. It was hard to take your eyes off the show-girls, whose bodies moved in spectacular synchronicity, but Thaw continued to slink in and around them to the extreme opposite side of the stage.

As the music stopped and one of the girls flopped onto the lap of a delighted Stanford White, a gunshot rang through the nearly empty theater and echoed with the force of a cannon. Harry Thaw had come around from behind and fired a gun into White's back as the dancers screamed and White fell from his chair, taking the chorine with him, all enveloped in a huge cloud of smoke that billowed from behind the thick curtain.

At the sound of the blast, I gripped Mike's arm, surprised by the burst of gunshot. I hadn't remembered that the prominent architect had been murdered by Thaw.

'Relax, kid. That's how it happened in real life.'

The smoke began to clear as the music segued into a soft ballad. Thaw and White picked up the table and chair and followed the girls offstage.

From far upstage, against the darkened backdrop, a small spotlight caught a pair of legs – perfectly contoured, long and lean – dangling high above the boards. As the music got louder, a voice from the front row – probably Mona Berk's – yelled out the word 'Go!'

The legs kicked, like those of a child pumping a swing on a playground. Within seconds, the vision of the very platinum Lucy DeVore was in full view, her golden hair streaming down as she propelled herself forward and back across the length of the stage, her slinky teddy gleaming in the single spot that followed her movement. The swing descended slowly from the fly, with the motion of a smooth but steady pendulum as the ragtime rhythm picked up the pace.

Lucy turned her head to the audience far below her and started to sing the opening lines of the number. Her legs bent back beneath her and then carried her up out of sight again, sacrificing the words she was singing to the striking visual image she created.

As she drifted down and across to stage left, there was the sound of a loud crack. The seat of the swing broke away, and Lucy's scream pierced the back row of the balcony as she clung in vain to the hanging ropes that had supported her before she slammed onto the floor of the stage.

Chapter 18

Mike ran down the narrow flights of stairs from the balcony and vaulted over the railing into the first of the two side boxes that hung above the orchestra. He climbed into the second one, closest to the curtain, and reached for the metal ladder that was exposed to the side of the proscenium arch to climb down it. He was on the stage only seconds after Mona Berk, Ross Kehoe, and everyone else in range had come up to surround the still body of the teenager.

I had flipped open my phone to call 911 for an ambulance and police backup as I took the more traditional route down the staircase and into the front of the orchestra.

However surprised people were to see Mike Chapman, they responded well to his control of the situation. 'Get back. Everybody get back,' I could hear him shouting to the group that had crowded in around Lucy DeVore. 'Give her air.'

'Call for help,' I heard Mona Berk say.

'There's an ambulance on the way.'

Mike saw me from the stage. 'Coop, get up here. The rest of you, stand off. She's alive. She's breathing. Coop, don't let anybody touch her. Keep 'em away. She needs air. You – any one of you,' Mike said, gesturing to the small band of actors. 'Go out to the lobby and wait for the medics. Bring 'em right in here.'

I kneeled in beside Mike. 'Can you tell what's fractured?'

'The legs, obviously,' he said, pointing to where the bone had broken through the skin. 'I don't know about the neck or spine. I don't want to touch anything until there's an EMT here to check it. She hasn't opened her eyes yet. Just stay with her while I look around.'

Mike called to Mona Berk, 'Who's operating the swing up above?'

She, in turn, pointed at Ross Kehoe to give the answer. 'The fly crew. We've just got two guys up there today.'

'Don't let anybody leave. Make a list of everyone working here today,' Mike said, trotting into the wings to find his way up to the fly gallery.

I sat on the stage next to the shattered body of Lucy DeVore. I placed my hand over one of her outstretched arms and found her pulse – a very weak one – and I kept her hand covered in my own, stroking it and telling her she was going to be okay. She had not fallen in the same way that Talya had been thrown to her death – headfirst – so I tried to be optimistic that the injuries would not be fatal.

Mike seemed to have disappeared backstage. I could no longer see his navy blazer and shock of black hair against the dark metal grillwork of the theater walls and scaffolding. The people who had made up the cast and audience were split off into small circles now – Mona huddled with Ross Kehoe and Rinaldo Vicci, on her cell phone, explaining the situation to someone she had called; the actors obviously distressed about the injured teenager.

I looked to the flat ladders against the backstage wall for any sign of Mike, and saw only shadows from above. I turned my head to the theater entrance, hoping a crew of EMTs would be nearby again this time. And I checked Lucy's face, to see whether she had opened her eyes yet, but that had not happened.

Mike was back at my side by the time the paramedics arrived. I stepped away and made room for them as they began to check Lucy's vital signs and got to work.

I followed Mike to Mona Berk's little group. 'There's no one up there. Where the hell are those guys?'

'Look,' Kehoe said, 'it's just a skeleton crew we brought in for the afternoon. The Imperial's stagehands and techs don't come in till later in the day.'

'Bad choice of words, "skeleton crew". Who are they and where'd they go? Was this just a way to do it on the cheap? Avoid union labor?'

'It was supposed to be a simple walk-through, Mike. You think I wanted the kid to get hurt? The last thing I need is a goddamn lawsuit before I even close on the property. Look at them,' Mona said, pointing at the actors. 'All these morons need to do is start the story that this show is jinxed. The whole industry rides on superstition. I'll end up spending a fortune and never get this show off the ground.'

She wasn't much concerned about Lucy DeVore's life, especially if these events got in the way of ticket sales.

Vicci whispered something to Kehoe and they started to walk toward the ladder that went up to the fly platform.

'Hold it,' Mike said.

'I only asked to see what happened to the swing, detective. To see how the ropes holding it look like,' said Vicci, his accent thickening as he pleaded for Mike's understanding.

'I got Crime Scene guys coming to do that. Just stay off, got it?'

'But, crime . . . ? Who said anything about a crime?'

'Nobody yet. But this setup is going to be examined before any one of you touches anything. The swing, where'd it come from?'

Kehoe called over to Mona, 'Sweetheart, Mr Chapman wants to know about the swing. Where'd we get it?'

'The Brooks Atkinson Theater, Ross. Revival of Tom Stoppard's *Jumpers*, remember? The girl on the swing that was decorated with the crescent moon. Christ, isn't this one moving yet? Why don't they get her out of here and over to the hospital? This is such fucking bad karma for me.'

Mike was standing over the shoulder of one of the medics when he gave me a thumbs-up. They had secured Lucy's neck in a cervical collar and were getting ready to move her, which meant that it was unlikely she had sustained any spinal cord injury. With Mike's help they lifted her onto a gurney, which in turn fit on a collapsible set of wheels, carrying the young woman out of the theater and to the ambulance.

Once the most critical matter was dealt with, Mike turned his attention back to the producers. 'The crew, where are they?'

'On the street in the back. Grabbing a smoke. They're pretty scared,' Kehoe said, walking upstage to call out the back door.

Two kids in their twenties, dressed in jeans and filthy T-shirts, came back into the theater. Mike wrote their names and pedigree information in his pad and directed them to take him back up on the catwalk to see the pipes in the fly from which the swing had been suspended.

'You're not going to the hospital with Lucy?' I asked Rinaldo Vicci.

'I – I don't know what to do about the poor child. Perhaps you could tell me where they've taken her.' He rubbed his extended abdomen with one hand, again wiping sweat from his forehead with the other. 'I'm not really responsible for her.'

'Someone should be with her. The doctors will need an adult to sign a consent form for the surgery. Don't any of you care what happens to her?'

Mona held up her hands, as though telling me to stop talking. 'Wait a minute. I've got to speak to my lawyer before I even think of getting involved. Rinaldo, this is really in your lap. Isn't she eighteen? You told me she was eighteen, that we were just going to say sixteen for the publicity. You know her family?'

'Nobody. I don't know anything at all. She told me she's from West Virginia. She told me she's here alone.'

'Mr Vicci, I expect you can do better than that. Surely you must have some better information, something back in your office, perhaps?'

He was playing with the fringe of the lavender cashmere scarf he had tossed around his neck, on this mild spring afternoon. 'I'm thinking very hard, Miss Cooper. I'm thinking I don't know very much at all. This was all to be so informal today, you understand me?'

I was thinking that if I could pull the two ends of the

scarf a bit tighter around the neck he might cough up whatever it was he didn't want to tell me. 'Who brought her to you, Mr Vicci? How did she come to your attention? I want some explanation, some—'

'*Scusi, signora*. There would be notes in my office. I'm pleased to get that information for you and give you a call later on, but for now, she's just one of the many young ladies who knock on the door or someone refers to me.'

'Where are her clothes? There must be a bag with some identification. Someone to get in touch with?' I turned to the small group of actors and asked them to take me to the dressing room.

We walked behind the curtain on stage left, up a ramp to a cheerless communal room. One side of it was lined with mirrors, below which stood a ledge wide enough to hold makeup and hair supplies, with stools scattered beneath that. On the opposite wall were hooks and hangers. One of the girls from the dance number pointed at the black sweater and Capri pants that belonged to Lucy, and the tote bag that hung with them.

I dug around in the tote – pushing aside sunglasses, birth control pills, a strip of nicotine gum, and a container of mace – until I found a plastic wallet. There was thirty-four dollars in cash, an ATM card, and a New York State driver's license. The date of birth would have made Lucy twenty-one years old, a much more convenient age to do just about anything a beautiful young woman might choose to do in the big city. The residential address listed was on Ninth Avenue in Manhattan – no mention of any connection to West Virginia – and I guessed that whoever she really was, she had purchased the identification in some illegal joint, not too long ago and not very far from Times Square.

When I got back to the stage, Mike was standing in front of the orchestra pit, writing down names and numbers of the impatient angels who were waiting to get out of the theater. He turned his back and put his arm around me to explain what he had seen.

'Those kids don't know anything. One of them is doped up to the gills – it's amazing with all the marijuana in him he could balance on the fly without taking a header himself.'

'Who hired them?'

'The older one of them got a call last week from his cousin, who's on the crew at the Belasco. That guy didn't want to get in dutch with Joe Berk, so he passed the job along to these two, who are buddies. The script just tells them which pipe to move and when to move it. They have no idea who set the swing or when it was hung here.'

'You got the names of everyone in the peanut gallery?'

'Yeah, these mopes can go. Hubert Alden's agreed to stay to talk to us.'

'Which one is he?' I asked, taking a casual glance at the dozen people still milling about in the side aisles.

'The tall guy in the gray suit, trench coat over his shoulders. Looks like an ad for Brylcreem.'

Mike let the others go, still waiting for the Crime Scene Unit to show up. This kind of event – seemingly accidental – would not trump the day's other mayhem. I called my paralegal, Maxine, and dispatched her to the hospital to wait outside the recovery room for Lucy DeVore – no matter how long, no matter how late.

189

Whoever Lucy really was and whatever her story, this was not a time for her to be without someone to help care for her, and Max had tended more victims through trauma than almost anyone I knew outside of an emergency room.

We walked Hubert Alden to the back of the theater and introduced ourselves. He braced his back against the corner where the walls met and folded his arms, taking us each in as we studied him.

'The medical examiner told us you called this morning. About Natalya Galinova. I'm the detective handling her case.'

'I'm grateful to you for that. Is there going to be any problem having her – well, her body – released to me to take home?'

'I've got some questions, naturally. And we're waiting for her husband to sign the appropriate paperwork. Under the circumstances it's a bit unusual for someone who's not related to be making the claim.'

'We've had a professional relationship, detective. I've supported Talya, as an artist, and I've been very generous to the dance company, too.'

'This is what I'm a little confused about,' Mike said, furrowing his brow and making circles in the air with his right hand, in his best Columbo imitation. 'Exactly how does that partnership work?'

Alden's description of his patronage was cut-and-dried. He denied there was any sexual involvement with Talya Galinova.

'So what are you in this for?' Mike asked.

'I've made a lot of money, detective. I'm fifty-two years old – an investment banker. Married briefly but

190

no children. My grandmother was one of the most important opera singers of the last century. It's in her honor
that I support great artists.'

'Who was your grandmother?' Mike asked.

'Giulietta Capretta, before she became an Alden. Do
you recognize the name?'

Mike shook his head in the negative.

'And you, Ms Cooper?' Alden said, pushing away
from the wall and walking down the aisle toward the
exit door.

'I've heard recordings of her that my father had. Singing
with Caruso at the old Met, if I'm not mistaken.'

Alden flashed a smile at me, imitating his grandmother
for us, as he wagged a finger, and proceeded to roll all
his *r*'s in a perfect trill, much like Rinaldo Vicci did.
'"Alas, young lady, you can have no idea how big my
voice is if all you've listened to are the records. When I
made recordings, they had to turn my back to the horn,"'
Alden said, gesticulating grandly with his long arm, '"or
I would have ruptured the mechanism." That was
Giulietta's rebuke to the poor folk who never actually saw
her perform in person.'

Alden was playing to me and I could see that Mike
was annoyed. He got a few steps ahead of Alden and me
and waited impatiently for us to catch up.

'So that's what makes you so generous? Granny's
memory?'

'That's not enough for you, Mr Chapman? The Aldens
have been patrons of the arts for a very long time,' Alden
said, continuing to walk with a swagger, tugging at the
lapel of his coat to keep it in place on his shoulder. 'They
were part of the cabal responsible for the building of the

191

old Met. Broadway and Fortieth Street, 1883. Back when they were considered too gauche to be admitted to the Academy of Music.'

I had learned the story of the creation of the first Metropolitan Opera on my earliest trips to Lincoln Center. After the Civil War, the old guard who ran the academy, which had been the premier showcase for European and American opera performers in America until that time, had rejected the attempts at membership – and the petroleum money – of the nouveau riche: the Vanderbilts, Goulds, Astors, and Belmonts. The wealthy upstarts organized their own guild uptown, sending the Academy of Music into financial ruin and leaving on its site the Con Edison plant that still operates on 14th Street today. And opening night at the Met was so sparkling an event – women brilliantly gowned and jeweled – that the parterre boxes that held the rich patrons were thereafter called the Diamond Horseshoe. Undoubtedly, an Alden ancestor had been in that crowd.

'So in your particular case, what did the half a million get you?'

'Talya's attention, certainly. She was great company, Mr Chapman. Remarkably smart and uniquely talented, beautiful to look at, great to be with.'

'And her husband, he didn't get in the way?'

'Talya's husband hasn't been relevant for more than a decade. Lovely chap, as they say across the pond. He's been in a wheelchair since he suffered a stroke – he must be close to eighty years old – and I have to say he's getting a bit gaga. He's got an attendant around the clock and wants for nothing.'

'So what was the attraction there?' Mike asked.

'Money, when the old boy had it. But those days are long gone.'

'Friday evening, the night Talya was killed, were you at the performance?'

'No, actually. I wasn't even in town. I've got a place outside Vail, and I flew out for the weekend. I didn't even know she'd been killed until Sunday evening.'

Mike gestured toward the stage of the Imperial. 'What's your interest here?'

Hubert Alden sighed. 'You may know that Talya was pressing to play this role – the Evelyn Nesbit part – if the show got to Broadway. Joe Berk had been calling me to try to talk her out of it. Gave me the script to read. Have you seen it?'

'No.'

'There's another role we all thought would have been perfect for Talya. She just didn't take it very well when Joe Berk and Rinaldo Vicci told her about it.'

'Why?' I asked.

'It's the part of Evelyn Nesbit's mother, Ms Cooper. The next act of the show is really all about how Evelyn's mother took control of things after the murder. She was a very young woman, in fact – younger even than Talya was now. Thirty-something – quite glamorous herself and extremely manipulative. The Thaws bought her off – lots of mink, lots of jewelry. The second act is all about Evelyn and her mother, and what was known at the time as the murder trial of the century. Borrows heavily from that razzle-dazzle number in *Chicago*, but you don't often get an original thought on Broadway anymore, do you? And how can you lose an audience with a media circus, an insanity defense, and an attorney named – um . . .' Alden said, snapping his finger.

'Delphin Delmas.'

'Very good, detective. I guess murder really is your beat.'

'I take it Talya didn't like that idea.'

'The talons came out. She was furious with all of us.'

'But she's dead, Mr Alden,' Mike said. 'Why are you still in this game? You got another horse in the race?'

'I've backed a lot of shows for many different producers. I've watched the Berk family splinter itself into factions for years. Any time two of them are fighting over the same property, there's always a chance to step into that wedge and pick up a bargain. I've listened to Joe's tirades for as long as I've known him, so I thought I'd come see if Mona had anything going for herself.'

'She invited you?'

'Mr Vicci is the one who called. Rinaldo Vicci. Talya's agent.'

'Depends on which way the wind was blowing, didn't it, whether or not he represented her?'

'Talya? She'd come back to him. She always did.'

'Were you here today to see Lucy DeVore?'

'I didn't know anything about the kid. Didn't Rinaldo tell you that Talya had begged him for one chance to let Mona Berk see what she looked like in the leading role? Didn't he tell you that it was supposed to be Talya Galinova up there on that broken swing this afternoon?'

Chapter 19

'Can we stop for a hot dog? I'm starving.'

'Sure. But I've got no appetite. I'd like to go by Lucy's apartment and see whether there's any contact information for her relatives there.'

'I'll be quick,' Mike said, watching as the street-cart vendor fished two boiled franks out of the murky water in his stand. 'So how do you figure the swing?'

'I don't. Did you notice anything when you looked at it?' I said, taking the Diet Coke that Mike bought me.

'Yeah, but I can't tell whether it's just old rope or somebody intentionally hacked away at it. It gave out on one side and the wooden board – the seat holding Lucy – flapped back, dropping her on the stage like a rock. That analysis of the rope is a job for the lab.'

'And if it was a setup, the question is whether it was meant for Talya. Might even have been a safety valve – to make sure she was dead by today – in case the killer missed her at the Met Friday night.'

'Not a bad thought,' Mike said, drowning the second dog in a mound of sauerkraut.

'No thanks,' I said to a toothless man passing out cards

advertising an Eighth Avenue strip club. While Mike enjoyed his late lunch, I gave directions to a group of high school kids looking for video arcades and waved away a Jehovah's Witness who was hoping to convert me in rapid fashion beneath an overhead neon sign that advertised GIRLS! LIVE! NUDE! GIRLS!

'We stay here long enough, you could get lucky.'

'And you could get ptomaine poisoning.'

He wiped his mouth and we were ready to move on. 'You got an address on Ninth?'

I looked at Lucy's identification again and read him the number. 'That's close by. Should be in the forties.'

We cruised west on 45th Street, turning south when we came to Ninth Avenue, as we noted the descending numbers on the buildings. At the corner of 42nd Street, in front of the drab doorway of the four-story structure, bracketed by the graffiti on adjacent storefronts, Mike braked the car and pulled over to park in a loading zone.

'Jesus. I can't believe it. The Elk? That kid must be desperate.'

The flashing red neon sign above the grim entrance just said the word HOTEL. Both Mike and I had handled scores of cases there in our careers, and knew the more appropriate label for the shabby little place was *flophouse*.

'This is about as far from the Broadway stage as you can get in three blocks,' I said. 'You want to check? Maybe it's a mistake.'

Before the Disneyfication of 42nd Street, the area around Times Square had been full of joints like this. The Elk was the last one standing after a period of rapid development. It had a few permanent residents, and a dozen or so guestrooms in which a tourist might mistakenly show up in appreciation of the forty-dollar-a-night price for a mid-Manhattan accommodation.

But most of the rooms were rented by the hour to professionals of another sort who didn't mind that the only furniture in the cubicle was a bed and nightstand – no phone, no TV, no air conditioner – and that the communal bathrooms were down the hall, shared by the usual assortment of hustlers, hookers, pimps, and junkies.

We got out of the car and walked up the staircase that led to a locked glass door. I stepped around a couple of winos and a methadone addict nodding out, following as Mike forged a trail for me around discarded liquor bottles and empty crack vials.

The man on the desk buzzed us in and Mike flashed his badge.

'Somebody call about trouble? I got no trouble,' the clerk said in his clipped Pakistani accent. 'Somebody call you?'

'No, no. We're trying to help a young woman who's been hurt. She may be staying here.'

'Hurt here? No, no,' he said, shaking his head with great conviction.

'No, m'man. Hurt somewhere else. An accident. We need to find her family. Her name is Lucy DeVore.'

'Ah. Miss Lucy. She get hurt? She going to be all right, detective?'

'I hope so. You want to tell me how long she's been here?'

'Of course. We don't want any trouble with police,' the clerk said, looking through his box of index cards for the handwritten notes on his long-term residents.

Stabbings, shootings, rapes, homicides – the denizens of places like the Elk brought those crimes along with them the way ordinary travelers carried luggage. Generally speaking, the law-abiding clerks who manned the desk were cooperative with law enforcement, knowing they relied on the quick response of the local precinct when the bullets started flying and bodies fell.

Mike looked at the notes scribbled on the card. 'Looks like she's been here about three weeks. Is that right?'

'Three weeks, sir. Very right. Very nice girl. No trouble.'

The spaces for previous address were all blank. There was nothing except the date in March that Lucy had arrived and the room number assigned to her – noting that it had the extra feature of a hot plate. The rate was two hundred fifty dollars for the month, far less than most people in this part of town paid to park their cars.

'She paid in advance?'

'Yes, sir. Cash. That's the red check mark on the card. Everybody does,' the clerk said, pressing the buzzer to admit a hooker as she waved her room key against the glass. She blew a kiss at him and took the hand of the raggedy-looking man who accompanied her inside, wagging her spandex-covered ass at him as he stopped behind her to catch his breath on the next flight of stairs. They were on their way, no doubt, to the two-hours-for-twenty-five-dollars 'short stay' rooms, from which so many of my cases had developed.

'Nobody bothered her here?' I asked.

'Oh, miss. Many people would like to bother her,' he said, laughing. 'She ignores everyone. Very nice to me. Very nice.'

'Anyone visit her?'

He shook his finger in my face. 'Not that way. No visitors. None at all.'

'We need to go up to her room.'

The clerk looked from Mike's face to mine. 'For sure it's okay? Miss Lucy coming back soon?'

'Not too soon,' Mike said, giving his card to the man. 'Anybody looks for her, you call me. And don't let anyone touch anything in her room.'

'But soon the next money she will owe.'

Mike reached into his pocket and handed the clerk a bunch of twenties. 'Nobody takes anything from Miss Lucy's room. That money goes toward the next month.'

'Yes, sir,' he said, putting the money in a locked drawer and handing Mike a key. 'Room three seventeen. You would like me to take you?'

'We're okay.' We walked up two flights of sagging wooden stairs and halfway down the long corridor. Mike unlocked the door and stepped inside. He flipped the switch and the bare overhead lightbulb turned on.

The life of the dazzling golden girl on the flying trapeze – Lucy DeVore, or whoever she really was – was entirely contained in a single wheeling bag that lay open in a corner on the floor and accessories scattered around the room. Most of her wardrobe was black – cheap cotton blouses and sweaters, jeans and slacks that were folded neatly on top of each other. Some dresses hung in the closet, short-skirted off-the-shoulder types that would have showed her off to great advantage. Three pairs of shoes and one pair of high-heeled boots were alongside the bed.

There was a table with two drawers that she had used as a dresser. On top of it was a plastic cosmetics kit –

buy two lipsticks, get one free – that Lucy had probably used this morning to get ready for her walk-through. It was crammed with a variety of stage makeup – powders, mascara, liners and shadows, and a range of lip colors from palest pink to burgundy. Beside that were her toothpaste and toothbrush and a dish with a bar of soap.

On the bedside table was a small folder with photographs in it. Lucy as Mother Courage, as Joan of Arc, as Blanche Dubois, as Dorothy on the Yellow Brick Road, and as Nellie Forbush, washing her man right out of her hair. In some of the pictures she looked like she was fifteen, while in others old enough to handle the mature roles. The stage was every high school or amateur community playhouse in a small town in America, and if her family had attended her performances, there was no sign of it in this keepsake album. It probably wasn't meant to be sentimental, but rather to show her range of roles to the people in the business whose attention she tried to get.

The last photo seemed to be the most recent. In it, Lucy was dressed in a black leotard and tights, wearing a scarlet felt hat with white sequins and a long black tassel that fell onto her face, covering her right eye. It was a tarboosh, the Moroccan cap originally worn by students at the University of Fez that had long been regarded as a symbol of knowledge and integrity. I brought the picture closer and looked for any sign of where it had been taken. She was leaning against a door, bracing herself with her hand on the large steel knob. Around its hexagonal perimeter, engraved in the metal, was a word – perhaps the name of the theater or building in which the photo had been taken. Lucy's hand covered everything except the first letter, which was *M*.

I showed it to Mike. 'See that *M*? Think this could have been taken at the Met?'

He studied the image of the unusual doorknob. 'The design looks too stylized. From an older period, I'd guess. How many theater names are there in town that begin with the letter *M*?'

'The Music Box. The Majestic . . .'

'I'll get a list.'

I put the small album in my pocket to take along, hoping something in it would be a help in finding Lucy's home.

Mike picked up the pillow and ran his hand under the bed covers. 'You live in a flophouse like this, you gotta have some place to keep a few valuables, no? Where could she have put them? People break into these rooms all the time. She would have looked like she had extra bucks to satisfy a night's habit for one of her neighbors.'

'I've had prostitutes who worked out of places in this area. Some of them paid for lockers up the street at the bus terminal just for that reason.'

There was no flight tag attached to Lucy's suitcase. If she had arrived in New York by bus, she would have probably been familiar with the Port Authority station.

I went back through the clothing again, looking in every pocket for another key or an address book or any connection to a human being.

I picked up the faux snakeskin boots and turned them upside down, shaking them as I did. Something fluttered to the floor. I unfolded the tightly wrapped paper – a one-hundred-dollar bill. In neat handwriting, on the cream-colored border of the money, was a telephone number, and after it the name Joe Berk.

Chapter 20

A secretary opened the door to Joe Berk's apartment and reluctantly led us up the staircase to his bedroom.

I had called Maxine after leaving the Elk, and learned that Lucy was still in surgery. She had suffered a concussion and had not regained consciousness before they took her into the operating room. She had fractured both hips, multiple bones in both legs, and one of her elbows, but other than a few vertebrae that had cracked, there was no threat of paralysis or spinal cord injury.

Berk was propped up in his bed, watching an old movie on the single television screen on the far wall. A nurse sat on the sofa, trying to occupy herself with something to read as we began to talk to her patient.

'Heard you caught the matinee today, Mr Chapman. How's the girl?'

'I thought you and your niece weren't on speaking terms.'

'I got friends, detective. Joe Berk has friends everywhere. The girl gonna live?'

'Looks good. The resilience of youth, I guess.'

'What do you mean "resilience"? She bounced?' He looked to the nurse for a laugh but didn't get one. 'Maybe it's my timing. You know, detective, I never saw a bad-looking nurse until today. Check out the sour puss on this one. The doctors didn't want me to have any palpitations, lemme tell you they found the right girl for the job. The one nurse I wouldn't want to play with, they book her double-time. You two here because of your great concern for me?'

'We're here to talk about Lucy DeVore.'

'What's a Lucy DeVore?'

'The girl you just asked me about. The girl who was hurt at the Imperial today.'

'The Imperial. Lemme tell you something else about that. You know the Shuberts built that one themselves, 1922? Not these guys today who run the organization. The originals – J.J. and Lee. Nobody like 'em.' Berk was brilliant at sidetracking the conversation when it wasn't going his way.

'I read the plaque. Let's get back to Lucy—'

'Me, I just buy up the theaters. Those guys built 'em. Fifteen, twenty, thirty – the most beautiful and elaborate showcases in the world. The reason we still have legitimate theater today, despite all the movie houses and home videos, is because of J.J. and Lee Shubert. I can't remember how many of those gorgeous stages they're responsible for, but there was a time when Broadway theater was the most popular form of entertainment in the city. It's coming back, detective, and it's Joe Berk who's keeping it alive.'

'You're doing a bang-up job, Joe. I'm more interested in how come Lucy D—'

'And you know who their architect was, the Shuberts? A guy with the godawful name of Herbert Krapp is the one who designed these dream palaces.'

'Mr Berk—'

'Krapp. Can you imagine it? Talk about a boy who should have changed his name. Forget Yussel Berkowitz. Forget Peter J. Schmuck. "Hey there, it's me – Krapp." "How do you do, ma'am, I'm Mr Krapp." What do you say to your family? "Don't worry about your future, kids, I'm doing business with Krapp."'

The nurse picked up her magazine and chose this moment to take a break, walking out of the bedroom to the staircase.

Mike stood next to Berk's side and shouted in his face, 'Cut it out, Berk. End of the road. Lucy DeVore says you're the man.'

'What are you talking about? My guys tell me she wasn't even conscious. Don't bullshit me, detective, or next time I call the commissioner, I won't be such a prince. You'll be working security down in Macy's basement.'

'She was talking plenty at the hospital, before they wheeled her into surgery. Told me about the money you gave her. Told the nurse taking her history you were her next of kin and gave this number as the phone to call. Am I close?'

Mike held out the hundred-dollar bill to show Berk, then picked up the receiver next to the bed to see whether the digits on it matched the private telephone number on the portable plastic handpiece. He gave me a thumbs-up to tell me they did.

Berk threw back the covers and sat on the side of the bed. He was wearing nile green satin pajamas, the bottoms drooping below his hips. He screamed for the nurse as loud as he could. 'You wanna be responsible for my goddamn blood pressure? Get Florence Nightingale back

205

up here before I bust my gut. I don't know any Lucy DeVore and I never did. You know how many people have Joe Berk's phone number? Sweetheart, you mind handing me the bedpan?'

'Hold that thought, Joe. Ms Cooper hasn't played doctor with anyone in longer than I can remember, and she won't be starting with you if I have anything to say about it,' Mike said, pushing me away. 'I don't buy your antics, I don't buy your sudden urge to relieve yourself, and I don't buy your denials. Lucy DeVore.'

'Shove it, detective.'

Mike took out the phony driver's license and held the girl's picture under his nose. 'Look at her, Joe. This kid is living in a rathole on Ninth Avenue, and the only thread that seems to link her to the Great White Way has your name on it and a direct line to your boudoir.'

Again Joe yelled out the nurse's name.

Mike reached for the brown alligator wallet on the nightstand. He opened the billfold and removed a wad of cash, spreading it in his hand like a deck of cards. 'All hundreds, Joe. Ben Franklins, every one of them. Want me to start checking serial numbers against the bill we found in Lucy's room, see if I get a run of 'em? This how you pay off your girls?'

Mike was wilder than I'd ever seen him before in such tame circumstances – not a street chase, not a shoot-out, not a dangerous confrontation with a violent perp. I knew he was angry and unhappy, but he was doing things he would never have done on the job before Val's death. Playing with a rich man's money never had a happy ending on a police blotter. I tried to take his arm to get him to put down the cash. Instead, he threw the fanlike fistful

206

of money onto the floor, watching it scatter around the room.

'You're a real tough guy, Mr Chapman. You think the commissioner won't take my call? You think he won't do what Joe Berk tells him to do with some dumb mick cop? Get that nurse up here to pick up my money.'

'Tell me how you met that girl. Don't you understand I'm not getting out of here until you've done that?'

Berk held on to his pajama bottoms and reached over for the portable phone. Mike got to it first and tossed it out of the room onto the top of the stairs, listening to it bounce to the bottom and settle on the floor.

'Say you got to the phone and let's pretend you dialed nine one-one. I'm what you got, Joe. I'm the friendly neighborhood guy on the beat. You're off the hook on the age thing, Joe. Nothing to worry about there. Lucy gave it up to the doctor. She was nineteen last winter. She's over the age of consent.'

Berk picked up his head and looked at the expression on Mike's face. Mike's bluff seemed to have found its mark.

'Who's nineteen? That – that kid today – the one you call Lucy?'

'What do you call her?'

'I don't know if we're even talking about the same girl.' Berk had flopped back onto the side of the bed. The slightest bit of exertion – his argument with Mike – had exhausted him in his already weakened condition.

'Stop feeling sorry for yourself, Joe. That great-looking young kid who had some kind of a future twenty-four hours ago is going to wake up in intensive care tomorrow with two brand-new titanium hips and legs with more screws in them than you've got hundred-dollar bills. I want somebody who cares about her to be standing there when she opens her eyes. That's all I'm looking for here.'

'Look somewheres else. I never laid a glove on her.'

Mike pulled a chair up under himself, turned it around so he could lean against the back of it, and faced Joe Berk close up. 'Where'd she come from? Why'd she end up in the Elk? That's worse than the ninth circle of hell, for Chrissakes.'

Berk rolled onto his back and leaned against the two pillows stacked behind him. 'Who gives a shit where she comes from? I don't know how they find me, but they do. Maybe it's a setup.'

'What kind of setup, Joe?' Mike said, softening his tone. 'You looking at Coop? There's nothing you can say to shock her, trust me. She's seen and heard just about everything.'

I was slowly moving back to the far wall, knowing that Berk would be more likely to disclose something he found embarrassing if I faded out of the room.

'She doesn't look as tough as you,' Berk said, lifting his head to stare at me.

'They got a whole wing at Attica named in her honor, Joe. A pavilion, packed to the gills. SRO in your business. Full of the most depraved men you'd ever hope not to meet in a dark alley. And they didn't wind up there because of Coop's charm. Where most women have a heart? She's got a pair of steel balls. That's how come you know when she gets excited – you can hear them clanging against each other from miles away. Feel free to speak your mind in front of her. I always do.'

Berk's mouth twisted in a half-smile.

208

'You were telling me you think someone set you up. You mean, with Lucy?'

'I got a weakness for women. Not babies, not teenagers, not little girls. I like the ladies. Nothing wrong with that, is there?'

Mike was silent. He probably had the same visual I did, which made the thought of getting anywhere near Joe Berk's satin pajamas repugnant at any age.

'And the truth is, the ladies like Joe Berk,' he said, raising the same half-smile as he patted his belly. 'A good-looking young guy like you might find it hard to believe they throw themselves at me, but they do. I know, I know – you're thinking it's the money or the casting couch or the connections. Lemme tell you, Mr Chapman, women are suckers for guys with a lot of class and a lot of clout.'

'Lucy DeVore, Joe. How'd you meet her?'

'Dancing. I saw her perform in something, a month or two ago. Somebody introduced her to me after the rehearsal and bingo, she was looking for my help.'

'Who made the introduction? Dancing in what?'

Joe's head was back against the pillow now, his eyes closed. 'I said a rehearsal, in a studio. Day in, day out, that's what I do every day to make a buck. You expect me to remember what house, what stage, what the tune was? It don't work like that, sonny.'

'She's pretty striking looking. Hard to forget that long platinum hair, longer legs.'

'What kind of stupid are you, Chapman? She's platinum this month because that's the name of the show she wants to be in. I met her, she was something else. Maybe dark-haired, maybe red. If she was blond, I might have shtupped her. I might have given her a run for her money.'

209

'Joe, look me in the eye. You telling me you had a shot at that sexy kid and didn't even make a stab at it?'

'May my late wife rest in peace. Izzy Berkowitz, too. Nothing.'

'What kind of help did she want?'

'What they all want. Put her in a show, make her a star. Hey, she was practically at the end of her rope when I met her. Back-to-back auditions, with every unemployed gypsy in the business showing up.'

'Was she living at the Elk then?'

'I don't make house calls, detective. I don't know where she was living. You'd leave this place if you owned it?' Berk said, waving his hand in a circle around the room. 'They come to me, Chapman.'

'Did you give her money?'

'Yeah, I gave her a few hundred bucks. Told her to get a decent meal, buy some clean clothes.'

'For nothing in return, no reason at all?'

'You the only one that gets to ask questions, Chapman? I'm just the answer man?'

'Your turn, Joe. Ask away.'

'You're so interested in my love life. Lemme ask – you and Ms Cooper here – you two an item?'

I had to bite the inside of my cheek to stop from laughing out loud. Joe Berk stopped Mike in his tracks and seemed pleased to have done it.

'Like you said, Joe, the broads like guys with class and clout. I come up short on both.'

'C'mon. You're a handsome kid, full head of hair, you're built like an athlete, and you got that kind of John Wayne swagger about you. You might even be smart – how the hell do I know. What's wrong with you, Ms Cooper?'

210

I walked up behind Mike's chair and tousled his hair. 'I've tried everything in the book, Mr Berk. He just won't give me a tumble. I'll have to come back and get some pointers from you when you're feeling better.'

'Think, Joe. Anything Lucy might have told you that would help us with her?' Mike had warmed up the old guy, now he wanted results.

'I've given you all the help I can. How do you figure Rinaldo Vicci comes into the act? You think he represents street urchins? I know my niece won't consider the girl for a role if I make the call, so I told Vicci to take her to the audition. He talks out of both sides of his mouth. See if either stream of his bullshit makes sense.'

Maybe if Mike pulled on the fringe of Vicci's cashmere scarf Rinaldo would remember that Lucy DeVore got to him directly from Joe Berk. Now I had to figure why Vicci had lied to me about that.

The nurse was in the doorway of the room, tapping the face of her watch to signal that she was about to cut short our visit.

Mike stood up and swung the chair back into place. He reached for the plastic drinking cup on the bedside table that Berk had been sipping from and crumpled it in his hand, tucking it in his pocket. 'Sleep on it, Joe. Anything comes to mind and you don't want to bother your pal the commissioner tomorrow, give me a ring. By the time Lucy's out of the anesthesia, she'll tell us the rest of the story.'

Berk cocked his head and opened one eye to look at Mike. 'Fairy tales, detective. Little girls make up stories like they were fairy tales. Watch out for that.'

I was headed for the staircase when I heard Mike tell

Berk he was still working on the murder investigation of Natalya Galinova. 'This patron of hers, Hubert Alden, you know him, too?'

'If I came from his kind of background, they'd call me a patron, too. It's all in the bloodlines, Chapman. You oughta know that by now. Sure, Joe Berk knows everybody.'

'Any idea why he was at the Imperial today?'

'What do I care? I'm still trying to figure out why he thought he was entitled to take Talya out to dinner after her performance last Friday. Maybe Vicci called him, maybe Mona invited him. They'd probably be looking for him to pick up the tab for your girl, Lucy, if they really thought she had a future.'

'The night she was killed?' Mike asked, aware that Alden had just claimed to us that he had been in Vail the night of the murder. 'I had the impression Mr Alden was out of town last weekend.'

'Why? Because he told you that's where he was?' Berk shook his head. 'If I tell you I'm the Count of Monte Cristo, you're gonna believe me? No, but him, you take his word for it.'

'You know different?'

'When I got to Talya's dressing room, she was still onstage. I picked up her cell phone to call my driver. I saw she had a message, so I played it back. It was Alden, telling her he'd pick her up and take her for a late supper if she gave him a ring.'

'How come you didn't tell us that when we talked to you on Saturday?'

'It slipped my mind, Mr Chapman. My short-term memory is bad.' He gave Mike his crooked smile, the one that expressed his delight at being a hard-ass.

'You didn't happen to collide with Mr Alden back-stage, did you, Joe?'

'I didn't stick around, buddy. I don't do time-shares with my ladies. I'm a very exclusive kind of guy.'

Chapter 21

Mike was sprawled on the sofa in my den while Mercer read to him from the delivery menu of PJ Bernstein's deli. I had just gotten off the phone with Maxine, who told me that Lucy was in the surgical recovery room. Her condition was guarded, and the doctors had decided to place her in what they called a controlled coma because of the concussion, the possible brain damage, and their ability to better manage her pain. It was clear she wouldn't regain consciousness for several days, and I told Max there was no reason for her to stay at the hospital any longer tonight.

Mercer had poured us each a drink. Just over an hour ago, the toxicologist had called to give him good news on the case of the two Canadian women. Large quantities of Xanax had been found in the residue of the blender and in two of the three drinking glasses that had been taken from the dirty sink of Dr Selim Sengor.

He raised his glass to toast the results and I swirled my Scotch around before enjoying its smooth taste.

'Cara and Jean are getting a bit stir-crazy. They were ready to hit the road and head for home,' Mercer said.

'Now I can put them in the grand jury first thing in the morning.'

'How about Sengor? You going to wait until his court date on Friday to give him the news?'

'Not a prayer. Eric's a decent guy,' I said, referring to his lawyer. 'I'll call him tomorrow, tell him I'm going to advance the case and ask him to surrender Sengor first thing on Thursday. I not only get to raise the bail, but I get it out of Judge Moffett's courtroom and upstairs for a Supreme Court arraignment.'

Mike was telling Mercer about the painstaking police work at the Met in the Galinova investigation while we ordered dinner and waited for the end of *Jeopardy!*. He removed Joe Berk's plastic water cup from his pocket, holding it by its base in his fingertips.

'Bag it for me, Coop.'

'What were you thinking when you took this?'

'When Berk said that he hadn't laid a glove on Lucy, it reminded me of the glove – you know, the man's glove the guys found at the crime scene at the Met. Serology developed two DNA profiles on that. Here we've got a little saliva from Joe's lips, just for comparison. Piece of cake.'

'I can't use this in court. You walked out of his house with it. And it's not like the night when we thought he was dead. This time you were standing right next to him.'

'It's just a long shot, for investigative purposes only. I'm telling you, we can call it abandoned property. The nurse had a whole stack of 'em there. He wasn't going to use this cup again. I just helped clean up after him.'

'Toss it, Mike. If we're going that route, we'll do it the right way.'

'And tonight's Final Jeopardy category,' Alex Trebek said, interrupting our legal squabble, 'is Geography.'

We each had areas of strength, and this was Mercer's. His father's longtime job as a mechanic at Delta Airlines had exposed young Mercer to a world far beyond his middle-class neighborhood in Queens. He had studied the maps and charts his father used to bring home to him and knew about place-names in foreign lands of which I'd never heard.

Mike put his twenty on the coffee table and walked to the kitchen during the commercial break. 'I'm going south on this one. Anything in the fridge?'

I had never mastered the basics of cooking and rarely had more than survival food, usually in the form of takeout from Grace's Marketplace, a block away. 'Your favorite pâté and some heavenly Stilton.'

The answer to the question was posted for the three contestants: 'In 1754, Horace Walpole coined this word, which refers to the original name of the country we now call Sri Lanka, and means "accidental discovery".'

'You can't trust this guy Trebek. He tells you it's geography and then he throws one right in the lap of the English Literature major,' Mike said, slathering the rich cheese on a cracker and biting into it. 'Coop's already spent the money on her next pedicure. You know this one, bro?'

'I couldn't do any better than that guy,' Mercer said, laughing at the computer software designer from Michigan who guessed, 'What is *Ceylonese*?'

'Well, for a time Sri Lanka was known as Ceylon, but that's not what we're looking for,' said Trebek. 'Sounds like an artificial fabric, doesn't it? You're thinking of *Celanese*, probably. Different spelling, of course.'

'What is *serendipity*?' I asked. 'If I'm right, Mike, I get you to come to the Vineyard with me this weekend.'

216

'If you're right, you get your forty bucks and another chance for me to tell you that you spent way too much time with your nose in the books and not nearly enough in the local frat house getting some practical experience.'

'You're exactly right about that, sir,' Trebek said.

'The ancient name of Ceylon was Serendip,' I said, picking up the two bills, 'and there was this wonderfully whimsical folktale about the three princes of Serendip and a lost camel, which Walpole came across in his reading. So he created this very expressive word, and now it's used for everything from the discovery of X-rays to penicillin, both accidental side effects of the things for which Wilhelm Roentgen and Sir Alexander Fleming were actually searching. You should spend more time reading and a little less on the bar stool at Sheehan's.'

'And you need to get out a little more,' Mike said, smiling at me as I got up to put more ice in my drink. 'You know, Mercer, come to think of it, there might be a better way – perfectly legal – to get DNA from Joe Berk.'

'You sound like a man with a plan.'

'I think, Detective Wallace, that what Coop needs is to take one for the team.'

'I *what*?'

'You should have seen the way that sleazebag was looking at her this afternoon. I'm telling you, Mercer, with very little effort and a little time on her back, she could wind up as the queen of Broadway. We'd kill two birds with one stone – get some valuable evidence from Joe Berk and improve Coop's disposition all at once.'

Mercer was Mike's best audience. He was glad to see

his grieving friend find humor in anything once again, happy that I was the target. 'Now don't go rejecting it out of hand, Alex. Taking one for the team has a nice ring to it.'

The doorman buzzed on the intercom to announce the food delivery.

'I'm about to wine and dine you with the best corned beef sandwich in town, and you're talking about farming me out to Joe Berk?'

'You mind if we eat in here so we can watch the game?' Mike asked, switching channels to the Yankees game. 'If Jeter or A-Rod asked her to take one for the team, Mercer, she'd have her clothes off before the question was out of their mouths.'

'Guess what? You'd do exactly the same thing for both of them, Mikey.'

I took the bag of food to the kitchen to plate the sandwiches. We ate in front of the television and then I went into my study to organize my presentation for the morning grand jury while the guys watched till we pulled out a victory in the bottom of the ninth.

The next morning, Wednesday, Mercer had Cara and Jean in my office at eight fifteen to prepare them for the testimony each would give separately to one of New York County's six daily grand juries, the groups of twenty-three citizens who were impaneled for a month to hear evidence and vote a true bill of indictment, if indicated, that would propel a felony charge on its way to trial. When the prep was done and the quorum was assembled in the ninth-floor jury room one flight above me, Mercer and I led our witnesses up to the waiting room.

I filled out the slip for the drug-facilitated-rape

charge, and was reminded by the warden that the jurors had not heard any other similar cases this month, which meant I would also have to instruct them on the law. Colleagues with grand larceny auto and commercial burglary cases let me jump the line, knowing my victims might be fragile and more nervous about testifying for the first time than those in less emotionally charged matters.

Jean was my first witness. She presented more straight-forwardly than Cara, and I stood behind the third tier of jurors in the amphitheatrically shaped room, next to the foreman, taking her through the events of the preceding week and pacing her so the stenographer could capture all the words of her narrative.

From my position in back, I could identify four or five skeptical citizens – those who turned their heads to look at me in puzzlement, those who leaned in to whisper to a neighbor in spite of directions not to, and one who just shook his head from side to side and stared off at the empty wall beside him rather than make eye contact with the victim.

It was not until the forensic toxicologist took the stand, reeled off her impressive qualifications, and then gave the results of her testing that most of the panel appeared to sit more upright in their seats.

'Are you familiar with the prescription drug called Xanax?'

'Yes, I am.'

'Would you tell the jury, please, what kind of drug it is?'

'Xanax is a benzodiazepine. That's within the class of pharmaceuticals known as sedative hypnotics.'

'What effect does a benzodiazepine have on the body?'

'These drugs work on the neurotransmitters in the brain to inhibit the body's ability to function. It's used to relieve anxiety, to help people sleep. It sedates them,' Dr Babij said, going on to describe the specific scientific function of the drugs.

'What is the effect of taking Xanax with alcohol?'

'It's contraindicated, Ms Cooper. They are both sedative hypnotics, and because they interact with each other, they will potentiate – shall I say, increase – each other's effects. The desired reaction – sedation of the patient – occurs faster, longer, and with more severe results.'

When Dr Babij reached the discussion of the dosage that had been added to Cara and Jean's drinks, she extrapolated from the trace residue found in their glasses. She went on to describe symptoms she'd expect to find in the patient – everything from the nausea, vomiting, gastrointestinal upset that the jurors had just heard about, to falling asleep, loss of memory, and the possibility that these depressants would cause cessation of breathing.

'Are there tests that can be performed, doctor, after these drugs have been ingested, to help determine the amount of benzodiazepine administered?'

'Yes, if the witness has presented herself to a hospital in a timely fashion. We can check the blood or the urine. The drug is broken down in the body by metabolites. Some of the drugs are so toxic that they're evacuated from the body very rapidly. In this instance, we can get a reading from the metabolites because the women were treated so promptly after they awakened.'

Dr Babij studied her reports before looking up at the jurors to explain the results to them. She recited milligrams and numbers that were meaningless without interpretation. Her punch line would assure me of an indictment within minutes of concluding my case.

'Jean Eaken ingested enough of the benzodiazepine, mixed with an ounce of alcohol,' she said, 'to sedate a two-ton racehorse for the better part of a week. In my opinion, that young woman is lucky to be alive.'

The toxicologist repeated her analysis on the testing of the second victim. As I excused her from the room and stepped down in front of the jurors, I could see a change in demeanor on most of their faces, some 'tsking' at the close call and others shaking their heads in disapproval of Sengor's conduct. Their whispers would turn to serious discussion after I read them the appropriate sections of the Penal Law.

Drug-facilitated-rape statutes – new legislation to catch up to new-and-improved designer drugs – addressed serious crimes with severe penalties. I went over each element of the crime – evidence I had proved beyond the standard required – and left them to take their vote. Seconds later, the foreman buzzed the warden, indicating the conclusion of their very brief deliberation. The warden went in to retrieve the jury slip, then showed me the bold check mark confirming a true bill of indictment against Selim Sengor.

Back at my desk I dialed Eric Ingels's number while Mercer and Maxine made arrangements to fly Jean and Cara home to Canada.

'Eric? It's Alexandra Cooper.'

'Change of heart?'

221

'Hardly. You told Moffett on Saturday that I had no reason to hold your client without tox results. Well, I got them last night, presented the case to the grand jury this morning, have my vote, and I'll be ready to file the indictment tomorrow. I'd like you to surrender your client to be arraigned then.'

'What's the rush? I handed in his passport to Moffett's clerk on Monday, and we're on for Friday anyway.'

I didn't need to tell him that I had been burned by defendants who were foreign nationals before. The odds were too good that Sengor might try to flee in the face of felony charges with mandatory state prison time, and Lucy DeVore was an example of how easy it was to obtain false identification of every type in Manhattan. 'Seems to me your man has nothing but time on his hands. He's suspended from his job, so there's really no reason we can't move this along.'

'You just want to get the case out of Moffett's part.'

'You're not wrong, but he won't be keeping it anyway, Eric. It's getting wheeled out as soon as it's arraigned.' The calendar judge would literally put the names of six other judges in an old round wooden box with a handle to spin it, and we'd be sent before the jurist who was randomly pulled out of the wheel for motions and trial. 'I can't do any worse.'

'And if I can't reach Sengor?' Eric asked.

'The hospital's got him phoning in twice a day. They beep him, he returns the call. If they can find him, I'm certain that you will, too, Eric. That way he can surrender like a gentleman. I'll give you that. Ten o'clock tomorrow. Part Thirty.'

'Worst-case scenario?'

222

'We do it the old-fashioned way. Handcuffs and head-lines.'

'I'll try to find him. I'll confirm it with your secretary later today.'

'Thanks, Eric.'

Laura had held a call on my second line. It was Bob Thaler, chief serologist at the medical examiner's office. 'I'm looking for Wallace. Is he with you?'

'Yeah. He'll be back in a few minutes. What's up?'

'Tell him we got a hit on that attempt on the dog-walker in Riverside Park.'

'Fantastic. What do you have on the perp?' Cold hits – matches made from crime-scene evidence to DNA profiles by a computer, even when the police have no leads on a suspect – had revolutionized the investigation of violent crimes. 'Convicted sex offender?'

'Convicted of nothing. He was a suspect in the rape-homicide of a woman whose body was found in Fort Tryon Park eight months ago, but she was so badly decomposed there was nothing to submit for comparison.'

'Who is he?' I asked.

'Ramon Carido. Dominican, originally. Hasn't been in the country too long – and he's here illegally. He's also homeless, so far as I know. Got plenty of blood off the teeth of the dog that bit him. Seeped right into his gums.'

'Way to go. So even though the poor dog may have licked his chops?'

'He could have tried to clean his teeth all night, Alex. We just rolled back his gums and I found a great little sample of the perp's blood.'

'My dental hygienist would be proud of you. How'd you get Ramon's DNA?'

'Special Victims and Homicide did their usual canvass. The last person who saw the victim alive, going into the park for a run, recognized Carido from the local soup kitchen. Said he was one of the guys lurking around the fringe of the park that morning. Mercer's name is on the evidence tag submitted. Must have convinced him to offer up a saliva sample.'

'So he's in the suspect database. And he's homeless.'

'Have Mercer call me. We've got to figure some way to move on this before Mr Carido feels the urge to take a walk in the park again.'

Mercer was as pleased by the news of the identification as I was. 'I liked him for it the first time. He's slick, Alex. Had no problem spitting on my Q-tip 'cause he knew there was nothing left of the victim's body. She was dumped in a remote area of the park in the middle of hurricane season for more than ten days before she was found. Picked clean by local vermin, and everything else washed away by the rain and wind. Carido might even have checked the spot regularly to admire his handiwork.'

'Does it bother you that the attacks occurred in such different parts of the city?'

'Not at all. He probably had to leave the 'hood in Washington Heights 'cause word on the street was that he offed the Tryon jogger. Moved south to what Mike likes to call the People's Republic of the Upper West Side. Homeless shelters, folks friendly to panhandlers and derelicts, and the same kind of victim population walking, running, and sunbathing in a convenient park. He's my man.'

'So how fast can we find him?'

'Let me call the squad. He ponied up with counsel when I brought him in for questioning last fall and I know I've got the name of a Legal Aid lawyer in my file. You finish up on Sengor's indictment and I'll work on finding Ramon.'

By two thirty in the afternoon Laura had completed the paperwork for the filing of the charges against Selim Sengor. We had ordered in lunch from the Thai restaurant on the corner and the white cardboard containers had grown cold and developed leaks while I waited for Mercer to come back from Maxine's office, where he was making the calls, with the information we needed.

'Ron Abramson,' he said when he finally returned. 'I just tried the nice way, but maybe you can talk some sense into him.'

'How much do we need his help?'

'All the way. We don't have a permanent address of any kind for Carido, there's no file with Immigration and Naturalization 'cause he came in under the radar, and there's no mug shot 'cause he wasn't arrested. You gonna issue an APB for a six-foot-two Hispanic with no distinctive features or scars, maybe facial hair this season or maybe not, last seen wearing blue jeans and a black T-shirt? I don't even know if Ramon Carido is his real name – that's what he gave us and that's what we're stuck with. Good luck, Alex.'

Ron and I had started in our respective offices the same year. He supervised a pod of attorneys who handled violent felony cases, and there was little reasoning with him when he entrenched himself in a position for one of their clients.

I dialed the Legal Aid number and pressed his extension. We started with pleasantries and the conversation deteriorated from there.

'It doesn't matter whether or not I have a way to get in touch with Mr Carido, and it matters less whether I know where he is,' Ron said. 'You get nothing from us.'

'Ron, we've got a confirmed hit identifying Carido in the Riverside Park case. Whether you help us or not, we're going after him. It would be nice to think that another woman would be spared the trauma of a sexual assault by bringing him in sooner rather than later. If he's got a story that makes sense, I'll listen to you. I'm working with Eric Ingels on another matter and we've made a deal for a surrender in a perfectly civilized way, which is the same thing I'm offering your client.'

'You even think about going after Carido on the cold hit you've got and I'll take you to court on it, Alex.'

'What are you talking about? Of course we're going to find him.'

'Want to meet in front of Colleen McFarland?' Ron asked. 'I can be there in fifteen minutes.'

He knew McFarland was one of my favorite judges. Before her appointment to the bench, she had been one of the first women partners in the litigation department of one of the best law firms in the city, and a protégée of Justin Feldman and Martin London, two giants of the New York bar.

'I don't get where you're going with this, Ron. I've got a known perp and I want to get him off the street as fast as possible.'

'Your match came from the wrong databank, Alex. My

guy's never been convicted of a crime and his profile should have been removed from the suspect database months ago. Before you try using that information to lock him up on this, I'll get a court order to stop you. I'm not kidding around – I'll have you jailed for contempt.'

Chapter 22

I phoned Mike on my cell as I paced the corridor outside Judge McFarland's courtroom, walking among the drug dealers and predators who were waiting for their afternoon calendar calls in the six felony parts lining the long corridor.

'You keeping busy?' he said to me.

'Next time I tell you that the thing I like most about my job is that no two days are the same, or that it's never dull, or that it isn't like the movies because time and all other new cases don't stand still for the prosecutor even though the big murder investigation she asked for has dropped into her lap, promise me you'll smack me.'

'My pleasure. Where are you?' Mike asked.

'About to start a hearing that I hadn't exactly factored into my day. And you?'

'At the Met. The guys on the task force are tearing through the employee interviews. They're breaking down into categories – workers with ironclad alibis who never left the stage or were in the company of two or more other witnesses throughout the entire show, and a second group that needs a harder once-over; they're loners and

228

oddballs or guys who didn't sign in or out Friday night. Third are the ones who make themselves potential witnesses – saw somebody they didn't know in a hallway or stairwell, think they spotted Galinova getting on the elevator with another person.'

'How big is your pool of possible suspects?'

'We can rule out almost three hundred workmen. Solid guys, all professionals at what they do. They're of no interest to us. Gives us another hundred to monkey with. The lieutenant wants me to do the callbacks. Go at the weirdos a little harder than the first crew.'

'Anything new on the forensics?'

'That glove we were talking about – they've been retesting the preliminary because of the two different profiles I told you about, from skin cells inside and out.' The scientific technology had advanced to the point that with ordinary handling, cells would slough off and leave a genetic profile on almost any item of clothing that came in contact with skin. 'The one on the outer palm doesn't match the one on the interior. Thaler gave this assignment to Dr Bauman to work on, so he's got us swabbing all the first responders – cops and detectives.'

'That'll add a few days,' I said.

'Yeah, we've got to start by eliminating the first cop who picked up all the items. And every third-grader and boss who came along after that probably handled them. The DNA could come from the killer, of course, but it could also have been left there by anyone who held on to the gloves recently.'

I was trying to resign myself to the long timeline dictated by the laboratory work that needed to be done.

229

'Ten years ago, the first time you used DNA, how long till you got a result?' Mike asked.

'Two months, maybe three.'

'Yeah? Well, my first homicide had a six-month turn-around before we had even a preliminary profile, and you still had to fight the court to introduce it into evidence as a valid scientific result. Remember those days? Now we're impatient if we can't get a hit in forty-eight hours. We'll get it done, Coop. Mercer around?'

'Sitting in the courtroom, waiting for the fireworks to start. We're up here on that case of his from the weekend, in Riverside Park. I'll explain later.'

'Maybe we can meet up for dinner. Tell Mercer to bring the pooch that bit that asshole – I'd like to buy him a cocktail.'

Ron Abramson turned the corner from the elevator bank and held open the door for me. 'You want to settle this the easy way, before we go in?'

'Sure. You give us Mr Carido and we'll talk deals.'

'Not happening. I was hoping you'd see the error of your ways. I guess you've got no weekend plans, Alex. The Women's House of Detention can be a rough place to visit,' he said, smiling at me as we continued on to talk to the court clerk.

'Three hots and a cot, Ron. I've got very simple needs.'

He wagged a finger at me. 'No minibar. You'll be sorry.'

Colleen McFarland frowned when she saw us walk into the courtroom together. She looked at the remaining case names on her calendar and all seemed to be accounted for. 'New business, Ms Cooper, Mr Abramson?'

Ron pushed through into the well and let the swinging wooden gate slam back against my lower body. 'Yes, your honor. I've got an application to make. It's a matter of first impression and I'd like a ruling before Ms Cooper rushes ahead and winds up with some bad law.'

'Okay, let's add it to the calendar, shall we?' McFarland said, rising from the large armchair on the bench and directing the court reporter to take down the proceedings. 'Have you got a docket number?'

'No. There's no case yet, your honor, and that's the way I'd like to keep it. It's in regard to a Legal Aid Society client named Ramon Carido.'

'Who's going to start here? One of you want to give me some facts?'

Ron pointed to me and allowed me to describe the details of the attack, the subsequent investigation, and the serologist's cold hit.

'What's your problem with Ms Cooper's plan?' McFarland was smart and thoughtful, an attractive woman with wavy red hair and ice blue eyes that looked like they could cut through steel as easily as legal bullshit. Ron wouldn't have chosen to bring this issue before her without confidence in his position because she wouldn't hesitate to use her acumen to put him in line. And despite my friendship with her, she would be just as likely to rule against me and make no apologies for the decision the next time we went to Forlini's for lunch.

'There are two different databases involved, judge. May I distinguish for you?'

'I think I'm familiar with them, Mr Abramson, but I'll let you make your record.'

'The New York City Generalized DNA Index System is a forensic DNA database authorized under Article 49B of the New York State Executive Law. The legislature strictly limited the circumstances under which the State is entitled to collect, to preserve, and to disclose an individual's DNA records. It limits the genetic profiles to be maintained in the database *only* to people who have been convicted of specifically designated felony crimes.'

'That's the convicted offender database, then?'

'Yes, judge. But that's not where Ms Cooper alleges the match to my client was made. He's not a convicted offender. His profile isn't in that pool.'

'Tell me about that.'

'The medical examiner's office maintains another DNA system.'

McFarland was taking notes. 'What's that one called?'

'It's the linkage database, your honor. It's what you might refer to as a "usual suspect" or "suspect elimination" base. It's got everything from arrestees who've never been convicted of anything to bystanders at a crime scene who get caught up in a sweep.'

'By that you mean that biological samples are submitted to this second bank during investigations – by some lawful authorization, either by court order or voluntarily or—'

'Nobody gives DNA voluntarily,' Ron said dismissively. 'There's always an element of coercion when the police ask a person to give them a sample of their blood or saliva. Nobody wants to give their DNA to the government.'

'That's absurd, your honor,' I said, standing to address McFarland. 'It happens every day without police coercion. Thousands of people all over the country volunteer to submit samples to exclude themselves during investigations of violent crime, to help the police in

232

homicides or assaults involving family and friends, strangers who—'

She motioned me to sit down. 'You'll have an opportunity to respond, Ms Cooper.'

'Thank you, judge. I envy you, on behalf of all my colleagues at Legal Aid. At least one of us has the power to quiet my adversary with the wave of a hand. May I go on?'

'Certainly, Mr Abramson.'

'There is absolutely no legal authority for the existence of these records in the linkage database. Ms Cooper's efforts to use Mr Carido's profile – which should have been expunged from that computer system months ago – violates his Fourth Amendment freedom from unreasonable search and seizure and his Fourteenth Amendment right of bodily autonomy and informational privacy.'

And clearly violates what Mike liked to call Ron Abramson's Twenty-sixth Amendment right to be a pompous ass.

'I take it that Mr Carido was a suspect in some investigation or other several months back, is that right?'

'Yes, judge. But never charged.'

'With murder,' I said from my seat. 'He's still a suspect in an unsolved murder. We're not talking about a minor crime with a statute of limitations. We're talking about a rape-homicide that's still an open case.'

McFarland gave me her sternest look. 'You'll get your chance, Alex. Mr Abramson, were you Mr Carido's lawyer in that matter?'

'No, ma'am. One of the young women I supervised was the attorney of record.'

'And did she make a motion to expunge Carido's profile from the database?'

I shook my head in the negative while Abramson searched his file.

'Did she?'

'I'm looking, your honor. I can't find any record of that. But beyond that point, the legislature only authorizes disclosure of the DNA match in the particular criminal proceeding for which the biological sample was obtained. The prosecution wants to turn that legal provision on its head and open the floodgates, keep all the exclusionary samples and just test them whenever it strikes their fancy.'

Abramson was circling his arms in the air for emphasis now, looking more like someone doing the backstroke than an attorney making a argument in a court of law.

'So your concern here, if I understand you—'

'Is my client's privacy rights, Judge McFarland. Ramon Carido's DNA profile contains an extraordinary amount of personal information about him. It carries the entire physical component of his being, and this unregulated and discretionary attempt to use it by Ms Cooper and the NYPD is completely improper and inappropriate.'

'Are you done, Mr Abramson?'

Ron did the obligatory one-hundred-eighty-degree scoping of the courtroom before he sat down at counsel table, hoping that someone other than the three remaining-to-be-sentenced perps had witnessed his Clarence Darrow moment. 'Yes, your honor.'

'I'll hear you on this, Ms Cooper.'

'Thank you. Just to make this clear at the outset, judge, Mr Carido voluntarily provided the DNA sample at issue

234

here. At no point in the earlier investigation did he assert any claim that the preparation of the swab violated his constitutional rights.'

Abramson stared at the mural behind McFarland's head.

'The use of a linkage database is an essential part of the investigative process that begins when evidence is submitted by local police for DNA analysis. In almost every matter in which the identity of the perpetrator is unknown to witnesses or detectives, the attempt to gather biological samples for comparison – and significantly for exclusion – is as critical a step as trying to compare the material to that of convicted offenders.'

'How about the privacy issue?'

'Neither the police nor FBI nor prosecutors have access to the linkage database. It's the tool the serologists use to try to match evidence to unknown assailants. There's no dissemination of information to law enforcement agencies unless or until there's a hit.'

'Why don't you address Mr Abramson's argument about Carido's DNA profile? Is your point that once he gave his sample to the police, it remains in the database indefinitely?'

'I don't have to go that far, judge. The matter in which Carido gave a buccal swab is still an active and open investigation. He hasn't been excluded as a suspect. The fact is that the homicide investigation is the kind of case which will apparently not be resolved by this kind of forensic analysis because of the condition of the deceased's body, but there's no statute of limitations and the police are still optimistic they'll find the killer.'

The judge looked back and forth between us. I went

235

on. 'In fact, I don't think Mr Abramson can have it both ways. If he believes that the original homicide is a closed case, then Legal Aid no longer represents Ramon Carido. He's got no standing to make this motion.'

'I'm telling the court we're going to be Carido's counsel going forward for all purposes,' Abramson said.

McFarland was focused on the facts of the homicide. 'Well, if you don't need Carido's DNA to prove that original crime, why shouldn't I grant Mr Abramson's request?'

'There has been no motion by Legal Aid to expunge Carido's profile from the linkage database since the date it was entered. They've had months to take that step and failed to do so. Now you've got a confirmed match to a violent felony that he committed and the police are supposed to pretend it never happened? We have identified a predator who's clearly a danger to society and we have probable cause to arrest Ramon Carido, with or without the cooperation of Mr Abramson.'

'Have you got any law for me?' McFarland asked.

Abramson was back on his feet. 'There's a Kings County case, your honor. Carlos Rodriguez. I'll give you the cite.'

The old Brooklyn decision wouldn't be binding on McFarland, and she would welcome the chance to make new law. 'That's entirely distinguishable from the instant matter, judge,' I said. 'The victim and offender were known to each other. The issue of his identity and the DNA evidence were completely irrelevant to the investigation.'

'Did it go up?' she asked, referring to the Court of Appeals in Albany.

'No.' Thankfully not, I almost added. The decision in

236

the Kings County case was such a bad one for the prosecution – disallowing the use of the suspect's DNA profile – that the prosecutors wisely had never appealed to the higher court. 'But there are two other matters which raise similar issues that I'd like to submit to you.'

'Hand them to the clerk, Ms Cooper.'

'I didn't have time to pull them before I came up here.' McFarland seemed annoyed. 'You know the cases?'

'One is Waldemar – it's a Bronx decision. I can't recall the name of the other one.'

'Never mind. I'll find them.'

I had been more anxious to cut Abramson off before he stopped us from going after Carido than carefully marshaling the support for my position to present to the judge when we got here. If I had given McFarland the ammunition she needed to make an immediate ruling, it might have gone in my favor at that point.

'I'm going to put this over for a week,' McFarland said.

Abramson wasn't any happier than I was. This judge was never equivocal, and I assumed the adjournment was so that she could write an opinion on this still-evolving area of the law.

'In all fairness to my client, your honor, you're creating a much more dangerous situation for him. If there's going to be a manhunt, it always raises the possibility that the police will stage a confrontation with—'

McFarland poked at her sternum with her forefinger. '*I'm* creating the dangerous situation? I hardly think so. Quite frankly, Mr Abramson, I'm going to deny the motion in regard to your client, and I'm going to do that right now, from the bench. You can't expect the police to put the genie back in the bottle, can you? Since there was never an objection to the taking of a biological sample from Mr Carido, and since there was no request by your colleague to expunge that profile from the database, I'm going to deny your motion and allow the police to go forward with their investigation.'

'Most respectfully, your honor, then why bother with the adjournment?' he asked.

'Most respectfully, Mr Abramson, I'd suggest you let me finish my statement,' McFarland said. 'I think it's necessary to weigh the harm that could be done by allowing Mr Carido to remain at large. Your complaint is about the propriety of his profile in the databank, not about the validity of the DNA match, am I right?'

'Yes, but—'

'Balancing the potential harm to the public against that which your client might suffer, I'd have to come down in favor of using the biological evidence to charge him, sooner rather than later. He'll have his day in court.'

'And the adjournment?'

'The remedy you requested was rather extreme in this particular case, don't you think? But you raise some important concerns about how the linkage database is used now, how it will be used in the future, and about whether there is any appropriate mechanism in place for expunging a sample if it doesn't belong there any longer. I'd like to do some research on this, read the cases you've both mentioned. Perhaps you'd each like to submit briefs in support of your positions? That's why I'm giving you the weekend.'

I wanted to brief the matter this weekend like I wanted to empty Joe Berk's bedpan.

'And Miss Cooper,' McFarland said, 'I think what I'd

like to do is direct you to call the medical examiner's office. Tell the serologists that there are to be no further disclosures of any matches within the linkage database to anyone except known offenders for the next week or ten days – either to your office or the NYPD – until I hand down my decision. Nothing divulged concerning suspects who've been exonerated or from the so-called voluntary samples.'

'But, your honor,' I said, starting to protest before McFarland cut me off.

'Let's go off the record for a minute,' she said, pointing to the court reporter as she pushed up the large sleeve of her black robe with the other hand. 'Look, Alex, before you go crazy over this issue, how many cases are we talking about?'

'In a week's time, citywide? Maybe thirty, maybe a hundred.'

'That's submissions of evidence to the database, right?'

'Yes.'

'And hits? You're probably lucky to get five from the linkage database.'

'You're right, judge. Some weeks two, some none. Five would be a gift.'

'So don't make a stink. Get Ramon Carido off the street for the time being and let's slow this down so I can look at the bigger picture.'

'Give me two weeks, then, judge,' Abramson said. 'I want to consult with the other supervisors. We'd like to submit papers on this.'

Abramson and I were both trying to figure out what this meant for him. McFarland was not a Solomonic judge

– she rarely split the baby. She wasn't afraid to take a firm position, no matter how controversial, if she could ground it in the law. She was giving me a go at Carido this afternoon, but she might be doing Abramson a favor in the long run.

'We're back on the record. Miss Cooper, two weeks from today, ten a.m.?'

'Yes, your honor.'

Mercer walked me down the aisle and out of the courtroom. 'Where's she going on this? What do you think?'

'Call DCPI and get your press release out. I have no idea where she'll wind up, but at least we can get this psycho off the street now.' The deputy commissioner of Public Information could issue a release with a description of the attacker, and police could begin to sweep the parks and homeless shelters for Ramon Carido. 'And I'm going to have to find someone from the Appeals Bureau to help me out with a brief on this.'

'Hey, Alex,' Ron Abramson said, tugging at my elbow. 'You free after work for a drink?'

'Now that I don't have to pack my bags to go to Rikers, I guess I've got time to kill. I just don't think I'm in the mood.'

'Look, I had to do what I had to do. All my lawyers are unsettled about these databank rules, and I figured this was a good chance to get some guidelines. Got your attention, didn't I?'

'Another time, Ron.'

Mercer pressed for the down elevator and Abramson headed upstairs.

Laura got up from her desk and followed us into my

office. 'Eric Ingels called you. Says it's urgent.' She thrust the phone message with his number into my hand.

I dialed and he answered himself. 'Alex, I've got a problem with Dr Sengor.'

I flopped onto my chair. 'Like what?'

'Like he's not coming in. He won't surrender.'

'That's just another factor for the judge to consider when I ask for bail.' I was too tired and frustrated to worry about the extra day until his scheduled court appearance, pleased that the hospital was keeping him on a short leash by requiring him to check in twice daily.

'He wants to talk to you.'

'Who does?'

'My client. Dr Sengor.'

'Sengor wants to make a statement?' I shrugged my shoulders and looked at Mercer, repeating Ingels's comments so Mercer could understand what was going on.

'Not exactly. He swears he didn't commit a crime. He wants to talk to you.'

'You're going to let him?'

'I'd like to patch him in when he calls back. He's been phoning every fifteen minutes or so, waiting for you to come back from court.'

'Is he home? We can just set it up from my end,' I said.

'No, he tells me he's not. The apartment was hospital housing. He claims they don't want him living there during his suspension.'

'Fine. I'll be at my desk. Have him call my secretary on the hour. She'll hook you in on a conference line.'

I hung up and put Mercer to work. 'Let's get TARU

on this. How fast can they set up a triangulated phone call?'

The Technical Assistance Resource Unit was the NYPD's small crew of wizards who used state-of-the-art equipment to do everything from video surveillance to wiretaps and intercepts.

'Five minutes, with a bit of luck. I'll get that going if you give me Ingels's number. When Sengor dials in, you check caller ID and I'll run with that, too. And get someone from the DA's Squad down here to hook a recorder onto your phone. You'll want a tape of whatever he says.'

I called the squad commander, whose office was directly above mine, and then stepped out of the way five minutes later so that Vito Taurino, a detective I had worked with often over the years, could attach a device to the telephone receiver that fed a minirecorder. As long as one party to a conversation consents for a call to be recorded, the law in New York allowed me to surreptitiously tape the incoming call.

I dated and timed the header of the recording, sent Laura down the hall so that Mercer could use her console to stay in touch with TARU, and settled in to wait for the phone to ring. While Sengor and I spoke, detectives would be trying to identify his location by reading signals from cell satellite towers. If he stayed on the phone for ninety seconds, they would know the very street corner on which he stood.

'They're ready for you,' Mercer said. 'You're good to go.'

'Give me a heads-up when TARU tells you they've made him.'

Laura buzzed me from down the hall to tell me that Sengor had called on my line, and that she had patched Eric Ingels into the call.

'Dr Sengor wants to talk to you, Alex. Doctor? Can you hear me? Ms Cooper's on the line.'

The connection was bad. The crackling noise of the static made it hard to hear Sengor when he said hello to me. There was no need to recite Miranda warnings. The doctor wasn't in custody and his attorney had requested the opportunity for him to talk.

'You're making a very big mistake, Ms Cooper. I did not rape these women,' he said, barking each word into the receiver for emphasis. 'You have ruined my life, I want you to know that.'

I wasn't the one slipping mickeys into the drinks of unsuspecting women and then having sex with them while they were unconscious, but that never stopped a perp from blaming me for his problems. 'Doctor, is there—'

'I have lost my job, I've lost my home, I've lost my girlfriend, for what? What did I do? For what crime? You can't put my name in the newspaper just for your own career, for your own ambitions. It's *my* life you're ruining.'

'Eric, if your client is calling just to harangue me about the case, there's absolutely no point to this conversation.'

'Hold on, Alex, hold on. Selim? Can you hear me? Explain to Ms Cooper what you told me, explain how the girls were doing drugs before you got home,' Eric said. 'He wants to tell you what really happened.'

I looked at the second hand on my watch as Mercer stood in the doorway, holding the cell phone while he waited for results from the TARU detectives. I mouthed a question to him. 'How much longer?'

'They're not getting a signal. Be patient.'

'Miss Cooper? Are you listening to me? You know what would happen to my family in Turkey if this is public? Terrible disgrace. Disgrace to my mother, to my father – who is also a doctor. And what? Because of the word of these two silly girls? I'm asking you as a professional to drop this case. I've withdrawn from the hospital, no one was hurt, and if you don't prosecute, I'll be able to keep my license to practice medicine.'

Sengor hit the right button. A license to an endless supply of drugs to experiment on his victims. It wasn't a gift I was prepared to put in his hands. He rambled on and on, while I looked to Mercer for word of any results. We were going on four minutes and TARU had come up blank.

'Talk to your lawyer, Dr Sengor. There's no reason to go on with this conversation. You can explain whatever you'd like to the judge and jury.'

The call was terminated after six minutes and I hung up the receiver. Mercer was still on the cell phone, trying to get an explanation from the tech team.

'Did they have the right number?' I asked, checking the 212 area code and seven digits that I had taken down from caller ID against the ones on Mercer's pad. 'How come this works on TV and in the movies, but when I need it, the system fails?'

'They had everything right. They were scrambling like crazy trying to find the cell tower. The only problem is that your boy Sengor was calling from out of the zone – that's why TARU couldn't pinpoint his whereabouts.'

'What zone? What do you mean, "the zone"?'

244

'Sengor's calling from his father's home, Alex, in the old country. Bet you didn't know the area code in Ankara, Turkey, is also 212.'

Chapter 23

Within the hour, Mercer Wallace and a backup team from Special Victims were at Selim Sengor's high-rise building, a hospital-owned residence on the Upper West Side. While I waited for him to get back to me with news of when the young doctor had abandoned his home, I called the hospital's general counsel, who'd been monitoring him since his weekend suspension.

'You're telling me you had no idea Sengor fled the country?' I asked.

'I'm shocked, truly. We were beeping him two or three times a day, and ten minutes later he'd return the calls. I talked to him myself just this morning.'

'I've got detectives on the way to the apartment. I expect there are documents or papers left behind. Things that might help us track his flight route, maybe computer records. He'll be on the run.'

'I feel so embarrassed about this, Alex. You don't need to waste time with a warrant. We'll consent to letting you in. It's hospital property – I'll send someone from my office over to meet the detectives right now.'

'That would be a help. I think they're interviewing the super and doormen first.'

It was after five o'clock when Mercer called back. 'We got another collar.'

'A new case?'

'Nope. One of our perp's buddies. Seems Sengor skipped out of town over the weekend. Drove to Boston, flew out of Logan to London and then home. You're probably right about the phony passport. This other guy is also a psychiatric resident – maybe there's something in the water in that department. Dr Alkit's his name. Sengor gave Alkit his hospital beeper and the keys to the apartment.'

'So every time Sengor was beeped to check in . . .' I said.

'You got it. Alkit called him in Turkey, and he phoned the general counsel to report back, so they kept up the ruse that he was still in town. Sengor apparently figures that if he isn't here in the country, you can't go forward with the prosecution and there won't be any press. He thinks the Turkish authorities won't find out about the charges and he can keep his license to practice medicine over there. Guess he's never heard of Interpol.'

'Where'd you find this guy Alkit?'

'Your man in the counsel's office sent over an assistant to authorize us to go into Sengor's apartment. Dr Alkit was already in the bedroom, boxing up some of his buddy's things. Next to the door, packed and ready to go, was a carton of videos.'

'Videos? What do you mean?'

'Home movies, Alex. Videotapes that Dr Sengor made.'

'Porn?'

'Worse than that. Sengor had a camera concealed in the bookcase opposite one of the beds in his room. Just

247

ordinary video equipment propped up between two medical reference books. That's what Dr Alkit was dismantling when we arrived. I opened it up and whipped the tape into his VCR. Sengor recorded himself having intercourse with Jean Eaken.'

'Oh, that poor woman. What does—'

'She looks lifeless. She's out cold, never moves a muscle. It's hard to watch, Alex. It's like, like—'

'I've seen it before, Mercer. Like he's raping a corpse.'

'Exactly. I'm taking the box of tapes, too. Thirty-nine of them. Each one dated and labeled, some filmed here, some in Turkey. You can tell those from the background shot and even the music playing on the radio. If they're all the same kind of thing, you'll wind up with a lot more victims.'

'And Dr Alkit? What are you charging him with?'

'Criminal facilitation – aiding and abetting Selim Sengor in fleeing the country,' Mercer said. The bail-jump violation applied even to defendants who had been released on their own recognizance, like Sengor. 'Tampering with evidence. This tape puts your doctor behind bars and locks the door for a long time. Alkit's blubbering like a baby. Just trying to help his friend. For some strange reason he feels these encounters wouldn't be crimes back home in Turkey.'

'They wouldn't be crimes because if anybody knew about them, Dr Sengor would be short his private parts. I'd better tell the district attorney what to expect. Call me when you get to the precinct.'

'Will do. I want to check a few of the other tapes, see if they're similar.'

'Be sure and have them duplicated first. I don't want

248

the originals compromised.' The best evidence would require working from copies of these tapes, so that stopping the footage, rewinding, zooming in for close-ups, and all the other wear and tear wouldn't damage the first-hand evidence of criminal conduct.

I called Rose Malone, Battaglia's assistant, and told her I needed to see him before the end of the day.

'Be here in fifteen minutes. He'll be finishing up with the asset forfeiture unit by then.'

'What kind of mood will that leave him in?'

Rose had been the executive assistant longer than anyone could remember and the best barometer of the district attorney's disposition from moment to moment. 'Right where you want him. The unit broke up a drug gang and we get to keep about one point two million dollars that was seized in the bust for our budget. He'll be smiling, no matter what you have to tell him.'

On the way into the executive wing, I stopped by the Appeals Bureau to ask for assistance on briefing the DNA database issue, as well as to check our extradition treaty with the Turkish government. It didn't pay to engage with Battaglia unless one was fully prepared with answers to the questions he was bound to ask. I was gossiping with Rose about the latest office romances, always fertile ground in a little legal village with a population of six hundred lawyers – most under the age of thirty-five – a support staff of many more hundreds, and the regular presence of thousands of New York's finest under the same roof every day.

As the head of Asset Forfeiture walked out of Battaglia's suite, he was smoking one of the DA's cigars and blowing smoke rings in my face. 'My first Cohiba, Alex. Amazing what a million bucks can do for my career. He told me to send you in.'

Battaglia didn't move the cigar stub from the center of his mouth. 'I hope you're not about to spoil my afternoon. It's been a banner day up until now.'

'Then I'll start with the good news. There's a DNA hit on the Riverside Park rapist.'

'What'd the *Post* call it? Canine Cop Caper?'

'That's the one. The suspect has been identified and DCPI is going to put out a release with a sketch tonight. He's homeless, so it may take a few days to come up with him, but they're optimistic.'

'Let me know the minute they get anything.'

'Of course. Paul, I think you need to know that this case has raised an issue about using the DNA linkage database. McFarland's going to hold my feet to the fire while I try to set a decent precedent for us,' I said, taking the risk that I was better off warning Battaglia that there was the potential for trouble, even if I didn't give him the whole blueprint yet. 'I'm going to ask the guys in Appeals for some help.'

'So what's the bad news?'

'The drug-facilitated-rape case with the physician and the two Canadian women? I filed the indictment today,' I said, as I steadied myself for the district attorney's response to my report. 'But Sengor's already fled the country. He flew home to Turkey.'

Battaglia dropped his feet from the desk and actually took the cigar out of his mouth.

'How'd you let the guy get away? I can't believe you did that. It looks awful for us.'

'I asked for substantial bail, Paul. Moffett bought into

the fact that he was a doctor with roots in the community and let him out.'

'Roots, my ass. Any chance of getting him back?'

'The treaty allows extradition for murder and rape, but the State Department liaison just told me there's never once been a return of a Turkish national. They'll send back Americans or other Europeans, but they won't give up one of their own. Sengor was on the phone from Ankara telling me he didn't even commit a crime.'

'You don't think it'll get press, do you?' Battaglia seemed as anxious to keep it out of the headlines now as the defendant did.

'More ink than you'll want, I'm afraid. The commissioner's going to take the case to Interpol, boss. He's going to ask them to issue a red notice on this.' The international notice system would rely on my indictment to try to arrest Selim Sengor with a view to encouraging the Turks to let us extradite.

'Damn it.'

'It gets worse. Mercer just seized a video collection from the perp's apartment. We're probably talking multiple victims – maybe dozens, here and abroad. Seems he drugged and raped them, recording the entire encounter with a camera hidden in his bookcase.'

Battaglia spun his chair around away from me, pretending to fiddle with documents on the table behind his desk. He liked the success of my unit's innovative prosecution tactics, but he hated discussing the details of bizarre sexual habits. 'Now what the – what the hell is that all about?'

'Paraphilia.'

'Para what?'

251

'Dr Sengor's a paraphiliac, if I had to guess from the box of tapes Mercer just picked up. As Mike likes to say, it's Latin for "sick puppy". It's one of the categories of sexual dysfunction in the *DSM*,' I said, referring to forensic psychiatry's bible, the *Diagnostic and Statistical Manual of Mental Disorders*. 'The guy acts out his deviant fantasies with unwilling victims. What gets him aroused is doing things he wouldn't be able to do to a conscious partner, like maybe anal intercourse or – well, we'll know as soon as we watch the videotapes.'

'But why put it on film?' Battaglia asked, still with his back to me.

'To create a masturbatory scenario, a way to reenact the events to stimulate himself when the night is over. To keep a trophy of the event.' Great. I'm talking dirty to the most powerful prosecutor in the country and he's pretending to be shuffling folders on his desk, looking for an irrelevant piece of paper that doesn't even exist. 'These guys lead double lives, Paul. Sengor's a licensed professional in a well-respected field, but he's obviously got a fantasy about necrophilia.'

'So how come he says he didn't do anything wrong?' Battaglia said, holding up a file from the bottom of a tall stack of yellowed papers and staring at a page of statistical information that was at least two years old. Anything to avoid eye contact with me in the middle of this discussion.

'Rapists who drug their victims don't see themselves as criminals. The women are with them by choice, the pills aren't administered by force – even though the victims aren't aware they're drinking the substance – their clothes aren't torn off them, and they're rarely injured.

252

It's delusional on Sengor's part, but that's the nature of this kind of assault.'

'Anything else on this?'

'Not for now.'

He wheeled his chair around to face me. 'Meanwhile, what's the progress on the case at the Met? The press is killing us on this. There are front-page stories every day.'

Like most high-profile crimes, Natalya Galinova's murder spawned a related series of features. There was a retelling of the dramatic death onstage at the Old Met of the great baritone, Leonard Warren, in 1960, as someone in the packed audience screamed out to the paralyzed cast and crew, 'For God's sake, bring down the curtain!'; interviews with suburban teachers and parents who worried about sending their children on Lincoln Center tours because the killer was still at-large in the neighborhood; and countless profiles of Galinova quoting the great, world-famous men who had partnered her or the other primas with whom she had shared a stage.

There was even a sidebar by Mickey Diamond, who had covered the first murder at the Met. Running out of fresh leads to keep the current frenzy on the front pages, Diamond revealed that the only time the *Post* had ever rejected one of his tasteless headlines was in that earlier case, when he submitted his story with a title captioned *Fiddler Off the Roof.*

'Lieutenant Peterson's got everybody working double shifts, Paul. You know how methodical he is.'

'I've got a black-tie dinner at the Pierre Hotel Saturday night for some committee my wife's on – I can't remember which disease. Odds are that somebody or other from the Lincoln Center board will be there. You've got to give me something to say about the progress of the investigation.'

'You'll have whatever I know by then.'

Prominent people tried to treat the DA as their private attorney. Church leaders called to press for leniency when parishioners were caught up in white-collar crimes, parents of elite prep school students urged the hush-up of teachers arrested in Internet pedophile stings, and well-to-do investment bankers promised treatment programs for offspring netted in campus drug sweeps. Battaglia had developed an enviable immunity to all the pressure, and settled for being in the know about every detail of a case before muscle was applied by outsiders.

'Alex,' Battaglia said as I started to get up to leave, 'those television monitors that were in Joe Berk's apartment. The commissioner told me about them, even though you saw fit to leave me in the dark. You ever find out what they were filming?'

'We didn't have any way to run with that, Paul. Especially once they disappeared. I just don't know what he could have been watching.'

'Have you talked to the tech guys about it?'

'Yes, of course. They're on standby to give us a hand. But first we have to know exactly where the cameras were concealed – I mean, in what building – and what Berk was looking at. We never got there.'

'I'm just wondering whether he could be a – a—' He stopped himself midsentence, not even wanting to say the word.

'A paraphiliac?'

I thought about the interiors Mike and I had seen on the screens in the brief moments before Mona Berk had interrupted us. 'Possible. Voyeurism's a form of paraphilia. Peeping, watching someone disrobe or engage in a sexual act. Depends where he had those cameras positioned. We thought it looked like dressing rooms or bathrooms, maybe in some of the Berk theaters.'

'So why didn't you follow up?'

'It didn't seem to have anything to do with Galinova's murder, Paul. The cops went over her dressing room with every piece of equipment they had. There were no cameras concealed there, at the Met.'

'Let me know if you come up with any dirt on old Joe,' Battaglia said, smiling as he chewed on the wet tip of his cigar. 'I'd love to have it in my arsenal.'

I could see where he was going now. He wasn't suggesting that Berk was involved in Talya's death. In Battaglia's world of power and privilege, it would be a useful chit to know that Berk had a personal point of vulnerability, something he might someday trade for information of value in another case.

'Sure, Paul. When I was in here on Monday, you mentioned that you had a lot of background on Berk. That you thought he'd been involved in some kind of illegal tax schemes.'

Again he removed the cigar from his mouth. 'Yeah.'

'He told Mike and me there's a messy lawsuit going on. His niece wouldn't let us get into the details at all. Do you know anything about it? Maybe it would give us a broader family picture if I understood it, now that we've also got this incident with the girl who fell from the swing.'

'You talk to her yet?'

'She's in what the doctors call a controlled coma. One

that they've medically induced. They don't want her to wake up till they've got the pain management under control. Then they'll assess the brain damage.'

What Battaglia didn't like discussing about sex, he more than made up for when the subject was financial fraud.

'Don't run off, Alex. He's quite a character. You have any idea what Joe Berk is worth today?'

'Not a clue.'

'He makes the rest of the Fortune 500 look like amateurs. I'd say he and his brother built themselves an empire worth twenty-five billion dollars. Real estate, theatrical properties, airplane leasing, almost as many hotels as Hyatt and Hilton combined. It's a phenomenal operation.'

'Why did you start an investigation of the Berk Organization, boss?'

'Somebody snitched – brought me in some good information.'

'About Joe?'

'Joe and his brother, Izzy, they were inseparable. Izzy was the real brains of the family, plus he didn't have Joe's big mouth. They shared one common trait.'

'What's that?'

'They hated the taxman. I'm not talking about shipping your purchases to an out-of-state address or minor scams like that. Izzy Berkowitz might be the shrewdest guy who ever took on the feds, back when the two of them started making money, more than forty years ago. He was doing leveraged buyouts in the 1940s, before anyone ever heard of them. Izzy had more money hidden offshore than Captain Kidd.'

'Legally?'

'That's the issue. What do you know about 1740 Trusts?'

Ask me anything about the variety of deviant acts that comprised section 130 of the Penal Law and I could cite chapter and verse as well as draw diagrams, but this was as foreign to me as Swahili.

'Never heard of them. 1740 – the year?'

'No, 1740 of the IRS trust and estate provisions. In the 1960s, Congress passed a set of laws that basically ended the tax benefits of foreign trusts for residents of the US. To get around the legislation, Izzy dreamed up a scheme that he got going down in the Bahamas. As long as he could prove to Uncle Sam that a foreign citizen actually set up the trust and kept a legal presence in the islands, he wasn't subject to US taxes. Izzy found some friendly local, put him in business, and used the millions generated in cash from that general partnership to lend it to the other Berk Organization trusts and companies.'

'That works with the IRS? The feds bought into it?'

'They did originally, but not anymore. By then the Berks were grandfathered in by the government when the law changed a decade ago. I went into it to try to break the damn thing up but ran into a stone wall,' Battaglia said, plugging the cigar back into the corner of his mouth. 'As long as the income is loaned to other Berk ventures or reinvested – get it? As long as Joe doesn't distribute the money to himself or his heirs – he sits pretty on top of his billions. No taxes, no obligation to even tell the IRS what's in the trusts.'

'Quite an arrangement.'

'I guess Joe's got the same idea as Izzy had. The Berk family plan is to die broke.'

'Broke? You've lost me. None of them is broke.'

'On the estate tax return, Alex. Izzy's heirs claimed he was only worth twenty thousand at the time of his death. That's what got me into the matter to begin with. The feds grabbed it from me – they always take the easy ones – but they made a really bad deal. They let Joe call his own terms.'

'Why?'

'If I knew the answer to that, I wouldn't have lost jurisdiction of the case. Joe paid ten million to settle the tax claims, and the IRS agreed never again to tax any of the Berks' oldest offshore trusts. Never.'

'Sweet deal. That's why there's no way of knowing how much money is actually at stake here.'

'And that's why Izzy valued the family's privacy so much. He hated Joe's flapping mouth.'

'It can't make Joe very happy that now there's a lawsuit within the family. It's bound to make some of this stuff public,' I said.

'Why do you think I'm watching the suit so carefully?' Battaglia hated to lose. If he could find a way back into an investigation that so obviously intrigued him, he'd be looking for the first crack in the door through which to insert his toe. 'The two youngest kids – Izzy's daughter and Joe's son. They're the ones suing.'

'So that would be Mona Berk – Izzy's girl. And her cousin, Briggs. Suing who?'

'Joe Berk.'

'Why, exactly?'

'Greed. Entitlement. Revenge. Pick your vice. Joe and Izzy built an empire in a single generation. The whole point was to pass it along intact to their heirs, blanketing the family in this curtain of confidential dealings.'

'What changed that?'

'After Izzy's death, Joe quietly started restructuring a few of the trusts. His older kids, and Izzy's, wanted some of the stock and cash transferred.'

'But who suffered? I mean, how many billions does it take to feed a Berk?'

'Joe had two wives. So did Izzy. The kids from each of their first marriages are all in their late forties and fifties, all close to each other – brothers and sisters, first cousins – and very involved in the business. The two you're talking about are both the offspring of second wives, and in each instance, there was a fairly acrimonious divorce. These kids are a generation younger and don't have much to do with their half siblings. Since Joe was the trustee of Izzy's estate, he began to shift the assets around, very quietly – mainly to benefit the older kids.'

'And Mona found out?'

'Joe's kid – Briggs – told her. Two years ago he was still estranged from his old man. That's when he told Mona what had been going on. I imagine it's why Joe made such an effort to bring his son back under his wing. To keep him close and get him to drop the lawsuit.'

'What amount did she sue him for?'

'About five billion dollars, Alex, for the invasion of her trust fund. She claims that Uncle Joe bled her accounts dry. The irony is that the deal Joe Berk made with the feds to pay up the tax claim put such a tight clamp on his settlement agreement that even in the discovery process of her civil suit, the judge hasn't allowed Mona's lawyers to get disclosure of the terms and amounts of the trusts. Nobody really knows how much money is at the base of the Berk empire.'

'Hard to believe she could want that much more money than what she's got.'

Battaglia smiled at me. 'Her lawyers whine to me that it isn't about the money. She just wants to be on the same footing as the other children – it's all about being treated like family, is what they tell me it's about.'

'I'll let you know when I find the chink in Joe's armor. And I'll give you the latest on the Met before the weekend.'

Two other bureau chiefs were lined up to see the district attorney as I said good night to Rose. It was almost six and the corridors were empty now, most workers on their way home, and many young trial lawyers hunkered down over their desks, assiduously starting a long evening of legal research or trial preparation.

Laura had left a note on my desk, clipped to three telephone messages and a crisp white envelope, hand-delivered from the hospital's general counsel, who'd been monitoring Selim Sengor's suspension since last weekend.

The three calls were personal, so I sat down to deal with the letter before I dialed to gab and make social plans with my friends.

As I tore an opening across the top of the sealed envelope, I could hear the noise of a sharp scratch against a piece of flint within it. The paper was immediately engulfed in a burst of flames, which licked at my face, setting fire to my hair and the collar of my silk blouse.

Chapter 24

I grabbed the sweater from the back of my chair and buried my head in it, trying to smother the flames. I didn't know whether it was my cries of distress or the acrid smell of smoke, but something brought two rookie cops running from the main hallway on their way to the elevator into my office. One of them grabbed my head and cradled it against his shoulder, then pushed me back to make certain the shirt was no longer smoldering.

'You okay?'

I nodded, trying to calm myself before speaking.

'Sit down till you stop shaking,' he said to me.

His partner had picked up the envelope to examine it.

'Be careful,' I said. 'They'll try to get prints off that.'

'You mean it's not yours? I thought maybe you dropped a cigarette and set fire to something on your desk.'

'No. The letter was jerry-rigged with matches. I could hear it scratching as soon as I ripped it open, but I didn't realize what was happening fast enough.'

The taller of the two cops squatted so that he was eye level with the desk, examining the envelope with the tip of his pen. 'Look at this, Pavone. This mutt glued a bunch of matchheads on one side of the flap, then stuck a piece of flint on top of the self-sealer. The minute you start to pull back on it, it's gotta erupt in flames.'

Pavone studied what was left of the parched envelope. 'You know who sent it? We'll call a unit and get you a sixty-one on this.'

'I – uh – I know whose stationery it is, but I'm sure he's not the person who sent it. It's a case I've been working on – I'll have the detectives draw it up, thanks.' The uniformed force #61 was the department's name for a criminal complaint form. 'I'd have to guess my perp stole some writing paper from his employer's office. Sort of a parting shot at me before he left town.'

'Can we get a bus for you?'

'I don't need an ambulance. It didn't get my body, I don't think. It just singed some hair.' I could feel the blister developing on the skin beneath my blouse, but fortunately the cops couldn't see that.

'Can we at least get you out of here? Give you a lift home?'

I could see the brass insignias on their collars. They'd have to pass my street on the way north to the 23rd Precinct station house. 'Sure. That'd be great.'

I locked the door behind me – it was a crime scene now – and waited until I was resting in the rear seat of their patrol car to call the captain of the DA's Squad. I told him what had happened and asked him to get Crime Scene downstairs to photograph the homemade device and send it to the lab for a workup. The janitor would let them in my office with a passkey. I also asked him to break the news to Paul Battaglia and spare me that encounter for the moment, and to explain to the district attorney that I was just fine.

By the time Mike and Mercer arrived at my apartment in response to my calls, I had already showered and washed my hair. I opened the door in an old shirt and leggings, with a pair of scissors in my hand, and went back to the bathroom to snip at the hair that framed the left side of my face, and then even out the uncharred pieces that hung on the right. I felt like I was thirteen again, cutting bangs for myself and hoping my mother wouldn't notice the hatchet job.

Mike stood behind me in the doorway. 'Smells like an incinerator in here. Take some more off the top, kid,' he said, lifting some strands from behind that I couldn't see for myself. 'Where's the blouse?'

'On my bed.'

'Mercer, you better voucher it. Jeez, lucky you don't wear polyester,' he called out from the other room. 'There's a hole the size of my fist in this. You'd have been instantly deep-fried. Let me see your chest.'

He had walked back into the bathroom. I opened a couple of buttons and showed Mike the burn in the hollow below my shoulder.

He whistled at the ugly mélange of colors that had already developed there. 'For once it's a good thing you're so flat – uh, so small. Another inch of décolletage and we'd have had roasted marshmallows. Little ones. Tasty little ones. I mean, probably tasty.'

'Your empathy is heartwarming.'

'Want me to rub on the butter?'

'That remedy went out with the dark ages. Cool water. I stood in the shower for ten minutes, cold enough to

263

form icicles, I think. It'll be fine.' I glanced at the burn in the mirror – a mild second degree, I figured, and went back to cutting my hair.

'My way is a helluva lot more soothing than a frigid shower, but you're the boss.'

I joined the guys in the den five minutes later, where Mike pronounced my self-administered hairstyling a complete failure. 'She's got that whackier-than-Sharon-Stone-looking, finger-in-an-electrical-socket-just-for-kicks expression, don't you think, Mercer? Too punk to prosecute.'

'Not to worry. The first person I called was Elsa. She'll open the salon for me at seven thirty in the morning.' My beloved friend and hairdresser would repair the char-coal-fringed blond coloring and Nana would clip me into better shape.

'You got some kind of screwed-up priorities, kid. First the hairdresser, then the police? Where's your camera? If you're not going to see a doctor, we better get a few shots of the injury.'

I went back to the bedroom to get my digital camera and handed it to Mercer when I returned. 'This is a big mystery to you, Detective Chapman? Sengor probably put the flare together while he was sitting at home and stewing about his arrest. Then he left it with Alkit to be delivered through the hospital messenger system. Nobody would blink at an envelope with the counsel's return address coming to my office by hand. There'll be a sign-in from a legit deliveryman at our security desk, all on the up-and-up, and Laura was probably still there to receive it. I'm just glad she didn't open it.'

'Show him some skin, Coop,' Mike said, as Mercer

positioned me against the linen-white wall in my hallway to take some photos. 'I brought you a get-well present.'

When Mercer was finished, we returned to the den together. Mike had fixed each of them a drink, and handed me an elegantly shaped bottle of amber liquid with a bright red ribbon around its throat.

'What's this?'

'Time for an upgrade. A hyperpremium Scotch for a hyperpremium broad. No need to get freaky. It's still from Scotland. Isle of Islay.'

I tried to pronounce the long name on the unfamiliar label before Mike took the bottle back from me and opened it, pouring an inch – neat – into my glass. 'Guy in my liquor store said it's got a lot of finesse. No kidding, that's how he described it. Said it's richer and older than the stuff you've been drinking. Damn, you're richer and older than when I met you, too.'

Mercer studied the bottle while I tasted the smoky single malt. He let out a low whistle. 'Slow down on that stuff, Alex. The man bought you a twenty-seven-year-old Scotch.'

'Are you crazy?' I asked Mike. 'That must have cost you—'

'Hey, is it any good? That's all that counts tonight.'

'It's divine,' I said, sinking back against a pillow, letting the rich flavor work on my frazzled nerves. I knew the expensive gift was one of Mike's ways of thanking me for trying to get him back on course. I savored it twice as much.

The television was on and Mike reclicked the mute button to return the sound as Alex Trebek announced the Final Jeopardy category, Famous Military Leaders.

I stretched out on the sofa with two pillows behind my head. 'Must be your lucky day. You can recoup your loss on this delicious extravagance.'

'Double or nothing,' Mike said, tossing two twenty-dollar bills on the floor. 'Winner buys dinner. What do you say, blondie? Anywhere you want to go – we can walk around the corner to Swifty's for some twinburgers, or I'll drive you down to Patroon, buy you the biggest steak in the house.'

I sniffed at the ends of my hair. 'Can you just see me in Swifty's? The best-dressed, most perfectly coiffed ladies in Manhattan, and I walk in like this? No, thanks. I'm too achy to go anywhere.'

Mike walked to the phone to order a pizza as Trebek unveiled the answer. 'Editor of the autobiography of the great American general Ulysses S. Grant.'

Two of the three contestants seemed to be too puzzled to even venture a guess, while the third one scribbled an answer on his screen.

'I hate when they sucker me in like that,' Mike said. 'This answer doesn't have anything to do with military history. It's right up your English-major alley once again.'

'Not even a guess?' Trebek asked the second contestant, who held up a blank slate.

'Maybe it's a trick question. Why would you need someone else to edit your life story? I'm going with Grant himself,' Mike said, talking to Trebek.

'Mercer, do you care to jump in here, or is this for me, to ease my pain?' I said, reaching out my arm for the forty dollars on the carpet near my feet.

'Go for it.'

'I'm so sorry,' Trebek said. 'That's not the correct answer. Who—'

'Who was Mark Twain?' I asked.

'. . . was Mark Twain? Can you imagine that?' Trebek said. 'The author of one of our finest American novels actually edited and published the memoirs of one of the greatest generals who ever lived. Quite something, isn't it?'

'They were really an odd couple,' I said, 'but they were fast friends.'

'You're one to talk about odd couples.'

The phone rang and I screwed up my nose as Mike tried to hand me the portable receiver. 'I don't want to speak to anyone. Let it ring.'

He looked at the caller ID and pressed the talk button. 'Alexandra Cooper's residence.'

I rested my glass on the floor beside me and waved at Mike with both hands, mouthing the word *no* as emphatically as I could.

'No, sir. I'm just the butler. Yeah, Mr B, it's Mike Chapman. She's – uh – she's actually across the hall at her neighbor's apartment. Can you imagine? She ran out of Scotch. Yeah, she's fine. She'll tell you about it in the morning.' Mike proceeded to give the district attorney a replay of my description of the fiery letter, as well as to talk about the likely suspects – Sengor or Alkit – who might have sent it.

'Whatever you say, Mr B. Sure, I can spend the night here, no problem. I don't think anybody's gonna show up later on Ms Cooper's doorstep with exploding anchovies on a large pie, but if it makes you feel better, I'll keep an eye on her,' Mike said. 'Yeah, I know what you mean. Sometimes she's more trouble than she's worth. I gotta agree with you there.'

I pushed up from the sofa to protest. 'There are two doormen downstairs, twenty-four hours a day. I really don't think—'

'Don't roll your eyes at me, blondie. Till we see if they lift any prints from what's left of that envelope in the morning, the district attorney wants to play it safe.'

By the time the pizza was delivered, I was hungry enough to chew on a slice while Mercer and Mike devoured the rest of it.

A little before nine, Mercer had a call on his cell from one of his Special Victims Squad colleagues, who was a few blocks from my apartment. He was returning from the DA's video unit with duplicate copies of Sengor's collection and asked if we wanted to review any of them before arraigning his pal, Dr Alkit, in the morning. Mercer went down to the lobby and returned with six tapes.

'You want to see what we've got?'

'Guess we'd better look at the one from last Friday. Are they marked?'

'Yes. These are all labelled,' Mercer said, picking out the right tape and loading it in my VCR.

Sengor must have activated the video camera at some point in the evening after his victims had been rendered unconscious. The first few seconds of film showed the empty beds in his room, the covers folded down to reveal the sheets. Mercer had been in the apartment the night of the arrest, so he described to us the bookcase opposite the bed in which the device had been hidden, wedged among a series of pharmacological textbooks.

In the background, I could hear the CD player

changing discs, and then Kris Kristofferson's plaintive voice asking someone to help him make it through the night. Sengor walked into the room carrying Jean Eaken's limp body in his arms. He was naked, and she was dressed in the casual clothes she had worn when I met her late on Friday night.

The doctor lowered his victim onto the nearest bed, adjusted the dimmer on the light switch to darken the room, turned to the camera – almost preening for it as he ran his hand down his chest and paused to admire his erection.

Jean Eaken never moved. Sengor slowly and deliberately raised her by lifting beneath her shoulders and removed her sweater over her head. He unhooked her bra and took her arms out of its straps, one at a time. He was mumbling now, talking to her as he undressed her, but the words were inaudible to me. He let her fall back in place and stood up, taking a drag from a joint – presumably marijuana – that was on his nightstand, before going back to the business of removing her pants.

Mike had seen enough. 'Necrophilia. I've never seen anything so disgusting. How can you watch him do this? The only thing different than having sex with a corpse is that this kid's body is still warm. I'm telling you, you people who do sex crimes, you're all out of your minds. At least the people I deal with are dead. Over and out. They don't see anything, they don't feel anything. The perp doesn't get to say, "It ain't a crime where I live, buddy." It's frigging murder, no matter where it happens. This stuff? How can you look at it? No wonder your love life's in the can, Coop.'

Mercer stopped the tape. 'Here's a guy gives us the

269

whole crime, gift-wrapped. We have to watch it – make sure there's nothing exculpatory on it. You know that.'

Mike was in the kitchen, his vodka in one hand, the other one rifling through the freezer for ice cream, the most likely food group to be found in my home. 'Yeah, but there's something about the two of you sitting in the den with this – this disgusting stuff – and the fact that you're watching it together like you're at the movies is really—'

'Those nuns in parochial school did a great job on you, Mikey,' I said. 'I'm surprised you can even say the words *sexual intercourse*, no less do the deed.'

'What makes you think I've done it, kid? You'd be the last to know. I'm telling you, watching that shit roused you up, see? You shouldn't even be talking like this.'

'Mercer and I have to watch this, and all the other tapes they seized, just the way you go to autopsies.'

'Yeah, well, I'll take homicide any day of the week. Let me know when you think you've seen enough to prove your case, will you? I know you like to give the jury a rock-crusher, but this one's out of the park.'

I walked into the living room to meet him. He dropped into an armchair and scooped out spoonfuls of chocolate chocolate chip from the container, his feet on my glass-topped coffee table.

'Now all I need is a perp to prosecute,' I said, easing myself onto another chair.

Mercer followed me out of the den, but stood behind Mike. 'I'll head for home. You want to bring these dupli-cate tapes down to Max? I suppose she and your interns can sort through them all and see if we've got more victims to search out.'

'Will do.' I got up to walk him to the door and kiss him good night. 'Thanks for keeping me company. It really was frightening when that little fireball flew up at my face. Have you seen anything like that before?'

'Who got the call to the governor's office on Third Avenue two years back? Iggy, wasn't it?' Mercer asked Mike. 'Remember that prisoner in New Mexico who set up fifty letters like that and sent one to the governor of every state?'

Mike shrugged.

'Yeah,' Mercer went on. 'Five secretaries all over the map got lit up just like you. The other intended bombs sat in stacks of correspondence and they all got tracked to the same inmate. It's not hard to do, Alex.'

'You'll let me know about the fingerprints in the morning?'

Mercer pointed at my hair. 'You take care of the "do" – the rest is up to me.'

'You ready for a refill?' I asked Mike after I closed the door and locked the deadbolt.

'Sure. We'll watch the ten o'clock news and then it's lights out for you.'

'That's fine with me, Dr Chapman. I'm really whipped. You can sleep in the guest room, you know.'

'This sofa's worked for me before. I'm cool with it.'

'I'll get a quilt to put over you. And how about a robe?'

'Pink's not my best look.'

'No, I mean, I'm sure I've got a – um – an old—'

'You think I want to wrap myself in some rag that one of your lovers left behind? No thanks – I might begin to feel entitled, then what the hell would I do? Hey, I've

271

had worse details than this. You just try to calm yourself down.'

I was yawning before the anchor turned things over to the weatherman and said good night as I went to put myself to sleep.

But by four o'clock, I was wide awake and rolling restlessly from side to side. I had been dreaming about Natalya Galinova, a nightmare in which her broken body appeared as it had when I saw her in the bottom of the shaft at the Met. It was such a vivid image that for seconds I couldn't figure out whether or not I was still asleep, so unnerving that I got out of bed and went into the bathroom for a drink of water to change the setting.

I wrapped a dressing gown around me and walked in my bare feet to the living room to see whether Mike had stirred. He was curled up on the sofa, the half-empty vodka bottle beside his empty glass. It was probably the way he had anesthetized himself on more than one or two nights since Valerie had been killed.

I pulled a pillow off the armchair and stretched out on the floor beneath him, resting my head on the soft cushion, tracing the pattern of the pale green design in the soft wool threads of the Persian carpet with my finger. I was hoping the monotony of the motion would lull me back to sleep.

Images of Jean Eaken in Sengor's videotaped assault were hard to erase. The Kristofferson lyrics that had played in the background also kept repeating. Let the devil take tomorrow, I thought, 'cause tonight I really did need a friend.

Nothing worked. I watched the sky turn from deep cobalt to hazy gray to a bright cloudless blue. Whatever demons I was fighting, the basic problem was that I had been disturbed enough by the week's events – and by the letter bomb – that for at least this time, I didn't want to be alone anymore.

At six forty-five, I decided to shower and dress. I accidentally brushed against one of Mike's legs as I stood and he picked his head up, squinting as he tried to get his bearings.

'Sorry. I didn't mean to wake you.'

He looked at his watch. 'Damn. I better put a move on if we're going to make you look presentable today. What's with the pillow? How long have you been out here?'

'Ten, fifteen minutes. I just got antsy, is all. I'll be quick.'

'I'd like to stop by my place and clean up, too. Okay? Something wrong that you were out here? Something you want to talk about?'

'No. I was just slept out, I guess. I'm not used to going to bed so early.' He couldn't see the expression on my face as I walked away.

On our way out the door, Mike stooped to pick up the newspapers. The front page of the *Times* had no mention of Selim Sengor, but the *Post* editors couldn't resist another banner headline: DOC CONCOCTS TURKISH DELIGHT – FLIGHT.

We were in Mike's car, parking near his tiny walk-up apartment on York Avenue, when his beeper went off. He returned the call and seemed pleased with the message.

'The man's glove that was picked up near where Galinova was dumped, at the Met? The one that gave up two different DNA profiles?'

'Yeah.'

'Inside the glove, the DNA from the skin cells is a perfect match to Joe Berk.'

'Joe Berk? What's the exemplar they used? What'd they have with his profile on it to make the comparison?'

'That plastic drinking cup you didn't want me to take from his apartment, Coop. You can cut your teeth on some more breaking law. Make it legal for me so it sticks in court. Hate to jam you up with a bad search, but the practice will be good for you.'

Chapter 25

'I asked you to throw the damn cup away. Why do you risk getting good evidence by being a cowboy?' I asked Mike.

'Hey, the first time we were in Berk's apartment, you were hoping to pick up some white hairs, weren't you?'

'I didn't do it then, did I?'

'Garbage. I took the cup because it was garbage. Argue that to the stiffs who sit on the appellate court bench and wouldn't know a crime scene from a cocktail party. Let's go – out of the car.'

'I'll wait for you down here.'

'Battaglia said to keep an eye on you. I got this far so there's no point in letting you be a sitting target on a street corner. Don't pout about Joe Berk's DNA. I got what we need, didn't I?'

I followed Mike up the narrow staircase that led to his fifth-floor apartment. It was a studio that he had long ago christened 'the coffin' because of its small size and dark interior. Since Val's death, that nickname must have made each homecoming a reminder of his loss.

'Just throw those things on the floor and have a seat,' he said, pointing to a chair in the corner of the room.

He grabbed clean clothes from the closet and dresser and went into the bathroom to shower.

The disarray in the apartment was startling. While his department car was usually littered with empty coffee containers and food wrappers, Mike's personal appearance – most often a blazer, button-down-collar shirt, and neatly pressed slacks or jeans – was ordinarily reflected in his home surroundings. I started to hang up a windbreaker that had fallen to the floor and stuff socks and underwear in his laundry bag.

But more disturbing than the messiness was that this intimate space had been transformed into a shrine to Valerie. There were photographs of her on every surface, and her belongings were crowded onto shelves – architectural design books stacked on top of Mike's collection of historical biographies, and the exotic shells she brought back from her tropical vacations. I didn't know whether Val had moved all these things into Mike's apartment, or he had retrieved them from her place and set them up here after her death.

I bent over to study a photograph of Val I had never seen before. It was a close-up of her face, beaming back at the photographer – Mike, no doubt – from beneath the brim of an NYPD baseball cap. I was ashamed to catch myself making superficial comparisons – how much more even Val's features were than my own, what a fine beauty she possessed. I straightened up and dusted off the picture with my sleeve.

And then there were the clothes – several pastel-colored crewneck sweaters stacked on a closet shelf beside Mike's darker ones, strappy sandals lined up next to his loafers, and a diaphanous robe in Val's favorite lavender hues that was still draped across the back of the wooden chair that he had offered me to sit on.

I was smoothing the covers on the bed that had been unmade, probably for days, when Mike came out of the bathroom. 'What are you doing?'

'We can come back later on and I can help you straighten things up.'

'It's not Buckingham Palace, Coop. It's the way I live, okay?'

'It didn't used to be.'

'A lot of things didn't used to be. C'mon. Twelve-minute turnaround. Not bad, huh?'

'Would you like me to – well, to sort of go through some of Val's things with you?'

He looked at me as though I had said something crazy, something unthinkable. 'Can you just leave it alone? I'm not ready. Can you make a goddamn effort to understand that? Can you get it?'

I opened the door and started down the steps. I don't think Mike would have said anything to hurt me intentionally, but the shot was painful. 'Better than you think.'

I scanned the Sengor story in the newspaper as Mike drove the short distance to 56th Street and Park Avenue, near the town house to which Elsa's salon had moved. We picked up enough coffee for ourselves and the early-morning staff from a deli at the end of the block.

Elsa buzzed us in through security and we took the elevator upstairs. She groaned when she saw my hair, before either of us could greet her, and we walked to the rear of the sleek salon where the colorists worked. We had been friends for years, and I relied on that relationship as much as on her talent and eye.

277

'You gotta be a magician for this job,' Mike said. 'But she's unbearable if she isn't blond enough, so give those charred ends a go.'

Elsa went into the supply room to mix a formula and came back with my stylist, Nana.

'Well, if it isn't Nana-from-Ghana,' Mike said, getting up to embrace her. 'This is like the hair ICU this morning, no? All hands on deck for Coop's toasted tendrils.'

Nana fixed her broad smile at Mike and looked at the nape of his neck. 'While you're waiting for Alex, I think I'd better shape you up, detective,' she said in her distinctive West African patois. 'Come with me.'

'I was hoping you'd say that.'

They walked to the front together and I told Elsa what had happened yesterday while she wrapped my ends in tinfoil to set the bleach.

After the color processing, Nana tried to even the damage that I had compounded after the explosion with my amateur clipping. It was almost nine when Mike and I left the salon to continue on downtown to my office.

Laura was waiting for me at the door when we came in, apologizing for having left the deadly letter on my desk.

'You couldn't have known any better than I did. There's no reason for you to blame yourself. Thank God it didn't get *you* – I'm helpless without you,' I said, trying to lighten the atmosphere.

'Battaglia wants to see you. He told me it's got to be right away, 'cause he's going down to Washington to testify at a Senate hearing on gun control. Don't even sit down, Alex. He means immediately.'

278

'You coming?' I asked Mike.

He sat at my desk and spread out a napkin beneath the powdered jelly doughnut he was dissecting. 'The man didn't ask for me. I'm dining now.'

Battaglia was packing his briefcase with papers, ready to leave for the airport.

'How do you feel?'

'Fine, thanks. It was a good scare.'

'You getting anywhere on the Met?'

'Not much further than I told you yesterday. Only development is that a man's glove found near the scene of Talya's attack has Joe Berk's DNA inside it.'

Battaglia's cigar wiggled at the news. 'Interesting.'

'Don't get too excited about that fact, Paul. I don't want to keep it from you, but there may be an issue about the admissibility We'll find a way to get a clean sample. Chapman may have jumped the gun getting this one.'

'That's why I like him. Take him a cigar for me, but forget you ever told me this little factoid. I only want to know about the clean one. I'll pretend this one's just a product of my wishful thinking.'

'Mike and I are going back to see Berk this afternoon. Hear what he has to say. I know I promised you something before Saturday, but—'

'That isn't why I was asking. Why don't you get out of town for a few days, if nothing's cooking on the case? Sarah can handle the Carido arrest if they find the guy,' Battaglia said, referring to my deputy. 'Your Turkish doctor's taken himself out of range and you've got Chapman to run the investigation at the Met. Stay out of harm's way for a few days. Relax.'

He was looking at my unusual hairstyle as he talked.

'I was planning to go to the Vineyard tomorrow night, to open the house for the season. I just hate leaving with all this going on.'

'Go tonight, okay? Then I don't have to worry about somebody watching your tail. If we need you before Monday, you can always fly in.'

We walked out of his office together and I thanked him for the time off, well aware that he was banishing me in hopes that the bad press would evaporate if I wasn't around to fuel the reporters with leaks and updates on the three high-profile cases that were hogging the headlines.

Mike had his feet up on my desk, reading the sports news while waiting for me to return from the executive wing. 'D'you show him your burn?'

'He didn't ask, so I didn't tell. He encouraged me to fly up to the country today, but that depends on what you think we've got going.' I tossed him the Cuban cigar.

'I'm with Battaglia on that,' Mike said, sniffing it through the wrapper and sticking it in his jacket pocket. 'We can surprise Joe Berk with a visit, and I can get back to helping out at the Met. I'll take you to the shuttle this afternoon.' There were no direct Vineyard flights this early in the year, so I'd have to travel through Boston and take the nine-seater Cessna twin engine from Logan Airport.

'Excuse me, Alex,' Laura said, standing in the doorway, 'there's a young woman at the security desk in the lobby. She read the story in the paper about Sengor and she wants to talk to an assistant DA about something that happened to her last month. She thinks she was drugged at a club.'

'By him?'

'No, no. She just decided to come forward because of your case.'

'Do me a favor. Find someone in the unit to talk to her, will you?'

Whenever an unusual MO became public, women who'd been reluctant to tell their stories to detectives or prosecutors often came out of the woodwork, eager to see if their claims would support criminal charges. In the case of drug-facilitated rapes, the failure to get prompt medical attention and testing most often proved fatal to the case. It didn't surprise me that the Sengor indictment would result in a rash of new complaints that would keep busy many of the forty senior assistants in the unit.

Five minutes later Laura buzzed me on the intercom. 'Your phones are wild today, Alex. This one's a Dr Thorp – from the New York Botanical Garden. You want it?'

'Absolutely.' I picked up the phone and introduced myself to the caller.

'I've been told to talk with you about my analysis of the leaf particles that the NYPD submitted to me the other day.'

'Would you mind if I put you on speakerphone? I've got the case detective with me.'

'That's fine, unless you'd rather come up here to my office to meet with me.'

There were very few places in the city as magnificent as the vast acreage of gardens and conservatories, but my most recent visits there had sated my curiosity for the

281

time being. 'Perhaps we can start this with just a call, if you don't mind.'

'I've had a look at your leaf, and frankly, you don't see many of these.'

'Why is that, Dr Thorp?' I asked, as Mike got out his pad and flipped to a new page to take notes.

'*Pycnanthemum torrei*, Ms Cooper.'

'Sorry?'

'*Pycnanthemum torrei*. This plant is quite rare. In fact, it's GI.'

I was shaking my head at Mike, who leaned in to speak. 'Look, doc. We gotta go through this in Pig Latin or what? *Ixnay* on the scientific lingo. I'm a cop.'

'That's just the way we do things in botany. GI – that means it's a globally imperiled plant. It's known as Torrey's mountain mint.'

Just the name of the leaf explained the distinctive odor that we had smelled at the scene. 'So, in Manhattan, would it be hard to find?' I asked.

'Not hard, Ms Cooper. Impossible. It doesn't grow on your island.'

'Where then?'

'There are only ten places in the world where Torrey's mountain mint survives, so far as we know. There's a site on Staten Island called Clay Pit Ponds State Park. You can check with the city's Department of Environmental Preservation. There was a big brouhaha last year over a large shopping plaza that was planned for the location. Pickets and protesters and green-lovers. This sweet little endangered plant held up construction of a hundred-million-dollar mall project.'

Mike was writing down the names. 'Where else?'

282

'High Mountain, detective. The mint thrives for some reason in the Preakness Range of the Watchung Mountains. Do you know where that is?'

I said, 'No,' while Mike answered at the same time, 'Yeah, doc. Across the river in New Jersey, right? I'll explain it to her. Anywhere else in the Northeast?'

'No. No. Just these two patches. We're keeping a close watch. We'd obviously love to find more of it.'

'Thanks a lot for your help,' Mike said, ending the conversation.

'So what don't I know about the Watchung Mountains that I should?'

'It's a nature preserve with some of the most magnificent vistas of the city. Now, if you'd paid a little more attention in your history class, you'd know that it's got some of the highest ridges anywhere along the Hudson, and that Revolutionary soldiers used those points for signaling stations against the British troops.'

'Nice to know, but—'

'And in World War Two, the army mounted mobile antiaircraft guns on top of High Mountain in case the Nazis made it over the ocean. They should have kept the frigging things there to welcome those Al Qaeda bastards in 2001. A lot of people I care about might still be alive.'

'Where in New Jersey is it, Mike?'

'I was serious, Coop. Right across the Hudson. I'll tell you what else is there. Rock shelters – caves that were used by the Indians for hundreds of years.'

'So?'

'So how about that it's not very far from where your spelunker friend lives.'

'My what?'

'Chet Dobbis. Artistic director of the Metropolitan Opera. Rock climber, wig collector, former lover of Natalya Galinova. Maybe he tracked in a little mint on his cleats.'

Chapter 26

Lieutenant Peterson was waiting for us when we arrived at the opera house. The task force members were still sprawled out across the elegant boardroom, their cardboard cartons seeming to have spawned dozens of offspring since my last visit. We grabbed two folding chairs from a pile against the wall and sat down to talk about the latest developments.

'What does Joe Berk's DNA give you?' Peterson asked.

'A reason to look at him again. May be the first step in developing probable cause.'

'We can't use that hit, Mike,' I said. 'We'll have to get back to that square some other way.'

'So I'll get him to spit at me. It probably wouldn't take much. But now Chet Dobbis looks as good as Berk does.'

'Slow down, Chapman,' the lieutenant said, standing up to reach for a box of index cards. 'When you called me with the news about that rare mint plant an hour ago, I sifted through these – we've made one for each of the four hundred permanent employees here. Forget the per diems. At least sixty men who work on the staff live in north Jersey, and another fifty live on Staten Island.'

'And how many of those guys are in the pool that still

285

haven't been excluded, who were supposed to be in the opera house on Friday night?'

'Roughly? About thirty of them live out in Jersey or on Staten Island. But now we've got to go back and double-check the residential locations of all the others, comparing them to Clay Pit Ponds State Park and the Watchung Mountains. That's in addition to the people in Galinova's personal life that you're looking at.'

'How many famous killers – I mean, sort of house-hold name killers – were fat guys?' Mike asked.

Peterson and I looked at him quizzically.

'Like David Berkowitz – Son of Sam – he was chubby. Bluebeard, in drawings, they always make him look hefty. Fatty Arbuckle – I guess the name says all you need to know. Think about it, though. Most killers are lean and mean.'

Peterson ignored Mike and went back to reviewing pedigree information on index cards while I tried to figure out where his non sequitur was going.

'Malvo and Mohammed – the DC snipers – they were lean. The Menendez brothers – skinny. O.J. – well built but trim. Ma Barker – no fat there. I can't think of a lot of fat murderers.'

'You never watched *The Sopranos*?' Peterson asked. 'Tony S., Big Pussy – they had a ton of overweight perps.'

'That's television. Dillinger – thin as a rail. Manson – malnourished. Bundy, Dahmer, that fertilizer salesman from Modesto who gave your namesakes a bad rep – all lean.'

'Maybe if you told me why you want to—' I started to ask.

''Cause over your shoulder, Coop,' Mike said, pointing

to the glass door, 'is a porky little liar who looks like a homicidal maniac, and I think he's after you.'

I turned my head to see Rinaldo Vicci, still swathed in the lavender scarf, standing outside the fancy room that had been commandeered for the investigation. We were on the level of the parterre boxes of the empty theater, so there could be no other purpose for which he was lurking. I smiled at him and waved him in, but he shook his head from side to side.

'Throw him a crumb, Coop. Go see what he wants.'

I got up from the table and let myself out into the carpeted hallway. The auditorium doors were open now, and the orchestra rehearsal of the triumphal march from *Aida* filled the lobby with the rich sounds of its music.

Vicci walked ahead of me to the floor-length window that overlooked the plaza and fountain. 'Thank you, Signora Cooper. I saw you come in earlier, and I had a few questions to ask you.'

He was one of those people who had trouble making eye contact. He looked at my face when he talked to me, but his eyes focused on a spot inches away from mine, giving them a bizarre cast and making it hard to gauge his credibility.

'Why are you here today, Mr Vicci? I mean, why at the Met?'

He motioned in the direction of the stage with the tail of the scarf. 'A young tenor I represent. He's going to understudy the role of Radames. Signore Dobbis has been gracious enough to let me sit in on rehearsals.'

Vicci took a few steps closer to the window and gazed out at the pedestrians who were enjoying the spring morning. 'The girl, Ms Cooper, I feel so badly about the girl. I've been calling the hospital, but they won't tell me nothing because—'

'Lucy DeVore?'

'Yes, of course. Miss Lucy. Her condition, they won't tell me since I am not a relative of hers. Is she going to live?'

'The doctors expect she will, Mr Vicci. Personally, I hope they'll bring her out of the coma in the next week or so. The rest of you are so uncooperative, I expect she'll be able to give us some useful information,' I said. 'She's not going to die, if that's what you and your cohorts were hoping. They're just trying to control the pain levels this way.'

Vicci coughed and spent seconds clearing his throat. It seemed to me he was stalling, as he reached for something in his pocket and seemed unable to speak. When he resumed the conversation, his accent seemed to have thickened dramatically and he clutched at the scarf. 'Of course I don't want her to die. What a shocking thought. A lozenge?'

'No, thanks. You were supposed to call me about Lucy after you checked in your office. Tell me what your file said about how she got to you.'

Vicci closed his eyes and rubbed his forehead between his thumb and forefinger. 'I'm in a very precarious situation, signora. I'm so afraid that if I gossip about things, someone will be angry with me.'

'What you tell me in the course of this investigation is confidential. Nobody will know the information comes from you.' We were standing in the most open, visible space within the opera house, but there didn't seem to be anyone in a position to notice. 'I understand from some

288

of the other witnesses that it was you who invited Hubert Alden to be at the audition the other day. In fact, we know that Ms Galinova – Talya – was supposed to be the person on that broken swing. Not Lucy DeVore.'

He stopped twisting the fringed edge of his scarf and almost choked on his lozenge. My comment had the desired effect. I wanted him to know other witnesses were talking to us, even though none had said as much as I would have liked.

Again, Vicci cleared his throat. 'This is a very – how you say – a very unforgiving business, Ms Cooper. Actors, singers, dancers – both the men and the women – every day of their life is an audition. Everybody they speak to, every appearance they make, somebody is judging them for the next leading role, maybe the next bit part.'

'Galinova wanted to try out in front of Mona Berk?'

Vicci made the sign of the cross as he bit his lip. 'Joe Berk would kill me if he knew I arranged for her to do this. That's why Talya and I made up the story that she fired me. It was Talya who called Mona. Mona's fiancé, actually – Ross Kehoe.'

'How did Talya know Kehoe?'

'From years ago, I think, when he worked for Joe Berk.'

'Ross Kehoe was an employee of Joe's, and now he's engaged to Mona Berk? I bet Uncle Joe isn't happy about that. What kind of job did he have?'

Vicci didn't seem to know. 'In the theater, he did things for Joe. I saw him around, but I can't tell you his title. Was nothing very serious, I can assure you.'

Hadn't Kehoe told us that he'd never met Natalya Galinova? Mike would know if that's what he said in our first meeting with him.

'And Lucy DeVore? Please, Mr Vicci, I need to know how she fits in with these people. I need to know who brought her to you.'

Again the coughing fit, the hand covering the mouth to delay the answer – maybe to filter it. Again the throat lozenge. 'I – uh – I told you I didn't represent her, that I was doing a favor for a friend, no?'

'You did. Now who's the friend?'

'It was Joe himself, Joe Berk who told me to take the girl around. Get her a job, get her on her feet. Most of all to find her a rich man she could – shall I tell you Joe's word? A rich man she could hustle.'

'A man like Hubert Alden?'

'Exactly, signora.'

'Because Joe Berk was involved with her?'

'No, no. I believe Joe when he tells me this. I know his taste in women, and is not this girl. But he was very unhappy with Lucy,' Vicci said, crushing the candy in his teeth. 'Miss Lucy was making a play for Joe's son – the baby one.'

'Briggs?'

'Yes, Briggs, Ms Cooper. Joe found out about it and thought she was trash – you call in English a gold digger. He tried to buy her off himself – give her money, threaten to keep her away from the boy.'

'Threaten Lucy with what? Threaten to hurt her, like what happened to her on Tuesday?'

'No, no. I'm sure he meant only to hurt her career, not the girl herself,' Vicci said, protesting the inference I'd made. 'Joe didn't need to do something that extreme. You know, he only had to tell Briggs he'd disinherit him if he stayed with the cheap showgirl. The boy isn't *pazzo*,

290

Ms Cooper. He's not so crazy he'd give up the Berk fortune for a hillbilly who can sing and dance.'

The music had stopped now and someone was calling out directions for a scenery change.

'What about the money, Mr Vicci? She was living in the Elk Hotel. It doesn't look like anyone paid her off for anything.'

He raised his head back and put his forefinger above his lip, sniffing as he did. 'Up her nose, Ms Cooper. Briggs, too. Most of the money was spent on cocaine. That's how come the boy dropped his foolish lawsuit. He wouldn't make it without his father's money, not at the rate he snorts white powder. He had to come back into the fold.'

'And Lucy's family. Do you—'

'Honestly, I tell you the truth. This I don't know. And I don't think *she* wanted anyone to know who she was or where she came from. She had a little talent, Ms Cooper, a nice voice and quite an able dancer. Mostly what she had to sell were her looks – and her body.'

'Let's hope there's something left to that when she starts to recover.'

A shrill scream blasted off the stage and rang out across the tiered lobby. I could make out the voices and sounds of men fighting with each other and hear the low rumble of something mechanical moving behind the scrim. 'He's a lying bastard,' were the only words shouted out clearly enough for me to understand.

I ran to the glass-doored boardroom and pounded on it to get Mike's attention. As I grabbed the banister to fly down the winding staircase, the flat metal curtain suspended behind the elegant velvet swag slammed to the floor to cut off the auditorium from the violent encounter taking place backstage.

Chapter 27

Mike overtook me and pushed past the security guard to open the door that led to stage right behind the curtain.

The crew looked like players on the field at Yankee Stadium whenever the dugout emptied if they believed that a Boston pitcher intentionally had beaned a batter. Six guys were restraining one of the hands, who was trying to pull away from them and free his arms. Others were arguing among themselves, pushing and shoving, paying no attention to the three supervisors who were trying to calm everyone down.

One man was lying on the floor, writhing in pain, his ankle twisted off to the side so that his foot appeared to have sustained a major injury.

Someone was standing at the control panel, moving levers, and the wagon on which we were standing – the entire stage-right platform – began to move away from the main stage. I steadied myself against the papier-mâché side of an Egyptian pyramid.

Mike grabbed the arm of one of the men in the melee and several of the other detectives who had followed him downstairs from the makeshift office helped to restore order. 'What happened?'

'An accident.'

'Maybe I'll have to ask for everyone's driver's license. Make sure you don't run over anybody with all this equipment. It's too frigging dangerous here at the Met. I'll try again – what happened?'

One of the men in carpenter's pants turned to walk away. 'Something moved when it wasn't supposed to. That's all. There's a reason we call this place the House of Pain. There's a lot of ways to get hurt if you don't watch yourself – the fly system, the electrical panels, and even the curtain slams down at high speed. It's not a matter for the police.'

'What moved?' Mike asked, aware that the decent workmen had wearied of the detectives who had been poring over their personal lives for the last week.

'That wagon,' he said, pointing to the stage on which we were standing.

The entire system of four rotating stages was electrical, not hydraulic. I could see the pulley cable bringing the giant platform – forty by sixty feet – back into place. It had been activated unexpectedly, and one man's leg had been caught as the right wagon shifted under the main stage.

Mike directed his attention to the injured man. 'You okay, buddy? We'll get you a doctor to look at the leg.'

He was sitting upright now, rubbing his ankle. 'There's a medical office here. They'll check me out.'

The man in the green-plaid shirt who had been restrained by his coworkers broke away from them. 'Buddy, my ass. Tell 'em who you are. Tell 'em or I will.'

The man with the twisted foot was bleeding from the side of his mouth. The shriek we heard when his leg was caught under the colliding wagons must have followed a punch.

Mike walked into the group of men and told them to step back. Several protested, not willing to leave him alone with their angry colleague. They muttered about the work that had to get done and the rehearsal that was in progress.

Detectives helped the injured man to his feet and watched him test his ankle. He shook them off and started to limp away.

'Harney!' the guy with Mike screamed out. 'Don't go too far. You better tell the detectives where you were last Friday.'

Mike and the other men from the task force quelled the crew and took the two combatants to opposite wings. We cleared the entire central area so the cast and crew could get back to work.

Another loud creaking noise and a giant gap yawned in the floor of center stage. I stepped farther back, away from the monstrous black hole it created as the boards rolled apart. Seconds later, raised by some kind of lift below the auditorium, the eerie funeral set from the Temple of Vulcan – the crypt in which Aida and Radames would be entombed, buried alive – rose onto the stage.

I turned my back to it and followed Mike to the door that exited stage right, to the medical office where the limping man had walked.

Mike told the nurse to give us a few minutes with her patient and she left the three of us alone in her room. 'You want to tell me what this is about, or do I start with the guy who threw the punch.'

'It's none of your business. It's outside the opera house.'

'That's not what it sounded like to me. Let me see your ID.'

The man lifted the chain from around his neck and passed it to Mike, as I leaned in to study it with him.

'Ralph Harney,' Mike said aloud. 'What's your date of birth?'

Ralph answered with the date that matched his credentials, as well as his street address.

'You still live in Hoboken?'

'Yeah. Right through the tunnel.'

Mike handed the card back to him. The picture was a couple of years old, and the scraggly facial hair he sported exaggerated his age and now made him look more dissipated.

'What's got your pal so angry? Were you working the performance on Friday?'

'I'm on the night gang. I don't come on till after the show's over. Part of the crew who break down the sets.'

'Well, did you do that on Friday?'

'Yeah.'

'So what's the beef? Why does he say you're lying?'

''Cause he hates my guts.'

'Any reason in particular?'

'His sister. I was engaged to marry his sister.'

'You broke it up? That's why he's angry?'

Ralph Harney didn't answer.

'Yo. I'm talking to you. You broke it up?'

'She got killed in a car crash.'

'And who was driving?'

A pause before he answered. 'Me. I was hurt bad, too.'

Harney picked up his head to show Mike the scar that trailed from the corner of his eyelid down across his cheek.

I thought I could see scratch marks – relatively recent ones – healing on the skin above his goatee.

'But the girl died. Any charges?'

'What?'

'Criminal charges. Speeding? Intox driving?'

'Nope. No charges. Like I said, it was an accident.' Harney was grimacing with pain. He pulled up the leg of his pants and the skin was sliced through to the bone. Blood had caked around the wound and dripped onto the top of his boot. 'Can you wait with this or what?'

'You shouldn't have walked on it. You don't want to compound it if it's fractured,' Mike said, stepping out to tell the nurse she could get to work on her patient.

We exchanged places with her and walked down the corridor to find the guy in the green-plaid shirt. Two of the other detectives had casually penned him in near the rear of the stage, where the loading dock opens into the garage, letting him smoke a cigarette. Mike signaled them to move off as we approached.

'Mike Chapman,' he said, holding out his hand. 'You're?'

'Dowd. Brian Dowd.'

'You want to tell me the story?'

'What'd Harney say? He's the storyteller.'

'That you've got it in for him.'

'He's a scumbag.'

'I'm sorry about your sister. He told us about that.'

'Told you that he killed her?'

'That she died in an accident.'

'You call it an accident when a guy's had five or six vodkas with beer chasers and then gets in the car to drive home? I call it murder.'

'Was he arrested?' Mike asked, testing the story Harney told us against Dowd's version of events.

'No, no, he wasn't locked up. You know why? 'Cause his body was thrown from the car is what he says. Got all disoriented and had a traumatic head injury is what he says. He conveniently didn't show up at the hospital till the next afternoon, when he'd sobered up and his blood alcohol didn't test off the charts anymore.'

Mike paused, understanding Dowd's rage at his sister's killer. 'How long ago?'

'Less than a year. I tried to get the car keys away from him that night. Harney was so wasted he could barely stand up straight. My sister promised me she'd drive but she couldn't control him either. She – her body – was in the passenger seat when they found her, same as always.'

'And this is somehow related to Friday night?'

Dowd dropped the cigarette to the floor and crushed it with his boot. 'I suppose he told you he worked late?'

'Yeah. The night gang.'

'Then how come he was downstairs in the locker room before the curtain went up? Eight o'clock, I swear to God. Drinking beer and playing solitaire.'

'Who were you with when you saw him?'

Dowd sneered at Mike. 'My word isn't good enough? You need a crowd?'

'Two would be a good round number.'

'I got new glasses. Haven't had them a week. I left them in my locker and had to go back downstairs. Everyone else on the stage crew was in his place. That's how come I was alone when I saw him.'

'And that's what you started fighting with him about just now?'

'Partly.'

'You must have enlisted a couple of coconspirators.'

'I didn't need anybody to deck that coward.'

'And somehow the wagon just started rolling, ready to crush his legs once he was down on the floor?'

'It's a busy place, this stage. Got to watch your step all the time.'

Mike had his hands in his pockets, walking toward the loading dock.

'Jerks.'

'You say something else?' Mike asked.

'Yeah. Your cop friends are jerks.'

'Anyone in particular?'

Dowd was taking deep breaths now. 'You think you've got us all figured out?' he said, making a sweeping gesture with his arm. 'You think you know everything about us, have a sample of our DNA?'

'That's what we've been trying to do for the last week.'

'Ralph Harney. Better check that one again, you're so fucking smart.'

'Something wrong with the information he gave us?'

Dowd laughed. 'Only thing wrong is that he didn't give it to you.'

'That's easy to check. I'll just see if there's a card for him upstairs. The detectives have interviewed almost everybody in the crew.'

'You're missing the point, Chapman. Harney isn't the one who talked to your boys. He had his cousin come in here in his place, the day he knew he was supposed to be questioned.'

'How'd he get past the security?' I asked.

'First cousins. Hal Harney. They look like brothers,

the two of them. Hal's in the same union, maybe a year older than Ralph. Works down at the Majestic.'

Mike was agitated now, running his fingers through his hair. We had been told the theatrical jobs were incestuous, that the union membership was passed along from family member to family member – fathers and sons, uncles and cousins – hard for an outsider to break in through the ranks.

'Showed his pass and walked right through the door. Like who's gonna realize it if you don't know Ralph well enough to tell the difference? So Hal sits for the interview with these crackerjack detectives instead of Ralph.'

'And it's Hal's DNA sample we've got down at the ME's office waiting to be tested,' Mike said. 'We don't have Ralph's.'

'That's why you're jerks,' Brian Dowd said, practically jabbing at Mike's chest with his finger. ''Cause Ralph knows it'd match up with what you got before. That you'd look at him a little more close, ask him who mauled his face the other night.'

'Got what before?'

'DNA. You've already got Ralph Harney's DNA. That's why he wanted Hal to sit in for him this time.'

'And why do you think we have his DNA?'

''Cause of that hooker that was killed up in the Bronx back around Christmas – the one that was strangled?'

'Hunts Point Market?' Mike asked, referring to an area of the borough that was notorious for the prostitutes who worked it around the clock.

'Yeah. Killed in a motel room near the Whitestone Bridge.'

'Why did the police get Ralph's DNA?' I asked.

''Cause the bastard went on a real bender after my sister died. Hit the bottle even worse than before. Nobody in the old neighborhood wanted anything to do with him, so he started picking up whores. Somebody got his license plate in front of the motel the night the girl was killed, and that's when detectives came to the house. My brother told me that Ralph stood in a lineup and they wanted him to submit to a DNA test. You oughta know about it,' Dowd said, looking at Mike.

'We work Manhattan. There's a different Homicide Squad in the Bronx. I don't have any idea what happened to the case, but I can find out.'

'Well, if Ralph had anything to do with it, the angels were sitting on his shoulder again. Never got busted for that one, either.'

'And you think he had something to do with Galinova last Friday?'

'If that broad took a bad turn and ran into Ralphie with his load on, I'm saying he's capable of making all the wrong moves. He's not right in the head. He hasn't been since my sister died. What'd he say about the scratches he's got, huh? What kind of answer does he have about those?'

The orchestra was playing again, and Brian Dowd was shouting at us over the music.

The prompter was seated in her box downstage, ready to call out the first word of every line to the leads in the production, who had gathered in the faux crypt on the main stage.

'How late are you working today, Brian?' Mike asked.

'I'm on till four,' he said. 'I'm here as late as you need me.'

301

Mike headed around the rear of the revolving wagon toward the exit on stage right, putting out his arm to stop me as a backdrop hung on an overhead pipe dropped into place from the fly above us.

When we got into the hallway and could hear each other, Mike slammed his hand against the concrete wall. 'That's the damn trouble with this kind of voluntary dragnet. Ralph Harney has the balls to get a stand-in for his questioning. Why? You gotta ask yourself why?'

'The "why?" seems pretty obvious to me. Harney didn't want the task force to think they were dealing with a murder suspect.'

'That scam is over. Go up and tell Peterson about this. He can call the Bronx squad for details on the case with the pros. I'll get Harney out of the medical office and march him upstairs for a little tête-à-tête with my boys. See if he'll give us some saliva – maybe even some of that blood that's clotted on his leg.'

'And if he won't agree to do it?'

'That's why I keep you by my side, Coop. You'll get me a court order.'

'You keep forgetting about that odd technicality called probable cause. You develop some of it and I'll give you whatever you need.'

'It takes so much longer to play by your rules.'

'What's the hurry? Cool your heels. Try and be useful – get an admission from him. If Harney was never arrested for the Bronx homicide, or if he's been exonerated as a suspect, then his DNA profile is only in the linkage database. He's not a convicted offender, much to Dowd's dismay.'

'So what?'

'That's exactly the issue Mercer and I were in front of Judge McFarland about yesterday afternoon. If Harney starts looking good to you, I'm going to have to go back to her on my knees next week. She's forbidden the serologists to make any comparisons from that linkage suspect pool until she rules on the authority for its existence.'

'That'll endear you to the lieutenant,' Mike called out, walking away from me toward the medical office. 'Why'd you try to fix a perfectly good system when it wasn't broken?'

'It wasn't my plan,' I said, turning to go back up to the boardroom, and practically bumping into the nurse with whom we had left Ralph Harney. She was coming from the corridor that led out to the garage exit of the opera house.

Mike jogged back toward us. 'Where's your patient?'

'I couldn't deal with him, detective. He insisted on going to see his own doctor. There was no way to fight it, so I just helped him into a taxi.'

'Ralph Harney walked out of here? You got a doctor's name, you have any idea where he went?'

The nurse was dumbfounded by Mike's irritation. 'I don't know anything, Mr Chapman. He just seemed in a terrible hurry to go.'

Chapter 28

The lieutenant was angrier than I had ever seen him. 'I got twenty detectives sitting on their asses up here, like they're Mrs Vanderbilt's invited guests for opening night. We got one squirrelly guy in this whole cast of characters – with a gimp, no less – and he's out the door before anybody's the wiser for it? It's more like a night at the opera with the Marx Brothers.'

He started shouting names as his men got to their feet, putting on suit jackets and remaking the knots in the ties that hung suspended from their shirt collars. 'Go pull Harney's cousin off his job and bring him up to the squad. Give him a feel for what a real interrogation is like,' he said to the first pair he spotted. 'Alex, can I lock him up for anything?'

'I'll try to be creative. Not for lying to the cops, if that's what you mean.'

'Yeah. What the hell? Everybody can bullshit us. We're just the dumb friggin' police department. You two – Roman and Bliss – over to Hoboken. Somebody want to get information on Harney's family and run with it? Relatives, friends, hangouts, watering holes, known pros locations. Move it.'

'Better have somebody call around to local emergency rooms,' I said. 'There's always a chance that ankle really was broken and he's gone in to get it X-rayed. No reason to assume he's skipped town.'

'Ever the optimist, blondie. I know you prefer to be ignorant about military history, but I thought the theater arts were right up your alley,' Mike said.

'And?'

'John Wilkes Booth. Shot the president in the Ford Theater, leaped onto the stage, managed to evade capture and get out of town despite the fact that he snapped the fibula in his left leg. Where there's a will there's a way. I don't think Ralph Harney is planning to stick around and make himself useful. You want me in on this, boss?'

'Nah. We screwed this one up on our own. You had something else planned, didn't you?'

'Joe Berk. See if he's missing one of his fancy gloves.'

'Keep running with your end. We'll carry this disaster as far as we can.'

The drive down Ninth Avenue to the theater district was familiar now. I called Mercer to see whether there were any prints on the letter and envelope that had been delivered to me. I knew he would get the lab director to jump the analysis to the top of this morning's pile of cases.

'Halfway there,' Mercer said. 'What was left of the stationery inside your flaming missive had Selim Sengor's fingerprints – three of them. On the envelope, we've got a partial of his gopher, Dr Alkit.'

Those would have been easy enough to compare quickly because both men had been arrested, so their print

305

comparisons were available to the expert. 'Any other partials?'

'A few on the envelope. I got somebody tracking down the messenger so we can roll his fingers, and then we'll check Laura, too.'

'Don't forget the DA's Squad has hers on file,' I said, reminding Mercer that all of the office employees had to submit to be printed during the security clearance process.

'Well, you can get this off your mind. Sengor's an ocean away and we've got Alkit under arrest. Whoever handles his case can up the ante with these new charges.'

'Thanks, Mercer. Speak to you later.'

We parked down the block from the Belasco and made our way to the entrance shortly before noon.

Two workmen were on ladders, spread in front of the marquee. They were putting up letters that would announce the next show to move into the house. The front doors were wide open and we walked into the theater to make our way to Berk's elevator through the side corridor.

The auditorium was dark, but the curtain was open and the stage was dimly lit. I could make out the shape of a large box, and Mike walked down the center aisle to see what it was.

'Must be a cheerful production moving in. That looks like a coffin.'

I walked closer and could see that Mike was right. As I got halfway down toward the front row, several floor-boards on the stage parted to reveal an opening – though one smaller than that at the Met. The thick white hair of Joe Berk was the first thing I saw rising out of the hole, as he – still in his robe and satin pajamas – was lifted up to the stage from a pit below it on some kind of hydraulic system.

'Ha! Hope you two sleuths didn't think you were coming to my funeral,' he said, stepping off the square platform as it locked in place. 'One-man shows – personally, I hate 'em. Short of Olivier and Gielgud – and that gal who's got all those talking vaginas – there aren't many stars with the talent to keep an audience in their seats.'

Berk walked over to the coffin and lifted its lid. 'Got one of these young magicians coming in. Big sensation in London. He does all the great Houdini escape tricks – the iron box, the packing case in a tank of water, the ring and the dove. There's a nut for you, Chapman.'

'Who?'

'Houdini. That's who. Harry Houdini. He was a rabbi's son. Hungarian,' Berk said, laughing at something he remembered. 'My mother had a thing for Hungarians. *Prust* – you know the word? Yiddish for "common". You talk about changing names? So this kid is born Ehrich Weiss. He wants to change it? Fine with me. I'm the last guy to fault him for that. But how'd he pick Harry Houdini? You're ashamed of being Jewish, so instead you want the world to think you're a wop? Nuts if you ask me.'

Mike's political incorrectness was in the amateur ranking compared with Berk's.

'Why the coffin?' Mike asked.

'It's an original, from Houdini himself. This is where he performed his act for years. The stage of the Belasco. We got all his hokey cabinets and props for more than half a century. There's eighteen trapdoors in the floor of

307

this place. I can disappear into the pit and come back up laid out in that casket in thirty seconds. Wanna see?'

'No, thanks. I'll take your word for it,' I said. My own brush with premature burial had given me a strong aversion to such games.

'Chapman, you think Houdini didn't have tricks?'

'I'm sure he did, Joe. I don't much believe in magic.'

'Smart boy. Right on this very stage he used to do the coffin-escape gimmick. He'd let people from the audience come up and inspect the box, examine the screws that held the lid down, and then secure them with sealing wax. Did it hundreds of times and nobody ever called him a fake. What do you think, detective?'

'You got me, Joe.'

'Come look at the fittings in the bottom here. It's ingenious. You'd never spot it unless someone showed it to you. The screws on the lower part look like they're holding the bottom edge in place. But see? They're just fitted into dowels that slide off the edge. He'd stay in the coffin as long as he thought the audience was enjoying the drama, escape from the bottom, through the trapdoor on which the coffin had been placed, then stroll out onstage whenever he was good and ready.'

Berk let the lid slam down on the empty coffin. 'Illusions, Mr Chapman, that's what my world is all about.'

'And suckers still being born every day. That's why we're back to see you. I'm sick of illusions.'

'You're running hot and cold on me, sonny. I got to get back up to bed. I'm not quite myself yet,' Berk said, shuffling in his slippers toward the elevator.

'We'll follow you up.'

'Never mind, never you mind. What is it now?'

'Gloves, Joe. One of the guys on my team found a man's glove at the Met – in the hallway where Natalya Galinova struggled with her killer.'

'She liked gloves. Long silk ones, like the ladies used to wear in my day.'

'Not hers. Your glove.'

'Mine?' he said, hyperventilating as he rested himself against a packing crate in the wings off stage right. He blew his nose with a tissue and tossed it in a garbage can in the far corner. 'What are you, another Houdini? A mentalist? Who told you they're mine?'

Mike wasn't ready to admit he'd taken something of Berk's – improperly – that had yielded a DNA profile. A pack of high-powered lawyers would probably settle on our shoulders before we could leave the building.

'I could take the shirt from your pajamas, your skin cells would be all over it, just from the way your body rubs against it.'

'You'll take nothing of mine, Chapman.' Berk was ready to walk again.

'I could pick up that Kleenex you just threw away and the lab could use it to match to the gloves we—'

'My snot? That's what you're gonna resort to in order to find out what Joe Berk is made of? Go ahead, detective. That's your element, maybe, like dirt from the street. You're welcome to it.'

'Suppose I can prove – maybe not today, but next week or the week after – suppose I could prove it was one of your gloves?'

'Then what? Then you're gonna say I used the gloves to kill Talya and left one of them behind for you to

309

find, right? I'm not that stupid. And I wouldn't waste a pair of my good gloves on a hysterical broad who'd seen her best days on the far side of a stage curtain. Too expensive. Too hard to replace a well-made pair of gloves.'

Berk looked back to see if Mike appreciated his humor.

'Friday night. You remember Friday, Chapman, don't you? I didn't need no gloves on Friday. It was a beautiful spring night, my driver puts me right in front of the plaza at Lincoln Center and I walk fifty yards to the theater. What gloves? Who says they're mine?'

Mike didn't answer.

'Maybe I oughta go through my closet, detective. See if anybody stole a pair from me. You'll show me the glove, won't you? I can probably tell you where and when I bought them, how much I paid. Then we can figure out who took the damn thing from me and see if you're capable of solving that kind of crime. Larceny,' Berk said, dragging out the first syllable of the word to mock Mike.

'Depends who has access to your clothes, I guess. Maybe one of your relatives – someone close enough to get into your drawers. It might be the time to ask about, say, your family.'

'Don't forget half the coat-check girls in town. They could have lifted my gloves, too. Every time I went to lunch this winter, every time I went to dinner. You gotta do better than this, Chapman.'

'I'd rather talk about folks closer to home.'

'Talk fast. I'm not feeling good.'

'Your son. The young one.'

'Briggsley? What about him? You think he's a glove-snatcher, detective? He's got an allowance, he can buy the whole goddamn glove department of any store you can name. Bergdorf, Saks, Harrods, Dunhill.'

'There's one other – uh – illusion, I guess you'd call it, that I'd like to clear up. It's about Lucy DeVore.'

'The swinger?' Berk said, taking deep breaths again. 'The girl on the swing. Don't bullshit me that she's talking, detective. You contribute as much money as I do every year to that hospital, they'll tell you the status quo of anyone you want to know about. They get her out of that coma, I'll be the first to know.'

'There are a few people around town who saw your son with Lucy. People who'll say that they were hooked up with each other until you got in the way. I thought maybe that would remind you about exactly where it was you saw Lucy dancing the first time. About how it was she came to your attention.'

The hyperventilation had turned to disgust. 'You got no reason to bring my boy into this. He's a good kid, detective. He doesn't have the eye for women that I do, but he'll grow up. You leave him alone.'

I knew Mike didn't need Joe Berk's help to get an address for Briggs. He was just pushing the old man's buttons to see whether he could find a hot one. 'I only want to ask him a few questions. I know from the night of your accident he had the key to your place.'

'Yeah? That makes him a crook? So my niece was in here, too, that night.'

'That was after the murder, Joe. Mona was here after the glove was found at the Met. You're telling me I can't talk to Briggs?'

'I don't want to see his name in the papers, okay? He's out in Los Angeles for a week or two. He's helping his brother close a big deal for BerkAir. He comes back, be my guest.'

Berk shuffled over to the elevator and pressed the button, waiting for it to open.

'You send him out of town to get over the girl?' Mike asked.

'He's like his old man, detective. The girls love him. Two weeks out in Malibu he'll find someone more his type. More my type, too. You need somebody to pick up the pieces of what's-her-name's broken bones? Lucy? Talk to Alden.'

'What?'

'Hubert Alden. That's his kind of trash.'

'You were pretty sure of that when you suggested to Mr Vicci that he dangle Lucy in front of Alden at the audition.'

Berk stepped in the elevator and turned to face us. 'That wasn't the first time Alden saw the girl. I know my players, detective. You look surprised. Did he tell you something different?'

Mike's expression must have given him away. 'You're certain of that?'

'I'm not a mentalist, sonny. I'm no Houdini. The girl was two-timing my kid with Alden. I saw it with my very own eyes.'

The doors closed and Joe Berk vanished without telling us when or where.

Chapter 29

'We can stop for lunch, swing by your apartment to pick up whatever you need, and I can still get you to the airport for the three o'clock shuttle to Boston.'

'That's fine. What are you in the mood for?'

'Fresco,' Mike said. 'Can you get us in?'

The Scottos ran a superb restaurant on East 52nd Street, packed with a power crowd at lunch as well as in the evening. I called and Marian sneaked us into a table in the bar, skirting us past folks who'd reserved the prime tables in the main dining room.

'Don't be doing one of those salad things on me,' Mike said, opening the extensive menu. 'The food's too good.'

'You're right,' I said, asking the waiter for cavatelli with sausage and broccoli rabe, while Mike ordered the grilled bronzino.

As hard as I tried to bring the conversation around to how he was dealing with Valerie's death, he wouldn't allow me to go there. As soon as we got off the subject of work, he snapped back into an introspective – almost sullen – mood.

Mike waited in the car while I went up to my apartment to change out of my chalk-striped business suit and heels into a turtleneck sweater, slacks, and my driving moccasins. The Vineyard would be cooler than the city, especially at night. I kept enough clothes there so I didn't have to carry a suitcase back and forth, and had only a small tote with some things I'd bought for the house since my last trip.

At that hour of the afternoon, the ride to LaGuardia was only twenty minutes from the Upper East Side. We talked about our impressions of the characters we had met in the case, and what secrets each seemed to be hiding from us, and then I asked Mike how he planned to spend the weekend as we approached the US Airways terminal for my flight.

'I'll see what Peterson turns up on Ralph Harney. We've still got to cross-check background and alibis on all the guys who live on Staten Island or near the Watchung Mountains.'

'How about Chet Dobbis?'

'I want to do him myself. Try to get to Hubert Alden's office, too. See what he's like in his natural habitat.'

'It wouldn't be the first time someone who presents himself to us so cleanly has a seamier side. You'll call me if you get anywhere, won't you?'

'Sure. When does Joanie arrive?'

'Tomorrow. She's flying up from DC, so we were supposed to meet in Boston and go over together in the morning. I'll call her to explain when I get there.'

'You don't mind being alone tonight, do you? Your letter bomber's behind bars.'

I smiled at Mike. 'You didn't give me much choice, did you?'

'Bring me a doggy bag, Coop.'

'I know. Fried clams from the Bite,' I said. Mike had spent a lot of time with me on the Vineyard over the years, and agreed that the most delicious clams in the universe, as I liked to brag, were served from a little wooden shack in Menemsha, owned by my old friends the Quinn sisters.

'And give my love to the Baroness von Clam,' he said, referring to the nickname he'd bestowed on Karen Quinn, who flirted with him notoriously whenever we showed up for lunch.

'Will do.' I said good-bye and walked through the revolving door to buy my e-ticket at the kiosk. I couldn't remember another occasion when Mike had dropped me off without parking the car and hanging out with me until flight time, but then everything seemed slightly different these days since Val's death.

I made my way through the metal detectors and sat – shoeless – to be wanded and patted down by the security crew. The plane was late coming in from Boston, so there was a delay in the servicing before we boarded.

I sat alone at a window seat for the smooth fifty-minute flight, then repeated the check-in process again at the busy Cape Air counter, which rolled out its tiny Cessnas to the Vineyard and Nantucket, Hyannis and Providence, with impressive order and timeliness.

The flight was full – a pilot and eight passengers – so I settled quickly into place in the cramped cabin. I tucked my legs in front of me to make room for the man who took the seat next to me, separated by a space so narrow that one could hardly describe it as an aisle, and made the mistake of engaging him by thanking him for waiting while I got comfortable and fastened my belt.

315

'What are you reading?' he asked.

I held up the book jacket. '*Daniel Deronda*.'

'That's the author?'

'No, it's the name of the novel. George Eliot wrote it – her last book.'

The two propellers were revved up to maximum speed as we started to pull away from the terminal. Their noise and the likelihood of bouncing around in the air pockets frequently encountered at the low altitude of Cape Air's short flights made conversation difficult most of the time. That and the fact that I was reading an obscure Victorian novel probably known only to English literature devotees and librarians these days should have been enough to ensure that my seat partner left me alone.

As the plane vibrated on the deeply potholed runway, my neighbor leaned his head in toward me. 'What do you do?'

'Excuse me?'

'I asked what you do for a living.'

I gave him my best grin. 'I'm a single mom. Four kids.'

I had gotten from coast to coast and from New York to Europe several times without ever having to make small talk to guys sitting next to me after giving that answer. It was a foolproof conversation killer with lonely businessmen angling for a pickup.

'That's great. How old are they?'

He was either lying or dumber than he looked. 'Six, four, and the twins – they're two. I've cornered the market on diapers.'

I smiled and put my nose back in the book until he spoke again. 'I love kids. You have pictures?'

'They're in my tote. I gate-checked it.' I assumed he

was a comic or a pedophile, seemingly undaunted by my imaginary brood. But I liked his face, despite my initial instincts. His nose was crooked and he had wire-rimmed glasses that sat too far down on its bridge to look comfortable, but showed off the gray-blue cast of his eyes.

'What kind of mother are you? Can't believe you don't have snapshots in your wallet.'

We climbed slowly up out of Logan. If this guy was planning to chat me up the whole way, it would be a tedious thirty-three minutes.

'It's so rare we're apart that I don't need pictures to remind me. Can't ever have a moment's peace with four of them demanding attention. Feed me, change me, blow my nose, feed me again. You know how it is.' If that didn't make it clear to him, I didn't know what would.

The wingtip caught the edge of a cloud and the plane started rolling in the clear-air turbulence. I turned my head to stare out the window into the thick white mass we had just entered.

'You a nervous flier?'

'Not at all. I don't mean to be rude, but I think I need to nap for a bit. Just tired,' I said, leaning my head against the small window and closing my eyes. It seemed to be my only line of defense.

I actually slept for twenty minutes, shaken awake on the rough descent through the thick clouds over the Elizabeth Islands. We set down on the short runway of the Vineyard airport and taxied to the terminal.

My neighbor offered his hand. 'By the way, I'm Dan Bolin. I've got my car here, if you need a lift.'

'Thanks a lot,' I said, rubbing my eyes. 'I'm all set.'

'Your name is?'

'Stafford. Joan Stafford.' I hoped Joanie didn't mind that I had saddled her with four hungry little mouths to feed. And there I'd been with Mike a few hours back, wondering why people find it so easy to lie to us.

The steps had been lowered and the passengers were descending from the center of the plane. Dan Bolin waited for me to get off, but as I took my time walking back to the terminal building, he waved good-bye and headed for the parking lot. I had arranged for my caretaker to leave my car there for me, so I stopped in the Plane View restaurant and loitered over a cup of coffee to give Bolin the chance to be out of my way.

There was just enough daylight left for me to enjoy the stunning vistas as I made my way through the familiar curves and hills of Chilmark. The old Grange Hall, the dirt road cutoff to Black Point Beach, the calm glade of Abel's Hill cemetery, the seventeenth-century stone walls that lined the pasture of the Allen sheep farm, and then the sun setting on the water at the town landing by the Stonewall bridge. I could race the remaining two miles to my sanctuary, the old farmhouse that sat high over Menemsha Pond with a commanding view of the rich green landscapes and the blues of Quitsa and the Vineyard Sound far beyond.

My gardens were prepped and dressed for spring. The forsythia gave off a golden glow on either side of the gates marked by granite pillars, and the crushed white quahog shells that served as driveway dressing brightened the grassy surround. An array of pastel-colored tulips stood on either side of the front door, while sprouts of daffodils haphazardly dotted the yard and punctuated the formal plantings, which had not yet bloomed along the bordering

318

walls. All of these hearty April flowers seemed to be taunting the deer to come and taste them.

No matter how severe the stress, no matter how profound the problems I encountered at work, when I reached my Chilmark home, it was as though every pore opened and relieved me of the pressure building up inside. I didn't forget the images in crime scene photos or the details of an autopsy report, but somehow I could put them in perspective and be restored by the beauty and peacefulness of this one place on earth I loved above all others.

The inside of the house had been readied for my arrival, and I smiled with pleasure at the personal touches that welcomed me back. In every room there was a small bouquet of flowers from my own gardens, dry logs were laid in the fireplace – flue open and matches on the mantel next to my collection of old ivory crustaceans – crisp new linens had been laundered to refresh the palette of my bedroom, and a pint of my favorite clam chowder from the Homeport was next to a pot on the oven to be heated for dinner.

I called Joan Stafford to explain the change of plans and told her I'd pick her up at the airport at noon. I took a steam shower and wrapped myself in a warm robe before moving into the living room to light the fire and settle in with the evening news and an old Barbara Stanwyck movie. When I got hungry, I warmed up the chowder and then watched the second half of the flick with a glassful of Dewar's.

Despite the fact that some of the perils of the job had found a way to the island from time to time, and that even my home had been the scene of a frightening

319

intrusion, the changes that I had made to my security system over the years kept me comfortable here and completely at ease. I slept well, lulled by the steady noise of the crickets and awakened only by the early-morning light through the glass panes of the French doors in my bedroom, with the cries of robins searching for worms in my wildflower field.

My first foray out was to the Chilmark Store, for the morning papers and a cup of coffee that I drank, picking on a cinnamon bun, while rocking in a chair on the deck. I greeted islanders who had been longtime friends – fishermen, painters, construction workers, post office employees, waitresses, and the librarian – asking and answering the obligatory start-of-season questions about how the winter had gone. For all of us who lived or worked on the western tip of the island, past Beetlebung Corner, this general store was our lifeline – the center of the universe for food, supplies, news, and gossip.

Back at the house, I took my ten-speed bike out of the barn and set off for the Aquinnah Cliffs on State Road, glad for the first exercise I'd had in a week, coasting down past the dunes of Moshup's trail and saving my energy for the last winding hill on the way back to my house.

I called to check on Joan's flight, which was scheduled to land on time, so I put the top down on the vintage Mustang and drove to the airport, nested in the middle of the island within the state forest, to pick her up.

Joan's exuberance was hard to contain in a confined space, and she began blowing kisses to me the moment she emerged in the doorway of the small plane and made her way down the short stairway.

I stood behind the gate at the edge of the tarmac and

she dropped her bag to hug me as she stepped out of the way of the other passengers.

'It must be love,' I said. 'You look stunning.'

'Love – and then, of course, Kenneth. You like the highlights?' She spun in place, referring to the legendary hairdresser who had given her a new look.

We locked arms and walked inside to the rack where the luggage was delivered. There was no such thing as traveling light for Joan.

I picked up her duffel bag and started toward the car. 'You won't need half of whatever is in here.'

'I've brought some things for you. I know, I know – not necessary, but I did. And you've got to read my manuscript. I'm almost halfway done with the new book. That's in there, too. I didn't know if we'd be going out so I brought some extra clothes.'

'And Jim? How is he?'

'He's the best. He's wonderful, Alex. And he sends lots of love.'

We had been pals for a very long time and there was nothing that relaxed me more than curling up on opposite ends of a sofa with women I trusted and adored – like Joan and Nina Baum – to unload my problems and listen to theirs, or simply to dish about guys, clothes, kids, and anything else that came to mind.

'You'll catch me up on what he's doing. It's your call: we can go out for dinner tonight – the Cornerway, the Galley, the Beach Plum, Bittersweet, the Outermost,' I said, ticking off my favorite restaurants, 'or we can stop at Larsen's Fish Market and ask them to cook and split a couple of lobsters for us. Then we just take them home and chill them until it's time to eat.'

'Perfect. Let's go out tomorrow night. Have you got any really great wine?'

'Some Corton Charlemagne.'

'Whoops. Sorry I asked. Jake's favorite, if I remember correctly? Let's stay home and stuff ourselves in front of a roaring fire. We can drink you out of his leftover vino, darling, and then you can order something entirely new. We're over him, aren't we?'

'I'm trying, Joanie. Let's not go there.'

We drove into Menemsha, the commercial fishing village that was my favorite part of the island. Along the dock where steel-hulled trawlers off-loaded their catch, old-timers watched from the wooden benches along Squid Row.

Betsy Larsen was in the kitchen, cooking lobster and working the raw bar, and her sister Kris was behind the counter. It would take twenty minutes to make our dinner, so Joan and I ordered a dozen oysters each and carried them out to eat as lunch down on the jetty, at the bight that led out to the sound.

We reached the house and I parked in front of the barn, opening the trunk to take out Joan's bag.

She was already on the step and called out to me as she pulled on an envelope that was wedged in between the screen and doorjamb.

'Did you do this?'

'What?'

'It's addressed to me,' Joan said, tearing open the sealed paper.

I came up behind her and saw the daffodils bunched in groups next to the granite step. They were soaking in four brightly colored pails – children's plastic sand buckets

322

– lined up in graduated sizes, each full of the bright yellow flowers.

'"For Joan,"' she read aloud to me. '"Hoping to see you and the kids before too long." It's signed Dan Bolin. I don't get it, Alex. I don't know anybody named Dan Bolin. Does this make any sense to you?'

Chapter 30

'I think it's romantic.'

'It makes my skin crawl. Creepy, not romantic.'

'It's exactly what you get for lying to the guy. Especially, may I add, for using my name and giving me the added delight of mothering four little monsters. I almost asked him to join us for dinner tomorrow night.'

'Spare me,' I said. The Temptations were singing 'I Can't Get Next to You', as I added two logs to the fire and opened the second bottle of wine. 'It was a weird thing for the guy to do.'

'That's the difference between us. You're always seeing perverts and madmen where I would find adventure and, well, sexiness. Thanks for giving him *my* name.'

'Sexiness?'

'Well, it was a very sexy move. Admit it. To drive all the way up here from Edgartown with flowers for you. Have you forgotten how it's supposed to feel when a guy hits on you? Especially when he's creative about doing it?'

Joan had called the phone number on the note that Bolin left at the door before we sat down for dinner. He had recognized me from the photographs in the paper and the evening news stories after the arrest of the Silk

Stocking Rapist several months earlier. He knew I was pulling his leg from the first answer I gave and decided to play with me.

'In my business we call it stalking. Now I'll be up all night worried that the guy might actually find you in the DC phone directory. How's that for guilt?'

'You've been in your line of work too long.'

'How did he know where I lived? That's not in the book.'

'It's a friendly island. He told the kid who pumps gas in Menemsha that he forgot which driveway was yours and got a very cheerful and accurate set of directions.'

'So what did you say to him?'

'That we have a full house this weekend. I promised I'd pass his number along to you and maybe you'd call him next time you're here. It's against my better instincts, Alex. I'd much rather check him out.'

'You don't know who he is or what he does or whether—'

'You said yourself he had a nice face – intelligent and sensitive.'

'So did Ted Bundy have a nice face. You'd better take your nightcap and go upstairs to bed before you come up with any other clever ideas.'

Joan slept late on Saturday morning while I took my coffee out on the deck and started reading the draft of her new novel, a brilliantly perceptive tale of obsession and revenge among Southampton's toniest social set. It was fun to try to identify the people she skewered in the book with her witty dialogue and clever observations. By the time I showered and dressed, Joan had come down, ready to plan the day.

'It's fabulous. You just nail the whole scene so perfectly.'

'Did you finish?'

'Not yet. Why?'

'The legal stuff, the part about the husband changing his will? I want you to tell me if it's accurate.'

'I hope you had some help, Joanie. I haven't touched trusts and estates since my law school class. It's a really arcane specialty.'

'One of the T-and-E partners at Milbank, Tweed talked me through it. I just wanted to be sure it makes sense to you. Looks like a glorious day. How about a walk on the beach?'

'I'm game. Grab a sweatshirt from the closet in your room and take a scarf. The sun feels great but the wind is really kicking up.'

The ride to Black Point Beach took half an hour, the slowest part of the drive on the winding dirt road – full of ruts from the winter storms – that cut off into the woods and led out to the private stretch of pristine white sand that bordered the Atlantic Ocean. There were several cars parked near the walkway across the wetlands, so we took off our shoes and trekked across the dunes to the east, our footprints the only trace of activity in that magnificent meeting place of land and water.

This was the spot I came to whenever I needed my spirit and strength restored. It had been the favorite place on earth for my fiancé, Adam Nyman. We came here days after his accident to scatter his ashes, so that he seemed forever a part of this landscape, a vista that took my breath away each time I visited again.

Joan knew that, and she knew from my stories that the last time I sat high above the shoreline on this very dune, I had brought Mike Chapman here to comfort him, to try to console him, after Valerie's accident. I tried to stop thinking about the cases and personalities that had occupied all my waking hours during the week – Talya Galinova, Joe Berk, Ralph Harney, Hubert Alden – but it was hard to do even in this setting.

I warned Joan to stay on the path, pointing out the poison ivy to the right and left. We were making small talk, I supposed, as she tried to distract me from the more serious connections this beach conjured up in my heart and mind.

'You know who we had dinner with in DC last week? Cynthia Lufkin.'

'She's amazing, isn't she.'

'Smart.'

'Very smart.'

'Gorgeous,' Joan said, wrapping the scarf around her neck against the fifteen-mile-an-hour winds whipping off the water.

'Beyond gorgeous. And extremely generous. I'm a huge fan.'

'It kills me that on top of all that she's really nice, too. Don't you hate that?'

'It's a rare combination,' I said, laughing at Joan's comment as I reached the crest of the tallest dune, watching the blue surf pound against the packed sand.

Joan passed by me and backed down halfway to the beach, putting up her hands as though to stop me. 'Enough about Cynthia. Time to talk about me. Will you sit?'

'What's going on?' I zipped my sweatshirt and parked myself on the ground.

'Look, I know what this – this beach – means to you, and I've got something terribly important to ask you. And it's the only place in the world I can even raise this question to you, because it's only here that you can give me an answer and know whether, emotionally, it's an honest one.'

'What are you talking about?'

'How long have Jim and I been engaged? It seems like I've waited longer than anyone besides Sleeping Beauty to get married, right? Well, we'd like to do it this summer. And we'd like to do it on the Vineyard.'

'Nothing could make me happier. Are you crazy? What's to ask? I'll put up some tents just in case of weather, the gardens will be at their peak, I've got the best caterer. Joanie, I can't think of anything that would please me more than throwing a wedding for you.' I started to get up to embrace her and she pushed me back down onto the sand.

'It's not that, Alex. I mean it's not *just* that. Jim and I would like you to marry us.'

'Whoa, whoa, whoa. Prosecutors aren't judges. What are you thinking?'

'I know you're not a judge. Leave it to Jim to come up with this. He's done all the research. Did you know that in Massachusetts all we have to do is make an application to the governor, with a letter of recommendation and twenty-five bucks, and whoever it is we choose can be the celebrant of the wedding?'

'I had no idea. I've never heard of such a thing.'

'You get a one-day pass, that's all. A cousin of Jim's did it on Nantucket last year and it was the most divine wedding I've ever seen. Please tell me you'll do it, Alex?

What could be more perfect than being married by my very best friend? You'll write a personal little ceremony—'

'You're the writer,' I said, searching for excuses.

'Hell, you're the English Lit major. You've written more summations – longer ones – than half of my stories. It's not about the writing. It's the intimacy of it, that's what Jim and I want. We've each been divorced, so religion doesn't seem to be a big piece of this. We'd just both love to have my best friend celebrate our vows.'

My eyes welled up with tears.

'My dear, dear Alex. I'm not trying to make you cry. We want you to be part of our joy, of our marriage.'

I stood up and this time she let me embrace her. 'Don't worry about the tears, Joanie. I can't think of any greater compliment than this.'

She grasped my elbows and pushed me back. 'But you've got to look at me, Alex. The hardest part of asking you to do this is knowing what a flood of memories this will open up for you and bring back. It's inviting you to look in the face of everything that you and Adam were about to embark on when he was killed. It's your magical hilltop and your home and—'

'And this time it's your turn, Joanie. I couldn't have faced this ten years ago, I'm certain, so you're right to be concerned. For a long time after Adam's death, I didn't go to weddings, not anybody's. Hell, I couldn't even bear to look at ads for gowns or jewelry or china in all the magazines. I used to bawl when the Tiffany catalog showed up in the mail with endless pages of wedding and engagement rings.'

She followed me down the dune and to the edge of

the sand, where the bubbles in the surf sat like froth as the waves rolled back out to sea.

'You never forget, Joan, that's for sure. But all of that pain is in a different place now,' I said, turning to face her. 'I never come home to this island without imagining what it would be like if Adam was here with me, and I never will. But the memories of being here with him are wonderful ones, the best ones of my life. And celebrating your marriage ceremony would be just about the happiest assignment I've ever had.'

'So it's a yes?' she said, walking east toward Quansoo, the adjacent beach, where we could see people gathered around what looked to be a giant excavator.

'If you really want to put this event in the hands of an amateur, I guess I'm it.'

'Excellent. We've got to figure out what we're wearing. We can go shopping together for dresses next time I'm in the city.'

'What else can I help with?'

Joan's mind was racing now. She'd clearly been holding back until she raised the issue of the ceremony with me. 'We've got to tie up some rooms at the island inns.'

'How many people?'

'You know if it were up to me, it'd be a cast of thousands. Jim wants it small and cozy. We're somewhere between his forty and my closest five hundred. Think you can get Mike to come?'

'Joanie. I know what you're thinking.'

'You always do.'

'He hasn't even started to grapple with Val's death. Mercer and I are just beginning to draw him back into work again, so give him time to adjust.'

'Give him too much time and some lucky girl will be in there offering just the right kind of solace.'

'I work with him, Joan. I've never had a better partner, someone I could trust as much as I do Mike. He and Mercer cover my back, they think with me, they're the very best in the business. If we take this in a different direction, that entire professional relationship goes by the boards. You're hopelessly romantic.'

'Somebody has to be, don't you think?' she said. 'What's going on up ahead?'

'They must be opening Tisbury Great Pond.'

'What do you mean?'

The southern shore of the Vineyard, almost twenty miles of barrier beach, was dotted by a series of ponds, large and small. 'Those oysters you like so much? They come from that body of water,' I said, running up the nearest dune and pointing out the Great Pond. 'A century ago, the Wampanoags figured out the importance of the moon and the tidal changes in getting saline water from the ocean into the clam and oyster beds in here.'

'What'd they do?'

'They used to come down here with oxen and dredge an opening out to the sea. Now the local shellfish constable oversees things. They use heavy earth-moving equipment to make an artificial channel into the pond every spring, and a couple of other times a year.'

'That's a huge gap they've created.'

'Probably sixty, seventy feet across.'

'What's everyone looking at?'

'The local newspaper said the opening was supposed to be yesterday. But it doesn't always take the first time they try. The Native Americans were so damn smart about the tides.' We were side by side on the dune, staring out at the ocean. 'Mesmerizing, isn't it, the ebb and flow? If it's high tide and you've got a four-foot sea, but the pond is only three feet high, the water rushes right back in and fills the trench. The beach tends to heal itself, so it usually takes twenty-four hours – and a bit more shoveling – to make sure the gap stays open.'

'Wouldn't you like to watch?'

Joan and I walked the last quarter of a mile. The giant black excavator had blocked from view the rescue vehicle that had lumbered over the sand to park beside it.

We jogged the last few yards and joined the huddle of men standing around the small truck, its open back revealing a vinyl body bag.

'What happened?' I said, recognizing one of the volunteer firemen from the Chilmark station.

'Some smartass decided to test the waters last night. Inaugurate the opening of the cut by putting on his wet suit and bringing his surfboard down to the beach. Got caught in a pretty fierce rip and disappeared. Rescue crews searched half the night with no luck, till just about daybreak. He – his body – just got thrown back up here an hour ago. Nothing to see, Alex,' he said, trying to steer me out of the way. 'Nothing left to do but say a prayer.'

I nodded to Joan and we started back over to Black Point.

'Talk about putting a damper on a lovely afternoon. Don't you ever feel spooked by this?' she asked me.

'By what?'

'By death, Alex. How death seems to follow you wherever you go.'

Chapter 31

An early April thunderstorm ripped through the Boston suburbs south of Logan Airport and kept the plane on the tarmac for close to three hours on Sunday evening. It gave me even more time to reflect on Joan's remark, as I had done throughout the lazy weekend we spent together after leaving the beach. Police, prosecutors, pathologists, and serologists – all of us whose professional lives were absorbed with understanding the secrets of the dead – seemed to be surrounded with more than our share of violent happenings.

Instead of reaching LaGuardia in time for the dinner I had planned to enjoy with a couple of my law school friends, I watched Joan race off to catch the last shuttle to Washington and waited on line at the taxi stand to get a cab back into the city.

'Welcome home, Ms Cooper,' Benito said, stepping out to the curb to open the car door for me. 'I have your mail and some dry cleaning in back.'

I followed the doorman inside, waiting while he went into the storage area to get the bundle of magazines and plastic-wrapped dresses that had been delivered over the weekend.

It was ten thirty by the time I sorted through the bills, a postcard from Nina Baum, and the flood of invitations to charity luncheons that heralded the spring season. I started a tub running with steaming-hot water and sprinkled some bath salts in it, watching them foam up as the tub began to fill.

I was standing at the bar, pouring myself a shot of my new single-malt Scotch and smiling at the remembrance of Mike's gesture, when the apartment suddenly went black.

Feeling my way back to the bathroom, I turned off the faucet and then slowly guided myself around familiar pieces of furniture, into the kitchen to find a flashlight and the fuse box.

I yanked at the heavy metal door of the box, standing on tiptoe to see what had blown so that I could flip it back on. All of the switches were aligned, and I played with a few of them to see whether anything made a difference, but no lights came on around me.

With the same baby steps that got me from room to room, I went to the foyer of the large apartment and pressed against the peephole in the front door. I was reassured to see that the overhead hall fixtures were still working, which meant that the entire building didn't have the problem that I did.

I grabbed my pocketbook and dug out my cell phone, taking it into the living room, where the great expanse of windows caught whatever light reflected from the street lamps many floors below. I dialed the concierge desk to ask whether the two doormen could find the superintendent or a handyman, but the number was busy.

On the fourth try, I connected with Benito. 'No problem, Ms Cooper. Don't worry about anything.'

'What do you mean, no problem? I've lost all my power. No lights, the refrigerator is off, the clock radio. What is it, Benito? Do you know?'

'It's all the apartments in the A line. You and everybody else in A.'

'Up and down the whole building?'

'First floor to the penthouse. They're all yelling at me, like I had something to do with it.'

'Are they working to restore it?'

'You could call me back in half an hour. The super says he's gonna have somebody here to check it out very soon. A crew from Con Ed is coming. Maybe we'll know something by then. Maybe you'll already have it back on. Or you could just go to sleep, Ms Cooper. He gonna have it back on before the morning.'

My hallway neighbors, David and Renee Mitchell, usually didn't come back to the city from their country house until Monday morning. I had a spare key for their apartment, for the times I occasionally walked their dog, Prozac. But I decided it was foolish to try to get inside in case they were home and already asleep.

I stretched out on my sofa in the den, nursing my drink, ready to nap against the background of routine city noises twenty floors below – cars honking at one another, the distant sound of an ambulance siren, and the rumblings of the private carting services that lurched through the streets at odd hours of the night. There was no point undressing in case I had to leave the apartment or let a workman in to check the system.

I dozed for half an hour, awakened – I thought – by scuffling sounds outside my door.

I walked to the foyer again and looked out through the peephole, but saw no one.

'Benito?' I asked, calling the desk again.

'Yeah, Ms Cooper?'

'Any progress?'

'They got a guy working on it in the basement now, Ms Cooper. You wanna come down to the lobby and wait here?'

'Why?'

'I dunno. You know Mrs Melsher? The old lady with the walker? She got scared alone in the dark. She's down here keeping us company.'

'Thanks, Benito. I'm fine.'

'I'm going off at midnight. Want me to leave a wake-up call with Willie for you?' he said with a laugh. 'It's not enough we gotta be the weathermen for you guys, deliver messages to each other, sign for your deliveries. Now I gotta play hearts with Mrs Melsher and leave wake-up calls for the guy on sixteen who has to catch an early flight and the lady on twelve who's having root canal at eight a.m.'

'See you tomorrow.'

I went into the bedroom and laid down on top of the covers, pulling the throw over me. The lights flickered and the illuminated dial of the clock radio glowed for several seconds, but the room went black again and I closed my eyes to try to sleep.

It was one o'clock when the phone rang.

'Hello?'

'Sorry to disturb you, Ms Cooper. It's me, Benito. The super asked me could you come downstairs, please?'

336

'Why?'

'Look, I'm only doing what he told me. I'm calling all the A apartments. He has me working a double shift here,' Benito said, pausing before he brought up the deadly reference. 'He don't want me to be saying this to everyone, Ms Cooper, 'cause we don't want no kind of panic. But – like – think of nine-eleven. We don't want people stuck upstairs if there's some kind of electrical fire.'

I was bolt upright. 'Fire? He thinks it's a fire?'

Benito clucked his tongue in annoyance. 'I'm not saying there's no fire. It's a just-in-case kind of thing. Nobody told us what it is yet. The first guy that got here, he's started at the bottom. They're gonna check every hallway, go inside and check your electrical panels.'

'I really don't want to leave the apartment. I'd rather be here,' I said, thinking of the valuables I had around the place.

'Don't worry, Ms Cooper. The super's coming with him. The guy won't be in there alone. It just could be a really dangerous thing.'

The thought of getting zapped like Joe Berk or asphyxiated in a fire smoldering behind the apartment walls was enough to move me. I didn't need the reference to the unspeakable tragedies of 9/11.

'And you can't be using the elevator, Ms Cooper. They had to shut that down.'

'Why?'

'You're asking a lot of questions I can't answer. I guess that's how come you're a lawyer. Somebody smelled that kind of electrical-like, rubber-burning smell. We don't want to panic nobody, but they says you should come downstairs.'

I threw my purse in the bottom of my linen closet, put my keys and cell phone in my pocket, and tossed on a leather jacket in case I decided to leave the lobby for a friend's house as events developed closer to morning. The last thing I brought was the flashlight.

The twentieth-floor hallway was quiet, and as I passed the elevator bank I paused to sniff the air to see whether I smelled anything unusual. If there was something on fire, that odor was overwhelmed by the remains of a neighbor's curried takeout, in containers still sitting next to the trash compactor.

I opened the door to the stairwell and was surprised to find that it was pitch black. I backtracked into the hallway and flipped open the phone to call the concierge desk again, but the number was busy.

After three more attempts and growing impatience, I pushed open the heavy fire door and shined the long, narrow beam of the flashlight into the deep tower of stairs and grabbed the steel handrailing to begin my descent.

The supposed fireproofing of the emergency staircase served as a sound barrier as well. The only noise was the clicking of my loafers against the cement steps. I picked up speed as I rounded the landing on nineteen, becoming more sure-footed as my eyes adjusted to the darkness.

When I reached eighteen, I stopped in my tracks. Someone was breathing heavily, not far away from me, perhaps winded from going up or down the stairs. I tried to stay calm, assuming that it was a neighbor in some sort of distress.

'Hello?' I swiveled in place and turned the beam above me, in the direction from which I had just come, but saw nothing, and no one answered.

I grabbed the door handle to get back into the well-lit landing of the eighteenth floor, but it was locked. I flashed the beam below me and seeing no one, I went as fast as I could down the stairs to seventeen. Again, I tried the door for reentry, throwing my body against it as I pushed, but with no success.

Now the sound of my own deep breaths and loud heartbeats made it impossible for me to tell whether there were other noises.

I gripped the rail and dashed down farther, to sixteen, and now I could hear the footsteps racing from behind me, rubber-soled sneakers or shoes squeaking as they quickened coming toward me.

'Who's there?' I screamed out, sounding as panicked as I felt, knowing that my shouts couldn't penetrate the thick walls to alert adjacent tenants.

I leaned forward and slid my arm along the metal railing, trying to take two steps at a time but fearful of falling. As I turned on the next landing, I swung the light upward. Someone taller than I, dressed completely in black, with only the slits for eyes showing out of a ski mask, was trying to overtake me.

I let go of the support to reach into my pocket, bracing against the wall with my right arm to keep my balance, the friction of the leather jacket slowing my descent. Still clambering down and still shining the beam ahead of me, I felt for the redial button on the cell phone and pressed on it.

A gloved hand clamped around my neck, squeezing it with tremendous force, while the other hand locked on my shoulder. The person powering them knocked me to the ground as I tumbled to the next landing and rolled to a stop with my back wedged into the corner, wheezing to catch my breath.

'Benito!' I screamed as the shiny silver cell phone dropped out of my pocket and slid across the floor.

I could hear a faint voice calling out from the little device, 'Hello? Hello? Who is it?'

The figure was standing over me now, pulling on my legs, twisting me onto my stomach and trying to grab the hair at the nape of my neck to hold my head still.

I thrashed and kicked at him, screaming again to Benito. 'It's Alex Cooper. I'm in the stairwell, Benito. *Fire!* Benito. *Fire!*'

I was yelling as loud as I could, knowing from years of professional experience that someone was more likely to come to my aid if I screamed 'fire' and not 'rape'.

The man had one knee on the floor and the other planted in the middle of my back as he reached for one of my arms, stretching at the same time to try to grab for the phone. He made a weird, grating sound – like the tip of his tongue hissing against his front teeth – as his chin grazed the top of my head.

'In the stairwell, Benito,' I screamed again, unable to remember exactly which floor of the building I had reached. 'I'm on – I'm not sure, Benito. I'm think I'm on sixteen. Help me! *Help me!*'

My assailant couldn't have it both ways. He had to release my arm to snatch the phone from the floor. As he did, we both heard Benito giving commands in Spanish to one of the handymen, directing him to run up the stairs to find me.

The attacker dropped the phone and I heard it clatter down the steps. Then he kicked me once in the side so that I remained writhing on the floor, doubled up in pain. He took off into the darkness above me, and thirty seconds later, somewhere on a high floor between the landing and the penthouse on thirty-five, I heard one of the heavy emergency doors open and slam shut behind him.

Chapter 32

I was able to crawl down the steps to retrieve my phone and dial 911 before the building workmen reached me.

By the time the sergeant and two uniformed cops from the 19th Precinct arrived in the lobby, the team of Con Ed repairmen had restored power to the A line and started the elevators running again. There was no electrical fire and it would be hours before they could determine the reason for the blackout.

The sergeant took me up to my apartment while the cops called for a backup unit to go through the building from top to bottom.

I poured each of us some Scotch and we sat in the living room, his police radio on the coffee table so that we could hear the conversations back and forth as the guys searched the staircases and hallways in vain.

When the doorbell rang, Sergeant Camacho walked to the door to let his men in.

'Yo, sarge. I didn't know you and Coop had hooked up. Am I breaking anything apart here? A cocktail? Last dance?' Chapman was leaning against the entrance to my apartment, gnawing on a toothpick as he held the door open with his foot.

Camacho blushed and started to protest that he'd only responded to a call and was starting to fill out the paperwork on my complaint.

'Relax, pal. Take it easy. Not enough I spent the last six hours checking out a jumper off a project rooftop in East Harlem, now I got blondie seeing shadows in the stairwell. The least you could have done is invite me to the after-party, too,' Mike said, walking into the den, toward the bar. 'Mind if I turn in the brew for something more refreshing?'

'Good news travels fast, I guess.'

'The commanding officer of the Nineteenth called in an unusual on you. Lieutenant Peterson heard it on the scanner and told me to get my ass over here ASAP. And by the way? Peterson says the CO thinks you've got Munchausen syndrome. That you make these whacko stories up just because you like my company.'

'The only thing I like better than your company is a good night's sleep. I'm forgetting how that happens.'

An unusual report was filed in matters that might be of some significance to the commissioner and higher-ups in the department. The fact that a prosecutor working on a high-profile matter had been rousted from her home during the night and had been the target of an attempted assault would be of interest to everyone.

'You know your guys are coming up empty, don't you, sarge? I just saw one of them in the lobby and there's no trace of an intruder.'

I bit into my lip and tried to calm myself.

'This place is big. If it wasn't the midnight shift, we woulda had more guys on duty, bigger response to sweep the building. Do it faster.'

'It can't be that difficult. He fled up the stairs. He eventually had to go down to get out of the building, didn't he?' I asked. 'You're telling me nobody saw him?'

Mike sat opposite me, his hand on the knee of my jeans. 'Give the guys time to canvass people. Maybe we're dealing with a pro. He got in without anybody knowing about him, could be he slipped out that way, too. You okay?'

'Considering the alternative? I'm great.'

'You have any idea what this guy was trying to do to you?'

I glanced at the sergeant, afraid he would think I was crazy if I said what I really thought.

'C'mon, Coop. Tell me.'

'You don't really believe I was flushed out of my apartment randomly, do you?' I looked back and forth between their faces but neither answered. 'You think this perfectly prepared – I don't know what to call him – lunatic? Will that do? A guy dressed completely in black, head and hands covered – no ID, no trace evidence. You think he just happened to be there when my lights went out? Not for a minute. This has to be connected to something I'm working on.'

'Did he talk to you? Say anything that suggests he knew who you were?'

'Talk to me? It wasn't a pickup, Detective Chapman. The plan was obviously to kill me by choking or—'

'Whoa. A little dramatic tonight, aren't we? Kill you?'

'I called out to him, thinking maybe he was a neighbor. He never answered. All he wanted to do was overtake me and pin me down so that he could – well, he could do whatever it was he intended to do to me.' I rubbed my neck. 'I'm telling you he gripped me so hard that if I hadn't gotten away from him he'd have stopped my breathing within seconds.'

The sergeant was emboldened by Mike's skepticism. 'Maybe, ma'am, he was just coming along behind you and fell on the staircase. My guys are knocking on—'

'Oh, my *masked* neighbor? The one who dresses for blizzards in April? The clumsy one who can't stay on his feet?' I stood up and walked to the front door. 'Why am I wasting time with you two? Sergeant, I'd like you to take me down to the lobby so I can see who these guys are from Con Edison.'

'Coop, stay here and I'll bring up their supervisor so you can satisfy yourself that none of them have anything—'

'I wasn't talking to you, Mike. You might as well go home and keep wallowing in your own misery. No need to take *me* seriously.'

Mike grabbed me by the elbow and pulled me away from the door. 'Wallowing? Is that what I've been doing for three months? Is that what Val—'

'I'm sorry. That's not what I meant to—'

'You don't usually have any difficulty expressing yourself. I get your point.'

'I apologize, Mike.' I squared off to face him directly. 'I'm scared and I'm tired and I'm the one who's feeling sorry for myself tonight. Please accept my apology.'

'Whoever did this to you was either inside another apartment or out of the building by the time the first RMP got here.'

'Mike, will you forgive—'

'It's not the time for this, Coop. The sergeant doesn't

345

need to know my backstory, okay? These Con Ed guys who are here—'

'You've seen them yourself? They're legit?'

'There's bad wiring, they say, that took the electricity in this whole line down.'

'Bad, like it's damaged? Or like it was intentionally altered?'

'It's two o'clock in the morning. Bad is all they know so far.' Mike took a slug of vodka and adjusted the collar of his jacket.

'You know more than you're telling me.'

'I always know more than you give me credit for, kid, don't I?'

'I'll give you an acknowledgment in my next legal brief. What is it?'

'It doesn't take a law degree to know that the source for all the electricity in the building comes in through the basement. The basement is accessible from within the building, isn't it?'

I nodded. 'From the garage, too. And from the outside, although I assume those doors are locked at night. It's huge. There's a storage room, a laundry room. I've never even been inside the custodial area.'

'Working a toaster oven is high tech for you,' Mike said. 'Once inside that boiler room, a guy with a few high school vocational classes under his belt could easily find the main electrical panel that connects to the A-line apartments and with not much more than a pair of needle-nose pliers, put you and anyone else he wanted out of business for the night.'

'And the elevator banks?' I asked. 'Was the super really ordered to shut them down?'

346

'Yeah. You can smell the burnt rubber in the basement. They had to take that precaution with both banks of elevators.'

'You believe there was a man after me, right?'

'I'd believe you if you told me you saw a UFO, kid. I'm not the enemy here,' Mike said, steering me back to the living room sofa to sit down. 'Face it. This building is a block long. You've got the north and south wings, two elevator banks for residents plus the freight elevator, and two sets of fire stairs. All your stalker had to do was make the place go dark, then walk up the staircase and wait for all the pigeons to come out of their cubbyholes. It's not the *how* that's hard to figure, it's the why.'

'Security cameras?' the sergeant asked.

'Too snooty here,' Mike said. 'Management wanted them installed after an incident a few years back. Coop's neighbors were up in arms. Invasion of privacy and all that crap. No cameras.'

'All he had to do after the attack,' I said, 'was go back up to one of the floors above me and walk across the hallway to the other side of the building—'

Mike took over from there. 'Take off his mask and gloves, drop them and the black sweater in the garbage chute, and walk down and out like any other respectable citizen, unnoticed because of all the commotion that's going on in the lobby and outside the building.'

'The CO has a man on each entrance of the building. Everybody passing through this morning will have to stop to be identified, residents or not,' Camacho said.

'Can't wait till I get my eviction notice,' I said. 'Talk about a nuisance tenant.'

347

'Give me your keys.'

'What?'

'Your keys. I'm going to take the sergeant downstairs to see where things stand while you grab a few hours of that sleep you say you need. I'll let myself back in for a nap. Better than wallowing alone at home.'

'Mike, I feel like—'

'The keys,' he said, holding a hand up in my face to stop me from going on. 'Rest up 'cause we got an early-morning meeting with Joe Berk.'

'I'm not sure I have the fortitude for him first thing in the morning. He's so crude. You got something I don't know about?'

'I've been working on that photograph of Lucy DeVore. You know, the recent one, looks like it could have been taken since she got to New York.'

'Wearing the fez, leaning on a doorknob with a word inscribed in the metal that begins with the initial *M*?'

'Yeah, that one. So first I stopped by the task force operation at the opera house. Not even close. There's nothing that looks like the same design or lettering on anything at the Met. So I got a list of the other legitimate theaters from one of the old-timers who works the box office, for all the Broadway houses that begin with *M*. I started at the Music Box.'

'What a beauty, isn't it? It was designed to house musicals by Irving Berlin. That's why my father always loved to go there – reminded him of his childhood.'

'Too delicate. Not a match. So I tried the Majestic.'

'That one's huge.'

'No good. Forever *Phantom*. Even threw in the Martin Beck. Nada. And there used to be a theater called the

Morosco, the old broad told me, but it was demolished a long time ago.'

'I can't think of any others.'

'I couldn't, either. But the same dame told me about the Brooks Atkinson, whoever the hell he was.'

'A critic. He wrote theater reviews for the *Times*.'

'Yeah, well, that was built back in the 1920s. And it was called the Mansfield then,' Mike said, not even trying to suppress a smile. 'Why you'd name anything for a critic is beyond me. I still thought it was worth checking out the original fixtures despite the change on the marquee.'

'I take it you found your doorknob.'

'Nope. But hanging in the theater lobby was a whole bunch of blowups of famous actors from forty, fifty years ago, celebrating at Sardi's after some kind of award show. In one of them, you can see Yul Brynner, Zero Mostel, and Richard Burton, each raising a glass, with Joe Berk smack in the middle of the group. And on top of his foul-mouthed fat head is the same, exact kind of tasseled red fez that Lucy DeVore was wearing in that photograph we found in her hotel room.'

Chapter 33

When we left my building in the morning, detectives were still canvassing neighbors, crime-scene technicians were going over the exits and basement for trace evidence, and the lobby was abuzz with curious tenants who wanted to know about all the police activity that they paid so dearly not to experience.

'Speed it up, blondie. You're getting the fish eye from the super,' Mike said, pushing me through the revolving door and pointing to his department car, parked at the curb at the end of the driveway.

'Are we calling to say we're on the way? Seven thirty's a pretty unsociable hour for a drop-in.'

'We'll get Berk's pump working early. Might be good for him.'

We stopped in front of the Belasco, right opposite the manhole that had jolted Berk's heart just a week ago. Mike rang the buzzer of the apartment's front door and several minutes later, a woman's voice asked us to identify ourselves. It was a different private-duty nurse who admitted us to the office at the bottom of the winding staircase.

'Mr Berk's having a bad morning. I can't allow you in without permission from his physician.'

'I've got some medicine that might help him breathe a little better,' Mike said, ignoring the white-capped sentry and climbing the wide steps two at a time.

I shrugged at the nurse and followed.

The patient's nile green satin pajamas had been replaced by a pair of magenta ones, but all else looked the same. Berk came shuffling out of the bathroom, wrapping the tie of the robe around his waist. He was obviously startled to see us in his bedroom.

'You're pariahs, both of you. What's left of me that you want this time? Here,' he said, holding his arm straight out ahead of him, pushing up the sleeve. 'My blood? Take it. C'mon, drain it out of me. Maybe I'll get a deduction for a charitable contribution.'

Berk walked to his bed and settled himself back into it.

'You read the papers, Joe? Anything besides *Variety* and the stock ticker?'

'Why? You gonna give me a current-events quiz?'

'Ms Cooper here indicted a doctor last week. That sicko was drugging women to knock them out in order to have sex with them.'

Berk pulled the sheet up under his chin and looked over at me. 'That your case? Quite a headline you got yourself. Your boss probably would have liked it better if you caught the guy.'

There wasn't much Berk missed.

'But her boss did make an interesting point, Joe. The doctor liked to go to the movies. Foreign flicks and local ones, too. Apparently he preferred that to the stage, no offense to you. So he made his own. Filmed himself raping women who didn't have a clue what was happening to

351

them. And that fact got District Attorney Battaglia kind of wondering about you, Joe – about—'

'That prick didn't like me from the old country, Chapman. He's looking to get me any which way he can.'

'Battaglia asked Ms Cooper whether it was possible you had the same kind of perversion the doctor has?'

Berk raised himself up and guffawed in Mike's face. 'Perversion? What does he know from perversion? Let me tell you, young man, Joe Berk never had to put anybody out to get laid, detective. I like 'em talking to me and smiling at me and telling me they never had it so good before. I give a shit if they're lying? Makes us both feel good. Tell Battaglia to stick that in his cigar and smoke it. I told you before, Chapman, the girls can't get enough of old Joe.'

'No, no, no. Not that part, Joe. The movies. Coop and me,' Mike said, looking over at me and pointing a finger. 'Don't correct my grammar now, kid, okay? Coop and me, the first night we were here, mourning for you a little prematurely, we saw the video screen setup you had right in this room. Four monitors, and three of them weren't tuned in to the evening news. They were – well – where were those cameras shooting, Joe? What were you watching, and did whoever it was on the other end of the lens know she was being watched?'

Berk was squirming under the covers now, gulping for air like a fish out of water.

'We gave you a pass the first time we met you here, Joe. We felt bad that you'd taken such a hit from stepping on the sewer cover. Coop and me, we didn't figure these televisions,' Mike said, sweeping his arm in the space behind him, where only the ordinary set remained today, 'we didn't figure they had anything to do with the murder of Natalya Galinova. But now I don't know. I just don't know.'

Berk seemed to be struggling to speak.

'Mike, go easy. Let me get the nurse,' I said, turning and walking to the top of the staircase to call her to come up.

'Coop's a softie, Joe. Every now and then, something cracks through that armor she wears over her heart and gets inside and shoots directly to her brain, dulling its action for a few minutes. Me? I don't buy your bullshit. You're gasping for air 'cause you're grasping for straws. Too much time in the theater is what you've had. You're all about artifice and make-believe.'

I stood in the doorway, watching Joe as he stretched his hand out to get Mike's attention. 'Listen to me. Those monitors, they were so I could see my shows, check the productions without leaving home. That's all—'

'I'm sick of your lies. Those cameras weren't focused on any stages. They were in bathrooms or dressing rooms. They were in places nobody expected to be spied on. You don't have to help me, Joe. I'm good at legwork. I'll walk the soles off these shoes but I'll find your goddamn secrets before too long,' Mike said, walking to the far side of the room and pulling open a cabinet drawer as he passed by a bureau. 'And with any luck, I'll find your videotapes, too. 'Cause I gotta figure you were filming your show-girls, your dancers, your hookers – whoever it was – just the way that perverted doc was recording himself with every victim. You had somebody set up a camera system connected to your bedroom so you could play with your-self whenever the mood struck you. I gotta think you sat here alone in your slimy pajamas and made believe you had one of these girls right here in the room with you, keeping alive the myth of Joe Berk.'

Berk tossed back the covers and tried to swing his legs over the side of the bed. 'Don't touch another thing in this room. Get out of here, both of you.'

'The tapes, Joe. I know there are tapes somewhere around here. Am I getting warm?' Mike asked, walking toward one of the many closet doors. 'Am I getting closer?'

The nurse came in the room just as Berk lifted a small figurine – a statuette of Napoléon – from the bedside table and threw it at Mike's head. It didn't come close to hitting him, but it shattered the mirror on the wall behind the bureau.

'Bad arm you got. And seven years of bad luck to go with it.'

The nurse was trying to calm her patient and get him back in bed. The slight exertion of throwing the brass piece seemed to have exhausted Berk.

'You're a fool, Chapman. I've had guys thrown off the force for less than this. You're way out of line.'

'I hate being lied to, Joe. I hate murder most of all—'

'I never killed anybody. You're being stupid about that.'

Mike stood on the other side of the bed, while the nurse took Berk's pulse and adjusted the pillows behind him.

'Then why do you keep lying to me? You aren't honest about the little things, so now I got to worry about what you're hiding, I got to focus on what's your connection to the big things. Like why did Galinova have to die?'

Berk closed his eyes and tried to take a few breaths.

'Why did you keep lying about Lucy DeVore?'

Berk didn't speak.

'There's no point lying. That coma she's in was medically induced. She'll be out of it later this week. Paralyzed, maybe, but I expect she'll have good reason to want to tell us the truth. This photograph, Joe. Look at it.'

Berk didn't move.

'Open your eyes. It's your hat, isn't it? Lucy's wearing your hat?'

Berk cocked an eye and examined the photograph. 'The fez? C'mon, detective. You're gonna bait me, I expect you to do better than that.'

'I've seen pictures of you with a hat just like that.'

Joe Berk was smiling. He had the upper hand again, or so it seemed. 'Once. I had one of those on my head once. Sardi's. A Jewish boy with a fez on his *keppel* for four hours? It seemed like a lifetime to have to wear it that long. Forty, maybe fifty years ago. Gave a million dollars to a hospital for crippled children that year, trying to buy my way into the theatrical community. In return, for one night I was an honorary member of the Ancient Order of the Nobles of the Mystic Shrine. That's what your fez is, Mr Chapman.'

'What? Shriners?'

'Of course, Shriners. The industry used to be full of them. The theaters were their playground. Yul Brynner, you kids remember him? Maybe not a real king, but what a prince. He told me that night I reminded him of Jackie Gleason and his pals at the Raccoon Lodge. Ridiculous looking. I couldn't wait to get the damn thing off my head.'

Berk closed his eyes again and his voice faded. 'You

355

want a fez? You want to know who put that hat on Lucy's head? Check with Hubert Alden. He's got a thing for those red tasseled caps.'

Chapter 34

Mike walked me into One Hogan Place and took me directly to the ninth-floor District Attorney's Squad, the hand-chosen NYPD detectives who were assigned to Battaglia to work on major investigations led by some of the six hundred prosecutors on our staff. The captain wasn't there yet but a team had been brought in to assist on last night's attack and I spent the first three hours of the day being debriefed by them about the entire week's happenings so they could partner with Mike and Mercer if the events of last night at my apartment were indeed related to our investigation at the Metropolitan Opera House.

Mike left us to return to midtown, intent on bringing Hubert Alden down to me for questioning later in the day.

At noon, when we completed the first grueling round of detail, I went into the restroom to wash my face in hopes of reviving my flagging spirits.

On my way back to my own office, I ran into Mike getting off the elevator. He was carrying a tall vase of flowers that obscured his face as he made his way down the corridor.

'Are you crazy? That must have cost a—'

'Don't worry, kid. They're not from me,' he said. 'Security wouldn't let the poor delivery guy in the door after your express letter bomb incident.'

I followed him past Laura's desk and made room for the dramatic arrangement of spring flowers – stargazer lilies and hydrangeas, deep-fuchsia anemones and pale pink long-stemmed roses.

'Open the card,' Mike said.

He caught my hesitation.

'Open it. I'm not all that curious about your admirers, Coop. I just want to make sure the note doesn't explode in your puss.'

I unsealed the small card. 'Alex – to make up for the daffodils, and for alarming you with my doorstep delivery. Dan Bolin.'

'What could possibly be in that note that makes you turn red?' Mike asked, reaching for it.

I dropped it on the top of my desk. 'That's ridiculous. I'm not blushing. I don't even know the guy.'

'A hundred bucks' worth of petals and you don't know him? Imagine what'll happen when you start putting out for him. Why is he sending stuff like this if you don't know him? We gotta put him in the suspect pool for last night?'

'Joan knows him. I don't mean she knows him, but she's talked to him. He was on the Vineyard this weekend.'

'You're not making sense with this "know him but we don't really know him" stuff. Guess I picked the wrong weekend to take a pass on your invite. You do a three-way or something to deserve this?'

Laura was standing in the doorway; when she started

to talk to me, I stepped toward her and Mike picked up the card. 'Mike, Mr Alden is downstairs. Shall I have them let him up?'

'Yeah, he didn't want to accept my hospitality for the ride. Told me his driver would bring him down here. Given the choice, I'd pick the backseat of his limo, too,' Mike said. 'So who's this Bolin guy?'

'Oh, Alex? A gentleman named Bolin called this morning and asked if it was okay to have flowers sent here. Something about not wanting to upset you by asking for your home address, but I gave him this one.'

'That's fine, Laura.'

I bent over the desk, trying to make order out of the scattered folders and newly accumulated mail, but Mike knew I was just avoiding his glare.

'You didn't answer me. Who's this guy you know but you don't know? Where does he live? What does he do? Where was he last night?'

'Look, it was a harmless flirtation on his part. I sat next to a guy on a plane for half an hour and he tried to ask me out. Not interested.'

'The florist and I would both have to say you didn't make that very clear, did you? Don't you think we have to talk to him, put him in the mix?'

Laura was still in the doorway, probably feeling responsible for the appearance of the flowers, disliking as she did any tension between Mike and me. 'He sounded like a perfectly nice man, Mike. I wouldn't have given the green light if I'd known—'

'Can we leave him out of this entire discussion unless it becomes necessary to go in a new direction?'

'I don't know why you're protecting him, Coop.'

'That's not what I'm doing. I'm trying to keep him out of my personal life – and my business – until this murder investigation and all its offshoots are resolved.'

'Maybe last night had something to do with Dr Sengor's case,' Laura said, trying to be helpful.

'Sengor's in Turkey, his accomplice is in jail—'

'What if he had more than one accomplice?' Mike asked.

'Joan Stafford thinks I'm paranoid. Maybe it's from hanging around this place too much. Both of you see suspects everywhere.'

Laura turned away from us when we heard Hubert Alden's voice from the hallway. 'Is this Alexandra Cooper's office?'

Mike lifted the flower arrangement and started out of the room. 'I'm putting this on Laura's desk for the time being. Doesn't exactly look like a serious prosecutor's lair with half of the Versailles gardens looming between you and your target.'

He walked back in the room followed by Hubert Alden, who removed his hands from the pants pocket of his well-tailored navy pinstripe suit and rubbed them together as he surveyed the gritty surroundings of my small office – cramped, in need of a paint job, and decorated with court exhibits that were reminders of cases won and lost over the last decade.

'And you're a bureau chief, Ms Cooper?' Alden said, watching a peeling paint chip on the ceiling as though it were about to fall on his shoulder and mar the surface of his jacket. 'I can't imagine how the Indians live.'

'One of the perks of public service. You never have to waste time thinking about how to redecorate.

360

Whichever shade of gray the city uses every twenty years is fine with me. I'd like to thank you for coming down here. We have a few more things we'd like to discuss with you.'

'Has there been a resolution yet about the release of Ms Galinova's body from the morgue? I'm flying to Europe at the end of the week and it would truly set my mind at ease if we could get her out of the morgue and put her to rest with some dignity.'

I made a note to call the ME's office. 'I should be able to finalize that.'

'If you're leaving town, that is,' Mike said, settling into the chair next to Alden.

'How dramatic of you, detective. Now, what do you know that you think might put the brakes on my plans?'

'I remember standing in the back of the theater with you the day that Lucy DeVore had her tragic – well, let's still call it an accident. And if I'm not mistaken, that's when you told us you were not in New York on Friday night, when Ms Galinova was murdered. Did I get that right?'

'Exactly so. I spent that weekend at my house in Vail.'

'Maybe dead dancers don't talk, but cell phones can still tell tales, Mr Alden. There's a message on Talya's phone,' Mike said. I knew he was bluffing now because her phone had never been found. We were only going on Joe Berk's statement that he claimed to have listened to Hubert Alden's invitation to take the ballerina out for a late supper the night she went missing. 'Your voice, offering to pick her up that same evening.'

Alden raised his head, looking out the window over mine, face-to-face with a gargoyle who laughed back at him from the building cornice across the narrow street, its tongue extended from its wide stone mouth.

'Dinner, Mr Alden? That ring a bell?'

'I never got an answer from Talya. I made that call from my office, late in the afternoon, I think. Naturally, I would have stayed in town if she'd responded that she wanted to see me. I keep the company plane at Teterboro, in New Jersey, right over the George Washington Bridge.'

'You didn't happen to stop by the opera house on your way to the airport, did you?'

'Mr Chapman, I was scheduled to fly out at around seven o'clock that evening. I didn't stop anywhere, because I was anxious to get into the Vail airport before they shut it down for the night.'

'But it's your own wings, no? You tell the pilot it's ten or it's midnight, and that's when the flight goes.'

'We were wheels up before Natalya went onstage, detective. The first act started at eight p.m., didn't it?' Alden was steaming now, unhappy about the implied accusation and perhaps also unhappy that we may have heard something more intimate in the phone conversation than he had revealed to us. 'The flight records on both ends will confirm my departure and arrival times.'

'Those records will tell me about the movements of the aircraft, Mr Alden. Whether they account for where you were that night is another matter.'

Alden leaned forward with his elbows on the arms of the wooden chair and shook his head while he looked down at the floor. 'You brought me down here for this? You'll be embarrassed when you get the answers you're looking for.'

Mike could shift gears as suddenly as moods. He

backed off the subject of Galinova's murder, and sensed from our first conversation with Alden that he would be more comfortable talking about his theatrical ancestors.

'I'll be first in line to apologize if I'm wrong, Mr Alden. I mean, there it was in your own voice, the night of the murder. I had to ask you, since you didn't tell us about your dinner invitation the first time we talked. And the main reason we asked to see you again is that we really wanted your help about something else, something that involves Joe Berk.'

Alden seemed to perk up now, pleased to shift the attention back to Berk.

'I'm figuring you might know some of this because of your grandmother, the opera singer, and 'cause your grandfather was such a patron of the arts. You know anything about the Shriners?'

Alden looked at me to check my expression, and I met his glance with a smile. 'Why do you ask?'

'Obviously, I can't tell you exactly why, but let's just say Berk hasn't been too candid with us, and maybe you can help me understand why.'

'Candor isn't part of Joe's vocabulary. What is it about the Shriners?'

'Who are they? What do they have to do with the theatrical community?' Mike asked the general question to start Alden talking, but I knew he would work his way up to the red tasseled fez.

'The Ancient Arabic Order of the Nobles of the Mystic Shrine, detective. A nineteenth-century offshoot of the Masons – you know about them, don't you?'

I knew that Freemasons were opponents of divine right kingships, attracted by the freedom of early craftsmen,

363

spiritual heirs of the men who built the world's great monuments – the pyramids, Solomon's Temple, the Roman aqueducts, and later the medieval cathedrals.

'Fraternal organizations,' Mike said.

'Yes, but with a firm set of beliefs that are centered in the freedom of man. You had Voltaire and Ben Franklin, George Washington and Mozart, all espousing democratic ideals and benevolence. By the mid-nineteenth century, most towns in America had at least one Masonic Lodge, not just for fraternal purposes, but for philanthropic goals as well.'

'And the Shriners?'

'They first of all had to be Masons, but their order evolved from a more exotic heritage – the seventh-century Order of the Mystic Shrine,' Alden said, looking over at Mike. 'You'd actually be amused by their original purpose.'

'What was it?'

'To maintain law and order, to help local governments fight crime. They were a kind of primitive posse when they originated. It wasn't until the nineteenth century that their mission changed.'

'I hate friggin' posses. Last thing I need is a bunch of amateurs trying to do my job. What did they change to?'

'In my grandparents' time, the Shriners really became the playground for the Masons, associated with most of the popular entertainers of the day. And all very taken with the exotic symbols of the original Middle Eastern or Near Eastern Shrine associations.'

'Why so?'

'Because that's where the movement originated, centuries ago. When it was revived in America, there were two men who cofounded the order in the 1850s. One was a stage actor and the other a medical doctor – William Jermyn Florence and Dr Walter Millary Fleming. They had this idea to use the organization to entertain people, while at the same time being charitable, raising money for medical research.'

'But what did you say about the Middle East? What symbols are you talking about?' Mike asked.

'William Florence played in performances all over Europe and northern Africa – in many of the same theaters where my grandmother, Giulietta Capretta, later sang. He went to Algeria and Cairo, bringing home with him some of the rituals from the shrines there, some of the trappings of the early orders that flourished in the Middle East.'

'Like what?'

'Islamic motifs, in everything from the architecture of their meeting places to the details in the interior design. These American Shriners didn't construct theaters for their entertainment and lodging, Ms Cooper. They actually built mosques. And they gave them Arabic names, all over the country. Bektash Shrine Temple in Concord, New Hampshire; Syria Temple in Pittsburgh; the Ararat Temple in Kansas City; the Aladdin Temple in Columbus, Ohio; the Sphinx Temple in Hartford; and the Rameses Temple in Toronto. More than half a million members nationwide.'

'A hundred years ago? Mosques all over this country?'

'Indeed. And the leaders were all known as imperial potentates and grand masters, again in the Arabic traditions.'

'You mentioned design elements, too,' I said. 'What was distinctive about them?'

'Colors for one thing. The mixtures of red and yellow and green are very evocative of the culture. Certain symbols are constants, like the crescent moon crossed with the scimitar, arabesque grillwork in many of the building features, and always mosaic tile work on the walls and ceiling – lots of glazed terra-cotta, usually with a foliate imagery—'

'Hold it, buddy, will you? You make a study of this stuff?' Mike was trying to take notes as Alden talked.

'I inherited the entire theatrical collection that had been in our family for decades. It's part of my genealogy, detective – it's in the blood. Nothing I had to study.'

'What do you mean you inherited something? Like what?'

'Scores of photographs – George M. Cohan, Sophie Tucker, Lillian Russell – they all performed with the Shriners. I've got a unique assortment of signed playbills from opening nights and events, and even costumes they wore at major events.'

'What kind of costumes?' Mike asked.

'From opera, from Shakespearean plays, from lodge meetings—'

'I don't mean that. I mean what did the Shriners wear?'

'Suits just like us. Only the potentates got the fancy robes,' Alden said.

'And on their heads, what? Hoods?'

'It's not the Klan, detective.'

'So what'd they wear?'

'Surely you know the tarboosh, Mr Chapman? The famous red fez?'

'Yeah, yeah. I know it.'

366

'From the University of Fez – the symbol of learning and integrity.'

'You inherit some of those, Mr Alden?'

'I certainly did. I'll be glad to show you anything you like.'

'You keep them?'

'At my home, detective. I've got a media room filled with memorabilia of my grandparents. Quite colorful.'

'And the letter *M*, Mr Alden – you know, from the alphabet. Does that have any significance in these Shriner designs?'

Alden didn't miss a beat as he held up his fingers to tick off his answers. 'Quite likely it does, if you tell me what you mean, what it is you're looking for. Obviously, there are words like *mosque* and *minaret,* and the name of the Masons themselves. Fez is a city in Morocco. There's another *M* for you. I don't follow your question, Mr Chapman.'

I kept thinking of Lucy DeVore, smiling at the camera in her red tarboosh, her hand on the doorknob that bore the distinctive letter *M*.

'If these shrines were so popular all over America, how come they built one everyplace in the country except Manhattan?' Mike asked. 'How come there's no Shriners' theater right here?'

'I hope you don't mind being corrected again, detective, but one of the most immense, ostentatious mosques ever created was opened here in 1923, on a prime piece of real estate dead in the center of the city. Still standing, Mr Chapman, right in midtown on Fifty-fifth Street, and I'll bet you've been inside it dozens of times.'

'There's no mosque on Fifty-fifth Street,' Mike said.

'What's the name?'

'Mecca Temple, Miss Cooper. Maybe that's the *M* you've been looking for. Mecca Temple of the Ancient Arabic Order of the Nobles of the Mystic Shrine.'

Chapter 35

'Where on Fifty-fifth Street?' Mike asked, Alden's suggestion an affront to his pride in his intimate knowledge of the city over which he kept watch. Each street, each avenue, each grid evoked the memory of a crime scene Mike had worked. 'There's a synagogue over on the southwest corner of Lex, but there's no mosque.'

'West Fifty-fifth, between Sixth and Seventh avenues,' Alden said, pleased with himself that he had us stymied.

I closed my eyes to envision the block and thought immediately of the large theater there that I had been to more often than even Alden could have guessed.

'City Center?'

'The City Center of Music and Drama, Ms Cooper. Next time you have tickets for a show, stand across the street and crane your neck to look up to the very top of the building, maybe twelve or fourteen stories high. You can still see the words *Mecca Temple* carved into the façade.'

I have stood on the sidewalk at the entrance to City Center scores of times since my first childhood visits and never once noticed the carved letters so far overhead.

'But it's – it's been a theater for longer than I've been

alive. Before Lincoln Center was built, it was home to the New York City Ballet and Opera.' I was taken aback at the thought that this cultural treasure had a history that wasn't familiar to me – and, I was sure, to many other theatergoers.

Mike wanted to leave for the building at once. He walked to Laura's desk to use her phone, and when I heard him ask for the desk sergeant at Midtown North – the precinct just a few short blocks from City Center – I knew he was calling to send a patrolman around the corner to examine and report back on the shape and design of the doorknobs in the old showplace.

'I can't believe I never knew about that.'

'It's ancient history, Ms Cooper. Does it interest you?'

I tried to keep Alden chatting without letting him know that the reason for my heightened interest was because of a possible link to our investigation. 'I've studied dance all my life. I see the Ailey Dance Company there every year, and, of course, it's where American Ballet Theater does their fall series. And all the Broadway revivals they stage – who doesn't know City Center?'

'Then I must arrange for you to meet the director. I'm sure you two would be sympatica – she's a brilliant young lawyer who also used to dance. Arlette Schiller, do you know her?'

'I don't,' I said, one eye on Mike as he reentered the room. 'But I'd certainly like the introduction.'

'So how long was Mecca actually Mecca?' Mike asked.

'The temple opened in 1923, with grand wizards and potentates from all over the country. Quite an engineering marvel it was, this massive sandstone cube topped by its extraordinary dome. The main steel girder that supports the balcony is the longest one ever used in New York City still to this day – six stories tall if you were to lay it on end – delivered by ship to the harbor and snaked uptown on a caravan of trucks.'

'But just for Shriners?'

'Originally, detective, yes. There was the auditorium, of course. It's right around the corner from Carnegie Hall, as you know. But even back then, no one was allowed to smoke at Carnegie Hall. Since cigar smoking was a big part of the lodge activities, the auditorium was built with all sorts of huge exhaust fans in it, to accommodate the practice as well as to help draw stage business away from Carnegie. Mecca's theatrical section seated almost five thousand people, if you can imagine that so long ago. The rest of the shrine's rooms – banquet halls, lodgings, ceremonial shrines – well, they were all quite private.'

'So what happened to the place?' Mike asked.

'First came the Crash of Twenty-nine, and then the Great Depression. It was no better for the Shriners than for anyone else in the country. Even though they considered themselves a philanthropic organization, they couldn't claim a tax exemption because they rented the auditorium to outside groups. By the late 1930s, the banks foreclosed on the loans that had been used to build Mecca.'

'So the mosque went into bankruptcy?'

'It did indeed, after a very short life. Sat empty like a forlorn Arabian palace in the middle of this urban landscape. Before all the skyscrapers went up in midtown, you could see that fantastic dome from miles away in every direction. The government got the property by tax foreclosure and put the building up for auction in 1942.'

'Who bought it?'

Alden smiled. 'The City of New York itself turned out to be the highest bidder. Stole the place, even by the standards of those days, for one hundred thousand dollars. The claim on it was more than six times that amount. It was the genius of LaGuardia.'

'What?' Mike asked.

'Mayor Fiorello LaGuardia. The rest of the politicians wanted to tear the building down and replace it with a parking lot.'

'Except for LaGuardia?'

'Yes, he'd long had the idea to create a great municipal theater, with cheap tickets so that the arts could be more available to the ordinary citizen. He didn't want it to be like New York's commercial theaters, so he aimed to build a constituency made up of colleges and schools, philanthropic and professional groups. The mayor wanted shows to start at five thirty in the evening so people could come straight from work, save the train and bus fare. He had some wonderful ideas to support the performing arts in New York.'

'And let them be more accessible than Broadway?'

'By far, Ms Cooper. When City Center opened, you could sit in the balcony for thirty-five cents or pay top dollar – literally, a dollar ten – for the orchestra. Broadway seats cost three times as much.'

My phone rang and Laura answered it, buzzing the intercom. Mike reached over and picked it up. 'Yeah, sarge?'

He listened for a few seconds and hung up the phone. 'No doubt about it. This time *M* is for Mecca.'

'I'm quite pleased I could help you solve your puzzle, detective. Anything . . . ?'

'When's the last time you were there, Mr Alden?'

His forehead wrinkled and his dark, thick eyebrows met as one. 'It's been weeks, Mr Chapman. Several weeks.'

'Exactly when?'

'Look, if you're back to playing "gotcha" again, I'd obviously prefer to check my office diary.'

'Why'd you go?'

Alden looked to me. 'They have this wonderful Encore series – Broadway shows.'

I knew the series, which had proved to be enormously successful for the center year after year.

'It was a performance of *Bye, Bye, Birdie*. That's amusing, come to think of it.'

Mike was too focused on Lucy DeVore posed in someone's fez, leaning on a door handle in the Mecca Theater, to be easily amused. 'How so?'

'*Birdie* was really the first musical to bring rock'n'roll to Broadway.'

'Spare me the lyrics. Coop's likely to break into a dance. What of it?'

'There's a scene in the show where the characters go into the wrong room and break up a Shriners' meeting. Remember that?'

I didn't.

'Tarbooshes and flying tassels everywhere. I'm sure there are plenty of them in wardrobe over at City Center. You don't need to see mine.'

The one on Lucy's head had distinctive markings. A crescent and scimitar – whose meaning I now understood – over some Arabic design. We'd be able to tell whether it was a costume from a Broadway performance or the real deal from an antique mosque.

'How about backstage, Mr Alden? You been backstage lately?'

Again the man's brow furrowed as he tried, it seemed to me, to second-guess the direction Mike Chapman was going before he supplied an answer.

'I've been backstage dozens of times, detective. I'm a—'

'Yeah, I know. You're a friggin' patron of the friggin' arts. I've bought more beers at Yankee Stadium than you've got playbills, but it doesn't get me in the locker room to pose for pictures with the boys after the game. Dancers. You been backstage here lately with any of the ladies?'

Mike was losing the bigger picture to close in on the image of Lucy DeVore. Hubert Alden had no idea where Mike was headed.

'Upstairs, certainly.'

'Whaddaya mean? In the balcony?'

'No, no. There are nine or ten floors of studios in the office tower behind the auditorium, Mr Chapman. Some of the most spectacular dance studios in the city are housed there, rented out to many of the companies for rehearsal space.'

'And you've been up in there recently? Where exactly?'

'I'm surprised that Chet Dobbis didn't explain all of this to you when you talked to him about Talya Galinova.'

'What's for Dobbis to tell?'

'Before he came to the Met, Chet was the artistic director at City Center. He knows every inch of that place from the top of the dome to the crawl spaces in the basement.'

Mike looked at me to see if I was following Alden's point. 'What does that have to do with Galinova?'

'Well, of course I've visited Talya at City Center. So

did Dobbis, so did Rinaldo Vicci, so did Joe Berk. Talya's rehearsal studio was there, Mr Chapman,' Alden said, making the connection between Lucy DeVore's accident and Galinova's murder a bit less tenuous in my mind. 'She spent much more time in that building than she did at the Met.'

Chapter 36

There was no point keeping Hubert Alden in my office any longer. His information was pointing us in a new direction, reweaving many of the same characters into a new tapestry, giving us another venue to explore – one that was familiar to most of them.

As Mike walked Alden to the elevators, Mercer Wallace came into my office carrying a bag full of sandwiches.

'Heard you were busy doing your StairMaster workout early this morning,' he said, unpacking the late lunch he brought for each of us. 'I figured after that you could even stand a bag of chips for a change.'

'Feed me, m'man,' Mike said, returning to the room and reaching for the roast beef hero, biting into it as though he hadn't eaten in days. 'How was your weekend?'

'I think I've been in every homeless shelter and soup kitchen in the city since you left town. Still looking for Ramon Carido,' Mercer said. 'He must be living under a rock in the park, and it has gotta be driving him crazy. This beautiful spring weather – every jogger and biker and stroller is out there on his hunting ground, stoking his imagination. I doubt he'll ever go after a dog-walker again.'

'Coop missed all the local news while she was on the Vineyard. Every station showed that sketch of him around the clock.'

'Reward money's up to twenty grand from one of the victims-advocacy groups. Some mutt'll turn him in for the loot before too long.'

'So you worked all weekend while I played hooky?'

'And lucky thing you did, Ms Cooper. May I say that for once you are no longer the favorite prosecutor of the Manhattan Special Victims Squad? I don't want to be a snitch, but somebody drew a mustache and horns on that picture of you holding my baby boy last Christmas. You look downright evil.'

'Easy come, easy go. What now?'

'The guys are really pissed at you because of the order from Judge McFarland in the Carido case.'

'You mean not being able to try to match their DNA evidence to the linkage database? Two weeks and we'll have a whole new set of rules. Good ones, I hope.'

'In the meantime, we caught six new squeals since Thursday night.'

'Yeah, I saw the complaint reports on Laura's desk this morning. Four of them knew their attackers. DNA won't make the difference in those cases. Tell the squad to work those cases the old-fashioned way – with their brains.'

'Well, they need the databank in the other two. In fact, when you look those reports over more carefully, you'll see that Saturday night's break-in down on Allen Street may be part of a pattern. We want to try to link it to an open series in Tribeca.'

Mike had finished his hero and was working on his

second bag of nachos. 'She's not going to win any popularity contests in the Homicide Squad either. Same beef.'

'I didn't go up to court intending to try to make new law, guys. It was a command performance.'

'Yeah, well, don't go calling nine-one-one again any time soon,' Mike said, wiping the mustard from his cheek with the back of his hand. 'Some dick is likely to tell you to stick your DNA up your—'

'Laura? You just reminded me, Mike. Laura?' She poked her head through the doorway. 'Would you call down to the supply office? They need to issue me a new cell phone. Beg them to let me keep my old number, okay?'

'Got it.'

'I had to turn mine in to the detectives this morning so they can make a record of the exact times of the calls I made from my building last night,' I explained to Mike and Mercer. 'They have to check with Benito, too. Maybe he heard whether my attacker said anything while the line was open.'

'I thought you told me he didn't say a word.'

'That's exactly what I told you. And I'm sure of it. They just want to double-check, in case I'm mistaken.'

'Guess you got zero credibility, Coop. Those cops trust you about twice as much as you trust your witnesses. It's good medicine for you. What'd you think of Hubert Alden?' Mike had finished his bottle of root beer and reached for a swig of my Diet Coke to wash down the food.

'Same as I think about anybody who throws a curve like that one. You and I had such tunnel vision about the Met as the geographic center of this investigation. There's something way too slick about Alden, and I worry that

378

maybe he's just steering us away from the progress we were making,' I said, as Mike started to tell Mercer about the rehearsal studios at City Center.

'Progress? You still got a ballerina in a refrigerator down at the morgue and me itching to put cuffs on Joe-do-you-know-who-I-am-Berk. Progress is when I ratchet those little metal bracelets on somebody's wrists.'

'When do we check the place out?' Mercer asked.

Mike looked at his watch. 'It's almost three o'clock. Let's get up there while there's still someone to show us around. Where are your wheels?'

'Bayard Street. Near the sleazebag bail bondsman's office.'

'I'm in front of the building. Let's use mine. Chow down, blondie.'

The ride up Avenue of the Americas was slowed by traffic. I tried to nap in a corner of the cluttered rear seat of Mike's department car. I didn't have to count sheep – I had an even longer list, it seemed, of suspects who had eluded the long arm of the law this past week: the Turkish doctor who drugged his victims; Ramon Carido, the rapist who'd been bitten by a dog; and Ralph Harney, the stage-hand who'd gotten a stand-in rather than provide us with a sample of his DNA.

'Ralph Harney,' I said aloud. 'You think he knows enough about electrical stuff to have been the guy who blackened the apartments and waited for me last night?'

Mike cocked his head and looked at me in the rearview mirror. 'He's a stagehand, not an electrician.'

'But he's worked around all that elaborate stage wiring for years. Had to pick something up, the jobs are so inter-twined,' Mercer said. 'Worth looking at. The guys he works with could tell us how much he knows.'

There was a hotel loading zone half a block east of City Center. Mike pulled in and parked the car.

As we approached the theater – the great expanse of sandstone capped by its monumental dome – a huddle of young women walked out of the building, stopping on the sidewalk to talk among themselves. Their long legs resting in the turned-out position of dancers, towels around their necks, suggested they had just finished the day's warm-up or class.

Behind them, another woman rushed out of the door, seemingly agitated that her path was blocked. She shifted from one side to the other, nudging the girl closest to her in order to pass by and run out into the street to flag down a Yellow Cab. She tossed her large black tote into the rear seat and climbed in after it.

It was impossible to tell whether she ignored the three of us or simply didn't hear Mike Chapman call for her by name to get her to stop. Mona Berk slammed the door of the taxi and took off down the one-way street.

Chapter 37

The two security guards inside the lobby were less than impressed with Mike's gold shield. They kept no sign-in book at this entrance, although there was one on the 56th Street side, where the center's offices were located. And no, they had no idea who any of the women were who had left a short while ago.

One of the men called upstairs to have someone from management escort us inside. While we waited, I stepped back out on the sidewalk to look at the front of the theater. The words *Mecca Temple* were too many stories above for me to see – as Alden had suggested – but the other Islamic architectural motifs were impossible to mistake.

I noted as if for the first time the arcade of horseshoe arches in the tawny sandstone, the attached columns and capitals framed by the traditional Arabic *alfiz,* and the colorful glazed tiles that set the building apart from the low brick structures on either side. The massive façade was dotted with lancet windows, again in the Moorish style, which must have provided the only natural light to the areas behind the auditorium seats in the upper balconies.

Inside the foyer, Mike and Mercer's impatience was clear as they paced between the advance ticket sales window and a wall on the far end, postered with coming events.

'Detective Chapman? Ms Schiller sent me down to answer your questions. My name is Stan,' the young man said, extending his hand to each of us. 'How can we help?'

'We're investigating the homicide that occurred at the Met ten days ago.'

'Miss Galinova, of course.'

'We understand that she rented studio space here for class and rehearsal.'

'Yes, she did. We were privileged to have her.'

'We're going to have to look around. We need to see where she worked, whether she kept a locker here, any record of her comings and goings or who might have visited her. People she mixed with, dancers who might have noticed her guests, men who—'

'Perhaps we can schedule an appropriate time to do this. I hadn't realized how much ground you need to cover.' Stan tried to reach an arm out to stop Mike from entering the lobby, but he was too late.

'We might as well get started,' Mercer said.

Mike had climbed the six steps that led to the rear of the auditorium, so completely different in style from the Met and other theaters we had seen. Mercer and I stepped up behind him for a look.

I had never seen the old house empty. Tier after tier of red velvet seats spread outward like a great fan, with shiny brass railings that ran along the aisles. The stage with its arched proscenium looked enormous; above and around the ceiling was the lacy grillwork typical of Moorish design – large perforated stars arrayed as cutouts above the orchestra and over the balcony seats – and gleaming ivory paint accented with rich gold metallic trim.

'Coop, take a look at the seats.'

Below the armrest of each seat on the aisle was an intricately engraved panel, and in the middle of each one was the letter *M*.

'Miss Galinova had nothing to do with the auditorium, detective,' Stan said, pushing up the sleeve of his shirt to check the time. 'I'm leaving for the day at five, but if you'd like me to take you up to the office tower, I can give you an idea of where she worked.'

He led us out through the lobby. 'If you don't mind walking up a flight, we can actually connect through to the other space from within the theater without going outside to the Fifty-sixth Street entrance.'

'We saw a woman leaving as we pulled up,' Mike said. 'Mona Berk. D'you know her? She have an office here?'

'I have no idea who she is. The name means nothing to me.'

I walked beside Stan on the broad staircase as Mike and Mercer hurried ahead. 'Very grand looking, isn't it?' I said as we reached the mezzanine.

The wide expanse was unlike the cramped spaces in Broadway theater lobbies, with beautifully stenciled coffered ceilings and thick carpeting.

'When the Shriners built Mecca Temple, this was one of the gentlemen's lounges. It was their smoking lodge, actually. Lots of sofas and sitting chairs, spittoons beside them. Marble floors with Moroccan carpets. The old boys

383

were very interested in their comfort and elegance. Watch your heads, please.'

We all stooped to exit the auditorium area and emerged into a dingy hallway that led to the office tower.

'Careful where you walk. This is the only way through to the studios, and it has to be kept unlocked. It's the only fire exit on this side of the building. But it's worth your life to get through here at the moment,' Stan said, guiding me around piles of gels and high-top sleeves that once covered the spots from recesses overhead. 'We're replacing a lot of the lighting equipment, modernizing to a digital system.'

The path was cluttered with all the backstage theatrical magic that brought the stage alive, and Mike was annoyed at me for tiptoeing around the mess and slowing him down.

'Sorry, Mr Chapman. Mecca was entirely gaslit when it was built in the twenties. Between that and the smoking habits of a lot of the performers and workmen, we've always had to take extraordinary precautions against fire.'

A few corridors away we reached a bank of elevators.

'I'll take you up to seven. That's where Ms Galinova liked to work.'

The age of the old theater showed itself far less gracefully in the areas out of public view. Walls were in bad need of a paint job, occasional corners graffitied in bright colored markers by members of visiting dance companies whose signatures provided a riotous splash of color against the drab beige paint.

'Did she have a dressing room?' Mike asked. 'A place where she could be alone?'

'City Center isn't like the Met. We don't have a star

384

system here. There are changing rooms, certainly, but nothing with Galinova's name on it. Is it possible she found an empty office to park herself in? Well, just try a few of the doors – there's always something available. Dusty but available.'

Dancers – women and men – brushed by us as they passed out of a class. They all looked like teenagers – perfectly toned bodies, unlined skin covered with sweat, most of them in black leotards and tights topped by colorful woolen leg warmers.

'This is Julio Bocca's Argentine company. Fabulously talented young people. I think the oldest member of the corps is seventeen,' Stan said, waiting until they cleared through. The accompanist was still working on the timing of a tango and the music drifted into the corridor and followed the dancers down the hall.

We walked into the studio they had just vacated and I was aghast at its dimensions and décor. 'This is fabulous,' I said to Stan. 'I've never seen rehearsal space like this in the city.'

'Do you dance?'

'No, no. But I've studied ballet for years, taken lots of classes.'

The room was unusually large, in length and depth. The painted ceilings and even the door frame were rich in architectural detail and color. What was most unique for a Manhattan rehearsal studio was that there were no columns at all, a completely open space in which the dancers could stage numbers as they would be performed in a theater.

Mike wasn't listening. He headed directly to the far end of the room and climbed a few steps, seating himself in an oversize wooden chair, carved with elaborate stars and crescents that I recognized now as symbols of the Middle Eastern influence.

'What about this?'

'The potentate's throne, detective. It was in these old lodge rooms that many of the secret rituals of the Shriners were conducted. In almost every one of these studios, there's an altar or shrine that played some part in the daily life of the members. I don't have a clue what went on in here, but most of us are just grateful that all this rich detail survived what the city did to the rest of the common space,' Stan said, gesturing back to the hallway.

Mike was down the steps and back to the door. 'Where else did Ms Galinova spend time?'

Stan passed him and retraced his steps in the hallway. 'This dressing room is for the women. I suppose that's the one she had to use.' He looked over his shoulder at me. 'Although I can't imagine for a minute that a prima like Galinova enjoyed sharing it with anyone else.'

From within we could hear the voices of the dancers, speaking in Spanish, and the sound of the running water from the shower.

Mike nodded at me. 'Your territory, Coop. Check it out.'

I pushed open the door and entered the room.

The first area had been converted into a small lounge. Several sofas and chairs were against the wall, and three of the dancers – barefoot and robed, waiting their turn for the shower – were curled up and chatting with one another.

I passed by them to another section of the room.

Instead of lockers, there were only open cubbies for their belongings and a coatrack on which their clothing hung.

The last chamber was the bathroom area: several toilet stalls, a row of sinks, and one entire wall that was mirrored. There were backpacks on the floor, magazines and iPods stacked beside them, and makeup on every flat surface.

One of the girls emerged from the shower, wrapped in a bath sheet with her head turbaned in a towel. She excused herself as she slid in front of me, and I pressed my back to the wall to let her pass.

My hands were flat against the surface, a smooth, glazed tile that was cold to the touch. I looked around and noticed the same old ceramic squares – undoubtedly the original 1920s design – covering the wall opposite the showers and creating a border along the ceiling edge and floor.

I walked to the empty shower stall, which was also elaborately tiled, then turned to study the dark blue and pale green of the mosaics worked into a white ground. What had Hubert Alden called the typically Islamic motifs? A foliate design, he had said.

I ran my fingers over the beautiful image. The flowers looked familiar to me – their shape and colors – and I tried to recall where I had seen something like them.

Foliate, of course. Beautiful flowers. They were tulips, Arabic style, created specially for the Mecca Temple. And the other time I had seen them was on the monitor in Joe Berk's bedroom.

The images we suspected Berk of watching – of stealing for some personal perversion by means of a hidden surveillance system – must have come to him from a camera that had been surreptitiously installed here in the dressing room used by many of the dancers who rehearsed at City Center, including Lucy DeVore and the late Natalya Galinova.

Chapter 38

The eight dancers looked at me as though I were crazy when I asked them to get dressed so that I could bring a man into the lounge. '*Por favor – vistase! Avance! Tengo que traer un hombre aqui.*'

I raised my voice, urging them to step out into the hallway, and even though I added a few '*por favors,*' they didn't move.

I walked briskly past the cubbyholes to the door, again calling to them to dress themselves because a man was entering.

The three who had been changing wrapped towels around their slim bodies and stood speechless as I called to Mike to come into the bathroom.

He was too embarrassed to even make a joke, so he marched behind me to the area near the showers that the girls had been smart enough to clear.

'Look familiar?'

'Twenty dollars, Coop. The question is, What was Joe Berk looking at when the monitor in his bedroom caught these tulips?'

'I'll take your twenty. *Who* was he looking at? That's the answer I want.'

Mike ripped back the opaque shower curtain and stepped into the wet stall. He was trying to find signs of a concealed device, and repeated his search in each of the three cubicles.

I watched him run his hands around the tops of the metal frames, and in the last booth he came up with what he wanted.

'You got it?'

'Not a camera. But there's a recess drilled in the wall there. Can't see into it – we need a ladder. But it feels like there's a mounting that could have held a small camera, and it's slanted so that focus would be on the tiled wall in the background. C'mon, let's move. Be sure and thank the young ladies on your way out. We're going back to Berk.'

Mercer and Stan were waiting for us in the hallway, and Mike took Mercer aside to explain what we had seen.

'Are you done now?' Stan asked.

'Haven't even started yet,' Mike called back to him. 'Who's the best tech guy you know?'

Mercer answered. 'Vito. Vito Taurino. Right, Alex?'

'The guy's a genius,' I said. 'Docs all Battaglia's wiretaps and video surveillance. The kind the courts allow.'

'We gotta find him now. Yesterday. Get him up here.'

'I'll call Battaglia. But could someone really transmit video images from inside that shower stall?' I asked.

'It's all wireless now, Coop. It's called microwave technology – and I don't mean the kind you cook with. We used it in that murder investigation at the social club on Mulberry Street. You just need a board camera the size of a computer chip – the lens sits flat up on it – and mount it almost any place with brackets, like in that recess. Wire it through the back of the wall. Or maybe there's a dropped ceiling in the bathroom. Vito can check.'

Mercer took over the explanation. 'Run that up to an antenna.'

'But where?' I asked.

'Just stick one on top of the building. Any building.'

'Better yet,' Mike said, talking to Mercer. 'How about this dome? Stick a Yagi right on top of this mother, point it at a repeater, get the popcorn ready and—'

Mercer snapped his finger. 'You're at the movies.'

'Slow down. What's a Yagi?'

'It's a kind of antenna,' Mercer explained. 'You can direct them, orient them so they're facing repeaters, and the repeaters carry them the distance, to wherever the monitors are waiting.'

'There are repeaters all over town,' Mike said. 'On top of the Empire State Building, Thirty Rock Center, the George Washington Bridge.'

'Think nine-eleven,' Mercer said. 'When the towers collapsed, even your cell phones went dead downtown 'cause all that relay equipment was on top of the Trade Center.'

I was beginning to understand. 'And the camera just rolls all the time?'

'Probably motion activated,' Mike said. 'Someone steps in range of the lens and it's showtime.'

The bathroom door opened and one of the enraged Argentines called Stan over for an explanation. He tried to mollify her but clearly wasn't successful.

'You two try to get some answers from Berk. I'll take Stan back up to the main office and see what other

391

information they've got that might help. If Galinova was renting rehearsal space, there have to be records of the dates. Somebody must have information about when she was here and who else hung out around her. You'll be back to me?' Mercer asked.

'Yeah. We'll stay in touch.'

Stan tried to free himself when he saw us walk away. 'If you're leaving, you'll have to go out the Fifty-sixth Street side. The theater's dark tonight. The entrance you came in is closed after five.'

We left Mercer in the hallway. Stan was surrounded by three agitated dancers, as we waited for the elevator that returned us to the first floor. A small arrow pointed in the direction of the 56th Street exit and we followed the snaking corridors to make our way out.

The narrow, dark passages of the ground floor of the old building were lined with posters that re-created the theater history of the past few generations. I hurried to keep pace with Mike's long strides, past the life-size and youthful Lenny Bernstein – 'vital music performed under a stimulating young conductor'; Mike Todd presenting Maurice Evans in *Hamlet* with the top ticket price of $2.40; and the 1948 image of George Balanchine and Lincoln Kirstein, whom City Center had invited to establish a resident ballet company – which later became the New York City Ballet.

It was after five o'clock and workers were beginning to emerge from office buildings up and down the street. Mike cut a path through the crowds and I followed in his wake, down 56th and south on Sixth Avenue, then around the corner until we found the car.

The ride to the Belasco was slow, rush-hour traffic

blocking each intersection as we crawled down Seventh Avenue behind commuter buses and an army of Yellow Cabs.

I called the DA's Squad office to ask the captain how soon he could make Vito available to us, so I could urge Battaglia to back me up if he was in the middle of another case.

'He did an eight-to-four today, Alex. I can beep him but he was going off to his kid's Little League game. He may not call in for a couple of hours.'

'Can we have him tomorrow?'

'No problem. He's doing another day tour. He'll be in the tech room when he comes on. Just call him and tell him what you need.'

'Thanks a lot.'

'You got a green light?' Mike asked.

'You and Mercer can figure out where you want him to start.'

'Depends what we get out of Joe Berk now.'

'He's just going to deny it again,' I said.

'Then you're gonna have to get a search warrant. He can deny all he wants but you and I saw those tulips on the screen in his bedroom the first time we were there. If I have to choke the old bastard, I'm gonna get answers this time.'

'You've got to keep it calm. He tunes you out when you go wild on him.'

'Wild? He hasn't seen me even halfway to vicious yet. I've been saving up for this kind of encounter.'

Mike got out of the car and slammed the door. We walked up the street to the Belasco and headed for the entrance to Berk's apartment just west of the theater.

Mike stepped aside to let me enter and I was startled to come face-to-face with a man in a dark suit and sunglasses who was standing at the elevator controls.

Before I could say my name he had pressed the button and told us to go right up.

I was surprised to have such easy access, and I smiled at Mike as we rode up to Berk's office. As I pushed open the door, which was ajar, I could hear loud voices – a lot of them – and it was clear that the man downstairs who let us in assumed we were on the list for whatever party was in progress.

Mike followed me inside, and I scanned the dozen faces but saw no one familiar in the grand office, ringed with its bizarre collection of Napoleonic memorabilia.

My eye was drawn to the top of the staircase, outside Joe's bedroom, where Mona Berk and Ross Kehoe were engaged in a lively conversation with a man, clinking their cocktail glasses together and laughing at whatever story Kehoe was telling.

The young man seated in Berk's desk chair had just uncorked a bottle of champagne when he spotted the two of us entering the room.

'Come on in,' he said, getting to his feet and walking over to greet us. 'I'm Briggs. Briggs Berk. Joe's son. Have we met?'

'Chapman, Mike Chapman. This is Alexandra Cooper,' Mike said, choosing not to further identify us as police and prosecutor in case the kid didn't know about our involvement with his father. 'We're here for Joe.'

Briggs put a hand on Mike's shoulder and laughed. 'We're all here for Joe. What are you drinking?'

'No thanks. We'd like to see him, if we can. I need to

talk to him for a few minutes. I don't want to break this up but it's kind of urgent.'

'Talk to him? Can't help you with that, Mike. If you want to see him, the viewing doesn't start till tomorrow afternoon. Frank Campbell's, three o'clock.'

Campbell's was the most famous funeral parlor in Manhattan, known for its tasteful wakes and services for well-to-do New Yorkers.

'Right now,' Briggs said, 'the only place you can see Joe Berk is the morgue.'

Chapter 39

'I didn't know you guys were cops,' Briggs said, blanching as he planted the champagne bottle on his late father's desk and led us into a small study off the main room. 'I'm – uh – I'm sorry for – uh—'

He didn't seem to know for which offense he was apologizing, but the display of Mike's shield had sobered his disposition.

'We've got to make a couple of calls. You mind leaving us alone in here?'

Briggs closed the door behind him and must have signaled the reveling mourners to quiet down. Mike called the ME's office and reached the attendant on duty.

'Get me Dr Kestenbaum,' he said to the clerk who answered the phone.

'Talk about dancing on the grave,' I said. 'What a disgusting display.'

'You expected better from the Berks? I just want to know who pulled the plug on him. Too many happy people in there. And pretty ironic that he and Galinova are sleeping together again, side by side.'

'No wonder Mona was in such a rush to get here for the celebration.'

'Hello, doc? Chapman here. You got the Wizard of the Great White Way ready for his surgical debut?' Mike winked at me. 'What do you mean, who? Joe Berk. I'm talking about Joe Berk.'

Chapman listened for several minutes and then repeated the conversation to me after he hung up. 'They're going to do the autopsy tonight, but his death has all the signs of a stroke. Damn, I would have bet the odds he didn't die of natural causes. Especially before I got to rattle him.'

'I wonder what Joe's medical condition was. I mean, I hope that we didn't—'

'Don't go feeling all guilty on me, Coop, like we brought it on by aggravating him this morning. Kestenbaum says it's a logical aftereffect of the electrical event.'

'Electrical event? He makes it sound like a Broadway production. Meaning what?'

'Berk survived the jolt from stepping on the manhole cover. But apparently people who live through that experience can develop clotting in the blood vessels along the path that carried the current through the body. So it's not unusual to have a – what'd he call it? – an arterial thrombosis in the first few weeks after the accident. A stroke is what killed him.'

'And I was just beginning to feel we were so close to connecting Berk to Galinova's murder, to figuring out what was going on between them.'

'Let's keep at it. Suppose he did it, suppose he's still the main suspect? There's stuff to tie up here,' Mike said, opening the door to the office.

It looked as though several people had left while we

were in the study, but Mona Berk and Ross Kehoe had come downstairs to talk to Briggs. Before I could get any farther, the elevator doors opened and the squat figure of Rinaldo Vicci burst into the room.

'Briggsley, my boy,' Vicci said, rolling his *r* in dramatic fashion, ignoring both of us and embracing the young man. 'I came as soon as I heard the news. It's impossible to believe. Such a force, such a great life force.'

Mona let them talk and walked over to us, glass in hand. 'Some things are just meant to be, Mike, aren't they?'

'Seems to me you could have waited another few days before starting the celebration.'

'You know, in my head I had it figured he was dead a week ago, the first time I got the call. Sort of like a dress rehearsal,' Mona said, smiling. 'Made it so much easier to take when I got the news today. It wouldn't become me to fake my grief, would it?'

Briggs turned back to us. 'Mona told me why you were here last week. This really isn't the right time to be bringing a criminal investigation into my father's—'

'Oh, yeah? And you're giving death etiquette lessons while you got a party going on here? Let me start by extending my sympathy to you. Sincerely. You can't imagine quite *how* sincerely because of how unfortunate the timing of your father's passing is for me. I had bigger plans for him.'

'Why don't you tell us what happened today?' I said.

A semicircle had been formed now. Briggs in the middle, facing us, with Mona next to him and Ross Kehoe stroking her back as he watched the scene. Vicci was on the other side of Briggs, his hands clenched and poised against his lips, as though in prayer. There were four men and one woman gathering across the room. Mike told them to be sure not to leave before giving us their names.

'I'm so tired I can't even think straight,' Briggs said.

'When did you get back to New York?'

'From the coast? I took the red-eye Saturday night. I've been up since then.'

'Did you see your father yesterday?'

'Yeah. Yeah, I was here. Look, do I have to answer your questions right now? I mean, I'm sure my lawyer would like to be here.'

'Your lawyer? You in some kind of trouble?' Mike asked facetiously.

Ross Kehoe answered for Briggs. 'Not a criminal lawyer, Mr Chapman. Obviously, Briggs had to get Joe's attorney over here right away. There's a lot to attend to, a lot of financial matters to work out.'

Kehoe had left Mona's side and was trying to create some physical distance between Briggs and the two of us.

'We don't mean to upset any of you any further. We'd just like to know – well, how Joe died and who was with him,' I said.

'He was alone,' Briggs said. 'I mean, the nurse was here. She's the one who found him. She said he'd had a bad night.'

That didn't make me feel any better about having dropped by to stir things up in the morning.

'Your visit with him on Sunday – was it just a regular – well . . . ?' I didn't even know how to phrase the question. I couldn't imagine anything normal about the Berk family, but I didn't want to put the word *confrontational* on the table.

Mona started to speak. 'My uncle loved Briggs. Why don't you sit down?' she said, turning to her cousin, who seemed to be wilting before our eyes.

Kehoe picked up the conversation. 'Detective, the kid's been through a lot. None of his siblings give a damn about him. He and his father were getting along really well these past few months. How about a couple of days to let him absorb this?'

'Whatever the doctor says. Take some Tylenol, get plenty of rest, and, by the way, lay off the buckets of champagne. They don't mix well with formaldehyde.'

Mona was trying to keep Briggs calm, so I asked Ross Kehoe, 'What did the nurse say about Mr Berk's death?'

'Only that she checked on him at about eleven a.m. He was complaining of a headache and she put him back in bed for a nap. When she went in to bring him some food an hour later, she couldn't wake him up.'

'Did his physician—'

'Yes, of course. The nurse called nine-one-one. EMTs arrived first but it was all over. Joe's personal physician was here within the hour.'

'You and Mona?'

Kehoe held up his hands. 'Hey. Briggs called Mona to tell us about it and we came over because of how Mona feels about Briggs. Joe and Mona in the same room would have been a recipe for disaster.'

'How'd you get along with Joe?' I asked.

Kehoe put his hands in the rear pockets of his jeans. 'Which day of the week?'

'Didn't you work for him once?' Mike asked.

'That's right. I had no beef with Joe. He was good to

me back then. No surprise he didn't like to think of me marrying into the bloodline, but he treated me fine.'

Of all the people in the room – and all those we had met in the course of the investigation – Mike seemed to get the most out of Ross Kehoe. Something about his blue-collar background, the rough edges of his city accent, reduced what Mike liked to call the bullshit factor. I imagine his appearance had changed once Mona came into his life – finer clothes, expensive suede loafers that he sported today, a stylish haircut – but the basic bones looked as much like a cop's as did Mike's.

'What'd you do for Berk?' I asked.

'Everything. Met him in one of his theaters. My old man was in the union – you know the way this business is. Joe thought I could do things – I don't want to blow my own horn – but I was kind of a jack-of-all-trades, and I could deal with his temper better than most.'

'What did you do for him, exactly?'

'Stage crew kind of stuff, originally. A couple of years back, before I met Mona, I was his driver. That's when we got kind of friendly. He even put me into some investments. Some good deals that I scored on. Mona likes bling – and it got to the point I could buy it for her myself.'

'Joe fire you?'

'Nah. I just left. It wasn't gonna work with me getting so close to Mona.'

While we were talking, I saw Mona Berk walk away from Briggs and start back up the staircase, nodding to Rinaldo Vicci to join her.

I elbowed Mike, who followed after them.

Mona paused on the fourth step and turned to face

him. 'Once again, it's time for me to tell you to get out of here, if you and your girlfriend don't mind.'

Mike kept jogging up the stairs.

'Detective, where do you think you're going?'

'I just need to check out something in Mr Berk's room.'

She raised her voice. 'Where's your warrant, detective?'

'Where's your standing?' he said to her as she tried to catch up with him.

'What do you mean, standing?'

Mike was at the top of the stairs. 'This is Joe Berk's place. And since Uncle Joe has gone to meet his maker, you haven't got any more legal right to tell me to get out of here than Houdini does. You got no standing.'

'Ross, is that true?'

Kehoe shrugged his shoulders. 'I'm not getting into this one. I'm not a lawyer, babe. I don't know who's right here.'

'Briggs? Say something, goddamn it,' Mona screamed to her cousin.

I dashed up the stairs to try to broker a deal but Mona raced past Mike into Joe's bedroom and pulled the door shut behind her.

'Wait a minute, detective, will you? What do you want? What are you looking for?' Briggs trudged to the bottom of the steps and held on to the banister. 'I want to be there when you're looking around my dad's stuff, okay? Don't you think that's fair?'

'*Fair* isn't in my vocabulary for you or for anyone else in your family – for this whole cast of characters. You're all so used to dealing with make-believe that you don't know when to wake up and tell the truth.'

Mike walked to the bedroom door and turned the

402

knob. Neither one of us should have been surprised that Mona had locked it when she went inside.

Mike kicked and pushed against it, but the heavy oak panels didn't budge. Briggs climbed the staircase while Ross called out to Mona to be reasonable and open the door.

Rinaldo Vicci went to Berk's desk and pulled out the top drawer. '*Piano, piano.* Slow down, everybody. Calm yourselves.'

Vicci walked to the bottom of the staircase and Mike trotted down for the ornate brass key. He put it in the lock and the door opened.

The room was empty. Even Berk's bed had been stripped of its linens and all the medications on his nightstand. The only things that looked out of order were a few open dresser drawers and a closet left ajar.

Mona Berk had taken the private elevator – the one that had ferried showgirls directly to the bedroom for David Belasco and the late Joe Berk – and left the building. I couldn't imagine what she might have taken with her.

Chapter 40

Mike was ripped. He went first to the closet and started looking through it, pushing hangers apart, pulling shoe boxes off shelves and tossing them on the floor.

'You got to stop this, Mike. You can't do it.'

'Take a hike, Coop. This time he's really dead and I can do—'

'You don't even know what you're looking for.'

'Why? Those jerks on the Supreme Court were so many light-years ahead of me? I'll know it when I see it, isn't that what they said? It works for me, too.'

Briggs was in the doorway, oblivious to Mike's reference to the famous opinion on pornography rendered by Justice Potter Stewart more than thirty years ago. 'What . . . ?'

Now he looked like every other junkie crashing down from a cocaine high. His eyes were red – not from crying, we knew – and he was sniffing constantly. His hand was shaking as he tried to find a surface on which to rest it.

'Alex, go ask Kehoe where his beloved went. Tell him to get her on the phone, pronto,' Mike said, rifling through dresser drawers. 'Briggs, d'you ever go to the movies with your father?'

'Shows. Mostly shows, you know? Broadway.'

'Do what I told you, Alex.'

I didn't want to leave Mike alone in the room with Briggs. I didn't want him flipping out at the kid.

'Go. Get Kehoe. I'm talking home movies, kid. Ever see the monitors your father had in this room?'

Mike waved me out. I guess he hoped Joe's son would speak more candidly about his father's habits if I wasn't there.

'I don't know what you're talking about,' Briggs said as I walked away to the top of the stairs.

Vicci was on his cell and Kehoe was using the phone on Berk's desk.

'Excuse me, Mr Kehoe. Why don't you give Mona a call?' I asked. 'We've got a few more questions for her.'

He covered the receiver with his hand. 'Let her cool down. She's on her way home. I can handle this more diplomatically than Chapman, okay?'

I stepped to the side and called Mercer to bring him up to speed. He was still at the City Center office tower, which was basically closed down for the evening, and he was waiting for our return in one of the management offices in which Stan had set him up.

'Call Peterson for me. Ask him to get a team to sit on Mona Berk's loft in SoHo. The address is in the DD5s. Keep an eye on her till Mike figures out what he wants to do next. And maybe the lieutenant ought to set somebody up over here. I may need to draft a warrant 'cause Mike's convinced Berk has videos or more photographs – something to give us a break. It wouldn't hurt to have someone safeguarding this place overnight.'

'You know what Peterson's going to tell me. No manpower.'

'Let him pull some of the guys from the Met task force before they knock off for the day. It's important.'

Rinaldo Vicci was saying good-bye to Kehoe as I approached them. 'Please, Mr Vicci. I'd prefer that you don't leave yet. Detective Chapman may have a few questions for you.'

'But, signora, I've got a client performing at the Winter Garden tonight. Second lead. I promised to meet with him backstage before he goes on.'

'We'll do our best to get you there on time.'

Vicci unwrapped his trademark scarf and walked to the sofa to make another call.

'Would you mind introducing me to these other people?' I asked Kehoe, taking a small writing pad from Berk's desk.

'Sure. They're friends of Briggs. I don't know all their names, but there's no reason for them not to cooperate.' We broke up the foursome who still remained and I took down their pedigree and contact information. A short conversation with each and it seemed they had no connection to Joe Berk other than their relationship with Briggs.

'You think Detective Chapman wants me to wait around, too?' Kehoe said.

'I'll go up and check with him. We've actually got to get back up to City Center this evening. I was going to talk to Mona about that, too. Does she keep any kind of office there?'

'At City Center? No, she doesn't. Why do you want to know?'

'I saw her leaving the building this afternoon. I tried

406

to get her attention but she was already on her way here. I guess she'd heard the news about Joe. I was wondering what her business might be there.'

'She may have gone to see a rehearsal. Or maybe an agent called her to check out a client. You'll have to ask her about that.'

'Let me see what Mike's up to. I'll be back to both of you in a few minutes.'

Briggs and Mike were talking quietly when I went upstairs to the bedroom, the kid sitting on the side of the bed and Mike on a chair he had pulled opposite him.

Briggs was recounting the conversation he'd had with his father yesterday.

'Do you mind if I—'

'C'mon in,' Mike said. 'Doesn't look like junior here knew about the monitors. Claims he had no reason to come into the bedroom. Wasn't here very often.'

'Hardly ever.'

'But you were having dinner with your father the night of his accident,' I said.

'Yeah. But we hadn't been getting along too well before that. We'd made that date a few weeks earlier. I – I waited for him to come downstairs. I always did.'

'Tell Ms Cooper why you came back from California.'

Briggs looked up at me. 'Rinaldo – you know Mr Vicci? – he'd been calling me about Lucy. About Lucy DeVore. He told me the doctors expect her to be conscious this week. He – um – he thought I ought to be here, like in case she had anything to say about me. He's – well – he's like a very nervous kind of guy, Mr Vicci.'

'Did your father know why you were coming home?'

407

'Nope. I didn't call him until yesterday morning. Only Rinaldo knew, and Mona. My cousin Mona.'

'Why'd you tell her?' I asked.

'We were just getting to that when you came in. Seems Briggs here wanted to talk to his father about his will. Get the old boy while he's down.'

The young man's head snapped up as he looked at Mike. 'He almost died last week. I wanted to – um – to make sure things were straight between us, let him know he didn't have to worry about me screwing up the fortune he'd made.'

'Make sure you were still in the will? So tell Miss Cooper why you called Mona.'

''Cause my siblings and I don't get along. They hated my mother and they hate me. Mona's the only one in the family who's been decent to me, even when my father had no use for me.'

'She wasn't mad at you when you dropped the lawsuit the two of you had started against Joe?'

Briggs looked over at me. 'Who told you about the lawsuit?'

'Give the DA some credit for doing her homework, kid. Ms Cooper's not as dumb as she looks,' Mike said.

'Did you and your father argue yesterday?'

He didn't answer.

'Were you fighting about your inheritance?'

'I didn't want to do anything to upset him. He – he looked bad,' Briggs said. 'I felt really sorry for him. Right up through the night of the accident he was really strong. He was in good shape. All of a sudden, I see him this way. He looked so weak and unhappy. I didn't mean to start a fight.'

'But you did?' I said softly.

'I don't want to talk about it. And I don't want you looking around in here anymore until my dad's lawyer comes over.'

'We've got some detectives on the way who are going to spend the night here, Briggs. They're going to make sure no one touches anything of your father's,' I said.

'So you'd better come downstairs with us, okay?'

He stood up and followed us out of the room. Vicci and Kehoe were waiting for Mike in Berk's office. It was after seven o'clock and each was ready to get on his way.

Mike asked a few questions before letting them go. Both embraced Briggs and told him they'd see him the next day.

Within minutes after their departure, the doorbell rang. Briggs opened it and two men, both detectives who'd been called in from their respective squads to work on the Met task force, introduced themselves to Briggs and came inside.

'Hey, Michael,' Frank Merriam said, slapping Chapman on the back. 'Counselor, top of the evening to you, too. Heard you had a rough night over at your place, Alexandra.'

'You know me – any excitement to keep Chapman on his toes.'

'You pull this detail, Frankie? Sorry about that,' Mike said. 'Till we find out who the executor of the estate is, Coop's afraid someone's gonna run off with whatever Joe Berk has here.'

'No need for apologies. Overtime, my good man. Back-to-back tours in the big city? Doesn't happen often enough

409

for a guy in the 123rd. Just tell me where I can get the best steak and a couple of brews when I stroll out for my dinner.'

The portly, red-faced Merriam worked in one of the three precincts that covered Staten Island. The city's fifth borough was part of the same police department, but it seemed like a different planet. To cops who spent a career working the streets of Manhattan, the 123rd might as well have been in the Cotswolds.

'Those men we saw going out a few minutes ago. You happen to get the name of the tall guy? The younger one?'

Mike answered. 'You mean Kehoe? Ross Kehoe.'

'That's the moniker. I thought he looked familiar.'

'You know him?'

'Not a drinking buddy, if that's what you mean. Remember the Kills?'

The expression *kills* derived from an old Dutch word meaning 'channels', dating from the period when New York was once New Amsterdam. The Kills was the body of water separating Staten Island from the New Jersey shoreline, and Mike and I had come to know it well.

'Sure.'

'We had a homicide – body washed up near the Outerbridge Crossing. Probably a hit, somebody who got whacked, but was dressed up real nice to look like a suicide.'

'How long ago?'

'Two, maybe two and a half years.'

'Who died?' Mike asked.

'Construction worker. Had something to do with one of the unions and some mob heavies. You've met my partner, Vinny, right? He thought Kehoe looked good for it. Four or five guys who grew up with the union boss. Seemed like they'd do anything for him, and Kehoe was one of the slickest in that pack.'

'Grew up where?'

'Staten Island.'

Mike and I looked at each other before he spoke. 'Where's Clay Pit Ponds park?'

'You oughta come hang out with me sometime. I'll give you a tour. None of this blackboard jungle you live with in Manhattan. We got beaches and golf courses and lakes. We even got us a wildlife refuge now.'

'Clay Pit Ponds park, Frank? C'mon.' Mike was serious now, and I thought of the Staten Island site of the rare Torrey Mountain mint plant that had been found on Talya's pointe shoe.

'Southwestern part of the island.'

'Near the Kills? Kehoe have any family there?'

'He did then. His mother lived off Woodrow Avenue. I think he had a sister who may have gotten the family house when she kicked the bucket, but I didn't follow it close like Vinny.' Frank was exploring the niches that ringed Joe Berk's office, looking at the bizarre assortment of Napoleonic objects.

'The homicide Vinny was working – he ever clear Kehoe?'

'Nah. The ME gave us an inconclusive. Body was in the water too long for a cause of death so we never got no murder charge to go with.'

'Listen to me, Frank. You guys out on Staten Island, news reach you yet about this stuff they call DNA?'

'Only lately. Don't Nab his Ass – DNA – Don't Nab

411

his Ass until you get his spit or his sperm. That's what the captain always tells me. Right, Michael?'

'Did Vinny get a DNA sample from Ross Kehoe?'

Frank put down the Empress Josephine's tortoiseshell hair comb to turn around and face Mike. 'What do you think, buddy? You cross the Verrazano and it's all amateur hour to you? We get a few homicides every year, a handful of rapes. Sure, Vinny got DNA. That's how come I saw Kehoe. He had to come into the station house to be swabbed one night. Cool as an ice cube. Never gave us a bit of trouble.'

'And the deceased?'

'Nothing left of what was once his body to compare to anything or anybody. Waterlogged bones inside of a zoot suit. Fishes and frogs got to him first.'

I walked to Joe Berk's desk and picked up the phone to call Serology.

A technician answered and I identified myself. 'I've got an urgent request. I need you to drop whatever you're doing to examine two samples tonight. I need you to make a comparison to some evidence in the Metropolitan Opera murder case.'

The tech rambled an objection while Mike smiled at me, the biggest grin I'd seen on his face in months. 'That's the Coop I know. I can hear those steel balls clanging against each other even while you're standing still.'

'Well, either you call Dr Thaler at home or I will, but we're going to get this done before your shift is over tonight.'

The tech continued his protest.

'I know there's a court order forbidding comparisons of crime scene evidence to suspects in the linkage database, and you have my word that I'll deal with the judge first thing tomorrow morning. In person. If anybody's held in contempt of court, you won't be the first one behind bars. That'll be me. I'm going to give you the names and case information and you tell me how fast you can get this done, okay?'

I told him what he needed to know, then hung up the phone and grabbed Frank Merriam in a bear hug.

'Some globally endangered mint and a few skin cells on the outside of a man's glove,' Mike said. 'Didn't look like much at first, but it's beginning to smell a little bit like probable cause.'

Chapter 41

'No one in or out upstairs,' Mike said to Frank, putting the key to the bedroom door back in the desk. 'Lawyers should be crawling all over this place by tomorrow morning. They'll be more of them carving up Berk's empire than there are maggots on a dead rat.'

Briggs had agreed to go back to his own apartment to spend the night.

Frank had taken off his trench coat and settled in behind Berk's desk.

'Watch out for the ghosts, Frank.'

'And exactly which ones would they be, counselor?'

'Belasco's ghost. The theater downstairs is supposed to be haunted. Now that Berk's dead, there might be two spirits floating around. Could be a traffic jam, with the size of those egos.'

'Well, Alex, you know me and floating spirits. Sounds more like a cocktail than a fright.'

I drove the Crown Vic back uptown to City Center while Mike made some calls. He found out that there were two detectives on a fixed post in front of the loft where Mona Berk and Ross Kehoe lived, but the guys had no idea whether they'd arrived there before or after

Berk went inside. They had no sightings of either resident.

'Beep me the minute you see anything,' Mike said before he hung up. 'They're right, though, Coop. It's dinnertime. Eight o'clock. If Berk and Kehoe are out eating somewhere, they may not show up for hours. I gotta assume Peterson has her office covered, too.'

He dialed the lieutenant's number, but someone else in the squad answered. Peterson was out on his meal, so Mike passed the message along to the colleague who had answered the phone.

I took Eighth Avenue uptown. We needed to go east on 56th Street, since only the entrance to the office tower – not the theater – would be open at this hour of the night.

I was parking the car when someone entering the building caught my attention. 'Did you see that?'

'What?'

'Going into City Center. Wasn't that Chet Dobbis?'

'Can't tell. I just caught the back of his head.'

I locked the door and threw the keys over the hood to Mike. 'I'd swear it was Dobbis.'

'He used to work here, according to Hubert Alden, before he went to the Met.'

'But no longer,' I said, crossing the street to follow him inside.

The guard sitting behind the desk smiled at Mike and me as we walked in. We had no idea where we were going but he didn't seem to care.

'Excuse me,' I said as Mike flashed his badge.

'Go right on ahead,' he said, not looking up from his solitaire hand.

'You give new meaning to the word *security*. We're looking for my partner, Detective Wallace. You know where he is?'

The guard picked up a piece of paper and pushed the phone to Mike. 'He said for you to call him when you got back. The director is letting him use her secretary's desk. Just dial extension two-nine-nine.'

'And that man who just came in before we did?' I asked. 'Was that Mr Dobbis?'

'Was it who?'

'How long have you worked here? Was it the former director, Chet Dobbis?'

'Sorry, miss. I've only been here two months. I'm real bad on names.'

Mike hung up the phone. 'Let's get Mercer first. He's meeting us back at that ladies' lounge on the seventh floor.'

The corridors were empty and we wound our way around to the elevators and up to the rehearsal studios. Mercer was waiting for us there.

'Check it out, Alex. I don't want to embarrass anyone.'

I walked in and turned on the light. No one was inside, so I opened the door for Mike and Mercer.

We went to the showers to reexamine the room using a flashlight that Mike had brought in from the car. There was a small recess above the molding in the opposite wall and it looked like a hole had been drilled in to support the kind of microcamera that Mike and Mercer were familiar with from their surveillance cases.

'You want Crime Scene to take some pictures of these spots, don't you?' Mike asked. 'They've got to do it before

Vito comes in tomorrow to dig behind it and see where the wiring goes.'

'I already called. They're not going to come out on a job like this tonight. They've got their hands full with a homicide in Inwood and a drug raid that turned into a shoot-out. They told me to secure it till morning,' Mercer said. 'They'll have a crew here first thing, and they can document whatever Vito finds.'

'Can we close it off?'

'Yeah. Before Stan left for the night, he got me the janitor. Soon as we're done he's going to lock it and put up one of their "out of order" signs on it. That should work. I'll call him when we get downstairs,' Mercer said as we started back to the elevator.

'You know Merriam? Frankie Merriam?'

'Heavyset red-faced guy from Staten Island?' Mercer asked.

'Map of Ireland on his mug – that's the guy. We gotta bring you up to date on what he says about Ross Kehoe.'

'So let's go grab some dinner. What we need to do is sit down and sort out all these pieces. What's close by?'

'Michael's,' I said. 'On Fifty-fifth Street, a block away.'

The restaurant was a favorite of literary lions and media heavyweights, but it was after eight thirty, so we'd be able to nab a table in the quiet garden room in the rear.

'Walk back the cat,' Mike said.

'What?'

'That's what the three of us have to do. Walk back the cat.'

'What do you mean?'

'Military intelligence, Coop. Spook-speak. Say somebody shoots the king or blows up the embassy. After it

417

happens the cat walkers go back and look at all the intelligence they had before the event, apply the stuff they know after the fact to whatever happened. Uncover the moles, find the motive.'

'I'm for that. We know a hell of a lot more than we did before the weekend. Did Mike tell you that I swear I saw Chet Dobbis coming into this building when we pulled into the block?' I asked Mercer.

'No, but now that explains what Ms Schiller's secretary was waiting around for while I was hanging out for you.'

The elevator doors opened on the ground floor as Mercer continued. 'One of the other secretaries came by so they could walk to the subway together, and I heard her say she was staying late, waiting for Mr D to get here. She had to let him into the theater before she left. Some kind of proposal he was working on. It never occurred to me they were talking about Dobbis.'

'So that's only ten minutes ago?'

'Yeah.'

'Let's check the theater. What the hell is he coming back here for – and at night, when no one's around?'

Instead of turning right toward the security desk, we retraced our steps through the narrow hallway, piled deep with soon-to-be-discarded equipment that we had navigated earlier in the day. The heavy door that separated the office tower from the original Mecca Temple building was open, and the three of us threaded our way behind the mezzanine seats, our footsteps padded by the thick carpeting of traditional Moorish design that covered the entire space.

The vast auditorium was darkened, except for a few

rays of light that came from off to the side of stage right. I could hear a man's voice from the pit below, and we all stopped so that Mercer, the tallest of us, could peer down from the steep rake of the balcony to see who was speaking.

He motioned us to the top of the staircase and whispered, 'It's Dobbis. His back is to us so I can't hear what he's saying, but it looks like he's talking to someone in the wings.'

We continued down the wide staircase from the old Shriners' lounge, descending to the rear of the once-elegant lobby of the old theater. The doors leading to the street were all locked and covered with metal grating, while those that accessed the auditorium were closed over.

Mike put his finger to his lips and led us down the side of a corridor that abutted the theater. It seemed to be taking us as near to the stage, to the front of the orchestra, as we could get before revealing ourselves to Dobbis.

On a signal to each other, Mike and Mercer pulled open the two doors that stood catty-corner in the cul-de-sac of the hallway. Mike took the one that led toward the stage and I was behind Mercer as he moved into the auditorium toward Chet Dobbis.

'What the—' The startled Met director stepped back and dropped into a front-row seat, beneath the glistening white-and-gold detail of the ceiling that shone against the dimly lighted house. 'I'm so thankful you're here.'

At the same moment, I heard someone running behind the black-curtained area in the wings. I looked from Dobbis, whose sincerity I doubted at this point, back to the source of the footsteps.

Mike streaked across the middle of the stage in pursuit of the shadowed figure, and Mercer doubled back out the door we had entered together and up the steps to join in the chase.

I started toward Chet Dobbis to ask the reason for his gratitude when the theater went completely dark. The thick gray steel fire curtain dropped from the fly down to the floorboards with the alacrity of the blade of a guillotine.

Chapter 42

Dobbis stood up and I could see the silhouette of his body moving in my direction as I turned back to the exit to push it open. 'Miss Cooper, wait!'

I yelled Mike's name and let the door slam on Dobbis as I entered the dead-ended corridor. It was too dark there to see anything except the shiny silver barrel of a revolver that was pointed at my face.

The man holding the gun was Ross Kehoe.

At the instant he started to speak to me, Dobbis barged through the door, which smacked against my back and knocked me into the wall.

Kehoe grabbed my neck with his left hand and pressed the gun barrel to the side of my head, just below my right ear. 'Walk, both of you. That way. Lead her, Chet, if you don't want me to blow her brains out all over your back.'

The icy feel of the cold metal bore against my skin sent a chill through my body. I twitched involuntarily and Kehoe tightened his grasp on the nape of my neck.

This was the gloved hand that had clamped on me from behind in the darkened stairwell of my building last night, only now I could feel the rough surface of his thick fingers pinching my smooth skin.

'Don't fight me. You won't win this one,' Kehoe said as he pushed me ahead of him. His voice was harsher now, more guttural than it had been in Mona Berk's presence. This was Ross Kehoe, street thug and stagehand, before she had tried to gentrify him. Why hadn't I thought of him when I was jumped from behind in the dark, his lean, sinewy body a perfect match for the masked man in black?

Dobbis moved quickly along the darkened corridor and out the door into the lobby. Ross Kehoe told him to head up the steps, so he began to climb the broad staircase first. I looked over at the grating that barred the exit doors but could see nothing toward which I could make a successful run. 'Move, Alex. Follow him up.'

Kehoe growled his commands at me. He freed my neck so that I could go up behind Dobbis, but the gun barrel nudged at my back with each riser I mounted.

I started to turn right at the top of the stairs, toward the door that led to the adjacent office tower, the one through which Mike, Mercer, and I had entered the back of the theater. But that wasn't the way Kehoe planned to take us.

Kehoe reached out with the gun and tapped me on the arm. 'Left. Go left.'

Dobbis was standing still. I looked back and forth between the two men but couldn't figure the dynamic. Dobbis seemed as much a prisoner as I did, but he obeyed Kehoe's command immediately and walked the way he was directed.

I expected Mike and Mercer to emerge out of the doors beside the stage within seconds. The sound of our voices would certainly alert them that we were still in the auditorium.

'The detectives will be flooding the place any minute, Chet.'

'Shut up, bitch,' Kehoe said, slapping the back of my head with his hand. I coughed and bent over, turning to look at him. Dobbis walked on. Kehoe kept licking his lips with his tongue, then twisting it into the side of his mouth, making a sucking sound as irritating as a phonograph needle sliding across an old vinyl record. I'd heard that disgusting noise when he assaulted me last night.

'I told you to move,' he said.

I didn't wait to be hit again. I didn't know whether it was good for me – or very bad – that Ross Kehoe's anxiety seemed to be building, almost as much as mine.

There was a second staircase, not quite as wide as the one that led up from the lobby, and Kehoe told Dobbis to take it. 'I have lots more time than that, don't I, Chet?' Kehoe asked. 'I mean, don't you think the lady's an optimist?'

Were they in this together or not? I couldn't tell.

I kept talking, thinking my words would echo below in the great space of the open theater and that someone would be able to hear me sooner or later. 'What does he mean, Chet?' I asked.

The steps became more narrow and steep as we climbed behind the second balcony, several hundred seats held aloft by the largest steel beam in the world.

'Tell her. You can tell her,' Kehoe said with a laugh, again followed by that awful sucking sound, some kind of nervous reflex that got exercised more frequently when he was stressed.

The gun was still to my back, Kehoe playing with it from time to time, running the metal tip up and down

423

my spine whenever I had to stop to wait for Dobbis. I walked behind him through a doorway and into the balcony area, high above the stage. Another left turn and we were going up more stairs, narrower still, to the very back of the last row of seats in the theater.

Dobbis stopped on the highest step to catch his breath. 'When this place, Mecca Temple, was built in the 1920s, it was lit entirely with gas jets. And because they needed the gaslight and torches backstage to help the actors get around when the shows were on, and to light the stage itself, the designers had to be creative about ways to prevent fire from spreading.'

I looked down toward the stage, but even in the darkness, the height from these narrow steps and the incredibly steep rake of the upper balcony made the view dizzying. I grabbed the brass railing and held on to it.

Dobbis pointed to the steel trap of a curtain that had cut me off from Mercer and Mike. 'The idea here was to be able to transform the stage – in the case of fire – into a chimney, to separate it completely from the seats in order to protect the audience. The flames would be confined to the stage and shoot straight up, while the people in the audience would be safe. They'd have time to escape.'

I steadied myself and continued to look for any sign of life below. Dobbis went on. 'The curtain was made of asbestos originally. Replaced by steel.' He stopped talking and closed his eyes. 'This firewall is impenetrable.'

Kehoe prodded me to walk again. I clutched the railing so that I wouldn't lose my footing and fall, as we made our way against the red velvet drapes behind the last row of seats. Not far above my head was the ornate ceiling, with elaborate Arabic designs outlined in brilliant gold leaf that seemed to glow in the dark, like the perforated stars that sat recessed into the ceiling beside the unlit chandeliers.

I had to turn sideways to shimmy between the heavy drapery and the last row of seats. 'What does that have to do with—'

Dobbis was clutching the seatback of a chair, slowly putting one foot ahead of the other, since he barely fit in the narrow space. 'It means that when we redesigned the theater, in order to fireproof the building against an accident or an electrical fire backstage, we did it so that with a single button, the manager could isolate the stage completely. The steel curtain drops in three seconds flat —'

'I think she caught that, didn't she?' Kehoe said, mocking Dobbis.

'There's only another five seconds for anyone onstage to get off when that happens. But then the steel sides and rear drop – and if you don't know they're coming – you get caught in there, just the way your cops did. It's like a giant steel trap.'

'But *he* got out.' I was referring to Ross Kehoe, as I grasped the seatbacks and followed Dobbis's baby steps, coming to an abrupt stop behind him as he reached a cement setback in the middle of the row.

'You remember the way, Chet, don't you? Take those stairs.'

'I can't see anything, damn it. You should go ahead of me.'

Kehoe laughed. 'You could probably scale your way up the side of the Grand Canyon or the top of Everest and you're telling me you can't climb up there? Four more steps, Chet. Feel your way.'

Chet Dobbis leaned over the opening and crawled. Kehoe squeezed behind me as I followed Dobbis, still hearing no noise, no sign of rescuers, coming from below.

Kehoe padded like a panther in the darkness, familiar with his surroundings and secure in his footing.

'They'll get out, too,' I said, sounding no more confident than I felt. 'Soon.'

Chet Dobbis was at the top, reaching out a hand for me to stand up in the dusty confines of a storeroom full of antiquated stage lighting equipment. 'It won't be that easy for them, Miss Cooper. If I had to make an educated guess, I'd say Ross has sealed the whole place off. Killed all the electricity down there. In half an hour, it has an automatic disengage system built in, but thirty minutes is a long time to wait.'

Kehoe pushed me aside and lined up behind us. There was a slice of a footpath between stacks of plywood scenery that had been left leaning against walls and cardboard cartons that were labeled with show titles, costumes and props abandoned on top of them.

'They've got cell phones,' I said, remembering that Laura had not gotten one to replace mine before I left the office this afternoon.

'Easier to get through from outer space than from inside that metal enclosure,' Dobbis said. 'Nobody knows that better than Ross.'

'Why?' I asked. 'Why does Ross know?'

''Cause that was my job, girl,' Kehoe said, sneering at me, the same irritating noise coming from his lips. 'You

426

kept asking me what I did for Joe, didn't you? You think I'm some kind of jerk, don't you?'

Another door for Dobbis to open. Another step into a black chamber, like the poor man's equivalent of entering Tut's tomb. Once again my eyes gradually became accustomed to the greater darkness; the room was piled from top to bottom with theatrical treasures, if not the golden objects of a boy king.

Dobbis was feeling his way through the mess, his movement slowed by the overflow of old sets that were in his way.

'You didn't give me credit for being so smart, did you, Alex?' Again Kehoe clutched my neck with his bare hand, trying to shake an answer out of me. I could feel the calloused skin, the strong grip of a man who had labored as a stagehand for years before being rescued by Mona Berk from his working-class surroundings.

Kehoe squeezed tighter.

I had nothing to say. I hadn't seen a moment's chance to break away on this trek, and now I seemed to have lost the ability to resist against his brute force.

'Joe did. Joe Berk did. Saw me working backstage when I was just getting started. Still a teenager, brought in by my uncle, trying to get into the carpenters' union. Move it, Chet. One more door there, then up a flight. Don't you remember?'

'I've never come this far. Nobody's been there since this place was built.'

'Been where?' I asked, the words catching in my throat.

'Forget fucking carpentry. I figured that one out fast. I watched my old man's thumb get ripped to shreds by a saw while he was building a set for some bullshit play that didn't even stay open for two weeks. Tore the bone off down to the joint. Too much backbreaking work, and you're sucking in the sawdust all day long. It was the lights I liked. I liked controlling the whole operation with the flick of one switch. All the juice was in my hands and even old Joe Berk thought I was a genius.'

Another pitch-black chamber, this one hung with row upon row of faded costumes.

Royal robes and ballgowns, tutus and tulle skirts of every length, outfits for soldiers and cowboys and chorus girls and cancan dancers.

Dobbis leaned over and half crawled up another set of stairs. 'Joe Berk's jack-of-all-trades. You did all his dirty work for him.'

'You don't know half of what that old bastard was up to,' Kehoe said, waiting for me to follow Dobbis.

'Is this it?' Dobbis asked.

'Open the door.'

Chet Dobbis turned his shoulder to the black steel frame and pushed but nothing moved.

Kehoe removed a small silver gadget, the size of a can opener, from his left pocket. He pressed a button on it and the door slid to the side, allowing a slice of light from within to streak down the painted black cement steps.

'It's the dome of the old mosque, Alex. We're going into the dome.'

Chapter 43

One more long wooden staircase, its steps embedded with a row of tiny lights like the pathways that illuminate on airplanes to show the way to the exits in case of emergency.

At the top of the flight, awaiting our arrival, stood Mona Berk.

'Shit,' she said to Kehoe. 'What are you doing with her, too?'

'I didn't expect the cops to show up in the middle of this. I had to think fast.'

'Not your strong suit. Let's figure this out.'

Dobbis went first, and despite the danger to both of us, seemed to stand in place and look all around the room, taking in everything he could see.

Ross ordered him to move and when I reached the top of the landing, I understood what had stopped Dobbis in his tracks.

Overhead, in the center of the massive circular structure, was a large skylight. Through it streaked moonbeams from the cloudless April night. Adjacent buildings – large hotels, offices, and high-priced apartments that overlooked the vast space of the mosque dome – also cast down an eerie neon night-light.

And high above me, suspended from the rounded ceiling on lengths of shiny brass chain links, was a red velvet swing – the kind that sixteen-year-old Evelyn Nesbit swung on naked to amuse her paramour, the great Stanford White, and the kind of swing from which Lucy DeVore dropped, likely to die, the day Ross Kehoe walked her backstage for her audition.

'Over there, Chet,' Kehoe said, directing him to a sofa in a corner of the great dome that had been furnished to look like a hidden bordello.

When Dobbis took his seat, Ross passed the gun to Mona and told her to keep it on me while he tied Dobbis's hands behind his back with some strips of cloth that looked ready-made for the occasion.

I studied him now, out from behind me for the first time since he'd accosted me. He was edgier still, pushing Dobbis's limbs when the captive director didn't comply fast enough, licking his lips constantly and sucking in more air.

I tried to scope the rest of the room, not wanting to take my eyes off the handgun for many seconds. There was a bed, to the side of the swing, that was dressed in the lavish style of the linens in Joe Berk's room and had the same crest and monogrammed initials; an antique brass clothing stand from which hung a variety of lingerie and robes; a well-stocked bar with liquors, wines, and crystal glasses of every shape and size.

I started to walk back the cat. 'Where's the camera?'

'What?' Mona asked.

'That's what you did for Joe, isn't it?' I said to Kehoe, ignoring Mona Berk. 'You wired up places for Joe Berk. You're the electrical specialist – that's what you did in theaters, isn't it? You built him an entertainment system that let him watch anybody he wanted – women in dressing rooms, bedrooms, showers – and whatever the hell was going on here, in this . . . this playground you created for him.'

'Whatever turned him on, Alex. That's what he paid me for. Got to the age where Joe wasn't always able to do an evening performance after his matinee. Sometimes he just liked to watch.'

Kehoe walked toward me and motioned me back to an area with chairs and a sofa. 'You're next, Ms DA. Pick a seat. Make yourself comfortable.'

I didn't move.

'The bitch is so used to telling people what they're supposed to do, I don't think she takes orders well,' Mona said. 'Ross told you to get over there.'

I didn't know whether fear or exhaustion had the tighter hold on me. I was sweating and breathing heavily, but chilled as well and shivering from that. My head throbbed and my neck ached from Kehoe's angry grip.

As I sat on a straight-backed chair, Kehoe looked around the room for something with which to restrain me. Near the seat of the swing was a length of thick rope, wrapped in a coil, like a cobra waiting to strike. It reminded me of the cables used to hold weights attached to the fly gallery that dropped the scenery onto the stage.

For some reason, Kehoe stepped around that rope and walked instead to the clothing rack. He removed a silk wrap from one of the robes and came back to us, this time taking my hands and tying them tightly behind me. He must have had another plan for the big rope.

There were no windows in the giant circular dome, no

way to communicate with the world outside. I guessed there was a hole in the skylight overhead, because a draft of cold, fresh air blew down occasionally, rippling through me with another chill.

Kehoe had taken the gun back from Mona and they had walked a distance away from us to have a conversation.

'Don't you think someone will look up here?' I asked Chet Dobbis. 'What did you mean that nobody's ever been in this place? Why?'

'There was never anything up here when the mosque was built but an antiquated ventilation system. All the smoke, all the stale air – it was sucked up here by a behemoth of a fan and dispersed. By the 1940s the whole process had changed and that form of exhaust was replaced with more modern ducts that were installed downstairs. The dome? This has never been used for anything. It's – it's just ornamental.'

'Can we get out of here, Chet? Isn't there any way out?'

He had seemed resigned from the beginning to some kind of dreadful fate, timidly following Kehoe's directions, while now I could focus on nothing but finding a way to escape.

Dobbis shook his head and stared down at the floor. 'After I left my job here, Kehoe must have done this.'

'Done what?'

'There was a renovation of this cupola – first time ever – in 2003. Opened it up so they could get to the outside skin of the dome and replace the old Spanish tiles that had been part of the original installation. Arlette, the woman who replaced me as the center's director, told me they basically swept the place clean and shut it up again.'

'So Kehoe knew this whole space was vestigial, was of no use to anyone, and he engineered a way in for himself. With Joe Berk's money, and with access to all the nubile bodies Joe was willing to pay to perform for him.' And access, I thought, to the top of the dome, to install an antenna to transmit video images.

'Looks like he managed to do that. Who the hell would even find a way back here? And how? There's no way to open that door except electronically, Alex. He's got some kind of control, some electrical device that he pressed to let us in.'

'No other exits?'

'Nothing up here. One way in, one way out. I'm sure of that.'

'How about the firewall on the stage? Doesn't that set off an alarm to nine-one-one?'

'It was meant to, but not if Ross disabled it when he pulled the plug on the power and lights down there. He seems to have a separate system of his own in here.'

If an escape tactic wouldn't work, I needed to know why Ross Kehoe had called Dobbis to the theater tonight. I needed to know if there was any deal we could try to make with him and with Mona Berk to let us out alive.

'What does Kehoe want with you?'

He looked over at Ross and Mona, who seemed to be arguing with each other.

'I was stupid enough to believe him when he called me to come over tonight. Told me that Mona had an offer for me, wanted to give me a piece of a new production if I'd give them some advice in exchange.'

Dobbis picked up his head and I could see tears in his

eyes. 'I should have known he'd be setting me up for something.'

I leaned toward him. 'But for what? Do you know what that is?'

'He's going to kill me if we don't do something. He'll kill both of us.'

I didn't need a road map to figure that out. Every theater had its ghosts, and we were on our way to joining the cast of this one.

'I understand you. Why, though? I'm just a product of bad timing tonight. Why you?'

'He was setting me up to take the weight for Talya's murder when you and your team walked in,' Dobbis said, pulling in his breath to regain his composure.

'Did you?'

'No, dammit. Nothing to do with it.'

'Joe Berk? Or was it Ross Kehoe?'

'Talya knew about Joe's game. She knew he had a fetish for young girls, for taping them while they were undressing or making love or showering. Watching them is what aroused him, especially when they didn't know – they couldn't know – that anyone could see what they were doing. Mostly he liked to look at them when he was home alone. Sometimes when the company he was keeping wasn't enough to do the trick for him.'

'She knew because he did it to her?'

'Talya? She was too old for Joe. But she caught him at home with tapes of the young dancers. Videos of the girls in the showers and in the rehearsal studios who didn't know they were being filmed, and other kids who liked to perform for him, maybe right here in this room –

happy to be photographed from a distance, happy that he couldn't touch them.'

'How do you know?' I asked, thinking how right Battaglia had been to ask me whether Joe Berk was a paraphile.

'Because Talya told me. She didn't like me a lot, ever since we'd stopped being lovers years ago. But she trusted me – she always trusted me.'

'What did she tell you?'

'Talya wasn't very good at it, but she was trying to blackmail Joe. Trying to use that information to get herself a boatload of money – or a starring role in Joe's next big hit. I guess she wanted me to know in case Joe did something to threaten her. She wasn't thinking of murder or anything like that, I can assure you. But Talya was aware that if her plan backfired, Joe would have the power to make her life miserable.'

'Do you think Joe paid Ross to kill Talya that night at the Met?'

'I'm tired of thinking. It's not going to help us any to think at this point,' Dobbis said, raising his bound hands to his face and rubbing across his eyes as best he could. 'I should have been using my brain for the last week, while you and your detectives had *me* in your sights instead of Kehoe and Berk.'

'You were all in our sights, Chet. Every one of you. That's how it works till we're able to break down the information we've got. Maybe if you'd told us how much you knew about Talya, back then. Maybe if you let us know about Talya and what was going on in her relationship with Berk. There's a lot you've said just now that could have helped us last week.'

I despised his self-pitying whining. If he hadn't lied to Mercer and Mike, if he hadn't withheld what he knew about Talya and about Joe Berk, we wouldn't be together in this bizarre crypt that was unlikely to be opened until the next renovation, maybe fifty years from now.

'I didn't know enough to tell you anything. It was only tonight, only a minute or two before you walked into the theater, that Ross bragged to me about killing Joe Berk.'

'Today? He told you that he killed Joe today?'

Chet Dobbis threw back his head and looked up at the sliver of sky above us. 'No, no, no. You still don't get it, do you? Ross Kehoe killed Joe Berk last Sunday night, right in front of the Belasco Theatre.'

Chapter 44

I wasn't walking back the cat anymore, I was running with him.

Ross Kehoe – Joe's trusted employee, his driver, the genius with every kind of electrical equipment. That day at the Imperial Theatre, moments before he walked Lucy behind the curtain to put her up on the swing, it was Ross Kehoe who stood on the stage, directing the guy in charge of the lighting to give him something cooler, to bring down the brightness. Why didn't Mike or I realize then that Kehoe had a specialty, an area of expertise that had all to do with electricity?

Last night, when the lights went out in my home, when someone broke into or scammed his way into the building and shut down the power in the A line of apartments, why didn't I think of Kehoe's electrical prowess when I racked my brain for possible suspects connected to the investigation?

And when Joe Berk stepped on a manhole that was wired to jolt him into the great beyond, why didn't any of us figure that the man who used to chauffeur him would know exactly where to park the car, know exactly what sewer cover Joe would step on when he came out of his apartment to get across the street to go to dinner with his wayward son? How easy for someone with Kehoe's ability to cut the wrapping on the insulation in the power box – just minutes before Berk and his son left the Belasco to go to dinner – in order to mimic the tragic accidents that had electrocuted unsuspecting pedestrians in Manhattan in years past.

Of course Briggs had told Mona about the dinner plans. Of course Kehoe had the opportunity to stage – what had the ME called it? – an 'electrical event' and wait in the wings, on the dark street, to make sure Joe Berk was his only victim.

So Joe Berk had been meant to die last Sunday, just two nights after Natalya Galinova's murder. And shortly after his beloved Briggs had dropped the lawsuit against him, hoping for reconciliation. It was Briggs who had been escorting Joe out to the car on their way to dinner that evening, and undoubtedly Briggs and Mona who had been partners with Ross in Joe Berk's skillful execution.

None of them had counted on Joe's ninth life, short as it was.

Chet Dobbis was also sweating profusely. 'Joe Berk's accidental death was supposed to put an end to your investigation.'

'How? Why would—'

'Ross made that much clear to me tonight. Talya was killed on Friday. She and Joe were in the middle of a tempest – had been for days – fighting and feuding quite publicly. He missed her performance that night but showed up in her dressing room.'

Everything Dobbis said so far made sense.

'She disappeared at the Met that very evening. The

best Joe could do was say his driver would vouch for him. Even an idiot knows that one of Joe's employees would swear to anything to keep his job. That's worthless in a court of law.'

Dobbis was right. The chauffeur was always a lousy alibi.

'Joe's glove was found near Talya's body. That's what Ross told me. He said he heard it from Joe. Is it true?'

I nodded my head. A glove with Joe Berk's DNA on it – and a good chance now that the other skin cells on the surface would soon be matched to Ross Kehoe, whose profile was in the linkage database from the earlier homicide investigation on Staten Island. All the information in that database that had been rendered useless – paralyzed for the time being – after I appeared in court last week on the Ramon Carido case before Judge McFarland.

'You think Ross couldn't have gotten his hands on a pair of Joe's gloves and planted one at the scene? You think Joe would ever have missed them?'

'Not likely. He probably had—'

'Dozens of pairs. That was his style, Alex. More of everything. Whoever got through the winter without losing a glove somewhere?'

'But Talya's murder? Did Joe really know his way around the Met?'

'He'd been back there scores of times. He was an impresario, courting talent, courting stars. Of course he'd been behind the scenes. They could have been going to any one of the offices,' Dobbis said, pausing for several seconds. 'Like Ross said to me downstairs, they could have been coming up to my office.'

'And they were fighting on the way there,' I said.

439

'Two terrible-tempered people, both volatile and very physical. They argued and Joe became enraged. Struck her, maybe hit her too hard. She passed out and he panicked. Threw her down the shaft.'

'He was strong enough?'

'You only saw Joe after he was hurt. He was as strong as he was tough. It gave him the menace to back up his mouth.'

I was following Dobbis's story line until he reminded me that it was just the version that Ross Kehoe had expected the police to believe. It was Ross who had actually worked at the Met – worked at almost every theater in Manhattan at one point in time or another. And Ross who knew the place well enough to steal a white-haired wig that would help incriminate Joe Berk, too, having no idea the Met used animal hair to make the wigs.

'So then Ross set up Joe Berk's electrocution. Which would have been a neat way for the police to close the case, had it worked. The killer gets his just deserts. And that's why Mona Berk came to the Belasco the night Joe was supposed to die. She was going to leave enough evidence – videotapes, maybe – something connecting Joe to the threats that Talya had been making. Something that would have given him a motive to murder his diva. Case closed.'

Chet Dobbis raised his hands again to wipe away the sweat. 'You know he's going to kill us. You understand Ross has that rope here so that he can—'

He stopped abruptly, unable to speak the words.

'But why?'

'Because Joe Berk lived too long. One week too long. Joe spent a lot of time with you, with the detectives last week. Ross doesn't think any of you believe Joe killed Talya. He wants to take the heat off himself. He wants to make it look like I—'

Dobbis choked on his own words.

'See that rope?' he asked me.

I looked at the thick pile on the floor near his feet. 'He wants to make it look like you committed suicide?'

He nodded his head, and now the rivulets of sweat merged with the teardrops.

'I guess he figures that it's easy to make a case that Talya was on her way to my office when she was killed. Old lovers, everyone knew that. Make the case that I was jealous of Berk, jealous of Hubert Alden.'

'But why would he do it here, in the dome, if no one would find you?'

'That wasn't the plan. At least not until you showed up. He had the gun. He was trying to force me to go up to the fly gallery – backstage – just before you got there. He must have more rope. Think how easy it would be to hang me from the fly,' Dobbis said. 'Make it look like I killed myself.'

No wonder Chet Dobbis had said he was glad to see us when Mercer and I surprised him in the auditorium.

Ross Kehoe walked over to the bar, turned his back, and leaned against it.

'Make me a drink,' he said to Mona.

'Don't give me orders,' she said, looking petulant and unhappy.

'I'm doing all the work. Make me a drink.'

She walked toward the counter and poured from one of the decanters. They had been quarreling with each other, from the look on her face. Kehoe must have felt as trapped as Dobbis and I did. There was no need to fuel that mix of desperation and nerves with alcohol.

'Your arrival tonight makes things much harder for us,' Kehoe said to me. 'And that's why you're making it so much harder for yourself.'

'You don't know my partners very well. They're out of that steel trap by now and they won't leave this building until they've found me.'

Kehoe looked at his watch, took a sip of his drink, and smiled at me.

'The front entrance to the theater was completely barred,' I said. 'They know none of us went out that way, and if they go back the way we came in through the office tower, the security guard will tell them we never passed by there again.'

'You're giving that dumb bastard a lot more credit than I would. And I guess you don't know there's a series of exits right behind the stage. Three doors and a truck bay wide enough to fit a container shipment. That would be the logical way to take anybody out of here quickly,' Kehoe said, running his tongue round and around his lips. 'Those doors are the first things your buddies would have seen when the release went up on the firewall.'

I looked at Dobbis and he nodded in agreement.

'I guarantee you they'll look everywhere else before they even figure out there's an entrance to this dome,' Kehoe said, as Mona Berk took the glass from his hand and sipped at it. 'It sits in the middle of this city like a gigantic ball, and it's never had any use at all.'

'The noise—'

'You got a lot of degrees, maybe, but you don't know anything important, do you? Like everything else in a

442

theater, that door is soundproofed. Scream, Miss Prosecutor, and maybe a passing pigeon'll hear you up above, but nobody else will.'

He reached into his pants pocket and withdrew something. They were small objects that I couldn't see, but I could hear the metallic sound as he jiggled them together in his fingers.

Kehoe opened the chamber of his revolver. He lifted his hand to his mouth and I watched in horror as he kissed the tip of a bullet and placed it in the gun. He grinned at me and sucked in air again, kissing a second bullet and loading it in the chamber.

'I wasn't counting on two of you,' he said. 'I hate to waste the lead.'

I raised my head and tried to scoff at his arrogance, which frightened me every bit as much as it did Chet Dobbis. I knew there was no way out, but Ross Kehoe must have known that, too. We were all trapped here together. 'They're not stupid enough to think a woman disappeared from within a theater and simply couldn't be found anywhere.'

'Don't be so sure of yourself, Alex,' Kehoe said, pointing the gun at me and cocking his head, as though he was practicing taking aim. 'That theory didn't do anything to help Natalya Galinova get out of the Met alive, did it?'

Chapter 45

Two hours must have passed before Ross Kehoe and Mona Berk left the area where Chet Dobbis and I had been restrained. They had forbidden us to talk to each other as they whispered between themselves, reformulating their plans.

The only other noise I could hear came through the broken skylight above – the honking of car horns and the occasional scream of sirens, too far away to be useful to me.

Kehoe walked away from us and down the staircase. I was even more tired now and terribly frightened as I had watched Kehoe deteriorate throughout the night, fighting with Mona and then pouring himself a second drink.

My arms ached from trying to stretch at and work the binds behind me, but I sat up at attention when I heard what sounded like the door – our only connection to freedom – slide on its tracks. It seemed like Kehoe had left.

Ten minutes later the door reopened and Kehoe walked up the steps and back to us.

He spoke to Mona. 'Nobody down there. They've got the lights on now, but I couldn't see anyone.'

I whispered to Dobbis, 'How can he tell? What could he see?'

'Do you remember those perforated stars, the enormous ones over the proscenium with cutouts in the grillwork?'

They were the most beautiful part of the auditorium's design. 'Yes, of course.'

'If Kehoe walked around that entire dark chamber we came through, he'd reach the area behind those eight stars. When the Shriners built the place, that was an organ loft. Another anachronism, another empty space. But from behind those stars you can pretty well see the entire auditorium. And you can do it without being seen from below.'

Everything seemed to be working to Kehoe's advantage.

Mona got up from the bar stool and moved to the bed, stretching out on top of it. Kehoe walked over to us.

'You might as well rest. You need to save some energy to make your way out of here when we're ready to go.'

His back was to Mona, who had rolled over on her side. As he squatted to look behind me to check that the ties were still secure, he laid his hand on my knee, then ran his forefinger up the length of the inside of my thigh. I suppressed a gag as my eyes followed his dirty fingernail along the seam of my gray slacks.

'Go where? How?' I asked as he pushed up to his feet. Had he lost it entirely that he thought he could walk us out of this dome?

'Chet will tell you. This theater has more trapdoors and underground passages than the Vatican. Two, three in the morning, maybe we'll get moving. Might even have

445

to wait until tomorrow night.' Kehoe lifted the revolver and stroked his cheek with the barrel. 'Unless you get on my nerves too much.'

'And then what?' I asked. 'Cops will be looking for you everywhere. Your home, the airports, the train stations, the car rental—'

'You know, Alex, that's the nice thing about owning your own planes. BerkAir. Not that we intend to take you and Chet quite that far with us. Maybe a little insurance to get us to the right private field.'

'BerkAir to the Bahamas, no doubt.'

'Follow the money,' Kehoe said, sitting up against the headboard of the bed, next to Mona, to keep an eye on us. He rested the gun on his chest.

'Mona's money,' I said, wondering whether Joe Berk had fixed things in his will after Briggs dropped the lawsuit.

'I hate fucking rich people,' he said, rubbing his hand over Mona's backside and laughing to himself. 'It's just their money I like.'

If she had appeared to have been reclining calmly before he made that remark, Mona was on her feet and obviously restless again, looking for something, or someone, to be the target for her hostility. She paced back and forth beside the bed before walking to the swing that was suspended from the ceiling high above us. With one hand she grabbed the brass chain while she steadied the seat with her other one.

'Stay off that,' Kehoe said.

'Why?' she asked. I didn't think that Mona Berk was used to taking orders. She ignored him and pulled herself up on the swing, pumping her legs to get it moving.

'You want me to pull you off that or what?' Kehoe's mildest threat would have done the trick for me.

'I want you to get us out of here, Ross. That's what the fuck I want.' She was going higher and higher, disappearing for seconds against the backdrop of the dark walls as she flew by. I could see only the shiny brass chain making a dizzying arc as I tried to follow its motion.

Kehoe walked toward the swing and Mona kicked harder, nearly grazing the top of his head as he came closer.

When she flew back past him, Kehoe reached out and grabbed Mona's leg, pulling on it as he twisted the chain around and around with his well-muscled arm. Her head snapped forward and she wrapped her elbows tightly against the metal links to keep herself from falling off.

'Are you crazy?' she yelled at Kehoe. 'What's wrong with you?'

'Stop the damn thing!' he said, stepping away as the seat of the swing jerked up and down while Mona tried to unravel herself.

She came to a stop, threw her head back, and started laughing. 'You're nervous, aren't you? You're as goddamn nervous as I am, aren't you?'

I watched as she jumped off and walked over to Kehoe. I couldn't hear what they were saying to each other but I could see that they were arguing, which couldn't be good for any of us.

I was too wired to close my eyes, even though I was aching with exhaustion and fear. I looked over at Chet Dobbis, who had hung his head, slumped in his seat, and started crying – turning his face away from me when he caught me watching him. With every ounce of whatever strength I had reserved, I twisted and turned my wrists, pulling the silken strips as far apart as I could.

Kehoe and Mona had gone back to sitting against the headboard of the bed, fidgeting and whispering to each other, until it must have been after two o'clock in the morning. I looked over when I saw her stand up and start to approach, probably on a command from Kehoe to check on Dobbis and me. I stopped wriggling and held my hands in place behind me.

My heart began racing faster as I saw that Mona was holding the revolver.

'You don't need that with me,' I said. 'I'm too scared to make trouble.'

'You've caused more than enough for me and Ross already. Look what you've started,' she said, waving her hand with the revolver over her head. 'It's your fault we're trapped in here.'

I needed to calm her down as badly as I wanted to calm myself. I had no idea whether Mona Berk had ever held a gun before and I was even more frightened to think we were in the hands of an amateur.

'Ross seems to know what he wants to do,' I said, hoping she was annoyed enough to tell me what was in store.

'Maybe he did before he started drinking,' Mona said, looking over at him to see whether he was paying attention to her. He had gotten up to stretch and splash water on his face from the wet bar across the room. 'I should never have waited here for him. I should have left all this dirty work up to him to get done.'

'So how come you trusted Ross when you first met him?' I asked tentatively. Maybe I could talk her down.

Maybe I could convince her that she had so much more to live for than he did. 'I mean, wasn't he working for your uncle?'

'Like that would have mattered to me? Like I thought anybody in the world would have had an allegiance to Joe Berk for longer than the first paycheck?' Mona asked me. 'You know what Joe did to me? You people who think he didn't deserve to die a miserable death, you ought to know this. He paid Ross to break into my old apartment – even my office – to hook up some of his surveillance cameras so the mean old prick could know what I was up to. Not naked, not in the bedroom. Joe just needed to know who I was hanging out with, who I was seeing and what I was doing. So he'd have a reason to fuck me out of my inheritance. Any reason. That's how I met Ross.'

She was seething now at the thought of the old family history and I continued to try to shake off the chill as I shivered in the face of her rage.

'What do you mean?' My wrists ached and I could feel the blood accumulating above them as I stopped moving my fingers.

'Ross felt bad for me. Listened to Uncle Joe talk all the time about how he was going to screw me out of my share of the money. Came to me and told me what was going on, that he felt guilty about being the one to set up the works – you know, the electrical stuff. Told me what Joe was doing to me and to Briggs, too.'

So Ross Kehoe double-crossed Joe Berk. And did it with the perfect enemy to make it a win-win situation for himself. Could Mona really think Ross was in love with her, and could she possibly believe he wouldn't cross her, too, when the right time came? His contempt for the Berks was palpable.

'I could have killed the old bastard myself. This was all I needed,' she said, patting the gun barrel with her left hand.

I hated guns. I'd been around them a lot in all the time I'd worked in the office and had friends in the NYPD, but I'd never wanted to use them. I watched Mona's hands carefully, hoping to figure out if she was familiar with this one. I tried to tell if she knew it was loaded or not, whether it had a safety, and how to use it. If she was into guns, then I'd still be at a great disadvantage, even if I could finish loosening my bonds to try to take her on.

I vowed to myself to start going to the range to learn to shoot the very next time Mike or Mercer had to be there, if I got out of this alive.

'Why did Ross break into my building last night?' I asked her, trying to distract her from the weapon she was playing with so casually. 'Why was he coming after me?'

Mona Berk didn't answer.

'Really, I had no idea he'd done anything wrong. I – I still don't know why he's doing this now,' I said. I could kick myself for not figuring it out earlier, but I hadn't.

'Rinaldo.'

'Rinaldo Vicci?'

'Yeah. He called me this weekend,' Mona said. 'He thought he'd made a mistake while he was talking to you.'

'Me? He never said anything to me.' A sense of desperation had crept into my voice. It was way too late to convince her I didn't know anything bad about Kehoe until the confrontation just a few hours earlier. Now I couldn't look at him and think of him as anything else except a killer.

She glared at me. 'Rinaldo knew that Ross had told the police he'd never met Talya. That he didn't know her. But Rinaldo said he was alone with you at the Met the other day. He said he told you that he had seen Ross in Talya's dressing room.'

'No, no. Vicci never told me he saw them,' I said, stammering a denial.

'Well, he thought he had told you too much about Talya and Ross,' Mona said, dismissively. 'Rinaldo was just trying to suck up to me, like he was doing me a favor by covering up that connection. But when I told Ross about the conversation, it made him crazy.'

'Why? I just don't understand that.'

'Ross figured he was a few steps ahead of the cops. He didn't think they were onto him at all. It was you he was worried about after Rinaldo made that slip.'

'But—'

We both turned our heads toward the staircase because we were reacting to the very same noise. It was a low whirring sound at first, and if Mona hadn't looked that way, too, I wouldn't have been certain that it wasn't just a tingling in my ears, the result of my exhaustion.

But Mona heard it and seemed frozen in place.

I started to get up on my feet and she pushed at me, screaming Kehoe's name.

The noise was steady now and it was coming from the heavy metal door at the bottom of the stairs.

'I told you not to move, dammit,' Mona said, slapping me across the face with her left hand. Her shouts scared the whimpering Chet Dobbis, who rolled onto the floor and tried to crawl behind his chair.

Kehoe was back at her side within seconds. 'What? What the—?'

'It's the door,' Mona yelled. 'What's happening?'

I strained at the bonds, certain that the silk ribbons were shredding into strips and that I could slip my hands out now.

Kehoe reached for the gun and Mona threw her right arm back in the air, wildly discharging a bullet.

'You lied to me!' she shouted at her lover. 'You told me no one could find us here.'

My eyes flashed between the staircase and the gun in her hand. I could reach the bottom of the steps in seconds, but she and Kehoe – and the revolver – would get to me before anyone could get the door to open.

Whoever was on the other side of that door – theater workers who'd figured out this might be a place to explore, or better yet, the police – would be in greater danger if I drew the gunfire in their direction. On the other hand, I had no idea how they would be armed and how I could protect myself, Chet Dobbis, and them – if I didn't alert them to the fact that our captors had a gun.

Mona had gone into a panic, confirming my realization that she and Kehoe were not expecting any allies to come to their aid. I watched as she went running away from the door – from the approaching enemy – and farther into the large domed room. Kehoe ran after her, trying to overtake her so he could get his weapon back.

I used my right fingers to yank on the binds one last time, releasing my left hand and then freeing both. My chances of being killed were just as good if I didn't make a dash to get out, once Mona and Ross stopped fighting with each other for the gun.

As fast as I could move, I got to my feet and ran down the steps to the door. I threw myself against it and pounded on it with my fists. Perhaps it was my imagination, but there seemed to be the slightest of cracks where the solid metal panel slid into the wall. I banged again and again, until Mona Berk screamed my name from across the room and fired a shot that glanced off the wall next to my head.

I turned to look and saw Kehoe struggling with her to grab the gun. She was kicking at him but calling out at me. 'You'll get us all killed, you bitch,' Mona yelled. I dropped to the floor as she let go with another round.

'How could you trust someone who met you in the middle of a double-cross?' I shouted at her. 'It's not you he's after, it's the Berk fortune.'

'You keep your fucking mouth shut,' Kehoe said to me. Then he turned his attention back to Mona, who had run to the far side of the bed. 'Give it to me, babe. I can finish them off and still get us out of here.'

I was crawling up the stairs on my stomach, ready to make a run for the darker side of the cavernous room. I could see Mona pointing the gun right at Kehoe's chest and I inhaled, ready to give her some more emotional ammunition.

'You must have made a deal with Briggs,' I called out to her, crouching at the top of the stairs. 'The kid drops the lawsuit against his father that you two started, in order to get back in Joe's good graces. Then you make a deal with him to get your share of everything he stands to inherit, promising to keep him up to his eyeballs in cocaine and showgirls. But you had to kill Joe to make it work. You two had to kill Joe before he disinherited Briggs for some other indiscretion.'

'There aren't enough rounds left for you to fuck with this,' Kehoe said to Mona Berk. 'Give it back to me.'

'He's going to kill you, too, Mona. As soon as he's got your money.'

'Shut up,' she screamed at me frantically. 'I told you to shut up.'

'I can shut her up, babe. I want the gun,' Kehoe said.

'It doesn't matter now, Ross,' I said. 'It doesn't matter unless you can boost yourself up and out of that skylight on your red velvet swing. Don't let him fool you again, Mona.'

'They can't drill through that door. It's impossible. They'd never be able to get the kind of equipment they'd need to do it up here,' Kehoe said to her as she continued to back away.

'They're not drilling. They're opening the door,' I said.

He turned from her and looked down the staircase.

'Jaws of life, Ross.' The sweetest sound I'd ever heard. The hydraulic rescue equipment used by police and military under the most dire of circumstances – for excavating bodies from aircraft and automobile accidents, building collapses, military disasters – and occasionally for getting lucky and extricating live ones from the jaws of death. I had seen the Emergency Services Unit use it in the most extreme and dire circumstances, and I knew that it could get the job done here this morning.

Mona Berk held the gun with both hands and pointed it at me. 'Stand still. I've got nothing to lose if I shoot you now. You're the reason we're stuck in here, dammit.'

The flickering neon shining in from the cityscape above the skylight made the jerky movements of Mona Berk and Ross Kehoe appear like they were caught in the rays of a strobe. I watched from my squat as he lunged at her to get the gun.

Again, Mona screamed as he punched her jaw and the gun fired, by accident more than design.

The bullet must have hit something close to Chet Dobbis, who had tried to flatten himself on the floor. I heard him gasp and saw him struggling to get to his knees, his hands still tied behind his back.

I knew I'd be safer in one of the dark recesses of the domed ceiling, but it would leave Dobbis exposed to the feuding killers.

As he reached behind himself to the chair he'd been sitting on to straighten himself up against it, Mona Berk turned and saw him as clearly as I did in a beam of light that streamed in from overhead.

'Stop moving around, you idiot!' I heard her call to Dobbis as she aimed the gun and discharged another round.

This time he yelled out in pain. He had only been upright for seconds, but Mona had found her mark. Dobbis had been hit.

I pushed up and ran toward him. 'Get away from me,' he yelled.

There was blood coming from his right shoulder and I grabbed hold of his left elbow to start dragging him with me away from the wildly frantic Mona Berk. I was trying to keep count of the bullets that had been spent, assuming the revolver held six and not knowing how many more Kehoe had in his pocket.

'Give it up,' Kehoe said, trying to get his gun away from his out-of-control cohort. 'I won't miss.'

'We're never going to get out of here, you damn liar,' Mona said, refocusing her rage on her partner. 'You're going to get us both killed.'

I saw the flash of the gun firing and again the sound of the blast echoing within the domed room. Another shot followed immediately and I saw Ross Kehoe fall backward from the impact and heard the crack of his skull against the surface of the floor.

Mona dropped to her knees beside him and ignored me for the moment. Her bloodcurdling screams scattered all the pigeons perched on the edge of the broken skylight. The gunsmoke trailed upward and gave off an acrid smell as it drifted toward the skylight.

I dropped Chet Dobbis's arm and started in the direction of Mona Berk and the fallen Ross Kehoe. The bullet count was in my favor, and the whirring noise at the door behind me continued to give me courage.

As I passed the bar, I grabbed a crystal decanter and cracked it against the marble countertop, holding the jagged glass in my hand by the neck of the broken bottle, and making a run at Mona Berk, who was sobbing now, while Kehoe was silent and still beside her.

'The gun is empty, Mona,' I said. 'Put it down.'

She didn't look up the first time I said it. She was mesmerized, it seemed, by the pool of blood collecting on the floor next to Kehoe's chest, trickling toward her.

'Drop it,' I said, determined to get it out of her hands before anyone managed to enter the room.

As I neared them, I could see that Kehoe's chest was moving up and down, but Mona wasn't watching that.

She couldn't take her eyes off the blood as the rivulet reached her knee and the crimson stain started to spread on the leg of her pants.

I took a few steps closer to her and she lifted her head, bellowing at me like a shrew, from her kneeling position on the floor. No words came out – only a primal scream. When she picked up her right hand – bringing the gun up with it – I charged at her and knocked her off balance. The revolver dropped onto the floor and slid under the bed a few feet away, while the crystal decanter splintered into hundreds of tiny pieces as I lost my grip, and Mona Berk landed on it as she fell backward.

While she rolled back and forth in pain, trying hopelessly to brush off the shards that were embedded in the skin of her neck, I retrieved the gun and ran to alert my rescuers through the widening crack they were creating in the entryway. Then I untied Chet Dobbis and examined the wound that had grazed his shoulder, reassuring him – and myself – while I waited for the powerful spreader to open the heavy door of the great old forgotten dome of the Mecca Temple.

Chapter 46

'You certainly took your time coming to get me.'

We were sitting in the squad room of the Midtown North station house, a couple of blocks away from the City Center of Music and Drama. It was five o'clock in the morning and about the only time in Manhattan you couldn't find an open joint that was still serving liquor.

'It was a toss-up for Mercer. His SVU pals came up with Ramon Carido in a homeless shelter in Queens, and they wanted him to go out there for the collar. We thought we'd have good news for you on that score, if we ever found you again. Battaglia was so damn afraid to lose you – or to get bad press over losing you – that he got on the phone with Interpol himself. The local Turkish constables know where Dr Sengor's parents live, and any day now we'll have that pervert cuffed. Ralph Harney? Bronx Homicide's got him back in for questioning. It'll be a trifecta, Coop. Not a bad night for the good guys.'

'How come you won't answer my questions?'

'You know the drill, Coop. Major Case has to debrief you first.'

'Tell me something, will you? What were you really doing all those hours?'

'Classified. Top secret. No can do.'

'Were you there at the dome with Emergency Services?'

'I wanted to be at the door, right behind the ESU guys when they were opening it up. First time I saw a space, I was gonna yell it into you, Coop. Final Jeopardy answer. That's what I was gonna say. Only there was no room for me up there. Hey, loo, you got a bottle of scotch stashed in one of your drawers here? Give the blonde a break.'

'So what was the answer?' I asked. 'What kind of clue were you planning on giving me?'

'Phoebe Moses. That was the answer.'

'You win, Mike. It wouldn't have helped me.' I rubbed my eyes and tried to control my anxiety so that I would be useful when the detectives began questioning me.

'You don't know Phoebe Moses? That's twenty bucks from you,' he said, pouring the golden liquid into a coffee mug that depicted a homicide cop standing over a body, and the familiar slogan: Our Day Begins When Your Day Ends.

'Mercer?'

'You got my money.'

'Who was Annie Oakley? I figured if I told you that, you'd be ready for me to toss my gun in to you. I thought if you were still alive, you'd put it together with my hint and do something to help yourself. Shoot one of those bloodsuckers.'

I lifted the mug and sipped the scotch. I knew Mike was just trying to humor me, trying to take my mind off the dreadful events of the night. 'That's quite a stretch, Detective Chapman.'

'You gotta get over your phobia of guns. Kaiser Wilhelm, he even let Oakley shoot the ashes off a cigar

459

he had in his mouth. I'm telling you, Coop, Oakley was so good that she outshot the greatest sharpshooter alive, Frank Butler. And you know what? Even though she humiliated him in public – like you're always doing to me – he married her. He got over it.'

'You willing to take that chance if you teach me how to shoot?'

'I'll just settle for my twenty bucks.'

'Were there any rounds left in the gun?' I asked.

Mike shook his head. 'You can't shoot yet, but your math was okay.'

'Kehoe was sure you'd never find us in the dome.'

'He came close to being right,' Mercer said. 'We had a team scouring that upstairs area – but they just didn't go deep enough. Couldn't see anything, couldn't hear anything. Didn't look like people had been up there in ages. We couldn't even find anybody from the crew in the middle of the night who knew how to get to it, once we knew you were there. We finally had to wake the director up, but that was only after we got lucky.'

'Where did you think we'd gone?'

Mercer stood behind me and rubbed my shoulders. 'Most of us figured Kehoe had taken you out on the street. You know, kidnapped you and had you in the trunk of a car on your way out of town.'

'So when are you going to tell me how it went down? Who's my hero?'

'Have mercy,' Mercer said, looking over at Mike. 'Don't make her read about it in tomorrow's papers. It doesn't have anything to do with her debriefing.'

Mike started to explain. 'Once we got out of our trap on that stage, I told Peterson to send in the detectives who were sitting on Mona Berk's SoHo apartment. See if there was anything inside there – notes, tickets, maps, phone messages on the machine – anything at all that would give us some direction to look for Kehoe. Don't act so surprised, don't be giving me any of your gotta-get-a-warrant bullshit. We're talking exigent circumstances here, life and death. Your life. I wasn't looking for evidence to use in court, Coop. I was looking for you.'

'I'm the last one to criticize your techniques at the moment.' I lifted my mug to toast him.

'Turns out Kehoe had his own set of monitors in their apartment, so he could keep tabs on what old Joe Berk was up to. See whether Joe was still peeping at the dancers. Kehoe was hoist on his own leotard.'

'Petard.'

'Don't correct me just about now, okay? One of the monitors was rigged up to a camera inside the dome. The two detectives described to us what they saw – the unusual size and rounded shape of the room – and that Mona Berk was inside it at that very moment, lying down on a bed. Motion-activated sensor in the camera, apparently. But they didn't have a clue where it was.'

Of course the bed – and the red velvet swing – would have been in camera range, even if Dobbis and I were not.

'And we wouldn't have known either,' Mercer said, 'if Mike and I hadn't just been introduced to Mecca Temple. I mean there aren't a hell of a lot of large domed ceilings in town, but I'd never even have thought to start looking there without knowing about the video.'

'Was Kehoe conscious when they put him in the ambulance?'

461

Mike shook his head. 'He'll pull through, though. Scumbags always do.'

'So he has no idea that Serology matched the DNA on the glove near Talya's body to his profile in the linkage database?'

'We're gonna save that tidbit for his hospital arraignment, maybe tomorrow.'

I told them what Mona Berk had told me. It sounded as though Talya, in her attempt to blackmail Joe Berk, had figured out – or been told by Joe – that it was Ross Kehoe who had actually installed the surveillance equipment. The day Rinaldo Vicci saw them together, in Talya's dressing room and let Mona think that he had told me about it, was the moment of her confrontation with Kehoe – a tantrum that probably sealed her fate.

'Lucy DeVore,' I said, remembering the shattered body of the young woman who'd also crossed paths with the Berks. 'This means we don't get a chance to interrogate him about Lucy DeVore.'

'Mercer and I were talking about her a little while ago.'

'While I was at death's door?'

'Couldn't move those jaws any faster than they were going, kid. Remember what Hubert Alden said, that it was Talya who was supposed to be up there on the swing at that audition?'

'Yeah.'

'Kehoe must have rigged the swing to kill Talya. A backup plan for Tuesday, in case he didn't have the opportunity to get the job done at the Met on Friday night.'

'But Lucy. How could he just let her go up there knowing the seat was going to break?'

Mercer spoke. ''Cause Briggs Berk was infatuated with

her. Or thought he was for the last couple of weeks. So Mona and Ross Kehoe figured it was one less distraction to deal with, one less piece of the pie to share with anyone else. And at an open audition – a perfect place for an accident, in front of a dozen or more witnesses. With Lucy dead, it would have given them greater control – for the moment – over Briggs. He'd be less likely to squeal on them than when he was coked up with her. Although they'd have that fear to gnaw at them for a long time to come.'

'That's the problem with blood money. It's gotta haunt you forever. You're asking too many questions, Coop. Finish that drink so we can take you home,' Mike said. 'I can just hear Joe Berk now.'

'What do you mean?'

'You know, that obsession he had with people who change their names. Moses, a girl named Phoebe Moses. Why would she have changed her name to Annie Oakley? It's good to be Moses. That's what Joe would have said. I gotta find out why she switched to Oakley.'

'Forget about the Berks,' Mercer said. 'You put down that mug, Alexandra, and before we take you home, we're going to find the first greasy spoon in town that opens and get us all some food that doesn't come off a sidewalk coffee cart.'

'I got the place,' Mike said. 'As long as she's treating.'

'We're making progress.'

'What do you mean, Coop?'

'Ten days ago, when we started working on this case, you turned me down flat when Mercer and I offered to take you for breakfast.'

'Don't push your luck, kid. There'll be no ballet, no—'

'I only offered bacon and eggs.'

'No opera, no—'

Mercer held out his hand and pulled me up. 'We're hungry,' he said to Mike. 'Let's go.'

'No theater tickets. No Shakespeare, no musicals, no revivals, no—'

'You love Broadway. You've always liked going to shows with me.'

'That was before I knew about the ghosts, Coop. Too many ghosts in those theaters – way too many. And I still haven't even learned how to deal with my own.'

Acknowledgments

The great theatrical institutions of New York City are among our national treasures. It was my good fortune to be introduced to many of them as a young child, and they are still places I go often to be entertained and transported by actors, dancers, and musical artists.

In 1980, I was a young prosecutor – and a frequent patron of the ballet at Lincoln Center – when a thirty-year-old violinist named Helen Hagnes Mintiks was murdered within the Metropolitan Opera House between acts of a performance. There were more than four thousand people under the same roof that night, not one of whom saw her encounter with her killer, nor heard her struggle. Like all my novels, this one has at its heart a tribute to victims of violence, and to those smart and dedicated men and women – police officers, prosecutors, forensic pathologists and scientists – who make it their mission to bring offenders to justice.

The incomparable Beverly Sills gave me access to her magnificent 'home' – the Met – where I spent countless hours beneath and behind the stage. Judy Zecher's knowledge of the Big House and all its staff was breathtaking, and her passion for it is contagious. Arlene Shuler – a brilliant dancer-turned-lawyer who continues to revitalize City Center – enthusiastically arranged tours that awakened me to its stunning architectural and civic history.

There is a wonderful branch of the New York Public Library at Lincoln Center whose clipping files gave me extraordinary detail about Broadway, past and present, as well as about notorious theatrical performers.

The Shuberts Present 100 Years of American Theater, by the staff of the Shubert Archive and Gerald Schoenfeld (a legendary theatrical good guy) (Abrams, 2001), *Murder at the Met* by David Black (Dial Press, 1984), lively conversations with Barry and Fran Weissler, and the archives of *The New York Times* all supplied facts and color.

Thanks to my publishing family at Scribner and Pocket Books – Susan Moldow, Roz Lippel, Carolyn Reidy, Louise Burke, Mitchell Ivers, Sarah Knight, Erica Gelbard, and John Fulbrook. A special nod to Erin Cox, who is the best partner in publicity an author could ask for.

The best thing that happened to *Death Dance* was the strong, smart hand of my new editor, Colin Harrison. A superb author himself, Colin's generous guidance made this work into a better book.

Sigrid Estrada is an author's dream photographer – from deadhouses to kills to the theater world, she has always framed and shot me with her great eye and grand style.

Again my thanks to Hilary Hale and David Young at Time Warner UK for their encouragement, support, and friendship.

And to Esther Newberg, great agent, great friend.

My family and friends are my supreme joy, and my

encouragement, through the long hours I spend alone with Coop and Chapman. Most of all, my brilliant and beloved husband, Justin Feldman, believed in me from the opening lines of the very first book.

This one's for him – and the two most wonderful young readers we know and love – Matthew and Alexander Zavislan.

FINAL JEOPARDY

Linda Fairstein

The days of Assistant D.A. Alexandra Cooper often start off badly, but she's never faced the morning by reading her own obituary before.

It doesn't take long to sort out why it was printed: a woman's body with her face blown away, left in a car rented in Coop's name in the driveway of her weekend home. But it isn't so easy to work out why her lodger – an acclaimed Hollywood star – was murdered, or to be sure that the killer had found the right victim.

As Coop's job is to send rapists to jail there are plenty of suspects who might be seeking revenge, and whoever it is needs to be found before her obituary gets reprinted.

'Raw, real and mean. Linda Fairstein is wonderful'
Patricia Cornwell

COLD HIT

Linda Fairstein

A chilling new Alexandra Cooper thriller from the acclaimed Manhattan Assistant DA who lives the gritty and glamorous life that she writes about.

On a steamy August evening, after an exhausting day in court, Assistant District Attorney Alexandra Cooper is called to a sombre crime scene. Alongside her colleagues, NYPD detectives Mike Chapman and Mercer Wallace, she views the body – a young woman pulled from the water with her hands and feet obscenely tied to a ladder. But who is she? Her elegant clothes and manicured nails suggest affluent connections, but just how well-connected she is surprises even Alex.

From a luxurious Fifth Avenue apartment, to famous midtown auction houses, to the avant garde galleries of Chelsea, Alex, Mike and Mercer hunt for a killer in a world where priceless art meets big money in a lethal mix. Determined to crack the case, they know that sometimes they have to rely on luck, like a 'cold hit' which will match DNA from the crime scene with a suspect's DNA profile in the police database – or is it a more sinister kind of 'cold hit' which claimed this victim's life?

Other bestselling titles available by mail: